A Twist of the Knife

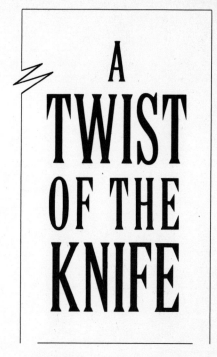

A TWIST OF THE KNIFE

Stephen Solomita

G. P. PUTNAM'S SONS
New York

G. P. Putnam's Sons
Publishers Since 1838
200 Madison Avenue
New York, NY 10016

Library of Congress Cataloging-in-Publication Data

Solomita, Stephen
  A twist of the knife / by Stephen Solomita
    p. cm.
  I. Title.
PS3569.0587T86 1988   88-9769 CIP
813′ .54—dc19
ISBN 0-399-13401-8

Printed in the United States of America

1 2 3 4 5 6 7 8 9 10

For M because I have to;
for Dake because I want to;
for E because I'd better.

A Twist of the Knife

1

When the rain began to fall, Attorney Street emptied almost as fast as the Half-Moon Social Club on the night Carlos Perez tossed a seven-foot diamondback rattlesnake through the front window. The rain ricocheted from the windows and walls and quickly rose at the intersection of Attorney and Rivington, backing over the curb and down into the basement apartment at 1672 Attorney. Bigelow Jackson, current occupant of that apartment, noticed a dark stain growing magically from the front door of his living room and dashed outside to clear the drain. For a moment the water ran freely and Big Jackson threw up his arms in acknowledgment of his victory, but then, responding to some deeper, inaccessible clog, the water began to rise again, quickly covering Jackson's shoes. Condemned to fight a holding action with towels and sheets, he turned to go inside, just noticing a man standing by the alleyway which ran between his building and 1684 Attorney. The man stood in a half-crouch, bent forward, hands hanging limply by his sides. His head rolled to the left, almost resting on his shoulder. To Bigelow Jackson, he represented the most common of all the exotic phenomena existing on the Lower East Side of Manhattan, the stoned-out heroin addict so deep in his somnambulistic world, he did not even notice the rain which emptied the neighborhood.

"Fucking junkie," Bidgelow screamed. He was so angry at the idea of the lake on his carpet, he seriously considered tearing the junkie to pieces, but it was raining very hard and his rug was getting wetter and wetter even as he stood there, so he contented himself with hurling one of several small flowerpots at the motionless figure. The pot bounced off the man's shoulder and broke into pieces on the sidewalk. "Now you get yourself gone, motherfucker," Bigelow Jackson bellowed. "I mean don't let me find your ass here when I come back." He slammed the door triumphantly.

Johnny Katanos, streetnamed Zorba the Freak, beamed inwardly, though he remained as still and lifeless as a statue. This was his craft, he thought. This was what he alone could do. Facing away from the enraged Bigelow Jackson, he'd had no warning when the flowerpot crashed into him, yet he hadn't moved a muscle, not even a twitch of the shoulders. That was his conception of how the waiting should be done—absolute patience in the pursuit of his goal.

Patience made the waiting easier, but the difficulty would emerge later when he had to come to life, to perform some action quickly and accurately. Muscles stiffened as the waiting time increased and any movement, no matter how carefully rehearsed internally, was likely to be jerky and unpredictable. The trick was in the breathing and Johnny, bent forward in a seeming trance, took each breath deeply, counting, forcing the rhythm so that he had to concentrate, so that his muscles would not cramp when he needed them most. Carefully, he divided his attention, alternately contracting and releasing the muscles of his upper arms. Four repetitions and then to the forearms and then back to the feet.

The windows overlooking Attorney Street are rarely empty. To the elderly, often without TVs or even telephones, the windows are at once entertainment and communication. An occasional "Hello" or "How are you?" produces a pleased smile as neighbors check up on each other. These old people watch everything on the street, silently cursing youthful predators, often in Yiddish. They are the last white people living on Attorney Street and they never leave their apartments after dark. Even so, the local street demons pick one of them off every week or two, rob and sometimes beat them as well, often for an imaginary treasure stashed in a mattress or beneath a dresser. Rosa Wertz, eighty-two, hidden behind a dark green windowshade, witnessed Bigelow Jackson's assault on the junkie and she continued to watch after Bigelow returned to the flood in his living room. She saw the junkie move slowly forward, stagger slightly, then turn and retreat into the alleyway, but as his route went directly away from her door, she simply returned to her radio, though later she would insist on telling her story to Officer Timatis who would only pretend to write it down. After all, the officer reasoned solemnly, who cares about a fucking junkie?

As Johnny Katanos shuffled back into the darkness between the two apartment buildings, he fought the urge to look up, to check for observing eyes. This was the most dangerous part of the plan, because there were many eyes assigned to watch this particular passageway, but he'd been standing in the alleyway for two hours and the few pedestrians racing toward shelter had ignored him completely. Even Bigelow Jackson, who knew Johnny Katanos well, had been fooled by a disguise consisting as much of a seamless junkie posture as of darkened hair and wispy beard. Crouched in a back doorway long ago boarded up and triple-locked from inside, Johnny felt sure that anyone coming to investigate would take him for a junkie, would dismiss him with a kick or an open-handed blow. But no one came, and only Rosa Wertz, now engrossed in radio psychiatrist Dr. Bella Effenhauser's explanation of the intricacies of pleasuring, had seen him and she was no threat to the plan.

It was near dark before the rain slackened into a fine, dense mist. In the alleyway, far from the few streetlights on Attorney Street, the gloom was relieved only by the dim glow of windows covered by sheets and blankets. In this darkness Johnny reflected, I am invisible. He jumped up to grab the lowest rungs of the fire escape and easily pulled himself up. Once again—but this time more powerfully—he felt the elation grow, felt the blood rush into his face and scalp until his ears burned red. For an instant he abandoned himself to the sensation. Then he began to climb.

The first two windows Johnny passed looked into empty apartments, though, technically, both were rented and the landlord, Miguel Evans, received a check each month from the occupants. These apartments served as a buffer between the unremitting avarice of the streets and the fabulous wealth of the fourth-floor factory where, each day, a half-kilo of heroin was broken down into small units and distributed throughout the neighborhood. It was not an operation that went unnoticed and many an upwardly mobile street hoodlum had hatched a scheme for the liberation of that wealth, but the businessman who owned the company, Ronald Jefferson Chadwick, had so far been able to stave off all threats. The doors of the lower apartments were always open, affording an unobstructed view of the stairs and hallway. Four heavily armed guards, one stationed in each apartment, were enough to discourage the greediest street criminal, and Mr. Chadwick felt quite secure.

This partially explains the Greek's unnoticed ascent. Two further reasons, Theresa Aviles and Effie Bloom, were holding open house on the other side of the building. They were encouraging the nymphomaniacal obsessions of seven ghetto criminals and just at the moment when Johnny hoisted himself past the darkened windows, Effie Bloom was pulling Enrique Vasquez' head between her huge, motherly breasts while five merciless criminals looked on. A seventh, Paco Baquili, commander in chief in the absence of Mr. Chadwick, emboldened by the privacy of a closed bedroom door, pressed his face between the hard, slender thighs of a grinning Theresa Aviles. This is just the greatest piece of luck, he thought. That asshole, Katanos, Zorba the Freak, had introduced the girls only one night before and they had come sniffing around the very next day. He sighed, inhaling deeply. They would show these bitches a good time tonight.

A large, Fedders air conditioner sat in a window of the fourth-floor factory, the only air conditioner in a neighborhood of ancient tenements where the electrical wiring was barely sufficient for the energy needs of a toaster. Johnny wasn't fooled. Even in the gloom, he easily picked out a wire running across the landing. It ran to a shotgun concealed in the empty air conditioner. Not very impressive in a world of lasers, but enough to permanently discourage the odd burglar or two. There was no sense in disarming the trap. He wouldn't be coming back this way, not according to the plan. Johnny had to force himself to go slowly. He could see the fifth-floor window and the two dark, canine shapes leaping against the glass. It was almost miraculous. He had been so quiet, so careful, and still they were waiting for him. He wondered what it would be like to have those abilities, to taste the surrounding world so deeply. The dogs were nearly perfect. Trained from puppyhood to respond only to their handler, they had been conditioned to victory, to the belief that no creature could withstand their attack. Their trainer had used declawed cats, old toothless dogs and once a staggering drunk to reinforce this conviction. Unfortunately, their greatest strength was their greatest flaw: Attack was all they knew. They would always come straight at you.

Calmly, unhurried, Johnny Katanos took off his jacket and spread it beneath the window to catch the falling glass. The window itself was protected by a barred gate and Johnny reached between the bars to break the glass with the butt of a long-handled hunting knife. The space between the window and the gate was instantaneously filled with the teeth of two enormous Dobermans. Their snarls were silent, however, and there was no barking. Their vocal chords had been removed so that they could attack without warning, without giving their target any chance of escape. Unless, of course, you knew they were there.

Johnny smiled for the first time. It was too easy. The dogs thrust their heads through the bars of the gate, so absolutely confident they made no effort to protect themselves. They almost seemed to offer their throats willingly and as they fell away, gushing blood, they were unable even to whimper. Johnny ignored them and began to work on the padlocks holding the window gate in place.

It was much warmer inside the building, warm enough to allow Johnny to acknowledge the chill that had penetrated to his bones. The door leading from the bedroom to the living room was closed, which meant the dogs' trainer would not have to enter the apartment to clear them out before Chadwick, who feared the animals as much as anyone, could enter. The Dobermans protected the fire-escape window leading to Chadwick's personal quarters. The guards, who were supposed to be in the second- and third-floor apartments, protected the doors. Johnny stepped over the animals, staying well clear of the bloodsoaked carpeting. The room smelled strongly of animal waste, strongly enough to cover the smell of blood. Opening the door, Johnny entered the darkened living room. It was getting close now. He pulled the tape away from his calf and took the automatic pistol into his right hand. The perfect familiarity of its weight against his palm made the blood rush into his face once again. He screwed the silencer into the barrel of the pistol and settled down to wait.

The party downstairs was in high gear. Patiently, dully, the lovers gathered about Effie Bloom, waiting for a turn. Effie lay on her back, having long ago abandoned even the pretext of passion. She pictured Johnny Katanos, cold as always, firing into the face of whatever man loomed above her. She timed these bullets to the slap of his groin against her belly. One cartridge for each thrust, for each grunt. This was rape. She could prove it by trying to leave. She wondered if they enjoyed what they were doing. Their faces were calm and concentrated, like men engaged in some complex work requiring every bit of attention. Content to twist her body as one would that of a department store mannequin, they did not even bother to speak to her.

Theresa Aviles, in the bedroom with Paco Baquili, was much more fortunate. Paco had been impotent, but had insisted, because he understood women and their needs, on performing orally and for an extended period of time. Theresa, as indifferent as Effie, was nevertheless convincingly passionate, erupting with provocative little cries of rapture every three or four minutes. And unlike Effie, Theresa never allowed herself to be moved by the injustice of the situation. When she finally pulled Paco's head onto her belly, she stroked his hair and whispered, "Do you want to kill me, man? You can die from too much pleasure. Like too much whiskey." The speech thrilled Paco who immediately launched into a story of his mother and the small town they came from in Puerto Rico.

At eleven o'clock the phone rang and Paco, naked, emerged from the bedroom. Grunting, he placed the phone to his ear, listened for a few seconds and hung up. Mr. Chadwick would return within forty-five minutes and the house must be made secure. Unfortunately for Ronald Chadwick, security, to Paco Baquili, meant sending out to the bodega for room deodorant. The girls were dressed and dismissed. The beer cans were picked up. In all events, as Paco understood it, the object was to appear as military as possible, considering the material at hand, and while this collection of ghetto freaks would never pass for Green Berets, by the time the boss walked in at midnight, the lower house had been restored to order and each of the defenders was in his proper place.

Ronald Chadwick was famous for his ability to sense danger, to taste it in the air, especially when large quantities of money were at stake. Still, when Paco Baquili opened the door with a smile which was echoed by that of DuWayne Brown sitting in the hallway with a shotgun in his lap, Ronald felt nothing out of place. Below the fourth floor, everything was as it was supposed to be and the players radiated confidence and security. Ronald and his escort, Parker Drabble, ignored all greeting and went directly to the fifth floor. The small suitcase, crammed with fifty- and hundred-dollar bills, seemed to push them forward. This was huge business even for them and if they hadn't been in such a rush, they might have noticed that something was missing. There should have been the sound of the dogs jumping against the bedroom door, just the scraping of the dogs' nails against the wood. But there was all that money. There was $550,000 in a suitcase in the safest place Ronald Chadwick had ever known.

Parker saw Johnny first and so he took the first bullet in the left temple. It was too late for Ronald Chadwick to stop the door from closing; he'd let go just an instant before the overhead light revealed his assassin, sealing himself into the room and thereby insuring his own death. He saw the right side of Parker's head explode and the process so absorbed him that he barely felt the bullet enter his own chest. It felt more like a blow, like a punch driving him back into the closed door. Then he was sliding toward the floor.

Without hesitating, Johnny lifted the still-breathing body onto his shoulder, walked calmly to the stairwell and tossed Ronald Chadwick over the railing. Pulling the pin from the hand grenade exactly as he'd been taught to do it, he listened carefully to the sudden commotion as the guards pounded up the stairs. Their voices rose and fell meaninglessly, excited shouts filled with fear and confusion. He waited until he recognized Paco Baquili's cry of astonishment, then dropped the grenade.

2

Detective Sergeant Stanley Moodrow, as his friend and commander, Captain Allen Epstein well knew, could be found in the Houston Street Killarney Harp Bar, an unfiltered Chesterfield smoldering in an ashtray, for at least two hours following any shift. Usually he drank Ballantine Ale, but on weekends, especially after a day's work, he drank straight shots of Cauldfield's Wild Turkey Bourbon, a thin, brown liquid that reminded Captain Epstein of the slop in the bottom of a morgue table after an autopsy. Captain Epstein considered policing to be an avocation particularly attractive to the mentally unstable—witness the high rates of suicide and alcoholism within the department—and Stanley Moodrow to be a fine example of this insight. It was irrelevant, of course. Arrest records, as he'd observed over the length of a twenty-two-year hitch, were unrelated to the abilities of the particular policeman. Stanley Moodrow, for instance, was regarded as ordinary by the department, yet, without him, Epstein would have been hard put to run his precinct at all.

"No," Stanley Moodrow muttered without bothering to look up. "Whatever it is you fucking want, the answer is no. I'm off duty."

Epstein, his face perfectly expressionless, sat down heavily. It was all so predictable. Moodrow's face reminded him of a puppy's before it grew into its skin. Small, nearly perfect features pressed onto an enormous expanse of dead-white flesh made him seem nearly devoid of emotion, even when he was annoyed, as he was just now. Epstein had once owned a dog like that, a bulldog puppy whose face hung in long, twisted folds, obscuring eyes and mouth. He didn't resent the sergeant's comment, because the sergeant was right. Epstein was asking for time that didn't belong to him and that entitled Moodrow to a nasty remark. "Stanley," Epstein said, "you wouldn't talk to me like that if I was a private citizen."

"If you were a private citizen, I wouldn't talk to you at all."

Epstein shifted in his seat, trying not to smile. "You got a point there." He belched loudly. "My ulcer again. Shit, it's just getting into gear."

Moodrow looked up with interest. "Do you know that Louis Armstrong took an enema every day? And Gandhi? Every fucking day?" He reached out to pluck at the barmaid's apron. "Get the captain a drink, OK, Rita?" The girl patted him on the shoulder and trotted off. "See, your problem is you're too damn fat. How many pounds you put on since you left the academy? Sixty? Eighty? It's gluttony." He settled back in the seat, watching Epstein's face. It was round and jolly, almost cherubic.

"It ain't the fat, Stanley," Epstein said. "It's the goddamn problems. You know how it is. The blacks around here can knock themselves off by the hundreds and the public don't care. Nobody cares. But let something change just a little bit and everybody goes nuts. Then I get problems and my gut jumps up and takes a good bite. Shit, I was just as fat in the academy. If your father was a cop, a little fat didn't mean a thing."

Epstein took the glass offered by the barmaid and sipped thoughtfully, just as if the brown liquid was ambrosia for whatever demon drove his ulcer. "The thing is, if I fix the problem, the pain goes away. It's as simple as that. Fix the problem and the ulcer goes away."

Moodrow pulled on his cigarette, inhaling deeply, then turned quickly toward the captain. "So what am I, Captain? The problem or the solution?"

Epstein laughed for the first time that day. "You're the solution, baby. The solution. Unless you don't solve the problem, then the solution becomes the problem all over again. But don't take it too seriously. Right now it's just a little, baby problem. It might never amount to anything. Correction. It probably won't amount to anything. Still, I want to be ready, Stanley, whichever way it goes."

There was a silence then. Both men looked around the bar as if noticing it for the first time. There were dozens of Killarney Harp bars in the city, each with a long steam table loaded with roast meats. The toilets all smelled of urine, even the women's toilets, though Killarney Harps were not places commonly patronized by women. The long wooden bars were scarred and stained and the bartenders spoke with thick brogues. The barmaids wore black trousers and white blouses and were usually moving into middle age. Rita Melengic, the waitress taking care of Moodrow and his captain, noticed the gap in their conversation and paused in her rounds to slide into the booth next to the sergeant. "Make room, make room," she commanded, slapping him with her hip. "Say Captain," she asked, "what kind of name is Stanley Moodrow? I mean it ain't no guinea name. It ain't no Jewish name. It ain't no Irish name. It don't even sound Polish, for Christ's sake." She stopped suddenly, out of breath.

To Allen Epstein, married twenty-five years, Rita Melengic had all the character of a generic aspirin. "How am I supposed to know?" he replied.

"Don't ya see his official record?" She threw him her best smile.

The detective broke in gently. "This is business, Rita. Go back to work."

"Sure, baby." But she held onto him. "You're still gonna take me home tonight, OK, Stan?" She looked closely at his face, but his features, small and efficient in his enormous skull, showed nothing. "I don't feel like sleeping alone."

Moodrow flashed the captain a defiant look. "Didn't I say I would? There's nothing happening that can't wait until tomorrow."

"Thanks, Stanley," she said, turning to the captain. "I just don't feel like going home alone." She scrambled from behind the table without waiting for a reply and returned to the wars.

The sergeant looked back at Epstein, his face once again expressionless. He straightened in his seat and the captain was impressed, as always, by the sheer bulk of the man. It did not seem possible for a man so heavily muscled to have such an ugly body. For a minute, he entertained the image of Rita Melengic lying under that great bulk—paralyzed, motionless.

"OK," Moodrow said suddenly. "I'll be the fish. Let's hear the problem."

"You remember Ronald Jefferson Chadwick?"

"Sure."

"The grenade was manufactured in Russia."

"Bullshit."

"The FBI says the grenade was manufactured in the Soviet Union. Something about the metal. The alloy. There's no doubt."

Sergeant Moodrow sipped his drink studiously, drawing his eyebrows into the center of his forehead, a gesture designed to make people think he was concentrating. He looked up at the captain, and replied solemnly. "So who gives a fuck?"

"What gives a fuck? I'll tell you who gives a fuck."

"No." Moodrow rose up, towering over the captain. "Don't tell me nothin'. A junkie buys a hand grenade and kills a pusher. He gets away with a bundle and he don't give a fuck either. We see it all the time."

"But not with a hand grenade," Epstein patiently explained. "We don't see any hand grenades at all. This is a Saturday night special part of town." He paused to let his message sink in. "All right, so nobody right this minute cares about a Russian hand grenade and some mutilated junkies. But let a hand grenade go off in a white department store any time within the next two years and the press'll be all over us. Not to mention the department. What I say is, let's check it out. Let's do our job. Go to the FBI. See what's doing with terrorists in this area. This is nut heaven, remember? Maybe it's some kind of Puerto Rican radicals. I want that nobody can say. 'How come you didn't do this? How come you didn't do that.'"

"I got a lot of cases right now, Captain."

"Just do this for two weeks. Let the other stuff slide. I want a complete report. For the files."

Moodrow, staring at the inch of bourbon remaining in his glass, sat down heavily. It happened more and more often lately. It was like losing a fight in the ring. No matter how determined you were, you couldn't make your hands go faster and you faced the inevitable end with tears in your eyes. The detective wished he was lying in bed with Rita and that they had finished making love—if they were going to make love—and that he was asleep and that he wouldn't wake up.

"Sure, Captain," he said. "You picked the right man."

In spite of his best and most earnest intentions, Stanley Moodrow did awaken on the following morning, though he had, in fact, forgotten his wish entirely. The sergeant, finished with the bathroom, sat at a blue Formica table in Rita Melengic's kitchen, pad and pencil in hand. If asked, he would assert his sense of well-being aggressively. Rita had seen this mood before. When given a problem, a solvable problem, he became so engrossed that he forgot to be miserable. Rita bustled about the kitchen, preparing for the coming day (or night, it being nearly 2 PM) while the detective played with his ideas. Lovers for three months, they seemed nearly married, although, within a day or two, if Moodrow stayed that long, Rita would be sick of the policeman, of the way he sat at the table, waiting to be fed. As if that was his right.

"OK," Moodrow said, scratching at the thick stubble under his jowls. "What do we know?"

"Is that a philosophy question?" Rita asked, pouring out the coffee. "It's too early for philosophy."

"What are you talking about?" He glanced at his watch. "Jesus Christ. It's after two o'clock."

Rita spooned butter into the frying pan. "Omelettes or fried with bacon?" She used her most businesslike tones. There were times when she simply could not resist the urge to bust his chops.

"Shit," Moodrow growled. "You're making me lose my train of thought. This is too important. We got five bodies in that house."

"Rye or white?"

Moodrow sipped at his coffee, holding his anger down. He looked Rita over calmly. A little broad in the butt. A little gray, but that was all right; at least that was more natural than hair dyes. Even the wrinkles on her face (and there weren't that many) ran up along the lines of her smile. She was what he called 'handsome' and, best of all, he didn't have to risk a damn thing. Whenever she wanted him she said so, and for his part, he enjoyed being with her and didn't miss her when he wasn't. "Listen," he said. "I need a little help with this hand grenade thing. Just let me bounce a few ideas, OK?"

Rita shrugged her shoulders. "We did the whole thing last night. One criminal kills another criminal. Who cares?"

"You're making a big mistake, Rita. A number one, fundamental error. Last night I was drunk. That's my excuse, but today I'm awake and sober. You get a job, you don't think about whether it's worthwhile or not, because that just takes away from the energy you need to do the job. You put all that aside and deal only with the problem. So, what do we know?"

Rita broke four eggs into a bowl and began to stir them with a spoon. "Somebody got onto the fifth floor of a dope factory, shot two men, killed three more with a hand grenade and wounded another. Then he got away with a suitcase full of something. Probably money. That's it."

"Not completely. It's possible someone else—one of the bodyguards most likely—but it could even be one of the cops investigating the blast took that suitcase. It's not likely, but it could be. Couple more things. We got two dead dogs and two padlocks picked off a window gate. We know the guy got in the apartment at least two hours before the shooting started. The footprints on the rug were dry, but the chair where he sat was still wet, soaked through. And he went out over the roofs, because the streets filled up right after the explosion. He used a 9mm automatic and a commie hand grenade."

"There's something else that's bothering me," Rita said. "Why didn't he shoot those dogs? He kills two dogs with a knife when he could just as easily have shot them." She broke the omelettes in half, scraping them onto two plates and began to butter the toast absentmindedly. "I think he likes contact. I think he likes twisting the knife."

Moodrow held up his hand. "Stop right there. Stick with what we're sure of. Speculation comes later. At 11:00, Ronald Jefferson

Chadwick, who just happens to be the heroin king of the Lower East Side, comes home. He's accompanied by his bodyguard, Parker Drabble, and he's carrying a brown suitcase. He goes up to the fifth floor without talking to anyone. Parker goes with him. Ten seconds later, Chadwick's body comes crashing down to the fourth floor which is the actual factory. All the soldiers run up from the second and third floors to gather round their fallen leader. Then a hand grenade follows the body and ka-boom, everybody's dead. Or almost everybody.

"Later on there's no suitcase. And nobody heard any shots, so that indicates a silencer. Pretty sophisticated. A 9mm with silencer. A Russian hand grenade. Not everyday equipment. On the other hand, Ronald Chadwick ain't your everyday pigeon."

"Now who's speculating?" Rita sat down across from Moodrow. She looked at her plate, then back to the sergeant. "How do we know the place was a factory? Did they find chemicals?"

"No, no. Not a factory like that. Chadwick'd buy a big piece, let's say a half-kilo of sixty percent pure. Then he'd cut it, bag it and get it out on the streets. We got scales, razor blades, mirrors, nearly a tenth of an ounce of heroin dust. We got eighteen pounds of quinine. Eighteen fuckin' pounds. That's very big business. Really. Chadwick was Rockefeller in that ghetto. He was the ultimate success. Even his death was right." Moodrow attacked his breakfast between sentences, stabbing at the soft eggs, then leaning forward to catch the food with his mouth before it could drop back onto the plate. "Something else, too. There was a booby trap on the fourth-floor fire escape, a trip wire attached to a shotgun. Very primitive. One of the soldiers warned us the minute we walked through the door. In the dark, that wire is invisible. If the killer went that way, he'd either have to know it was there or get his goddamn legs blown off. But that's no big deal. Do you remember the Ghetto Rangers?"

"The street gang?"

"Much more than that. Two years ago, the Rangers fought a war with Chadwick for control of the heroin trade. Now these were basically black gangs with black customers. Later on, after the war was won, Chadwick added some Puerto Rican personnel to his staff and expanded his territory, but at that time both gangs were black. According to the cops who worked on the case, twenty-two deaths resulted directly from that war. And that means we actually found twenty-two bodies. Who knows how many more are buried in those bombed-out tenements? It could be any number. Now you know how many times that war made the papers? Exactly once. Because two Ghetto Rangers happened to get blown away in front of a downtown restaurant.

"Sure, nobody cares if coloreds kill coloreds. People figure they deserve whatever misery they get. Only things're heating up. Hand grenades are a definite escalation and the captain wants to take a closer look. He wants to make sure the killer is just another criminal and not some crazy terrorist who's likely to take his action downtown."

Rita began to clear the dishes, piling one plate on top of another, but without thinking about it, Moodrow took them away from her and carried them to the sink. "Tell me, Stanley," Rita asked, "if it turns out to be one criminal killing another criminal, are you going to forget about it?"

"You mean a black junkie killing a colored pusher?"

"Yeah, that's what I mean."

"The captain wants to make sure everything's cool in his precinct. Business as usual. In order for me to make my captain comfortable, I have to find out who committed the crime. If I find out and I can prove it, I'll nail the motherfucker to the wall."

Rita blew him a kiss and laughed out loud. "Stanley," she said, "you're my ideal."

"You know how I'm gonna do it? I'm gonna say this guy had information about Chadwick's setup before he went to kill him. Exact, inside information. I'm gonna send two cops to check the alleyway for clothing or footprints. Anything to be able to say he got past the booby trap on the fourth floor. Also, I'd like to send two detectives to knock on every door in the neighborhood in case anyone saw anything, but this probably won't happen. No enough manpower. Not enough money. It's what we call very low percentage. But, from my point of view, all that's just so much bullshit, anyway. See, there's this guinea-Puerto Rican over at St. Stephen's named Paco Baquili. Now Paco's in very big trouble. For one thing, his arm's nearly torn off. For a second, he's damn near blind, though that particular problem might get better. But the worst thing is all that equipment, all that quinine and all that heroin is gonna fall right on top of him. He's the only one left. Now suppose I say that Paco knows who did this to him. I say it was an inside job and somebody wasn't where he was supposed to be and Paco knows who this person is. Of course, Paco would like to take his own revenge and that's natural. Very understandable. But still, if I can get him to tell me what that is, I'll be one very big step closer to solving my problem. See what I'm gonna do is . . .'' He walked up behind her and reached around to grip her breasts, pressing them back into her chest. ''I'm gonna put the squeeze on him.''

Paco Baquili did not count himself among the most fortunate of men, although, statistically, the chances of his being alive were very small. Only two feet away, he'd been staring directly at the falling grenade when it exploded and it was generally agreed by the staff of St. Stephen's that, especially from a moral point of view, he really should have been killed immediately. Yet (they felt) he'd gotten off lucky. Shrapnel had torn through his right arm, severing tendons in his elbow and wrist, neither of which, although the tendons had been reattached by the surgeons, seemed to respond to his desires. And he was blind as well, his head wrapped in layers of gauze bandages. The doctors assured him this blindness was temporary, but to a man facing thirty years in prison, loss of vision is tantamount to loss of life. Paco himself was an adroit and lifelong liar, so it was understandable if he tended to believe that doctors might also be liars. Then, too, this was a prison ward, as securely locked as the city jail; the doctors were employees of the prison system and, as such, liable to any cruelty. Hadn't they, just this minute, even though it was late at night and everyone else in the hospital asleep, allowed Sergeant Stanley Moodrow to enter his room, unaccompanied? Hadn't the sergeant locked the door behind him, snapping the lock loudly to make sure Paco heard it closing? Paco felt his predicament drop down over his face like a wet pillow.

"Jeez, Paco," Moodrow sighed, "what a break. One day you're up and the next you're fuckin' buried."

Paco's desperate grin spread from ear to ear. "So good to hear from you again, Sergeant Moodrow." He placed the policeman just off his left hand. "Long time, eh? How you been?"

"I was doing good before, but it's been pretty rough lately." The voice began to move toward the foot of the bed. "My boss has an ulcer. You know, he likes to take it out on the men, so once in awhile he puts a bug up my ass. Say, what happened to you? You're really a mess."

Paco instinctively rolled toward the sound, still smiling. "Some crazy bastard threw a hand grenade at me."

"You're lucky to be alive."

"I guess I'm ungrateful." Paco let his head drop back onto the pillow. "I don't feel like no lucky guy. I mean, my boss is dead. I don't even got no job."

The sudden, unexpected laughter made Paco jump, jarring his injured right arm, and his cry of pain, stifled almost before it emerged, blended nicely with the sergeant's happiness. "I'm sorry, Paco," Moodrow said. "I didn't mean to startle you. I keep forgetting that you're blind. Really. I'm not putting you on. It's just that, with all that time facing you. I mean all that quinine, eighteen fucking pounds. And five thousand little cellophane envelopes. And the scales. Do you have any idea how much powder we vacuumed off the rugs? What we pulled out from the little cracks in the floorboards? I could retire on this bust."

"But Sergeant," Paco said, desperately trying to follow the sound of Moodrow's voice as he wandered about the bed. "All that stuff belongs to Ronald Chadwick. Everybody knows who is the big boss in that district and it ain't Paco Baquili."

"Wrong, Paco." Somehow Moodrow had gotten behind the bed, his face directly over Paco's. "All your clothes are in the building. We got suitcases with your initials engraved. We got letters, credit cards. Hey, don't be modest. Ronald Chadwick's dead. It's all yours now."

Paco knew the silence that followed was meant to frighten him, but he was determined not to be the first to speak.

"Say, Paco." The policeman's voice was flat, emotionless. "How do you think the guy got up to the fifth floor like that?"

"Really, I don't have no idea, Sergeant. All I seen was Chadwick come flying down the stairs and then this explosion right in my face."

"Well, this guy somehow got past the dogs and through the gate on the window. He didn't trip the shotgun in the air conditioner. How did he know? You must have thought about it."

"Well," Paco explained, "you know I been in a lotta pain, man."

"I understand, Paco. Really. But you must have spent a few minutes thinking about the man who did this to you."

"Well, I have thought about it a couple of times. I think it might be someone out to eliminate the competition."

Moodrow sat down at the edge of the bed. He placed his fingers on the bandages covering Paco's right arm and began to stroke them gently. "And who would that be?"

Paco began to speak quickly, looking for the right words. "I believe the man would have to be Joseph Imoyeva, the African. He's the only one with the organization to handle our business. He has very good soldiers working for him."

Moodrow pressed down hard enough to bring Paco up into a sitting position. The injured man opened his mouth to scream, but could only manage a series of hoarse grunts. The sergeant, completely satisfied, dropped into a chair by Paco's right side and waited patiently for him to squeeze back the pain. The drugs Paco had been given to control his suffering had imparted a false sense of security, and he hadn't been prepared for the fire that swept up into his shoulder. The worst part was the inability to see it coming, to anticipate. Even now, he didn't know where the policeman was.

Moodrow cleared his throat. "You should remind yourself that you're gonna tell me what I need to know. Just the way you did before. I realize you want your own revenge. That's all you have left. But I also need. I need to talk to whoever dropped that grenade. Now you know fucking well nobody got in that house without having the layout beforehand. It just ain't possible."

"Sure," Paco agreed quickly, trying to smile. "That makes good sense to me. I go along with what you say one hundred percent. But how do I know which one it was ?'' Quietly, without interrupting, Moodrow removed the shoe from his right foot and raised it high in the air. ''There must have been a dozen guys who knew the layout. It might be any one of the soldiers. How am I supposed . . .''

This time Paco Baquili screamed. He screamed for a long time, then fell back, half-unconscious. He realized, dimly, that no one had come to investigate, no doctor and no nurse and that he was completely and utterly alone with Detective Sergeant Stanley Moodrow, who sat by his side, chuckling softly. ''Ah, Paco,'' the sergeant whispered. ''I really didn't enjoy that. I know my reputation among you people, but it's not justified and I'm going to prove that right now. See, I think that if I just whack that arm a couple more times, you'll tell me what I need to know. But, instead, I'm offering value for value, favor for favor. Give him up. You can't do shit from in here anyway. Look, I promise I'll try to give you a shot when I'm finished. I won't protect him. Also, if I can, I'll put some of the heat on him and take it off of you. But no more bullshit, Paco. Not one little piece of bullshit or I swear I'll tear that fuckin' arm right off your shoulder. I want the name.''

''Enrique Hentados.'' Involuntarily, without his even knowing it, Paco began to cry.

''How do ya know?'' Moodrow leaned forward eagerly.

''He's not around no more. Nobody can find him.''

''Maybe he just got lost for a few days.''

Paco panicked. ''Jesus Christ, man, I am tellin' you the truth. Only a few people knew about the dogs and that shotgun. Enrique knew. Shit, he was my mother's cousin, from my hometown in Puerto Rico. I got him that job as a favor. When I find him, I'm going to burn him with a torch until his flesh melts off his bones. I want him to die slow, man.''

''All right. Enough.'' Moodrow pulled a small notebook from his jacket pocket and began to fish for his pencil. ''Let's start with his relatives and friends.''

3

When forced to bulldog a problem, Stanley Moodrow could be as tenacious as any cop in the city, patiently shaking out a rumor or a witness until some tiny slice of truth emerged. He pushed when he could get away with it—pushing made things move more quickly—but he was careful to draw the line between good guy, bad guy, and civilian. No amount of pushing, however, had uncovered the slightest trace of Enrique Hentados, and Moodrow was a bad loser who tended to console himself with equal doses of alcohol and anger. On this occasion, though, seated in his customary booth at the Killarney Harp with Captain Epstein, he was more confused than annoyed. Confused and worried. He was convinced that none of the dozen or so people he'd questioned was lying to him. Enrique Hentados had simply disappeared.

Speculation had it that the kid had taken a huge amount of money from Ronald Chadwick and was living it up somewhere on the West Coast. This was ghetto nonsense. A boy like Enrique had only a limited number of possibilities. He could not take his loot and disappear into the heartland of America. A slight, dark-complexioned Puerto Rican, he spoke heavily accented English and had never really been one of Ronald Chadwick's soldiers. He was much closer to being Chadwick's mascot, a gofer who made sure the electric bills were paid and the refrigerator well-stocked with beer and cold cuts. Even if he had the physical strength to pick up Chadwick, who outweighed him by sixty pounds, Moodrow could not visualize him, hand grenade at the ready, crouching by the fifth-floor stairwell. It was inconceivable.

Initially, Moodrow had assumed that some rival to Chadwick's exalted position within the heroin community had used Hentados for information, then killed him to keep it quiet. But no other dealer had jumped in to occupy Chadwick's throne and Chadwick's suppliers were in a panic, desperately searching for retailers with sufficient capital. The price of heroin on the street, when it was available at all, had tripled in the week since Chadwick's death.

"Hentados is dead, Captain," Moodrow said, staring directly into Epstein's eyes. "There's just no place he could be hiding. But you know the funny thing? Not only don't I know who killed him, I don't even know why he was killed."

"So what, Stanley?" The captain drained his beer quickly, his stomach quiet for the first time in a week. He felt suddenly expansive, almost jocular. "Hey, look, everything's working out perfectly. You're pounding the streets, knocking down doors. It's great. Now we can go back to keeping order in the Seventh. Which is all I ever gave a shit about anyway."

"Oh, for Christ's sake, Captain." Moodrow picked at his sleeve, trying to brush away a large, dark stain. "Look at this. The goddamn thing's wet."

"Well, what do you expect?" Epstein sighed. "When you lay your arm in a puddle of beer, it generally does come out wet."

"See, Captain, it always strikes me as strange when every potential suspect in a case turns out to be innocent. It just worries the shit out of me, because I know it's gonna move some way I'm not ready for."

Epstein signaled Rita over to the table. "Say, what kind of lady are you? You let my friend's glass go empty like that?"

Rita put her hand on Moodrow's shoulder. She leaned over and kissed the top of his head. "Don't worry, Captain. I'll make it up to him later."

"Make it up to him now, Rita. Bring him a beer. And as long as you're going anyway, bring me one, too." He turned back to Moodrow. "So, what's next, Stanley? I have the feeling you're not finished with this one."

Moodrow shrugged. "I'm gonna see the FBI tomorrow. I still got a couple more names to check out from the list I made with Paco."

"And then?"

"And then nothing."

Detective Sergeant Stanley Moodrow's speculations were essentially correct and his fears entirely justified. Enrique Hentados would never turn up in Las Vegas, one arm around the waist of some impossibly blonde chorus girl. He slept a more peaceful sleep in a basement at 1109 Clinton Street, the third in a row of five burned-out brownstones, long abandoned, the open windows devoid even of their frames. In the early spring warmth, his body had begun to decay and the rats had caught the scent, digging fitfully. He wasn't buried deeply. It was understood by the occupants of these buildings, usually junkies looking for a safe place to fix, that one might use any upstairs room, but the basements, dark and damp, held secrets no sane junkie needed to know.

Enrique Hentados, a boy of limited intelligence, had worked very hard to please his cousin, Paco. After all, Ronald Chadwick had represented Enrique's only hope of success. He had been too timid, too small, ever to fight his way up. And things had gone well for him. He had had money in his pocket all the time and the promise of more to come. His clothes were clean and new, his trousers pressed to a knife's edge. And he carried a gun. Enrique Hentados, the worst shortstop in Cabo Rojas, Puerto Rico, had carried a pistol in New York and openly scolded the street urchins who strayed too close to Ronald Chadwick's home. He knew all the pushers. They spoke to him on the street, inquiring into the health of his mother and of Paco and Ronald Chadwick. He even knew the smaller dealers, including a newcomer to the heroin wars called Johnny Katanos, streetnamed Zorba the Freak.

Johnny's appearance on the drug scene had been sudden and, in its limited way, spectacular. He had been introduced to the Lower East Side drug scene by Jason Peters, a small-time black dealer he'd met in a bar on 27th Street. Jason had sold him small amounts of heroin on several occasions, but Johnny had clamored for more, always more, so Jason had agreed to turn him on to the wholesalers on Attorney Street, where heroin and cocaine were sold in a kind of impromptu flea market which assembled each day in a rubble-strewn lot one block from Ronald Chadwick's fortress. Johnny's success was nothing short of miraculous, even if his approach to business was unorthodox. He would buy for whatever price was asked and sell for whatever was offered. Accumulating profit and avoiding loss was never his aim. His target, right from the beginning, had been Ronald Jefferson Chadwick and Enrique Hentados had been no more than a highly specialized tool that, once used, would never again be needed. Besides, Enrique hadn't willingly turned against his boss. He'd tried very hard to preserve his integrity, but a man named Muzzafer had been much more determined and his need, in the end, had overcome Enrique's reluctance.

In some way, Muzzafer had been very sympathetic to Enrique. He'd felt a certain kinship with the boy because he, Muzzafer, knew exactly what it was like to begin at the bottom. He had spent his childhood in the Palestinian refugee camps in Jordan. At that time, his full name was Aftab Qwazi Malik. It is the earliest name ascribed to him, though, doubtless, there had been others before. His father, a leader, had struggled in the movement to oust the British and had been forced to change identities time and again. Muzzafer grew up in a world of rebellion and had caught the fever early on, so that, by the time he'd reached manhood, he'd married technique to desire and been hailed as an unqualified success. All by himself (though with the blessing of the PLO), he'd destroyed a concrete-reinforced, machine gun emplacement, along with the four Israeli soldiers manning it. It had been his entry into manhood, the Palestinian equivalent of the Italian ceremony known as "making your bones." After that he'd been sent to Syria for special training, and from Syria to a dozen operations throughout the world.

Probably the single biggest factor in the longevity of Muzzafer's career had been his physical appearance. No one, seeing him for the first time, could take him for a criminal of any kind. He stood five foot six inches tall and weighed a soft one hundred twenty-three pounds. His face was smooth, almost boneless, and was overshadowed by huge, liquid-brown eyes that in an attractive female might have been characterized as limpid. The effect of these eyes, offset by a narrow, full-lipped mouth, was to attract both men and women and the men who hunted for him, who had been hunting for fifteen years, considered him sexually androgynous. Nevertheless, it had been a decade since Muzzafer had been anything other than completely in charge of a project. The one he worked on now had been his creation right from the start.

It would have been most fitting if the conference which launched the course of action leading to the death of Ronald Jefferson Chadwick had taken place somewhere in the vast deserts of Arabia, in a bedouin tent, perhaps, spread with densely-woven carpets or a mud-walled hut as old as the Bible. The participants should have spoken in Arabic, in an obscure nomad dialect, and smoked from a hookah while veiled women, draped in black from head to toe, served heavily sweetened tea. The air outside the tent, shimmering with desert heat, should have been filled with the calls of camel drivers or the high, sparkling laughter of women drawing water from a well.

This was not the case. There was no conference, only a meeting of two childhood friends in a motel on the outskirts of Athens, Georgia. The men spoke softly and smoked Marlboro Golden Lights. They saw on green, vinyl-covered chairs, their faces close together, while the coarse yowling of Lucille Ball poured from the television speaker, a foil for potential eavesdroppers. They took a long time getting down to business, gossiping as old comrades will, repeating stories of mutual friends and enemies. They recalled the wretched poverty of the Palestinian camps in Jordan, the women and the adventures they had shared, the martyrs dead in Israel and Jordan and Lebanon, great victories in Munich and Jerusalem. They drank sherry, a habit picked up from the British, and as he filled their glasses, Muzzafer reminded himself of how much he hated the Moslem fanatics who threatened to overrun the Arab world. And they were not even Arabs, but Persians, the spawn of the mad Ayatollah. As he listened to his companion, nodding now and again, he wondered idly if, fresh from the final victory over the Zionist foe, he would be forced to take up the sword against the insatiable mullahs. He would, he vowed, never submit to their will.

"Ah, my friend, wake up." The fat man shifted in his seat. "You are dreaming and we must get down to business." He smiled, his jowls rippling. "You see? I have become just like an American. Always on a schedule and, what is worse, always on time." His name was Hassan Fakhr, though he'd checked into the Fairview Holiday Inn under the name Moshe Berg, a small joke on any Israeli antiterrorist who might someday investigate the meeting. He was obese, with a soft, fleshy nose and a lower lip which overshot his upper jaw, creating an impression of extreme stubbornness, though he'd come to his present position through his ability to yield ground whenever necessary. Hassan was temporarily attached to the Libyan Mission to the United Nations and enjoyed the privilege of diplomatic immunity, a fact which added considerably to his sense of well-being.

Muzzafer, though unprotected, showed no sign of being ill at ease. The meeting had taken place in the United States at his request. Both men held the American intelligence community in utter contempt.

"Certainly," Muzzafer said, raising his glass in mock salute. "To business. Above all else." He hesitated, though he knew Hassan understood his purpose. "Well," he continued, nonchalantly, almost diffident, "I wish to go to America."

"Ah!" Hassan raised a finger in the air, grinning happily. "But, unless I am mistaken, we are already in America."

"I'm serious, Hassan. I want to bring our business to America. They've escaped us for too long. I want to teach them to be afraid." He paused, letting the message sink in. "I'm *going* to teach them to be afraid."

"This has been attempted before . . ."

Muzzafer stopped Hassan with a wave of his hand. "The time is right, Hassan. I am determined. And I plan to do it in a way that's never been done before. Our methods will become a model for a completely new form of revolutionary struggle. We are not going to have contact with anyone outside of our group after we have armed ourselves. The FBI? The CIA? Our enemies work only through informants, through spies. If no one knows where we are or what we will do next, then we can't be sold out. It's that simple: No contact means no betrayal. We will not have to hit-and-run as we have in the past. We will remain in place and the pressure we exert will be irresistible.

"We will seek the destruction of life and property toward no other end than the destruction of life and property. We will feed the media with bullshit demands that are so sweeping and so vague, they can never be met. Think about it! An invisible organization with a name that has no meaning attacking random targets in one of the most crowded cities in the world. The Americans will be forced to realize that they can't escape the fate of the rest of the world. They can't hide behind their oceans while millions of our people starve. In Europe, they understand us already. The British, the French, the Germans, the Spanish—they know only too well and they leave us alone. Now it's time to teach America a lesson. You know, Hassan, Herr Marx tells us that 'religion is the opiate of the masses,' but Marx is wrong. Times have changed. Today, democracy is the opiate of the masses and we shall see how long their democracy lasts when they are really afraid."

Muzzafer stood up abruptly and began to pace the room. "I'm not speaking just to hear my own voice, Hassan. I'm determined to bring it off. Right now, America seems monstrous, virtually invincible, but they can be frightened, terrified, like any other people. When that happens, when they truly know that death may come any time they leave their homes, they will not hesitate to betray the Jews. Let's face the truth—without the Americans, the Jews will not last two years in Africa. We will drive them back to Germany."

Though his face remained passive, Hassan watched this performance with amazement. Muzzafer's eyes blazed. His hands swung through the air as if conducting his rage and his voice rose with each succeeding phrase. It was not an unfamiliar situation for Hassan and the outcome he feared most was leaving the room with Muzzafer for an enemy. But what if he was asked to join the project? He had dropped out of active participation in terrorist projects in 1980, precisely because he feared becoming addicted to the violence, and as a result, had been forced to walk a fine line. If these killers ever branded him a traitor, there would, he knew, be no place on earth secure enough to keep him safe.

Muzzafer walked to the bureau and took a manila folder from his suitcase. "Here," he said, walking back to the bed, "is my Army. My American Red Army." Laughing, he spread a handful of photos on the bedspread. "This first is Theresa Aviles. She was born Anna Rosa Gomez in the Dominican Republic, but raised in the United States. She joined a radical offshoot of the old Weather Underground, the Green Faction, while she was a student at the University of Maryland. In 1978, in what was really a pitiful attempt to raise money, she and her companions murdered two bank guards in Luther, Tennessee. She was captured immediately, but instead of turning informer, she stabbed a prison guard and escaped before her trial.

"This is her lover, Johnny Katanos."

Muzzafer held the photo up and Hassan, curious, stared at the dark, expressionless eyes, the prominent cheekbones, the incongruous boyish smile. "He looks like he doesn't care one way or the other. The rest of them are so intense. So sincere."

"Katanos looks like a little boy," Muzzafer said, "because he doesn't want you ever to know what he's thinking. He told us that he grew up mainly in institutions, in New York City, and he learned very young not to expose himself. To always hold something back. But he is in love with violence, Hassan. In Europe, he would pose as a drug dealer, work himself into a position of trust within some . . ." He paused for a moment, searching for the word. "Would you say drug 'ring' or drug 'gang'? In any event, once he understood the operation well enough to know where the money would be and when it would be there, he would simply take it. And usually in the most violent way possible. That is how he came to Algiers and how he met Theresa. He was living in Spain, in Malaga, when everyone caught up to him—the criminals, the French police, the German police and Interpol. He came to Africa through Gibraltar with his enemies one step behind him, then met Theresa and now he enjoys the protection of the Algerian government.

"Hassan, he is the hardest man I've ever met. Not a leader, of course, but a fantastic physical specimen. Perfectly willing to do anything asked of him, as long as it's violent and dangerous. I sent him to Haifa, to take care of a certain arms dealer who sold us defective rockets. He brought back the man's eyes."

Muzzafer held up another photo, taking that of Johnny Katanos from Hassan's hands. "This one is born Sarah Cohen, but is presently using the name Effie Bloom. She is a lesbian and very committed. She has read everything and will do anything, except sleep with a man for pleasure. After she assassinated the Grand Knight of the Christian Brotherhood of Georgia, Lester Hagen, she was sentenced to ninety-five years by an Atlanta jury. In prison, she killed another convict in a dispute over the favors of Jane Mathews, also a felon. Jane's father was a professor of Mechanical Engineering at Georgia Tech and it was expected that Jane, an A student in her junior year, would follow in his footsteps. Right up until the day she planted a bomb in Blair Hall. After she and Effie met, it was love at first sight, at least on Effie's part, so, naturally, when Effie decided to escape, she took Jane along. You probably remember the story. The bus taking Jane and Effie to Effie's trial was attacked by six of Effie's sisters. Effie and Jane were liberated and smuggled out of the country. If I remember correctly, there was quite a high body count on that particular adventure."

"Eight dead," Hassan grunted.

Muzzafer sat down again, resting his elbows on the table. "They will follow me. I'm sure of it. You see, right now they are living in a villa overlooking the Mediterranean, in Algeria. Very beautiful, my brother, but I have played a little trick on them. I have persuaded the

Algerians to expel them. Where can they go? The Americans are waiting for any opportunity to return them to prison, and this time precautions will be taken to see that they never again have any hope of escape. Effie and Jane would certainly be separated and this is Effie's greatest fear. It terrifies her.

"I will offer the chance to strike again and they will accept. What I need from you is permission to bring them into Libya, to have your doctors alter their features so they cannot be recognized from a poster or a prison photograph. I want you to supply them with documents and cash. We will remain in Libya for no more than a month and once we reach the United States, you'll never hear from us again."

Hassan smiled and relief flowed through him so quickly, his mood went from caution to euphoria without any seeming transition. "I don't think I will have any problem with this," he began. "Our friend, Muammar, is still angry over the death of his child, not to mention the attempt on his own life. As long as it's not an official Libyan project . . ."

"The American Red Army," Muzzafer explained, "will have no roots anywhere. Its identity will be as shadowy as its name."

Hassan reached into his pocket and removed his lighter, an old Zippo with a Marine Corps insignia on its face, and lit a cigarette. Offering the pack to Muzzafer, he asked, "Can I tell you what I really think? Can I be honest with you?"

"Go ahead." Muzzafer sat back. He knew what was coming, the obvious weak point in his project. "Let's hear it."

"These are not revolutionaries," Hassan said gently. His hands swept across the photographs. "Three amateurs, two of them lesbians, and a common criminal. You and I have been hardened by years in exile. By having to accept the leavings of other nations while the Jews squat on our homeland. We can accept the discipline, the isolation, but these college students . . ." He shook his head. "I know what you are trying to do and it's true that if your aim is to disappear, you will have to use Americans, but somehow you must find real professionals. You know very well that the most difficult part of any project is keeping the unit together. It's hard enough even when you have hardened professionals, with families that are easy to find. How do you expect to keep your Americans working in isolation for an indefinite period of time?'' He paused briefly. ''Within six weeks of your arrival in America, they will be bickering among themselves. Within six months, they will make you as much an amateur as they are. They will make you a criminal to match the one you're bringing with you.''

''You mustn't underestimate him, Hassan. I have never seen a man as eager as he is. Physically, he's one in a million.''

Something in Muzzafer's voice, in his enthusiasm, brought Hassan up short. He recalled the rumors surrounding Muzzafer's sexual preferences. He had never believed the stories, blaming them on the bad luck of Muzzafer's being dealt a soft body and a softer face, but listening to Muzzafer describe the abilities of the young Greek, he began to have his doubts. Not that he was upset. His relief at not being asked for anything he couldn't deliver allowed him the confidence to be objective.

''My friend, I don't care how dangerous he is. I don't care if he's killed a hundred people. If we've learned any lesson from our years in the struggle, it's to keep amateurs and common criminals away from our projects.''

''Listen, Hassan,'' Muzzafer said, his voice tight, ''there is nothing common about Johnny Katanos.''

Ten o'clock on a cold, Tuesday morning. The air so clear the skyline of Manhattan seemed etched in deep, blue glass. Johnny Katanos and Muzzafer sat in a black van parked by a meter across from a large, supermarket parking lot. Their position gave them a perfect view of the lot and they carefully inspected the cars entering and leaving.

They were looking for any sign of surveillance, nervous because the appointment they waited to keep (and which would not take place for hours) represented one of the few times their paths would intersect the main currents of international terrorism. On this day, for these few hours, they would be vulnerable to betrayal from outside the group. Of course, they could not have manufactured the instruments with which they would attack New York, nor did they have the means to smuggle weapons across borders, so the situation was truly unavoidable.

Still, Muzzafer had seen so many of his friends taken in situations like this, he couldn't stop tapping his fingers on the door handle, and Katanos finally reached out a hand to slow him down.

"Ease up, man. Relax. I'm the one gonna retrieve the merchandise. You're gonna take off, remember?"

Muzzafer smiled ruefully. "I think I fear the idea of betrayal more than actually being captured. You can sustain yourself in prison with your hatred, but it's hard to get over the sense that someone you trusted, that you called your comrade, sold you out.''

"Shit, where I come from, you expect your partner to rat. If he don't that's when you get surprised. Anyways, there's nothing we can do, but watch the drop. What's coming is coming and that's the end of it.''

"Maybe not the end," Muzzafer shook his head.

"What's more to do?''

"We can hope they didn't pick an asshole to make delivery.''

In January of 1961, Julio Rafael Ramirez had come to the United States to spy on the tens of thousands of refugees who fled Cuba after Fidel Castro's revolution. As these refugees were, for the most part, allowed to leave with nothing but the clothes on their backs, they were more than a little resentful, especially considering they had formed the bulk of the wealthy and middle classes under the dictator, Batista. Fidel was not unmindful of this situation. Suspecting that the American government might take advantage of their resentment, spurring the dissident expatriates on to deeds of sabotage and assassination, he asked twenty student supporters to go into exile with the refugees. They settled in Miami, Florida, and Union City, New Jersey, had gotten married, established businesses, had babies and christenings and first Holy Communions. Julio Ramirez, financed by the Cuban government, opened a barber shop on Kennedy Boulevard in Union City, never growing rich, but paying the bills all the same. This fall, from university student to barber, gave credibility to his tale of disenchantment with Cuban Marxism. Over the years, he'd established his roots within the community. He'd married, had children and continued to report each month to a representative of the Cuban Mission to the United Nations.

Unfortunately, Julio no longer enjoyed his work. He'd never really been an adventurous child, but as a young man—his imagination fired by a brother who'd gone to the mountains in the earliest days of the revolution—he'd seen Fidel's request as a golden opportunity to serve the cause of world socialism. He was fifty-two now, and while he hadn't exactly become a capitalist, he definitely preferred sitting at home with ''The Cosby Show'' to undertaking secret missions.

But Julio did what he was told, because his sponsors left him no choice. He could not return to Cuba and he didn't have enough information to interest the Americans. He'd realized long before, that his life, as well as the lives of his wife and children, would be worthless should the refugee community discover his true loyalties.

Fortunately for Julio's sense of well-being, he was not used very often. Instead of penetrating to the heart of Omega 7, Julio had remained on the outside, confining his efforts to membership in the most public religious and civic organizations. Havana saw him as a messenger, a mule to be used only for operations requiring the talents of a mule. On this particular evening, he'd been ordered to pick up a small ford van at Fort Hamilton Parkway and 99th Street, in Brooklyn, and deliver it to a supermarket parking lot in Queens. He was to wait inside the truck until a man in a green, corduroy jacket approached from the front with his hands in his pockets. The man would enter the van on the driver's side, whereupon they would proceed to a nearby subway stop and Julio would find his way home.

Perhaps Julio's sense of importance would have been less compromised if he'd known he carried enough plastic explosives in the cargo area to blow the little Ford back across the Hudson River, but the rear of the van was sealed off and the doors welded shut, so he had no opportunity to examine the merchandise. The sellers were, of course, Cuban, good friends of Muzzafer's and enthusiastic supporters of his projects, but the ordnance, automatic weapons, and a hodgepodge of special explosives, had been smuggled into South Carolina, along with 27 tons of marijuana, by Colombian guerrillas anxious to finance their own revolution. From South Carolina, it has been trucked as ordinary freight aboard a Penn Central trailer and received in Brooklyn by an attaché of the Cuban Mission, acting under the umbrella of diplomatic immunity. Then it had been left to cool for six months, just in case.

It is interesting to note that payment had been given long before delivery. It wasn't that the Cubans didn't trust Muzzafer. Actually, they would have financed the project from beginning to end if Muzzafer had been willing to surrender control. Of course, Muzzafer preferred to pay, parting with almost all the contents of Ronald Chadwick's suitcase. Then Julio Ramirez had been chosen to make delivery precisely because he was a nonentity who was not only unlikely to be caught, but who could tell his interrogators nothing in any event. The neighborhood in which the van was parked was predominantly Italian and Jewish. The neighborhood of delivery was Greek and Czech. There would be no Cubans to recognize Ramirez. To the all-white worlds of Bay Ridge, Brooklyn and Astoria, Queens, Julio was just another spic.

Julio was not unaware of his status within these communities and his nervousness was evident as he drove out the Gowanus Expressway toward Bay Ridge Parkway. More than once, the good citizens of Bay Ridge had taken the stick to their darker brethren. But Julio needn't have worried. The garage was located on an industrial block with an auto-parts store on one side and an aluminum warehouse on the other. There were black and Puerto Rican workers in abundance and nobody paid the slightest attention to him. Everything went smoothly, as usual. The keys to the garage worked on the first attempt and the van started immediately. Julio pulled the Ford out, replacing it with his own car, a dusty, green Renault, and carefully locked the garage door.

The van rolled smoothly over the ruts and dips on 86th Street and Julio was able to let his attention wander. He drove through Bay Ridge and Bensonhurst toward Sheepshead Bay. Easter was approaching and, with the first warm weather, the shoppers were out along 86th Street. Julio noted the small, family-owned clothing and furniture stores. On one block, Wo Fong's Cantonese Delight was flanked by Slim's Bagels and Gino's Best Pizza. Julio recalled his mother's cousin, Emilio Evans, who'd fled Cuba on a small boat in 1980. He'd wanted to work in Julio's shop and they'd taken a long drive by way of an interview. Newly arrived from a country where toilet paper was rationed, Emilio could not stop talking about the abundance of America. It wasn't even the supermarkets or department stores that impressed him so much.

The small shops, the butcher stores and fruit stands and hardware stores, often pressed one against the other in some obscure New Jersey neighborhood, seemed absolutely miraculous. Where did the money come from? Growing up in Cuba, Emilio had been led to believe that the majority of American workers lived in grinding poverty, but these Cuban-Americans not only had cars and color television sets, but videocassette recorders and ten-speed bicycles as well. They were sending their children to heavily subsidized state colleges while paying off thirty-year mortgages.

Julio turned north on Bedford Avenue and began the long drive through the center of Brooklyn. The shops on 86th Street gave way to blocks of single family homes set back on what were, for New York, substantial pieces of property. The owners were almost exclusively Jewish and the children played on immaculately kept lawns, the boys tossing Frisbees or baseballs while the girls gossiped on porch swings. The husbands were returning from work, driving Cutlass Supremes into driveways, trudging through unlocked front doors, attaché case in hand. A firm universe, established and secure. It did not seem possible that the Bedford Stuyvesant section of Brooklyn began just on the other side of Foster Avenue and was the start of the largest black ghetto in America. Bedford Stuyvesant, Crown Heights, Bushwick, Brownsville, East New York—a world of dark people which extended into Queens through Jamaica and Hollis and St. Albans right to the border of Nassau County, and included more than a million and a half citizens.

As Julio made the right turn onto Empire Boulevard and began to drive, his surroundings grew more and more threatening. Whole blocks of devastated four- and five-story tenements, their windows covered with gray, galvanized sheet metal, seemed to lean toward the street, almost beckoning him. Knots of men, gathered around aluminum drums filled with burning trash, threw grotesque shadows across the alleyways. Night was falling quickly and the old women scuttled down the streets, seeking the safety of locked doors. The total effect was demonic and Julio began to sense an awful malevolence. He felt like an angel strayed into hell and he fought his fear with anger and indignation. He remembered the white world, the Anglos who associated him with this horror. To them, if you were a spic or a nigger, this was your only world, the sum total of all your possibilities, and nothing you could ever achieve would rid them of this attitude. Julio became more and more impatient at the red lights, cursing under his breath and drumming his fingers on the steering wheel. By the time he saw the mouth of the Interboro Parkway, he could control himself no longer. He slapped his foot down on the gas pedal and shot free of the ghetto.

Unfortunately for Julio, black Brooklyn had had an identical effect on another good New Yorker, Dr. Morris Katz, who hit the accelerator of his Olds Regency at almost the same second, so that the two of them flew toward a space large enough for only one. Seeing this, they simultaneously jammed on the brakes, sending both cars into counter-clockwise spins. The two vehicles, as if their dance had been choreographed by Hollywood stuntmen, spun around each other twice before coming to a stop. Julio, furious, opened the door, leaped out and came within an eyeblink of being just the asshole Muzzafer, sitting in a parking lot ten miles away, was afraid of. But then he remembered himself for the first time since crossing Foster Avenue. He looked at his van and recalled that he was carrying an unknown cargo to an unknown group of terrorists on behalf of the Communist government of Cuba. Without a word, in a near panic, he got back into the truck, locked the door and drove off toward Queens.

The remainder of the journey was smooth and uneventful. New York parkways are dirty and gray and essentially featureless. There wasn't a great deal of traffic going north and Julio stayed in the right-hand lane, driving slowly and carefully. He took the Interboro Parkway into the Grand Central, an eight-lane highway connecting upper Manhattan, through Queens, to the further reaches of Long Island, and whisked past Flushing Meadow Park and La Guardia Airport, getting off at Hoyt Avenue, the last exit before the Triboro Bridge. Astoria, like Bay Ridge, was active and prosperous, bustling with shoppers, and the supermarket parking lot was crowded. He waited less than five minutes before being approached. The man was tall and moved very quickly, entering the van through Julio's door. Julio shifted to the helper side of the front seat. He was careful not to look directly into the man's face. There was no conversation, no "hello" and no "good-bye." They arrived at the elevated subway stop at 31st Street and Julio got out, heading immediately up the stairway to the train.

Johnny Katanos took the van back home to his friends. He drove slowly at first, wandering through quiet residential neighborhoods, eyes on the image in the rearview mirror. Then he began to turn corners quickly, without signaling, pulling immediately to the curb and snapping the headlights off. Though he could find no sign of pursuit, he persisted. Driving along 21st Street toward Long Island City, he turned into a closed carwash, accelerating through the lot to emerge on 20th Street heading in the opposite direction. He drove across the 59th Street Bridge into Manhattan, turned left onto Second Avenue, then swung quickly back onto the bridge toward Queens. He parked the van in a diner parking lot and went inside for dinner, watching all the time from a booth by the window. He saw nothing.

When he finished eating, he walked back to the van and began to drive straight toward his destination, going just fast enough to force pursuers to expose themselves, but not fast enough to attract the attention of ordinary policemen. He was convinced that they had brought it off, but he would not abandon his natural caution. Disaster, he believed, lay in wait around every corner, yet disaster could be avoided. It was a game he played. He would pretend that he had just that moment come alive, fully grown, and that his continued existence depended on constant vigilance. The minute he relaxed it was all over, and who could tell when he might be resurrected again? He tried to watch every window, every doorway. To be taken by surprise meant certain annihilation.

He drove to the end of Vernon Boulevard, then up onto the service road of the Long Island Expressway, passing the Brooklyn-Queens Expressway and Maurice Avenue before turning right at 61st Street. Two blocks past Flushing Avenue, he made another right onto 59th Road, a block of brand-new, three-family homes, some still unoccupied. As he spun the wheel, he pressed the button on a brown, plastic transmitter and the garage door on the third house swung open. With a final, backward look, Johnny slid the van neatly into the garage and closed the door behind him.

This was their place of refuge, a true "safe house." Its creation had been the topic of long debates in Algeria and, later, in Libya. Muzzafer had been accustomed to operating with the aid of local revolutionary groups, but in the United States they needed to be completely independent, which necessitated their finding a way to live anonymously. In Europe, most neighborhoods have been established for generations, many for centuries, and it would not be possible to move in without attracting attention, but in the constantly shifting neighborhoods of New York City's outer boroughs, a sense of enduring community is impossible to find. Anonymity is part and parcel of everyday existence.

Muzzafer had used this condition to his own advantage. They had rented apartments in a house at 461-22 Fifty-ninth Road, in Ridgewood, Queens, under three different names. Effie Bloom and Jane Mathews lived on the top floor, girlfriends from Indiana come to study at New York University's Graduate School of Social Work. John Katanos and Theresa Aviles, husband and wife, moved into the center apartment, Theresa telling the real-estate dealer that her husband was a long-distance trucker while she herself used to work at Citibank before she become pregnant. Muzzafer took the bottom floor, posing as an importer of oriental carpets, Muhammad Malik. It amused him no end to play the part of a Pakistani. Were Americans so unsophisticated as to be unable to tell the difference between an Asian and an Arab? Then he recalled that the British had one term to describe the Indian and the Egyptian. They referred to both as "wogs."

It was Muzzafer's habit to begin every meeting with a long story about life in the refugee camps of Palestine, stories which Johnny Katanos found both dull and amusing. Dull because they never varied—the same tale of injustice and deprivation was repeated time after time. Only the name of the characters changed, the characters and the towns and cities. The amusing part was the attention paid by the others and their obvious need to justify their actions. Having watched them in the performance of their duties, Johnny fully believed that they enjoyed what they were doing. Now why, he wondered, can't they allow themselves to know it? Why do they have to pretend it has something to do with "justice"?

The meetings were rigidly controlled. Heeding the warnings of Hassan Fakhr, Muzzafer had insisted the two couples not associate with each other outside the house, and that even their relationships inside be no more intense than those of ordinary neighbors. Nevertheless, he wanted them to have a strong sense of solidarity and purpose; hence the stories. He could see the enthusiasm in the eyes of the women, Effie Bloom, Jane Mathews, and Theresa Aviles, and though he could not read Johnny's face at all, he was not worried about Johnny losing his desire for action.

And in truth, Johnny had no real interest in this end of the business. The fact that the group was committed to spreading fear throughout New York City and had the means to do so was proof enough that his own aims would be well-served. And just as Muzzafer had no doubt that Johnny Katanos would remain loyal as long as there were projects and the weapons to execute them, Johnny was certain that Muzzafer would continue to increase the intensity of his assault on America until they were caught. He did not, of course, include himself in the "they." Nor did he exclude Theresa Aviles.

"The problem, as I see it," Effie began, "is that we don't have a hell of a lot of anything, so we have to find some way to stretch what we do have. That's if we want to appear to be what we call ourselves— an army."

"Exactly," Muzzafer said. "In fact, in some ways all antipersonnel devices already do that. You have a small core of explosive, surrounded by jagged metal. The metal is easy to come by and increases the damage tenfold."

Theresa's fingernails tapped the lace tablecloth absently. "I don't see any reason why we can't make antipersonnel devices. We're not idiots, are we?" She looked from face to face, her shoulders hunched up to her ears, a characteristic gesture. Theresa was a short, wiry woman, very intense and very nervous, who loved to talk of life in the Dominican Republic. Of the small farming communities, the warm winds, the brilliant tropical flowers. She could also speak of the poverty and degradation of a life without money or a real job. In this setting, in New York City, poverty occupied most of her reflections on her homeland. She was absolutely loyal to Muzzafer and totally in love with Johnny Katanos. The utterly distasteful sex in Ronald Chadwick's house had been Muzzafer's test for her and for Effie as well. Theresa understood it as a test and was proud to have passed with honors.

"A pipe and a handful of common nails with a couple of firecrackers in the middle. When I was a kid, me and my girlfriend blew up this boy's doghouse. Not with the dog in it, of course, but when the kid found out who did it, he never bothered us again." Effie Bloom, tall and rawboned, sat in a gray leather armchair which she'd pulled up to the kitchen table. It was her apartment, hers and Jane's, and she was very comfortable. "If we had enough pipe and enough nails, we wouldn't need very much explosive. It would hardly touch our stock."

"How much?" Muzzafer asked. "How much exactly? How many pounds of C-4 to how many pounds of nails to what length of pipe?" He nodded toward the kitchen where Jane Mathews was arranging mugs of hot coffee on a tray. "Shall we ask the expert?"

"Jane," Effie called. "Are you coming in or what?"

"Or what," Jane said, crossing the room to place the tray on the table. As a student of mechanical and chemical engineering, she was expected to answer any question on explosives. "There's milk and sugar on the side. Does anyone want cookies?"

"We were talking about manufacturing our own antipersonnel devices," Muzzafer said gently. Upsetting the relationship between Effie and Jane could easily lead to the destruction of his little army and he was careful never to criticize Jane in Effie's presence.

"I know. I heard you talking. First, you have to consider the diameter of the pipe as well as the length. You have to measure the thickness of the pipe walls, how much explosive pressure they can withstand. Will the pipe be anchored or loose? If it's anchored and one end is plugged, the energy of the explosion will be focused in a single direction and that's where you get the most bang for the buck.'' She smiled and laid her hand on Effie's shoulder. "Simple, right? Now all we have to do is find a pipe supermarket and order the plugged and anchored special.''

Muzzafer's mouth turned upward, a huge grin which only increased the sensitivity of his features. Johnny, watching the Arab closely, asked himself the same question Hassan had asked and answered it with the realization that if he saw Muzzafer on the street, he would swear the man was gay. No other possibility. Johnny flashed back to his early life, the years in juvenile institutions, sometimes for crimes, but more often because no one else would take him. In such a setting, unless he had someone to protect him, Muzzafer would be attacked every day of his life. The fantasy aroused Johnny Katanos and as he reached for his coffee, he let his left hand brush against Muzzafer's arm, noting that the Arab, though aware of the pressure, did not move his arm away.

"Why don't you take it, Jane? You and Effie,'' Muzzafer said. "Let's figure to use it in about three weeks. In the meantime, I want Theresa and Johnny to work with me on a little project. It's a payback for the help we got from Mr. Khadafy. It seems there's a certain Zionist living in Staten Island who has the ear of the American Defense Department. Our benefactors believe this Zionist played a big part in convincing Reagan to attack Khadafy and his family a couple of years ago. It's to be a simple assassination and our first public work.'' He raised his coffee cup in toast. "To the success of our efforts. May they all be as quick and as neat and as profitable as the demise of Mr. Ronald Jefferson Chadwick.''

5

Most New York City cops are committed to the belief that the rest of the world—not only civilians, but all federal agents and state troopers as well—regards them as inevitably corrupt and incompetent, as brutal morons equally willing to abuse a felon or accept a bribe. The psychology is "them or us," and just as blacks insist that whites can never comprehend the black experience, can never even come close, cops regard themselves as perennial outcasts, almost as outlaws in support of the law. Stanley Moodrow had long ago surrendered to this particular fantasy. Whenever he was forced to deal with outside agencies, he expected to be humiliated and his summons to the office of Agent Leonora Higgins at the Queens headquarters of the FBI was, for him, just another confirmation of his basic paranoia. He took it without flinching. The Manhattan branch, located at Federal Plaza near City Hall was less than two miles from the 7th Precinct, but apparently Moodrow's request for a briefing on local terrorist activity had been passed down the line until it came to rest in the lap of Leonora Higgins, one of two female agents in the New York area. Moodrow took it as an insult, clean and simple, and he fully expected Ms. Higgins to compound it by delivering a sharp lecture on the limitations of the New York City Police Department.

It was 8:30 AM when Moodrow began to drive out to Forest Hills, in Queens, and it was raining hard. The wipers, long overdue for replacement, smeared grease haphazardly across the windshield, forcing Moodrow to peer, squint-eyed, through a single patch of clear glass located just beneath the rearview mirror. Still, the sergeant refused to allow himself to become upset. Actually, he reasoned, he'd been lucky to get this Fairmount. The only other vehicle, a Plymouth Reliant, was notorious for stalling in wet weather.

He drove against the rush-hour current, heading out to Queens via the Williamsburg Bridge. The inbound traffic, buses and trucks as well as commuters, was backed up along the Brooklyn-Queens Expressway to the foot of the Kosciuszko Bridge. Moodrow stayed in the right lane, driving slowly. He passed the time composing obscene lyrics to the music of a Merle Haggard tune, "Are the Good Times Really Over for Good", while the radio squawked continually, spouting a series of near-unintelligible requests for police action. A traffic jam at the junction of the Brooklyn-Queens and Long Island Expressways brought him back to life. He could see the revolving amber lights of a tow truck at the Grand Avenue on-ramp and he quickly pulled onto the shoulder of the highway and began to drive around the problem. Two hundred yards ahead, a patrolman on traffic detail recognized the unmarked car and waved him through. The Toyota which tried to follow him wasn't as well received and the sergeant, glancing back through the rearview mirror, saw the driver rolling down his window, prepared to scream out his sense of the injustice done to him. The situation cheered Moodrow considerably.

FBI headquarters in Queens turned out to be a floor of offices in the old Lefrak Building on Queens Boulevard. The lobby was crowded and the bureaucrats, in regulation suit and tie, edged away from him in the elevator. He took it calmly, almost amused. Even the thirty-minute wait and the receptionist's abrupt manner failed to dampen his good spirits. There was a moment, however, as he entered the small office to discover that Leonora Higgins was not only female, but dark, chocolate-brown as well, when Moodrow's day nearly turned completely around. He stood for a moment, red faced, filling the door with his bulk, but then the absurdity of the situation overwhelmed him and he began to laugh, a crude, barbaric howl that had more insult to it than an upraised finger.

To her everlasting credit, Agent Higgins took Moodrow's ridicule without flinching. Tall and very dark, she stood, solemn faced, the light reflecting from high, prominent cheekbones, and absorbed his laughter. She would take this energy and store it for later use, a long-standing technique for enduring humiliation. She observed Moodrow's blocky silhouette in the doorway, and reflected on his rumpled, hounds-tooth jacket and stained tie. Her own navy business suit had been purchased at Lord and Taylor and was ironed nearly to a crisp. But this was, of course, irrelevant. She understood that she would never be granted any personal dignity by the white, Moodrow world, no matter what she did.

And she had achieved a great deal in her thirty-three years. The daughter of an accountant mother and a track-star-turned-junkie father, she had seen both sides—her mother, steady, going out to work each morning and her father, searching the house for money or nodding away in a corner. After high school, she'd agreed to enlist in the army in return for six-months' training as a paramedic. The army had kept to the bargain, putting her through a cram course in battlefield medicine before shipping her off to Vietnam.

On January 30, 1968, opening day of the great Tet offensive, she'd been stationed in a hospital in Phu Bai, a hamlet ten miles southeast of Hue. For the next week, she worked, day and night, as the soldiers poured into her station. Thinking of it now, her memory was a jumble of torn, moaning GIs, their cries punctuated by the slap of helicopter blades and the sharp, helpless orders of heart-broken surgeons. At week's end, just as she reached the limits of her endurance, the hospital had come under attack. Suddenly, wounded soldiers found the strength to get out of their beds and fight. Cold with anger, Leonora dropped her bandages and ran off to grab an M16. In fact, it was not an all-out assault by NVA Regulars, but a local guerrilla action involving fifteen men who chose to approach head-on, rifles blazing. Leonora had taken one man out at point-blank range, had seen three holes appear in a line across his chest. At first, the man's face had become puzzled, eyes turning inward, and then his life had gone. Leonora saw it run out as clearly as she saw his body jump backward and topple into the dust of the courtyard. She'd grunted with satisfaction, noting her lack of emotion, and had gone out to seek another yellow body for destruction. Later, she felt as if she'd lost something that had once been beautiful, but was now, like a withered flower, strangely repulsive, almost rotten.

After the war, she'd attended U.S.C. on a track scholarship, though she was never good enough for the better regional meets. However, she was more than happy to be getting a free education, while USC, for its part, was overjoyed to have found a female, black student who managed to maintain a 3.7 overall grade index. Leonora found she had a natural ability to recall almost everything she read. She combined this with a willingness to provide for the peculiar needs of her individual instructors. She scored 675 out of a possible 700 on her law boards and moved on to Stanford Law where her special talents proved even more effective. After graduation, she was heavily recruited by a dozen corporations, including the FBI. One company especially, the Chicago Consolidated Bank, under heavy fire for past and present deeds of discrimination against blacks and women, had offered Leonora a huge starting salary, as well as guaranteed advancement and an office with beige carpeting. Leonora chose the FBI because they offered her action and a chance to carry firearms, something no business could match. They promised her frontline experience in the bureau's antiterrorist arm and they kept their word, briefing her extensively before sending her off to apprentice under Agent George Bradley. Together, they headed a new intelligence-gathering effort directed at the hundreds of thousands of Indian, Pakistani, Arab, and Turkish immigrants pouring into the United States. Moodrow's information was to be part of this overall effort and Leonora was determined to make him fill that role, if she had to wait an hour for him to shut up.

It didn't take that long. A connecting door opened and a white, middle-aged man, Agent George Bradley, dressed in his usual pale-gray vested suit, stepped quickly into the room, cutting off Moodrow's laughter.

"I hate fat cops," he said to Leonora.

"What are you talking about, man?" Moodrow protested. "I ain't got an ounce of fat on me."

Bradley smiled indulgently. "Then why do you buy your shirts three times too large?" He pointed to where Moodrow's shirt hung over his belt. "Leonora, I think we'd better get this over with." He walked to the bookshelves and picked up a can of room deodorant. "Only half a can. Lord, the sacrifices we make."

Moodrow smiled eagerly. "You spray that shit at me, I'm gonna sacrifice your right arm." He took a step forward, but Leonora jumped between them, placing a gentle palm against Moodrow's chest. "Sergeant," she said, "why don't you be seated? We can get down to business in a moment. I apologize for having kept you waiting." She turned to George Bradley, her speech slow and controlled, her enunciation precise. "George, why don't you let me work with Sergeant Moodrow for now. If something important develops, you can always run him down at the . . . What was the precinct?"

"The Seventh," Moodrow growled.

"Yes, the Seventh Precinct."

Agent Bradley allowed his gaze to remain locked with Moodrow's for a few more seconds, then he glanced at Leonora. "Sure," he said, smiling broadly. He swung back to Moodrow. "So long, Stanley." He walked into his office, closing the door behind him, and turned on the lights. Moving quickly to his desk, his face composed, he removed a small tape recorder from the center drawer. Setting it next to the intercom, he switched both on.

In the other office, Moodrow slumped in a straight-backed chair, waiting patiently while Higgins rummaged about in a filing cabinet. "I hope you don't mind my recording this meeting. It's just standard procedure, really."

"That's no good," Moodrow responded. "You gotta learn to take notes. The tape's too dense. What if we talk for an hour? How many times could you listen? You should learn to use your instincts. Like a spider.'' He sprawled in the chair, legs far apart. The morning was almost half over and he was still having a good time. Just for an instant, he caught a glimpse of the reason for his exhilaration and her name, to his surprise, was Rita Melengic.

"Yes, I see," Leonora said. She sat down at her desk and picked up a thin, brown file. "Like a spider. Just give me a moment." She opened the file and began to read quickly. Moodrow watched without commenting, taking in her sense of composure and competence. He observed her hands, the nails at medium length, each perfectly trimmed and covered with clear polish. There was nothing fearful about her and Moodrow, realizing that he could not bully her, gave up the idea as easily as a two-dollar tip at the Killarney Harp. What the fuck, he thought, just another cop. She placed the file, still open, on the desk.

"How far did you get?" Moodrow asked.

"All we have is the actual crime."

Moodrow pulled several sheets of paper from his pocket and passed them across the desk. "Hold onto these for later." He paused, looking into her eyes. "The thing is, I'm not a federal agent. I don't know shit about Arabs. But what I do know is the Seventh Precinct and what goes on inside it. I been there twenty-three years, all my life. I mean, sometimes I don't go home for days. I stay overnight with some of the families in the neighborhood. I'm talking about civilians, not cops. I know all the bad guys and all the good guys. Anything goes on in the precinct, someone tells me where to dig for the roots. Except for Ronald Chadwick. Him I can't explain. For sure, he was set up by a kid named Enrique Hentados, but Hentados has disappeared. Now . . .''

Leonora interrupted, picking up her pen. "Give me some background on Hentados."

"It's in the new sheets. A Puerto Rican. Devoted to mom. He got his job with Chadwick through a cousin, Paco Baquili. Baquili's in my pocket. The way he tells it, Enrique was like a kid brother, a kid they let hang around. No way he could get inside that house with a hand grenade.''

"But if he knew the routine, Sergeant, it would seem quite easy for him to hide upstairs."

"Then where is he?" Moodrow pulled his cigarettes from his shirt pocket, handling the pack roughly. That was the problem with federal agents—by the time they had everything down, taped it and photographed it, the game was too boring to play. "You think a ghetto kid like Enrique Hentados can slip off to Rio with the loot? What would he do when he got there? The only hotels he knows about are the welfare hotels on Stanton Street. Rice and beans, Higgins. That's his universe, and if he was hiding somewhere in that world, I'd already know about it. And I'm not making any generalizations. A guy like Chadwick could bring it off. He could turn up in Los Angeles with a full wallet and strut for the next ten years. Not Enrique." Moodrow pushed his chair away and began to pace the room. Higgins remained seated, fascinated. "It's like the tape you're making. Taking notes forces you to listen for the important parts. That way you train your instincts. After awhile, you know when something's wrong, when they're lying. Look, how old are you? Twenty-four? Twenty-five?"

Leonora smiled for the first time. Was he trying to flatter her? "I don't get the point."

"The point is Enrique Hentados is dead and I don't have to find a body to prove it. Somebody used him and threw him away and it wasn't any of the big dealers. Shit, the whole neighborhood's in a fucking panic right now. Nobody has the money to take over."

"There's always the possibility that the killer was someone who had a grudge against Chadwick. Maybe he just evened up."

"Then where is he? People down there don't get revenge and just clam up. What's the point? If the killer was local, someone would be bragging about it right now. The guy came from outside. A fucking pro. This boy's so good, it's scary. And here's something else to think about." Moodrow leaned over the desk and tapped the back of Leonora Higgins' hand. "See, this guy likes to give pain. He shoots Chadwick and the bodyguard. Nobody hears nothin'. He's got the fucking money. Why doesn't he just take off? There's not a goddamn thing between him and safety, but he goes out of his way to set up some asshole soldiers two floors away. Did you get any pictures with your file? He blew the shit out of them. You know what I'm saying, right? Pieces all over the walls. If this guy decides to take his action over to Times Square, he's gonna cover New York with bodies.''

Leonora pulled her hand away, resisting a mischievous urge to wipe it on her skirt. ''I hear you, Sergeant, and I don't want you to think we didn't give serious consideration precisely to the point you're making.''

''Now you're gonna say, 'but,' '' Moodrow predicted.

''Exactly. But after examining the situation a little more closely, the use of a Soviet grenade, which is the only unusual factor in your scenario, is easily explained. The first thing we did, Agent Bradley and myself, was to contact General George Martin at the Defense Department. We wanted to know if any statistics were ever compiled on weapons smuggled back from Vietnam. I'm sure you remember that the North Vietnamese Army was supplied entirely by the Soviet Union and, of course, soldiers traditionally carry trophies home. General Martin told us that thousands of grenades, AK47s, sidearms, even rockets, were actually *confiscated* during the war years. Keep in mind there were hundreds of thousands of troops stationed there for most of the war, with virtually all of them being replaced every year. In the general's opinion, which he asked not be made public, it's unlikely the army recovered a tenth of what came across our borders. If you remember, about six months ago, a Texan marched into a Burger King restaurant in Amarillo wearing a string of Russian grenades around his neck. He wasn't even a Vietnam veteran. He got them from his son's army buddy.

''Even supposing that the attack on Ronald Chadwick did come from outside New York, that Hentados was used and then murdered, why can't the killer just be a talented thief with enough brains to operate outside his territory? I know I'm insulting you if I suggest you don't know that drug-related killings, ninety percent of which go unsolved, occur almost every day in New York and many of them are very, very grisly.

''So where does it go from here? While, technically, the hand grenade is a violation of federal statutes, we're confident that you're the man best able to close the Chadwick file, if it can be closed. All right?'' She pushed back her chair. The obligatory ''briefing'' was complete.

Moodrow stood erect, reaching out to shake hands. He noted, with some satisfaction, that her hand disappeared completely within his. ''That's just what the captain says. He also thinks it's just gonna go away. Well, what the fuck. I made my report and I guess you got plenty of work, listening to that tape and all. Now Captain Epstein'll feel much better. My guess is, he'll drop the whole thing. I mean, if the FBI's satisfied, then the NYPD must be satisfied. It only stands to reason, right? Well, it was a pleasure chatting with you.'' Moodrow leaned across the desk, whispering into the intercom. ''And you, too, asshole.''

George Bradley strolled back into Leonora Higgins' office, extending a cup of coffee. He smiled at her affectionately. ''Light and sweet?''

Leonora giggled. ''How'd I do?''

''So-so.''

''Really?'' Leonora felt her mood dissolving.

''He knows more than he told you. And he's right about instincts. Only they're not instincts, they're reflexes. You develop them by practicing. How did he know I was listening? Would you have known?'' His voice was kind, not cutting, and she took no insult, recognizing her own deficiencies. By age thirty-three, her age, Moodrow had had almost fourteen years of police experience.

Bradley continued. ''Anyway, you were right about one thing. There's nothing in it for us. It doesn't fit our methods. Let Moodrow solve it.''

Leonora nodded in agreement, tossing Stanley Moodrow aside. Without speaking, she got her coat.

They passed out of the building, Bradley opening an umbrella, and walked away from the shops on Queens Boulevard, back into the streets of Forest Hills, a solidly middle-class Jewish neighborhood. It was 11 AM and the streets were very quiet. There were some matters they never spoke about in a space where a microphone might be concealed. George had spent the early part of the morning with a Cuban, George Reyes, a double agent attached to the Cuban Mission to the UN. Reyes, a career intelligence officer, worked out of the Dirección General de Intelligensia and exchanged information on Cuba's foreign activities in return for cash payments made to a sister in Miami. It was Reyes who had told them, weeks before, of Muzzafer's contract to purchase arms. It was Reyes' understanding, though he had not met personally with Muzzafer, that an operation of some sort was being planned for the New York area. Over the next ten days, Higgins and Bradley had questioned two dozen radicals, all paid informants, in an effort to head off the coming explosion. They'd come up empty. Even the Israelis could only tell them that Muzzafer had passed from Algeria to Libya, along with several known fugitives, all Americans, apparently acting as a unit.

Bradley spoke first, his voice tighter than it had been in the office. "Well," he said, "the deal went down."

Leonora felt her heart give a small jump, as at the approach of some still faraway nightmare. "What did he get?"

"Plastics, automatic weapons, claymores. The full range. Most of it Israeli or American. Anyway, we've got the courier's name. Ramirez. A barber from Union City."

"Is he part of it?"

"Definitely not. He works for the Cubans and our bird insists that the DGI does not control this operation. However, Ramirez did meet, face to face, with someone from the group. He did not just leave the goods on a street corner."

Without thinking, Leonora Higgins linked her arm with George Bradley's. "Can we couple this with Moodrow's information? Maybe that's where the money came from."

"Sure, it's possible. You know, this is a strange business. A few rumors, a robbery, an informant's story and we all go wild. Our only option is to keep up the pressure and wait for something—or nothing—to happen."

* * *

By the time Moodrow got back to the precinct house on Broome Street, the rain had stopped, although heavy gray clouds still hung, as if pinned, to the tops of the East River bridges. Moodrow left the car double-parked on Pitt Street with the key in the ignition. Even in the 7th, it was considered bad form to steal a police car, especially an '82 Fairmount with extensive body damage.

The new 7th Precinct building, completed in 1981, combined the local police and fire departments, giving each more room and vastly improved communications equipment. For the first time, the cops of the 7th were tied into the central computer in Albany. After more than two decades in the old building, Moodrow had expected to miss the very small noisy rooms and the odor of mildew, but through an almost miraculous process, the new had come to resemble the old within a matter of weeks. The paint, municipal brown on municipal green, cracked, and now hung in sheets along the walls. The urinals, clogged with soggy paper towels, smelled of junkie vomit and the entrance hall still rang with curses and shouts, the endless complaints of criminals brought to justice. The phone system went out six times in the first week and New York Telephone had a team stationed there indefinitely. Somehow, two years later, the funds for the landscaping had disappeared into the bowels of the general budget and the walk-way turned into a sea of mud at the least drizzle. Nobody complained, except for Captain Epstein, who continued to retain fantasies of a smoothly functioning paramilitary organization dedicated to "crime processing."

Moodrow entered the stationhouse, trailing mud, and acknowl-edged the greeting of the desk sergeant, Officer Pannino. It was early afternoon and the action was light. Moodrow noted Detective Isaiah Abrams had Jose Rosa handcuffed to a hot water pipe. Rosa was a junkie-burglar and one of Moodrow's better informed snitches. He looked across at the sergeant, hoping against hope, but Moodrow ignored him and walked directly to Captain Epstein's office. Rosa would still be there later, even more grateful for any help Moodrow could offer.

The door to the captain's office was wide open and Moodrow stuck his head through. "Busy, Captain?" he asked.

"Stanley," Epstein smiled, "never too busy for my favorite physician. You've healed me completely. Fantastic." He gestured to the patrolman standing in front of his desk. "This here is Officer Bogard. I'm giving him the orientation lecture. Showing him the Seventh Precinct philosophy. Sit down."

Bogard tried to smile at Moodrow, but couldn't quite get it across. It wasn't that Moodrow was hostile or even indifferent. Bogard felt like he'd wandered into a veterans' reunion, though he himself had never been to war. There was a quality of experience here that eluded him completely.

"How much do you weigh, Bogard?" Moodrow asked.

"A hundred forty-five. Is there something wrong with that? I passed every strength test on the department exam."

"That's good, Bogard. You got a sap?" Bogard didn't respond, though he blushed noticeably. Blackjacks were common in the department. "You should learn to use one." Moodrow sat down, grunting amiably.

"OK," Epstein said. "Let's talk about crime. The people who live in this precinct are very poor, Bogard. I'm sayin' per-capita income is almost as low as the South Bronx. We got housing projects and we got tenements and we got crime. But that's OK, Bogard. The department doesn't expect miracles. Everyone knows we couldn't stop the crime in New York if we had a million cops on patrol. Prevention is for social workers. Down here we work on percentages. If the city-wide arrest rate for murders is thirty-four percent, which it is, then our rate should be thirty-eight percent. If it's eight percent for muggers, we go for eleven percent. Shit, Bogard, we don't have to worry about gettin' all the criminals. There are so many, they get each other. All we do is keep the numbers right and stay alive." He looked at Moodrow. "Anything to add, Sergeant?"

Moodrow crossed his legs, clots of mud dropping from his heavy, scuffed brogans. "The thing about a sap is you could use it against an unarmed perpetrator and not get busted by the department. Remember one thing: The department protects you against the outside, but they don't protect you from the department. You gotta be discreet. When you sap a guy, never hit him in the head. Go for the point of the shoulder or the collar bone. If his hands are up, slap his ribs. You wouldn't believe how fast they come around when you snap a rib.''

Bogard nodded toward Moodrow. "Thanks for the idea, Sergeant." Then he turned back to Epstein. "Will that be all, Captain?''

"Yeah, sure. Welcome to the Seventh. My door's always open.'' He watched Bogard leave, then rose to shut the door. "Beer, Stanley?'' Without waiting for an answer, he pulled two Budweisers from a small refrigerator and offered one to Moodrow. "How'd it go?''

Moodrow shrugged his shoulders. "It went. They listened, then sent me home. Just what I expected. All they know about is tape recorders and wiretaps.'' He snorted derisively.

"Don't take it bad," Epstein beamed. "You did your job and now it's over. It's time to go back to work for the Seventh. I got a big problem at the Asher Levy Nursing Homes on Jackson Street. The Puerto Ricans are harassing the old Jews, throwing stones. No big deal, but it's every day now and the goddamn rabbi's been in here three times. He wants to know what kind of Jew I am that I should let my own people be terrorized.'' He threw up his arms in disgust. "All right, I know it happens twice a year, like clockwork, but you got a special advantage here. See, you live in the fucking precinct. You know everybody.'' That fact, all by itself, branded Moodrow a maniac in Epstein's eyes. He had never known another cop to live where he worked. "Don't worry about bringing anyone in. Rabbi Tannenbaum will settle for a cease-fire. You just find out what's bothering the boys.''

Moodrow polished off his beer, tossing the empty bottle into the wastebasket. "Listen, Captain, I think I know who blew Chadwick away.'' He stopped briefly, acutely aware of having said more than he wanted to. "I interviewed thirteen people besides Paco and the story's the same everywhere. Understand? No disagreement on the particulars?''

Epstein nodded, signaling Moodrow to continue.

"There's this guy they call Zorba the Freak. Real name is Johnny Katanos. A Greek. Three months ago, Katanos got introduced to the scene by a small-time dealer named Jason Peters. Right away, he makes friends with little Enrique. They get closer than close. Like maybe even fags. Then one day Chadwick get ripped off and, just like that, Enrique disappears along with this Greek. You remember Ortiz? The little one with the tattoo on his back? He did a lot of business with Zorba, said he knew the guy couldn't be a cop because he was too cold. He says the only person Zorba ever spoke nice to was Enrique Hentados. Ortiz also thinks maybe they were getting it on together. I gotta say it, Captain. I ran down every one of Enrique's friends and relatives. They're all accounted for. Except this Greek."

Epstein pushed his chair away from his desk and got up to get Moodrow another beer. "You know, Stanley. I was hopin' this crap would go away."

"Now you sound like Agent Higgins. I hope you didn't mean all that shit you told the rookie."

"No, no." He pried the top off and passed the bottle over to Moodrow. "Of course not. I know it's only good when it's personal, Stanley. I been a cop for a long time. Like you. But this isn't personal. Some criminal got blown away. So what? You wanna spend the next six months tracking this Greek down?"

"But I could do it," the sergeant replied calmly. "You give me enough time and I'll find him."

"If he's still in New York?"

"He's here all right."

Epstein nodded in agreement. "Why argue?" he said. "He's not in the Seventh. We agree on that, too. Now here's the clincher. The fucking Jewish Defense League is threatening to set up patrols on Grand Street if we don't stop the attacks. You wanna see those assholes down here? Remember Crown Heights? We could have a goddamn war."

Moodrow dropped the empty beer bottle into the wastebasket where it clinked softly against his first. He knew that Epstein was correct. He, Moodrow, could probably prevent further trouble between the

Jews and the Puerto Ricans. The 7th precinct was his world. He'd never lived anywhere else. This was the Lower East Side of Manhattan, a neighborhood that never was. It stretched from 14th Street on the north to the Brooklyn Bridge on the south. Third Avenue and the Bowery separated it from Greenwich Village, while the East River formed its final boundary. Unlike the slums of Harlem or Bedford Stuyvesant, it had never been a "good" neighborhood. Most of its tenements, substandard from the first, were built between 1880 and 1915 to house the millions of immigrants pouring in from Eastern Europe. Czechs, Ukrainians, Poles, Latvians, Russians and 1.25 million Jews jammed into the 7th Precinct, until the streets exploded with humanity. Prosperity came slowly, but by the end of World War II, most of the immigrants had died or moved out to Long Island or New Jersey, leaving the Lower East Side to the Puerto Ricans who entered, not as aliens, but as full American citizens, only to discover that the living conditions, far from improving with age, had deteriorated so badly that some of the buildings—the top floors burned away by arsonists—seemed more like caves than homes. Rents, rigidly controlled by law, had fallen below the level necessary to produce a profit and rather than pay the taxes, many landlords had abandoned their properties to the derelicts and the junkies.

Over the years, for no apparent reason, many of the Puerto Ricans had come to blame their misfortunes on the few thousand Jews still remaining in the neighborhood. Concentrated in a small area along Grand Street by the East River, they controlled the only middle- and upper-income housing in the 7th Precinct, a fact bitterly resented by, for instance, those Spanish families staying on 6th Street between Avenues C and D where only three buildings remained standing. The Puerto Ricans referred to the area along Grand Street as "Jewtown" and every eight or nine months, one or another of the street gangs, ever in search of manhood, would begin systematically to harass the more affluent Jews.

This was very old news to Moodrow. Somehow, he'd never been identified with either group. The people of the 7th Precinct, Puerto Rican or Jew, recognized him as a man who pursued his own ends.

He was merciless to those criminals he chose to persecute and not much better to ordinary citizens when he was on a hunt. But they also knew they could come to him with a beef, that he would intercede if, for instance, Mrs. Perez' bodega on Rivington and Orchard was being systematically looted by junkies or if Mel Lipsky's son, presently at Riker's Island awaiting trial for credit-card fraud, was being threatened by that institution's resident homosexual community. He would handle this new problem as he'd handled all the others—by pursuing his aim doggedly, with a dedication that at times seemed almost mindless. Even as Captain Epstein rattled on, Moodrow began to choose a course of action. He would begin at the Boy's Club on Ludlow Street, a double storefront with three boxing rings and a pile of miscellaneous, sweat-soaked equipment. The Roberto Clemente Gym had produced three national Golden Gloves champions as well as an Olympic silver medalist and a host of professionals. Moodrow went there regularly to work out. He would spar with anyone. Dressed in sweatpants and sweatshirt, he towered over the young amateurs and the deal was that he would allow them to take their best shots without trying to hit back. He spun them around, leaned on them, sidestepped, pushed an elbow into a chin, took the punches on his arms— all with the freaky grace of a dancing bear. The kids loved the opportunity to try to deck the cop. No one under 185 pounds had ever done it, but there was still satisfaction in digging a left into Moodrow's ribs, hoping to produce some slight grimace. His appearances at the gym offered a welcome break from the endless workouts and the sight of the 265-pound sergeant waltzing with a fourteen-year-old lightweight brought rare smiles to an otherwise grim occupation. These were the best of the ghetto youth, the most highly disciplined of the street kids. They were not informants, but they, too, hated and feared the mindless violence of the criminals and junkies who haunted the Lower East Side, and they would point Moodrow in the right direction if they took to his cause.

"Well?"

Moodrow looked up to find Captain Epstein staring at him from across the desk.

"Well what?"

"C'mon, Stanley. What the hell have we been talking about?" Epstein smacked his palm against the desktop. He reminded himself, once more, of how much he needed Moodrow. "The Asher Levy Nursing Homes for Christ sake."

Moodrow shrugged. "Chadwick don't mean shit to me."

"Good," Epstein grinned broadly, already looking for some way to get rid of the sergeant. "By the way, did you tell that agent about the Greek?"

Moodrow returned Epstein's smile, trying to think of a way to get another beer out of the captain. "Fuck, no," he said.

6

The Meledy Soda Works built in 1924 and long abandoned, still sits on top of a small hill overlooking Countess Moore High School in Staten Island. A perennial eyesore in a middle-class residential community, the local economic planning board has, on several occasions, resolved to have it demolished, but has yet to come up with the money. It lies, appropriately enough, on Meledy Road, which runs one short block between Merrill and Richmond Avenues, and its second floor still offers a clear view of the Rockport-Central Housing Development, fifteen dwellings arranged in a neat rectangle on four streets— Hillman Avenue, Morgan Lane, Leggett Place and Jardine Avenue. The single-story ranch homes are only three years old and still retain the raw look of newly landscaped developments. The maples are small, and their trunks, wrapped with burlap, and the azaleas, though carefully trimmed, have yet to grow to the level of the windows. A thief would see these streets as threatening, as offering no cover, no place to hide, but what is danger to the thief is opportunity to the assassin.

Nevertheless, on the night Effie Bloom drove the van past Countess Moore High School, the residents slept peacefully, prepared to wait out the years necessary for the neighborhood to mature. There was no one awake to observe her passage along the deserted street, no one to notice her park beside the empty factory. She turned to Johnny Katanos squatting in the back. "Good hunting," she whispered, receiving a thin smile in return as he slipped through the rear doors, backpack in place. He move confidently in the darkness, going straight through the yard to a door in the southeast corner of the building. Bending back the already vandalized sheet-metal covering, he stepped quickly inside.

Most of the Meledy Soda Works consisted of a single, huge space, nearly three stories high, which held the machinery: enormous brass cookers and bottles by the thousands flowing along conveyor belts, that made the plant run. The machinery had long since been sold for salvage and the only clue remaining to the original use of the building was the broken glass covering the floor. Johnny moved through it without making a sound, pushing the glass ahead of him with the tip of his shoe. He felt the glass gave him an advantage because he would now be able to hear intruders from a long way off, while he, himself, would be absolutely silent. He kept one hand on the eastern wall as he slowly made his way north, pausing every few seconds to listen, straining for any presence beside his own. Within fifteen steps, he heard voices coming from the stairway and he flattened himself against the wall an instant before a match flared through a open doorway.

"Hey, baby, you wanna smoke?" The voice was heavy, a slurred, junkie croak.

"No, man, I'm cool."

"What you mean, you cool? How you cool? You crazy?"

A snore, loud and choking with a sudden hitch at the end.

"Shit, this honky sleepin' already. Hey, Jockamo, you sleepin', man?" A pause, punctuated by increasingly loud snoring. "We gon' take that mother off, man. Jus' like I say. He easy. Gon' be just like fallin' asleep. Damn, I bet we get four, five thousand . . . You listenin'? I say thousands. And it just be sittin' there waitin'. You got the piece, baby, so it be up to you."

Johnny's instructions had been clear and precise and, along with all the rest of the cell, he had agreed to them at the final planning session. He was to abort the operation in the face of unforeseen developments. Muzzafer had lectured at length on the danger of improvisation. "The changing of a plan," he'd explained, "always sets forth a new series of causes and effects which are necessarily unpredictable. The true revolutionary is able to postpone an action, because he or she understands that victory is inevitable and personal satisfaction is counter-productive. Ultimately, success depends on our ability to act as a unit in all phases of an operation. You Americans all want to be cowboys, standing at ten paces with your six-guns blazing, but you must realize that you face a mechanical beast, a computerized gunslinger, and if you cannot match his efficiency, he will destroy you merely to be able to add you to the 'solved' file of his IBM."

It took Johnny all of ten seconds to reject Muzzafer's reasoning. Even as he heard the voices, he felt the sudden rush of blood to his face and throat. Slowly, ears straining, he lowered the pack to the floor, pulling a long, black hunting knife from a sheath strapped to his ankle. He had known many junkies on the Lower East Side. They shot up, spoke for a few moments, then fell into a trancelike sleep. These two were like fat, cage-raised guinea pigs suddenly tossed into a crate with a hungry python and, from this point of view, Johnny Katanos' legitimate prey—an unexpected bonus for an assassin without politics.

Johnny moved slowly, silently, guided by the soft junkie breathing, until he was kneeling over the first man. He paused, waiting for the full rush of desire, then shot his hand forward, incredibly fast, closing off the mouth and nose. He experienced just a single pang of regret— it was too dark to look in the man's eyes. Then he pushed the knife into the soft throat below his hand, through the veins and tendons, taking the rush of hot blood as his reward.

"Whass happenin', man?"

Johnny's leg snapped out, almost without his will, straight to the source of the words, striking the man across the mouth and driving his head back into the wall with such force the hapless junkie never felt Johnny's weight pressed against his chest or the point of the knife as it thrust upward through the jaw tendons under his right ear, piercing almost to the center of the brain. Johnny twisted the knife back and forth, pushing against the junkie's hip. It was close, so very close, and the night had only just begun.

Then he was all business again, seeming to throw off his ecstasy like a topcoat. He dragged the bodies under the stairwell, feeling his way through the darkness, and began to climb toward the second floor, pausing every few seconds, listening, tasting the damp odors of dust and mildew. He stopped at the head of a long hallway—fifteen steps to an office door on the left, sliding forward, gliding through the broken glass. A deep calm washed over him, relaxing the bunched muscles in his shoulders, a sense of the deepest and most profound purpose. As a street kid, equally afraid of the institution and the alternative foster home, survival gave his life its only meaning. Now there was more to it.

The office door opened silently and to eyes accustomed to the absolute darkness of the inner plant, the room seemed full of light. One north-facing window had had several cinder blocks knocked out by vandals and the faint glow of the city made a small pool of light in the far corner of the room. Johnny dropped the backpack, opening it quickly to pull out the pieces of his weapon. He began to assemble them immediately, his movements smooth and rapid due to hours of practice, though he paused again and again, always listening, and he did not look through the window, not even to glance at the street below, until he was finished and the first bullet chambered. Only then, at 3:30, did he begin to sight-in on the small home at 18 Jardine Avenue, residence of the neighborhood's only celebrity.

Gerald Gutterman, three-term congressman and presently a judge in New York City's civil court was not primarily known for his contribution to American politics, though he felt that he'd given his whole life to the service of his country and his people. An ardent Zionist since his college days at New York University in the fifties, he'd begun raising funds for Israel right after graduation and, declared his enemies in New York's more liberal circles, he'd used his years in the House only to further the cause of the Jewish homeland. His name graced the letterheads of almost every Zionist organization and when he wasn't selling Israeli Bonds or haranguing congressmen, he was organizing Jewish teens for summer work in the various agricultural and manufacturing communes called *kibbutzim*. He was a tireless worker, always full of energy. By 4 AM, he would be out of his bed and into the shower. By five o'clock, he would leave his home, already absorbed in the coming day's activities and completely unaware of Johnny Katanos, rifle propped on a bipod, silencer secured, nightscope in place.

In some ways, for Johnny, the waiting, the anticipation was the best part of the operation. The moment of action would be gone almost before it occurred and he would be forced to occupy himself with disassembling his rifle and making good his escape. Now, eyes locked on the small, darkened home 250 yards away, he could afford the luxury of fantasy. He saw the congressman stepping out on the small porch, worked and reworked the scene until he could see every detail of face and clothing; saw his wife follow, clutching a robe against the early morning cold. She smiles at her husband, puts her arms around his neck, fingers linked, and pecks him playfully on the lips. They pull back slightly and just for a moment, Gerald Gutterman conjures an image from her girlhood. He sees a flash of copper hair, a firm breast, nipple almost piercing the palm of his hand, and then he is dead and the smile falls from the face of the old woman as the side of his head erupts, spraying her with bone and blood. Johnny Katanos rehearsed this moment again and again, changing the expression on her face: consternation, anguish, fear, especially fear, followed by a flash of recognition. He had her turn, somehow knowing his location, and their eyes lock, hers soft, gray, and his as black as the olives of Greece. Slowly, almost hypnotically, he slips another round into the chamber and takes careful aim.

At 4:15, a light went on at the rear of the house, in the bedroom, and then, a moment later, a smaller light in the bathroom. Once again, Johnny brought his attention to the doorway at 18 Jardine Avenue. He was using a Steyr-Mannlicher SSG, a .30-caliber rifle capable of placing a three-inch grouping in a small paper target at a distance of 500 yards, even with a sound suppressor attached. Finished with a Litton nightscope, a device able to amplify available light 40,000 times, it could, at 250 yards, in the hands of a professional, punch a hole in a mosquito's ass by the light of a single star.

But Johnny was not a professional marksman. He was a good shot, even a gifted amateur, but the Steyr-Mannlicher, the assassin's 'green-gun,' was too much weapon for him, and when his opportunity came, he missed his spot by half a foot. Gerald Gutterman came through his front door alone. He received no good-bye kiss from his wife who, in fact, had her own bedroom and was sleeping soundly, courtesy of the prior evening's dose of chloral hydrate. As it turned out, the only witness to the opening round of Muzzafer's war, was Peter DiLuria, a twelve-year-old newsboy out on his daily rounds. He was pedaling along Jardine Avenue, trying to pluck a *Daily News* from his canvas bag, when Johnny Katanos squeezed off his first and only shot. The bullet, six inches below its intended target on the side of his head, struck the judge just beneath his right collar bone, moved like a billiard shot from his ribs to his spine and then up through the trachea and into his brain, where it exploded with enough force to send his eyes sailing into the wet grass. There they lay, like two emeralds, waiting for Morris, the Guttermans' cat, who would find and eat them within the hour, a totally unexpected treasure.

The AMERICAN RED ARMY announces the execution of the Zionist-Imperialist dog, Gerald Gutterman, for crimes against the peoples of the world. The AMERICAN RED ARMY demands an end to the fascist United States Government's support of the Zionist state. The AMERICAN RED ARMY demands an end to the genocide practiced against the helpless peoples of El Salvador and Nicaragua. The AMERICAN RED ARMY demands that the Imperialist-Fascist United States Military remove its mercenaries from European soil and end its support of the illegal government in South Africa. The AMERICAN RED ARMY will never cease its activities until its demands are met. The VICTORY OF THE PEOPLE IS INEVITABLE.

Some days, as any worker knows, are better than others. There are, of course, no good ones, but, occasionally, one might, at least, pass quickly. A few, however, are so terrible, so degrading to the heart and spirit, that they require 50 milligrams of Valium and a pint of Jack Daniels just to get even. For Rita Melengic, Friday, March 23, fit neatly into the last category. Awakened at 9:15 AM by a desperate manager, she'd dragged herself out of bed, faced the reality of the bathroom mirror and gotten herself to the job by 11, despite having worked until two on the previous night. Her first hour passed uneventfully, but then, at 12:30, an effusive patron swung his arms into her path, knocking a tray of Budweiser drafts into her lap. Twenty minutes in a surprisingly (for once) clean lady's room, had served to dry the black, polyester pants all the barmaids wore, but her heavy cotton panties remained damp, exuding a faint odor of sour beer. Then, with the entry of six Ukrainian construction workers, freed from their day's toil by a sudden downpour, the pinching had begun. After an hour of pleading, Rita had had enough and simply refused to go near their table. However, in the spirit of good clean fun, one young man, his face smeared with soot, had taken a chair at an empty table, pretending to be angry with his comrades. When Rita passed by, carrying a tray laden with corned beef and brisket sandwiches, he turned quickly and with surprising strength, attempted to ram his left thumb into her rectum. All concerned thought this turn of events hilarious, until an incensed Rita smashed the offender with a Heinz ketchup bottle, opening a five-inch cut above his right eye and driving him, senseless, to the floor. His friends, even as they considered their revenge, found themselves surrounded by four off-duty cops who, while not exactly unsympathetic, knew of Rita and her relationship with Moodrow and could easily guess what the sergeant's reaction might be if they allowed five Ukrainians to kick his old lady's ass. The Ukrainians, recent immigrants from the Soviet police state, never even bothered to question the justice of the situation. They simply retrieved their fallen comrade and made a hasty exit.

Nevertheless, the bar's manager, Ramon Iglesia, had been less than understanding, declaring that pinches and pokes are part and parcel of a bardmaid's existence and, while not exactly to be encouraged, need not be met with first-degree assault, especially when the customers are still able to drink. Rita hadn't furthered her cause by calling Mr. Iglesia a "subhuman piece of shit" and, in fact, had, not for the first time, been fired on the spot. Her disposition was unimproved by the cold spring drizzle or the thought of Stanley Moodrow, who was waiting for her at home.

Thus she pounded up First Avenue, not even bothering to dodge the inevitable winos. She simply shouldered them aside, all the while imagining Moodrow, still in his underwear, waiting for dinner, or, better still, with the parts of his .38 Special spread across the kitchen table, a can of Schaefer in his hand. The image infuriated her and by the time she got to her doorway, she was ready to step on a butterfly, so it was not surprising that, upon finding a fully dressed Moodrow, pen in hand, writing doggedly, she responded, her curiosity excited in spite of everything, by shouting. "What the fuck do you think you're doing?"

Moodrow turned to her, deadpan. "I'm writing a letter."

"A letter? Who could you write a letter to?"

"Ann Landers."

"Ann Landers. " Almost a smile, "Are you kidding me? I'm not in the mood, Stanley."

Moodrow stared serenely into her eyes, face so straight it drooped. "I'm serious. I write Ann every month. I used to write to Dear Abby, but I had to quit her. Too conservative."

Rita hesitated momentarily, finally deciding that Moodrow was putting her on. Once again her voice rose. "Why would you write a letter to Ann Landers?"

He smiled for the first time, showing small, closely set teeth. "Listen, I got problems, too. You think I'm just a big, meathead cop, but lemme tell you something, Rita, this is America and in America anybody can write to anybody they want. Anybody."

Resigned, Rita sat down on the other side of the table. "OK, I give up. Read the damn thing."

"Dear Ann. I am a married man who has been married for nearly twenty-three years and the Lord knows how I do love my wife and my marriage is as good as they get. But lately something terrible has

happened because my wife stated that she is no longer happy with our sex life. What with six kids she says she has gotten so big that she can't feel a goddamn thing. Well you can imagine my surprise, as I have always enjoyed having sex with my wife, especially when she asked me would I consider doing it in her rear end because that way she could feel something again. Now I don't know what to do and I have made all sorts of excuses because to tell the truth many years ago I made a solemn vow to my dick. I said 'Dick, as long as there is pussy in this world I will never give you a shitty deal.' As you know a vow is an immortal thing and not something a man can just take back because his wife bends over, so I would appreciate your advice as soon as possible. I love my wife very much but am
TORN TO PIECES."

7

The assassination of Gerald Gutterman was referred to the offices of Agents Higgins and Bradley as a matter of course. Although they operated independently of the crime-solving process—the gathering and analysis of physical clues—they were automatic consultants on any terrorist activity in the New York area and had access to all reports, including the identities of confidential informers. Specific teams might be assigned to specific terrorist groups—Omega 7, the FALN, the PLO and, now, The American Red Army, but Bradley and Higgins formed a bridge between all the teams and thus were routinely briefed on any individual incident. Emerging from just such a briefing, an exhausting three-hour marathon in which all the physical evidence as well as autopsy reports on Gutterman and the two dead junkies, was examined in detail, each felt a presentiment of doom, a dark, hovering thunderhead waiting to descend. Their search, by the only method they knew—the pursuit of information through spies and informants—had produced no new results. The American Red Army remained invisible.

"It's almost like random killings," Leonora said as they left the building. "Like motiveless murder where no logical connection exists between murderer and victim."

"Worse." Bradley nodded agreement. "It's true that with the Hillside Strangler or Son of Sam, if they don't make a mistake, you don't catch them. But those killers were amateurs. They wanted to be caught, while Muzzafer is a professional with decades of experience and, as far as we know, has never been in jail for a minute. He won't screw up. Of course, it's also possible that he'll make contact with the international movement again—for supplies or money or maybe just for a chance to brag before his peers."

"Sure, but in the meantime, with the material they have, assuming Muzzafer is responsible here, they can cause unbelievable damage."

Bradley shrugged his shoulders. "What you say is true, but we can only play with what we've got. We don't have the manpower to begin searching New York City street by street."

They entered Ruben's Deli on Queens Boulevard, a black-and-white oddity of a kosher restaurant, and took a table in the back, ordering pastrami sandwiches, french fries and Dr. Peppers. The waiter, bent and gray, wrote laboriously. "You're saying french fries?" He asked, black eyes darting from Leonora to George Bradley.

George answered, clearly annoyed at having his attention pulled away from his problem with Muzzafer. "Is there something wrong with the french fries?"

"There is for some people," the waiter replied.

Leonora giggled. "Go ahead. Tell us."

"The french fries come straight from the freezer." He held up one finger in triumph. "Now the potato salad we make every morning. Fresh. You wouldn't believe how creamy."

"French fries," Leonora said, cheerfully.

"French fries," George echoed.

The waiter, outflanked, moved off to fill their orders, not even bothering to frown, and the agents resumed their conversation.

"There's two things to do," George began. "First, we get out some photos of Muzzafer, though what we have is pretty fuzzy and very out of date, even assuming he's wearing the same face. We can distribute them in the precincts and hope for the best. But, better yet, we can press that barber who delivered the weapons for the Cubans.

What's his name? Rodriguez? No, Ramirez. Even if he can't help us with Muzzafer, we can turn him, let him work for us for awhile. There's always the chance they'll use him again if Muzzafer needs to rearm.''

''You mean after he uses up everything he's got? By that time, we'll be investigating hot car rings in Hobart, Indiana.''

The waiter returned and spread the plates out on the table. The pastrami was too stringy, with the fat leaking over the edge of the bread, but neither of the agents complained, though both noted the fact. They waited, silently, for the waiter to move off.

''There's one other thing,'' Bradley said. ''I think it's time you go see that cop again. Moodrow.''

Leonora frowned. ''I was hoping we could put that one off. Wouldn't the captain contact us if something developed?''

''Maybe he knows something he's not telling the captain.''

''That doesn't mean I can get it out of him.''

Bradley sighed, hands rising automatically to rub his sore eyes. ''I realize it's all nonsense, but I don't know what else to do.''

Rita Melengic was a big girl, five foot seven inches tall and heavy-boned, a Czech from rural, farm stock, but she could not put her arms around her lover. Sometimes, lying beneath him as they made love, she fantasized him suddenly dropping down to cover her, almost to smother her, so that she felt, at once, protected and panicked. Two husbands and a dozen lovers had conspired to produce a bone weariness composed in equal parts of the terror of being alone and the pain given to her by her men. Not that she judged herself guiltless. She willingly accepted responsibility for her failures, coming to expect them to leave her life, as she expected that one day Moodrow would also leave. She could easily imagine herself trudging home with a stranger in tow, a young laborer or a drunken cop. She saw them arrive at her apartment, saw the clumsy preliminaries followed by hopeless, desperate sex when sex was even possible.

Still, in spite of these fears, she found herself thinking of Moodrow, more and more often as she went about her daily business. At times, she wondered if she was falling in love with him and, wondering this, she began to find the reasons. He never criticized her. He never patronized her. When she was sharp with him, and she often was, he flinched. And he was very funny when he drank, funny and truly crazy, his own man. Some of the older Spanish women spoke to him on the street as if he was the pope, according him the ability to pull off miracles of extra-legal law enforcement. But none of this explained the deeper kinship she felt for him, the kinship of two people who, though outsiders pronounced them strong and self-reliant, were so close to beaten that they could not begin to put it into words. Yet each knew of the other's plight, respecting the need for privacy, the need simply not to talk about it, and Rita waited patiently, expecting, sooner or later, to wake up alone.

For Moodrow, the problem was entirely different. He told himself, that, in fact, he didn't really care at all, that when, as it inevitably must, their relationship dissolved, he would simply go on his way, plodding toward retirement. He did not fear loneliness. He welcomed it because it served the self-image he most respected. Moodrow feared only retirement, which he equated with the end of life—a haze of alcohol and rapid decay. It was the way of his father and his uncles, the natural condition of men and women in life. He had never married, never even courted, content to attach himself to a succession of experienced lovers, like Rita Melengic. Sometimes they left. Sometimes he did. The longest lasted just under two years. Moodrow tied himself to his job, to a police department that was both adversary and ally, an enormous family with all the intrigue, the petty jealousies and backbiting, as well as the camaraderie and loyalties, that family life inspires. But, of course, and Moodrow understood this, unlike a family, he would one day be forced to leave the department, to retire.

Still, for all his self-reliance, for all his conceit, Moodrow was wrong about Rita Melegenic. On April 2, he woke up in a sweat, still trembling from the effects of a bad dream. At first, he couldn't remember the details, could only see Rita's face disappearing into a mist, dropping away while he clung to his perch, safe and sound. Then it came rushing back. He was holding her against his chest, his right arm around her waist. He wasn't afraid. She was so tiny, like a sparrow; he could hold her forever. Then he remembered that he was climbing a ladder and he got back to work, plodding upward. He was after Johnny Katanos who sat at the top of the ladder wearing Ronald Chadwick's face.

"Forget about me," the apparition called cheerfully. "Nobody wants me."

"I'm gonna get you, scum," Moodrow roared.

"Well, I'd like to get down," Rita said, ignoring Katanos. "This is really uncomfortable."

"How can I do that?" Moodrow protested. "There isn't any place."

"Are you crazy?"

Looking around, Moodrow found himself on a small platform. It stood at the top of the ladder, empty, surrounded by the dense, gray fog.

"Well," Rita said, "is it possible for me to stand on my own two feet? Or maybe you're hoping we'll grow together? Like Siamese twins."

Disgusted, Moodrow set her down, knowing there was something he was supposed to say, but not remembering. He stared into the fog, searching his memory, and then she was gone, breaking into pieces, arms and legs whirling away like maple seeds searching for the earth. There was no blood, no final scream. The scene was quite peaceful until he realized that she was gone forever. Then, before he could hurl himself after her, he woke up, panicked.

That morning, over breakfast, he offered to take her into his world, the cop world. He needed to share something with her, something that was important to him, and he made his offer while eating, which was, for him, most appropriate. "Say, Rita," he began. "I'm gonna put an end to the great Jewish persecution."

"You mean that trouble with the kids throwing rocks over at the Asher Levy Homes?" She spread butter over her toast, systematically covering every bit of bread before putting it back on her plate. "Have you discovered the identity of the master criminal who's been attacking our senior citizens?"

"It's not that funny. Seventy-year-old people get scared even when there's nothing to get scared about." He shoved a spoonful of raisin bran into his mouth and chewed slowly. "Anyway, I did run down the kid. A little Puerto Rican named Willie Colon. Willie's got a brother in the Sixth Street Gentlemen and naturally Willie wants to be just like his brother, so he proves his worthiness by throwing rocks at Jews. It makes sense, right? Just like everything else on the Lower East Side. Well, today I'm gonna put an end to this campaign of violence and hatred." He hesitated, watching her closely. "Wanna come with me?"

Rita fiddled with her coffee cup, spinning it in her fingers as she tried to grasp his intent. "Are you going to beat him up?"

"No, no," Moodrow giggled at the image of himself pounding on a fourteen-year-old. "This kid is only fourteen, Rita. He weighs about one hundred and twenty pounds. I'm not the sweetest cop in the department, but even I couldn't go that far. Except in extreme circumstances. Besides, it wouldn't do no good, anyway. I arrested the kid's old man three times for child abuse and wife beating. One time I had to take both kids to the hospital, unconscious. Another time I found his brother trying to wash some burns in the East River. Can you imagine? In the fucking river. No, this one can't be controlled by hitting, but I think I could shake him up. Actually, I'm gonna bluff him. Get me some sugar and some white flour. No, just tell me where they are and I'll get them myself."

They walked down Allen Street to Delancey, then turned east to the precinct. Moodrow was greeted again and again by the local shop-keepers, by the old ladies, by Puerto Ricans and Jews and Czechs and Italians. The street criminals honored him by edging into door-ways and alleyways, deserting their territories. At the precinct, Mood-row picked up an unmarked car and began to drive through the neighborhood, cutting back and forth through the narrow streets. They stayed south of Houston, Willie's home territory, searching care-fully—Norfolk, Suffolk, Clinton, Attorney, Ridge. After a fruitless hour, Rita suggested they try the area around the Asher Levy Homes. Perhaps the children were already at play.

"Worth a try," Moodrow responded shortly. He turned east onto

Grand Street, a wider, two-way street lined with small shops offering heavily discounted electronic and dry goods. It was already 4 PM and business was slow. A few shopkeepers were pulling down the steel shutters that protected their goods through the long night. Moodrow headed toward Jackson Street, noting the many elderly people making their way home. It was a perfect time for an attack. The small forms shuffling along the sidewalk seemed completely helpless and Moodrow kept expecting a shower of small rocks to come sailing over the rooftops, but twenty minutes of driving in a square between Montgomery, Madison, Jackson and the East River failed to flush out young Willie Colon. Finally, Moodrow, annoyed and showing it, spun up Clinton toward the mouth of the Williamsburg Bridge, crossing Delancey Street in spite of the hundreds of vehicles trying to get up onto the bridge. He laughed at the horns, then sobered up as he caught sight of his quarry.

"That's him. For shit sake, Rita, don't look at him. Jesus, just when I gave up. Now, listen carefully. After we park the car, you just walk along with me like you know what you're doing. I don't even wanna glance his way until we're right on top of him. He's a tough kid and he don't know I'm on to him, so he won't give up his dirt too easy. No, I don't think he'll run, but if he cuts out, I'll just get him another day."

Suddenly, Rita understood that he was talking to himself, that he was getting himself ready for action the way a fighter works up a sweat while still in the locker room. For a moment she was afraid, but then she became intrigued. She wanted to find out how it would end.

Moodrow continued the patter, gesturing broadly. He appeared lost in conversation, aware only of himself and Rita, until he came abreast of the small figure on the stoop. Then, with no warning, he turned on Willie Colon, hands on hips, and growled. "What the fuck you think you're looking at?"

For a second, Willie reverted to the infant attacked for the first time by an enraged father, fists raised, mouth twisted into a snarl, then he came to himself and played the street kid. "Nothin'," he said quietly. "I don't look at nothin'."

"You saying I'm nothing?" Moodrow demanded, face reddening. "Get up against the fucking wall, you little cocksucker."

Willie Colon, propelled by a push from one of Moodrow's huge fists, allowed himself to be pinned against the iron railing that ran up the stoop. He was afraid and greatly bewildered by the cop's sudden, furious attack, but as he had nothing illegal in his possession and he had been subject to harassment of one kind or another all his life, he felt it was far wiser to submit than to struggle, especially considering that this particular cop towered over him like some fairy tale giant. He expected nothing more than a quick frisk and a kick in the ass, figuring the cop was out to impress his girlfriend. He certainly didn't expect the plastic bag filled with glistening white powder which Moodrow pulled, as if by magic, from the front pocket of Willie's jeans.

"What's this, Willie?" Moodrow asked, his anger seeming to change over to joy.

Willie looked at the sergeant uncomprehendingly, totally confused by the turn of events.

"What's this?" Moodrow repeated. "Looks like we got ourselves a little dope dealer."

"I never seen that before, man," Willie protested. "That shit ain't mine."

"Then who does it belong to?" Moodrow asked quietly. "And how did it get into your pocket?"

"Somebody put that shit . . ." Willie stopped suddenly, caught in the obvious dilemma imposed by the situation. It was simply unacceptable for a fourteen-year-old street kid to accuse a cop of planting dope, so Willie made the prudent move—he stood mute. He had been on the street for a long time and began to feel a street revelation swelling up in him. The cop wanted something from him. If not, he would have arrested him without all the fanfare. In the back of his mind, though he never took his eyes off Moodrow's fists, he was already deciding what he would or would not trade in order to get out of the situation.

Rita, initially shocked by the fury of Moodrow's attack on what she perceived to be a defenseless child, got over her surprise just about the same time Willie got over his. She began to realize that she was watching an elaborate negotiation, a charade that had to be played through in order to discover the ending. Rita nodded as Moodrow's voice rose still higher.

"You little faggot," Moodrow roared. "You fucking *pato* cunt. I'll break your head if you say I put that shit on you. Get down those stairs." Moodrow yanked the boy down a short flight leading to what had once been the basement apartment. Rita followed, flinching as Moodrow kicked the door open and pushed Willie through. The small windows had not been covered and their eyes adjusted to the dim light quickly. The first room was fairly large and completely bare. Bits of rubble, pieces of wall and ceiling, covered the floor, except in one corner, where a narrow mound of broken concrete ran along the back wall. All three recognized it for what it was—a grave.

Surprisingly, Willie was the first to speak. "Say, man, what you got me for, anyways?" he whispered.

Moodrow pulled his eyes away from the heaped rubble, willing himself to the business at hand. "If you call me 'man' one more time, you little scumbag, I'm gonna break the middle finger on your right hand. You know my name. Use it." Willie responded by continuing to stare at the grave across the room and Moodrow, cursing the turn of events, made one more bid to get the boy's attention. "You know how much time you could get for this?" He held the bag up to Willie's face. "This ain't no juvenile bust. This ain't no slap on the wrist from some fag social worker. This is a goddamn adult felony and you're going into the men's detention block on Riker's Island. You got a chance with kids your own age, but I'm gonna talk to a friend of mine who's a sergeant of corrections and we're gonna put you in a cell with four, giant, nigger faggots and they're gonna fuck your asshole all day and night. Do you hear what I'm saying?"

Willie nodded, his attention once again focused on the cop. He felt a sudden thrill of understanding. He was being dealt with as a man for the first time in his life and, although he didn't really believe Moodrow would plant heroin on him, he was indeed terrified by the prospect of being made into a jailhouse punk. There were many stories of young kids being tried as adults for certain crimes, of children being incarcerated with adult felons when they were too young to defend themselves. Not happy stories at all and when Willie finally answered, he didn't have to force the fear into his voice. "I don't know what you want, Sergeant Moodrow. I don't know what to say."

Moodrow waited just a moment, fixing the child with a blank stare, as if trying to make up his mind about something. Finally, he spoke. "What's the captain's fucking name?"

"The captain?"

"Yeah, my captain. The captain of the precinct."

"Captain Epstein, you mean?"

"That's right. Captain Epstein. Now tell me what kind of name is Epstein? C'mon. Let's go." Moodrow, in his impatience, reached out to Willie.

"It's a Jew name. He's a Jew."

"And what do you think a Jew captain is gonna do when you lead a bunch of asshole kids in throwing rocks at his fucking people? Whatta you think he's gonna do?"

Relief flooded through Willie, flushing out the fear. This was going to be easy. Just a moment before, he had been convinced that Moodrow was going to ask him to set up his brother, who was dealing heavily. "I guess he gonna get mad."

"Yeah," Moodrow mimicked. "He gonna get mad. And then he comes and busts my balls. And I gotta take it because of some punk asshole kid like you. Some Puerto Rican piece of subhuman shit. Well, I swear to Jesus Christ I'm gonna put your ass in jail for the next ten years. And don't tell me you ain't the leader. You're right on top and, so help me God, I ain't gonna put up with it." Moodrow paused, looking around for some way to bring home the seriousness of the threat.

"Look," Willie cried, interrupting the sergeant's train of thought. "I let up on that shit, Sergeant. I don't care about them stupid Jews no way at all."

"And what about this?" Moodrow held up the small bag.

Willie hesitated, then took the bait. "We forget about that?"

"Just like that? No, I don't think so." Moodrow smiled. "I tell you what, tough guy. You go dig up that pile of concrete over there." He pointed to the grave. "Let's see what's underneath."

Rita saw the fear in the boy's eyes. Saw the adult leave and the child take over again.

"That's a grave, man," Willie whispered, lifting the back of his hand to cover his mouth. Instinctively, he began to back away.

"My name ain't 'man,' you little punk. Didn't I tell you what my name was?" Moodrow yelled, advancing on the boy.

"Don't make me do it. Please don't make me do it." He began to cry, a small stifled whimper and Rita reached out to restrain Moodrow. He seemed to notice her for the first time and regarded her with puzzled eyes. He felt himself torn between his business with Willie and his need to show Rita what it felt like to be a cop "Here," he said. "Watch it. Watch this." Quickly, his eyes darting back and forth from Rita to Willie, Moodrow began to tear the mound apart, flipping chunks of concrete as if they were foam movie props, releasing the smell of death until it filled the basement.

Rita cried out as the body began to emerge, a long, low groan of understanding. The head was twisted almost completely around and there were small, white maggots in the mouth and eyes. The flesh seemed folded on itself, like candlewax exposed to a sooty flame, but the coolness of the basement had kept the decay to a minimum.

Willie began to make the sign of the cross from his head to his waist to his shoulders, over and over again. "Jesus Christ," he cried out, at last. "That's Enrique Hentados, man. That thing is Enrique Hentados."

Moodrow stopped, his fury suddenly spent. He stared at Willie. "Say again."

"That's Enrique Hentados."

Desire flowed through the cop's eyes. They seemed happy, almost joyful, but he kept his voice hard. "That's gonna be Willie Colon if you fuck me up one more time. Now get out of here."

Willie didn't waste a second. He spun on his heel and flew up the stairs. Moodrow waited until the child was out of sight, then turned to Rita. "Go back to the car. Pick up the radio and press the button on the side of the microphone. Say, 'Car 205 calling precinct.' Then let go until someone comes on. Probably Bob Pellegrino. Tell him Sergeant Moodrow is in the basement at 165 Clinton with a dead body. We need a crime team down here right away. Tell him there is no danger. Can you do that?"

"OK, I can do it." Like Willie Colon, Rita was eager to get out of that basement, away from the sight and smell of Enrique Hentados. Moodrow, on the other hand, wanted nothing more than to be alone with the body, to examine the situation in private. He waited patiently for Rita to disappear, then returned to the rigid corpse and removed several more chunks of concrete, exposing the body completely. He went quickly through the pockets, finding nothing in the pants, cursing softly, then pulling two orange ticket stubs from an inside jacket pocket. Smiling to himself, he noted the name of the Ridgewood Theatre just before slipping them into his own pocket. Now the medical examiner would show up, complaining of the inconvenience, and the crime team would sweep the area for clues that would only be filed away. A remote crime. A minor annoyance on a Tuesday evening. Suddenly, he felt guilty. He had put Rita through more than he had ever intended. Suppose she left him, disgusted by the brutality? Well, he would make it up to her. He would put Epstein off for a few more days and they would take a little vacation. He knew people in Atlantic City. They would gamble, get drunk, make love. For a moment he was lost in the fantasy, but then, as he heard the scream of the approaching sirens, habit took over and he began to consider the death of Enrique Hentados.

8

In 1950, the Williamsburg section of Brooklyn, a mostly Puerto Rican neighborhood, stood face to face on its south and southeastern borders with the tense, black poverty of Bedford Stuyvesant. It was here, with Flushing Avenue as the border line, that the youth gangs of the 50s met to enact the rituals of passage that make a ghetto child into a man. They rarely used guns in 1950, content to batter and stab each other with baseball bats and chains and knives. In those days, car antennas (universally called aerials) could be snapped off a fender with one quick tug, like crushing an empty beer can. They made a singing sound, these aerials, as they whipped toward the flesh of an opponent. In schoolyard, on a dark night, they were completely invisible, almost magical.

The eastern and western ends of Williamsburg were heavily industrialized and supported businesses as large as the Knickerbocker and Schaefer Breweries and the Brooklyn Navy Yard, or as small as the individual warehouse-trucking operations on Heyward Street. These businesses formed the employment base for the Williamsburg community, a base that shrank continually. The three decades following World War II saw both breweries, the Navy Yard, and fifty other businesses close their doors forever, leaving Williamsburg with only a smattering of single-owner, garage operations—warehouses with virtually no heat in winter, no ventilation in summer and, most of all, no unions at any time.

Greenpoint, Brooklyn, lay directly to the north of Williamsburg. It was a working-class neighborhood, mostly Polish and Italian, into which the Puerto Rican community of Williamsburg expanded throughout the 1960s, pushing, little by little, along Kent and Wythe avenues, until it occupied all the area from the East River to Mc-Guinness Boulevard. This was not accomplished without bloodshed, as the indigenous population fought tooth and nail to save their wives and children from the ultimate indignity of having to associate with Spanish-speaking human beings.

But the Puerto Ricans had little choice. They were forced to expand because of pressure by still another ethnic group which began to move into Williamsburg in the early 1950s. Hasidic Jews, drawn by the strength of their leader, Rabbi Schoenberg, began to arrive in America shortly after World War II. At first, they settled on the Lower East Side of Manhattan, where they found help from the long-established Jewish population. But the Lower East Side was too crowded, rents were high in the small area that remained Jewish, and jobs were scarce. Besides, there were a great many Jews living there who did not follow Mosaic Law. These were Jews who ate bacon and whose children routinely dated gentiles. The rabbi had seen Jews like these in Europe. There was nothing new here. Nevertheless, he led his people on one last journey. He led them two miles across the Williamsburg Bridge into Brooklyn, into a neighborhood where there were no Jews of any kind.

These were wild-looking people. Dressed in ill-fitting black suits and white shirts without ties, they seemed to wear their black overcoats all the time, summer and winter. Thick, untrimmed beards and long earlocks combined with centuries of imposed isolation to create an insularity which the local population found entirely offensive. The Hasidim went to their own schools, shopped at their own stores, bought only kosher food and first and foremost, in a community where jobs were already scarce, offered employment to each other. The women shaved their heads on the day of their marriages. They wore long dresses and thick, opaque stockings, resulting in a general appearance which can only be called asexual, a certain and deadly insult to the young Spanish girls and their macho boyfriends.

So, the Jews came under immediate attack. The ghetto criminals of Williamsburg and Bedford Stuyvesant saw them as unarmed and therefore helpless, as traditional Jewish victims. What they didn't understand was that these people had no place to go back to, that their entire world had been destroyed, first by Adolf Hitler and then by Joseph Stalin and that, if necessary, they would have no choice but to die on the streets of Brooklyn. And the predators made still another error, another miscalculation based on ignorance. These people, these Jews, had seen their husbands, wives, parents, and children murdered by the butchers of Germany. They had seen their families shot and stabbed and bludgeoned to death. They had seen humans eaten by dogs. They had seen German soldiers throw living infants into burning ovens and they would not be intimidated by an eighteen-year-old kid with a Saturday night special.

After a time, they began to prosper. They bought up the small warehouses and established factories manufacturing sweaters and blouses. They purchased the row houses along Penn, Rutledge and Heyward streets. Schools were built and temples and even a grand, single-family home for the rabbi, the only one for miles around. It had a lawn with real grass, surrounded by a white wrought-iron fence and, to the Hasidim, gave the distinct air of a people prepared for a long stay. If they could not go back to Eastern Europe, if they could not make the Yiddish world come alive in its own garden, they would do their best to see it blossom in Williamsburg, Brooklyn.

Yet, over the next twenty years, the friction never died down, though it most often showed itself as a competition for political patronage. From the Puerto Rican point of view, the Hasidim had committed two unpardonable transgressions. First, they truly felt themselves to be superior to their darker, gentile neighbors and, second, they made no attempt to disguise their feelings. By the time Ronald Chadwick met his maker, the city of New York had been trying to mediate the

dispute for thirty years, but aside from physically separating the com-
batants in time of actual battle there was little the city could do. Still,
the politicians never gave up. There were votes on those streets, block
votes, and thus the citizens had to be appeased. The action of the city
over the Robert Wagner Homes was a perfect example of both the
dilemma and the solution. The homes contained two hundred heavily
subsidized apartments. Brand-new units, they represented the only
city-funded housing in nearly a decade, and the war for occupancy
began even before the old buildings resting on the site were demolished.

The most common charge was that, since everyone knows that all
Jews are rich and that these apartments were clearly meant for the
poor, the Jews should be excluded. This accusation led to the estab-
lishment of a special, though unofficial, fitness board to ensure that
only the poorest of the poor would be considered. The Hasidic community, on the other hand, agonized over their vulnerability should
they be forced to live door to door with the volatile Hispanics. The
city responded by recruiting almost every Jewish housing cop in the
city to serve as patrolmen at the Wagner Homes.

The negotiations went on for two years. There were dozens of
community planning board meetings in which great arguments were
made, in Yiddish and Spanish, as well as English. Finally, a bargain
was struck, as all parties had known would happen, in which the
apartments were divided evenly and Jews and Puerto Ricans and even
a few blacks shared each floor. All that remained was for the politicians to make their ritual observances, to consecrate the holy ground
while at the same time getting their pictures in the papers. The date
for the grand event was set for Sunday, April 1, at 10:00 AM. The
mayor, the president of the City Council, the borough president, Representative Herman Gonzalez and Rabbi Schoenberg, himself, would
all appear. There would be speeches and media people galore and,
just to make sure there was a nice crowd, a small block party was
planned for the afternoon.

Naturally, the sad history of the Robert Wagner Homes had gotten
plenty of attention in the local papers over the years and, just as

naturally, had not escaped the attention of the radical community, including the American Red Army. Several of the more public organizations, such as the Communist Proletarian Party had sent field operatives to assist the downtrodden minority in their battles with the Jewish community. Muzzafer, on the other hand, preferred to work more quietly. He had been so impressed with estimates of the size of the crowd, that he'd gone to the trouble to prepare a surprise for them.

The surprise involved a trip to New Jersey for supplies. Muzzafer led the foray, accompanied by Effie Bloom and Johnny Katanos. The three drove to the Vince Lombardi truckstop on the New Jersey Turnpike where, after a two-hour wait, they found what they were after. John Dalkey, truckdriver for Fairbanks Galvanized Pipe, Inc., returned to his eighteen-inch flatbed truck after lunch, prepared to make a small delivery of twenty-two pieces of inch-and-a-half by twelve-foot pipe, only to find a heavily rouged Effie Bloom, black bouffant wig rising grandly over dark, aviator sunglasses, waiting in the unlocked cab of his truck. She, with the help of a 9mm automatic, persuaded him to take a short drive into a swamp near the Bayonne Bridge. By the time he'd hoofed it to the nearest phone, Effie Bloom was well into Staten Island and about to cross the Verrazano-Narrows Bridge into Bay Ridge, Brooklyn. She was not followed. Two hundred and fifty dollars worth of galvanized pipe does not excite local policemen, though the information was recorded and, within twenty-four hours, the plate number had appeared on local hot sheets and the vehicle described as ''stolen.''

Of course, by this time, the truck had disappeared into a garage in Brooklyn and the plates had been changed. Because of her delicate touch, Jane Mathews handled most of the explosives. First, the ends of the pipe resting against the back of the cab were plugged with six inches of concrete. Then, after drilling holes in the pipe for the insertion of lead wires, small amounts of plastic explosives were placed against the concrete. Wires were run from the pipe through the back of the cab to a clock-timing device set under the driver's seat. Finally, thirty pounds of three-penny nails were pushed gently against the explosive, making the truck one, large antipersonnel device.

At 8 AM, the day before the opening of the Robert Wagner Homes, Johnny Katanos drove the truck into Brooklyn. It was the Jewish Sabbath and the streets were nearly empty. Just on the corner of Ross, across from what would become 148 Wythe Avenue, he flipped a swtich beneath the dash, cutting out the ignition. No amount of effort restarted the truck, though Johnny kept turning the key until the battery died down to series of pathetic clicks. Then, cursing, kicking the ground in disgust, he walked four blocks to where Theresa Aviles waited with the van. Exulting in their success, they jumped onto the Brooklyn-Queens Expressway and left Williamsburg behind them.

But their celebration was premature. By midnight, it was raining in New York, a cold, spring rain still catching the edge of winter, the kind that rips up cheap umbrellas and has pet owners cursing dogs who have to be dragged into the street. By 8:30 it was pouring hard enough to flood every highway in the city, and the politicians, after a hasty conference with all interested parties, decided to put the official dedication off for one week, though the new tenants would be allowed to begin moving into their homes.

Just as well. For at 10:00 AM, the American Red Army's bomb exploded, right on time, utterly destroying the facade and lobby of 148 Wythe Avenue. There were only two casualties. Patrolmen David Stein and Louis Hochberg took the full force of the explosion. After viewing the bodies, the medical examiner remarked that they looked like some giant had forced them through a paper shredder.

Rita Melengic had been playing the numbers—50 cents per day— since she'd gotten her first job at age seventeen. She'd won occasionally over the twenty years following, won $250 each time. She played 118, the date of her mother's death and each morning she bought a *Daily News* and checked the last three numbers of the previous day's take at whatever local racetrack happened to be operating. In her twenties, she'd added bingo at St. Joseph's and, after it became legal, an occasional lottery ticket, though she'd never won more than five dollars at the lottery. Yet, although she saw herself as a woman who gambled, none of her previous activities had prepared her for the experience of making twelve straight points at a Golden Palace craps table in Atlantic City, of turning two dollars into $9,192.

It wasn't just the money. She held the dice for fifty-three minutes, never diverting a single chip from the pass line to the more exotic wagering in the middle of the board. The other gamblers at the table kept offering advice, urging her to bet the six or the nine or the hard ways, but though the action swirled about her, she remained above it and they finally came around to her, cheering each successful point. After the eighth pass, the dice went off the table and the pit boss tossed them out without even looking at them. The other gamblers screamed their resentment, but Rita simply chose two new dice and resumed shooting. She felt strangely serene, though her whole body trembled with excitement. She was suddenly aware of the rows and rows of tables, each surrounded by gamblers and bathed in its own pool of light, small green islands tended by the caretakers, the stickman and his assistants. They wore plaid vests and dark green pants and their hair was cut, each one, just above the ear. She felt that she could see the whole city, all at once, as if she surrounded it while the dice threw themselves, making consecutive points of ten, ten, five and nine. Then, as she raised her hand one more time, she found it covered by Moodrow's huge paw. He pointed to the chips piled on the pass line.

"There's nine thousand dollars there," he said quietly, and she realized, with a start, that of all the voices raised to give her this or that piece of advice, she had never heard his, not once. He was just happy for her and she knew it.

"Should we keep it?" she asked, already sweeping the chips into her purse. "Are you sure it's nine thousand dollars?" But she had not doubt about it and no doubts about Moodrow when he removed four fifty-dollar chips and handed them to the young men in their plaid vests.

Later that night, as she sat astride his great body, her lust fully spent though she still held him inside her, she looked down and saw the same smile on his face. Suddenly, she slapped her palms down on his chest and the crack echoed in the small room. "It's perfect, you stupid cop,'' she said, the tears already running down her cheeks. ''Not matter what happens later, it's perfect tonight.''

They didn't go back to the tables. Instead, they let Reggie Reynolds, night manager of the Golden Palace, treat them to everything from parking to dinner. Reggie, who'd been born Morris Stern and raised in a four-room apartment at Clinton and Grand, had gone to high school with Moodrow, and though he'd left the Lower East Side right after graduating, he'd returned years later to ask Moodrow to remove an especially aggressive loan shark from the back of one of Reggie's uncles, his mother's favorite brother. The sergeant had turned the trick after a week of surveillance and apprehended the loan shark and two companions in the act of breaking a Puerto Rican truckdriver's thumbs. Several ounces of cocaine had been discovered in the trunk of the car they drove and what with possession of a controlled substance, possession with intent to sell, assault with a deadly weapon, atrocious assault, assault with intent to kill and weapons possession (a .45 automatic), Reggie Reynolds' uncle had faded from the consciousness of that particular loan shark.

Now Reggie was paying back and he saw to it that round after round of Chivas Regal appeared, as if by magic, at Moodrow's right hand. And Moodrow, anxious to oblige, put them away, three to Rita's one. Reggie kept bringing celebrities over to the table, fighters and baseball players and even the star of the Golden Palace, Kenny Brighton, a country singer from Alabama who was the current favorite on the Las Vegas/Atlantic City circuit.

Rita, watching Moodrow intently, as a woman always watches a lover about whom she is perpetually unsure, could not quite make out how drunk he was. The conversation at the table rambled back and forth, mostly gossip about various celebrities, until they were joined by Cedric Kingman, a lightweight prizefighter. Kingman's brother, an innocent bystander, had been shot dead on a Detroit street during a gun battle between two drug dealers. Condolences were offered and the conversation naturally turned to crime. All, except for Moodrow, expressed ritual indignation at a court system which plea-bargained major felonies into misdemeanors.

"C'mon, Stanley," Reggie said. "You must have some opinion. You just sit there like the great stone sage, like a Buddha in some museum. Let's hear what an expert has to say."

Moodrow cleared his throat and Rita knew, then, that he was quite drunk, though in control, and that he was about to launch into one of his special talks about crime. She waited for him to begin, gave him two sentences, then, leaning over to rest her head on his shoulder, she slid her hand down into his lap and began a gentle, determined massage.

Moodrow giggled, but an inappropriate giggle goes unnoticed at a table full of drinkers and no one changed expression as the sergeant continued doggedly on.

"You guys are amateurs. You read the paper and think you're getting the truth." He was slurring just a little bit, but, again, nobody picked it up. "Shit, you probably think it's like all clues, like that asshole with the funny hat, Surelick Combs or whatever his fucking name is." He stopped suddenly as Rita grazed him with the tip of a sharpened fingernail. "Jesus Christ." He looked around the table, giggled again. "But it ain't like that at all. There's only two ways you solve crimes, and that's either you catch them with the goddamn gun still smoking or you make somebody rat out." He paused momentarily to plant a kiss on Rita's cheek, then collected his thoughts and continued. "I don't wanna hurt you, Cedric, but let's say I catch one of the assholes that shot your brother. Now I know the guy is a middle-level dealer and I gotta get two things from him. First, I want the other guys responsible for the shooting and then I want the scumbag's boss. You know, you can't beat it out of them anymore. They're too goddamn tough. I mean, sometimes you could persuade a guy, but for the most part, you gotta make a deal, because if you don't, you never get them until they're on the street, shooting. Say for a second everyone at this table decides to smuggle in five pounds of coke. How do we get caught? Nobody knows who we are or what we're going, but let's say the courier gets popped coming through customs. Just by accident in a random search. If the agent that busts him don't make some kind of a deal, we're back in business tomorrow, but if he does make a deal, we all get busted.

"I swear it must be a hundred times I went up to a guy and said. 'Hey, listen, you're looking at ten to twenty, but I could make it three to five if you give me this name and this name.' Eventually I get it all and sometimes I put him back on the street and let him go work for me. And I mean work. I stay on the cocksucker's case every minute. If I didn't do it, I'd never bust anyone above street level. The guy who really gets fucked is the poor schmuck who loses his cool in a bar and plants a knife in his neighbor's ribs, 'cause ninety percent of the time that guy doesn't have anything he can trade and he gets the full dose."

Moodrow paused once again. The rest of the table was silent, held there by the obvious conviction in his voice. Finally, he looked around the table. "You wanna stop crime? Then make drugs legal. Forget tougher sentences. Let the ones who can't make it any other way get high or give 'em fucking jobs." He stood up suddenly, holding his jacket closed. "Now you gotta excuse us. Me and Rita ain't used to being up so late. We gotta get some rest."

"Yeah," Rita said, following innocently. "He's real tired."

9

The unexpected spring rain responsible for ruining the American Red
Army's surprise party in Williamsburg, continued through Sunday
and Sunday night, an unremitting downpour which did not die out
until late on Monday morning. By that time the highways in New
York City, as well as thousands of basements in the outer boroughs,
had been turned into a series of muddy-brown lakes.

FDR Drive went first. By 9 AM on Sunday, the underpass below
Carl Schurz Park was flooded with more than two-and-a-half feet of
water and the Drive was closed in both directions. A half dozen roads
followed—the Brooklyn-Queens Expressway; the Whitestone Expressway at the fork to the Whitestone Bridge; the Grand Central
Parkway in Kew Gardens and again at Hoyt Avenue; the Cross Island
Parkway and the Interboro at Metropolitan Avenue. The Belt Parkway, which runs along the Atlantic Ocean in southern Brooklyn and
floods in a heavy fog, was impassable. The ocean, in several places,
had reached out an arm to cover the roadbed.

Monday morning was a commuter's nightmare and switchboards
were jammed all morning with the excuses of those unable to face
the traffic. Some abandoned the roads, deciding to approach the island
of Manhattan by subway. They forced their way into trains that simply
remained, doors open, in the stations. The tunnels below were as

flooded as the streets above: Signals were jammed, switches stuck and third rails shorted throughout the system.

The majority arrived at their jobs about noon, wet and disheveled, harassed even beyond a New Yorker's ability to cope. Then, as they, scurried about, trying somehow to catch up, the temperature outside began to drop. It had been fifty-three degrees when the rain began. By Monday evening, it was twenty-six and falling. By Tuesday morning, it was sixteen degrees and what before had been merely wet, was now ice. The subways were barely running and all those commuters who'd been bitten on Monday, took back to the roads just as those who'd taken Monday off pulled out of their driveways. The backup at the bridges and tunnels began before 7 AM. By eight o'clock, traffic on the entryways to the great island was frozen as solid as the puddles on the street.

Even within Manhattan, patches of ice, untouched by an armada of orange saltspreaders, slowed traffic to a standstill. Fifth Avenue became a sea of buses surrounded by bright yellow taxis, as packs of dogs might surround buffalo. Passengers complained to harassed cabbies who could think of nothing except how slowly their meters ran when they moved along at a rate of four red lights to a block. Of course, the horns would not stop, not even when the traffic officers, huddled down in their heavy brown coats, waved ticket books threateningly.

And these New Yorkers had been waiting for spring since the end of the holiday season. In January, all along the northeast coast of America, the cold moves in, soaked through with humidity, driving those who can afford them into ankle-length mink or down coats. The good citizens run from office to cab to home, glancing up into the sky in search of the warm days to come. By March, they are already impatient; by April they are desperate for the few seventy-degree days that mark the boundary between unbearably cold and unbearably hot. These days rarely arrive before the very end of April, yet eyes persist in flickering skyward, hoping for the best and, failing that, filling the cabs and subways and buses with their lament: "Man, it is fucking cold out there."

But for Rita Melengic and Stanley Moodrow, the weather went

virtually unnoticed, even though it took them nearly ten hours to drive from Atlantic City to Rita's apartment on First Avenue. The Garden State Parkway was awash, with visibility down to near zero. They joked about it for awhile and then Rita fell asleep, her purse, stuffed with hundred-dollar bills, cradled in both arms. At times, in her sleep, she slumped against the door and Moodrow patiently tugged her across until her head pressed against his shoulder. Then he plodded on, slowly, persistently.

Rita woke at 6 AM, as they were rolling through Perth Amboy toward the Outerbridge Crossing into State Island. At her request, they stopped for breakfast in a small diner off the main road. At first, tired and silent, they simply stared at each other through critical, puffy eyes, but by the time they reached Staten Island, the coffee had made them more or less alert. Rita, somehow, managed to fix her hair without looking in the mirror, then elbowed Moodrow in the ribs.

"Say something, you fart."

"Me, a fart? Rita, I been constipated for twenty-two years." He waited for her come back, but she was too tired and so, impulsively, he blundered on. "How old are you, Rita?"

"You know how old I am."

"Tell me."

She shrugged her shoulders. "Forty-one."

"That's interesting," Moodrow responded, eyes glued to the road. "Let's live together."

Rita gave him a sharp look and he grinned, but refused to turn his head. "It sounds stupid to me, too," he said, finally.

There was a silence, in its proper place, but after a few seconds, it frightened Rita and she had to break it. "So how old are you?" she asked, just reaching over to gently stroke his arm.

"You know how old I am," he said. He was already sorry he'd opened his mouth. He recognized that he was supposed to ask the lady to marry him, given his feelings for her, not live with him.

"You're fifty," she said.

"We're too old to get married. It's ridiculous. It'll make us look like a couple of fucking clowns."

Another silence, while they listened to the hiss of tires on wet pavement. Until Moodrow put it on the line. "What if I said I loved you?" he asked.

She bit his ear, a quick, sharp bite. "We *are* too old."

"Sure, much too old. So what I'll do is, I'll get enough clothes out of my apartment and we'll try it for two weeks."

"Then what?"

"Who the fuck knows?" Moodrow groaned. "Maybe we'll go to Holland. For the tulips."

"Neptune, more likely," Rita said, "For the atmosphere."

On Tuesday morning, while Moodrow returned to work, Rita Melengic put her winnings in the bank—$8,786—in a money-market fund. Then, at noon, when she knew it would be busy and she, as an experienced waitress, would be most valued, she went back to the Killarney Harp on Houston Street and confronted Ramon Iglesia, the man who'd fired her. Not surprisingly, he broke into a huge smile, his anger long ago dissipated, and they spent the next hour having coffee and catching up on neighborhood gossip. Ramon had a new girlfriend, but she was still running around with her ex-lover though she, Irma, swore they were not going to bed anymore.

"But I heard she went up to his apartment," Ramon cried. "My friend told me she was up there for two hours. How could a woman go to a man's apartment that long if she wasn't gonna let him do it? Not for no two hours, because if she didn't give him no ass, he wouldn't let her stay there. Not for no two hours."

Rita gave him a long look, reaching for what he wanted to hear. She finally decided that he was in love with Irma and so she, Rita, would try to reassure him. "Haven't you ever had a woman in your apartment without going to bed with her?"

"Not without trying." He gave her an affronted look, drawing in an already weak chin. "Besides," he waved a finger in victory. "They already been lovers for three years. He ain't gonna go in a room alone with her for no two hours if she don't give him nothin'."

"Well, maybe there was someone else there. Did you ask her?"

Ramon perked up briefly, then allowed the anger to rise back into his hunched shoulders. "My friend told me she was alone with him."

"Was your friend inside? Don't be so quick to judge. You didn't ask the poor girl. Give her a chance, for Christ's sake. Anyway, I'm gonna let Stanley move in with me."

Ramon's aspect changed immediately, brightening until he fairly glowed. He reached out to squeeze her fingers gently. "That's so good to hear. You too beautiful to live alone." He looked around the room, noting the customers and waitresses engaged in their noon-time dance. "Hey girls," he called out over the noise of the bar. "Hey, Louisa, Rosa, Kathy. Come over here." And when they arrived he continued, explaining Rita's good fortune which began to seem better and better to her as the girls petted and kissed her. They were, all of them, veterans of the wars between men and women. Kathy and Rosa were married, unhappily, while Louisa, five-years divorced, merely screwed around, also unhappily. For them, any change, especially when viewed from a distance, had to be for the better. But it wasn't their opinions that mattered to Rita anyway; it was their obvious feeling for her, their warmth and affection. Then she told them about her winnings in Atlantic City and they fell back, awed and jealous. In their world, men and women were always coming together and falling apart, while cash was inevitably in short supply.

"What are you gonna do with it?" Louisa asked.

"Well I put it in the bank this morning, but I was thinking of having a party here on Saturday night after we close. I mean, if I get my job back." She gave Ramon a sidelong glance.

"No problem," he said. "I already been sending people around looking for you. But I got to be careful. I can't come myself, because your boyfriend is a cop. Jesus," he paused to wipe his forehead, a purely symbolic gesture of submission, "for awhile I was afraid you might send him after me. He's the biggest damn cop I ever saw."

On the Tuesday morning following the assault on the Robert Wagner Homes, Moodrow, relieved of any special detail, also returned to work, and picked up the thread of a large fencing operation, an ongoing investigation he and several other detectives had been pursuing for nearly three months. He worked at his desk in the detectives' room, a place he avoided as much as possible, not because he disliked his fellow detectives, but because he hated the noise—the cops yelling to each other across the room, the assorted criminals and complainants, some clearly psychotic, screaming their innocence to whomever would listen, and, most of all, the endless ringing of the telephones.

Still, he put in his time conscientiously, spending most of the morning on the hated telephone. Other detectives, involved in the same case, approached his desk from time to time. The team was looking for an informant who could introduce them to the fence, an Italian named Angelo Girardi, but after two hours of comparing notes and calling in favors, they were reduced to considering the possibility of bringing in an undercover cop from some outer precinct. All knew it would take months for a new man to penetrate the operation, and nobody was satisfied, when Moodrow, at twelve o'clock, pushed his chair away from the desk.

"Fuck it," he declared earnestly. "I'm gonna go have lunch and see if Rita got her job back. Take about an hour." He tossed some papers on his desk, walked out into the dayroom, shrugged into his coat and was halfway out the door when the duty sergeant looked up from his desk, peering over his bifocals.

"Hey, Stanley," he called out over the noise of the detectives' room. "The captain wants to see you."

"Well, for shit sake, Harry, why didn't you tell me before I got dressed?"

Clearly offended, Harry sniffed once, then buried himself in the stack of paperwork that lay on his desk, the same paperwork he'd been staring at since nine o'clock in the morning.

Helpless, Moodrow threw off his overcoat and trudged down the corridor toward the captain's office. Without thinking, he opened the door as he had a thousand times before, only this time Epstein's voice rang out before he was in the room.

"Don't you believe in knocking, Sergeant?" the captain asked.

Moodrow looked around Epstein's office, noting Agents Higgins and Bradley as well as a New York deputy inspector named Sean Flynn, a fourth generation Irish cop. He nearly laughed aloud, imagining the kind of pressure that could make an old-time Fed-hater like Flynn accompany two FBI agents into a precinct house. Nevertheless, in spite of his amusement, he started to back out of the room, understanding both that he was in some sort of trouble and that the captain needed to put on a show.

"Forget about it," Epstein said, just enough resignation in his voice to show he was playing his part. "You're in now. Why don't you take a seat."

Moodrow did as he was told, sitting absolutely immobile in a chair across from Higgins and Bradley.

"This is Deputy Inspector Flynn," Epstein said.

The deputy nodded once. "We've met before, Captain," he said crisply. "I had the honor of presenting the sergeant with a commendation about six months ago. For bravery, if I recall. A tenement fire."

"How you been, Inspector?" Moodrow asked.

"Still pushing, Sergeant. Thanks be to Jesus."

"Well," Bradley interrupted. He knew the dialogue was meant to annoy him. A message of solidarity from the troops. "We've only got a few minutes, so let's get right down to business." He addressed Moodrow directly. "First, we'd like to know how you're doing on the Chadwick case. Are you close to making an arrest?"

Moodrow looked at Epstein, received a slight nod, then spoke out. "We closed it out. Nothing but dead ends. Nothing solid."

"Then how about something liquid?" Bradley asked, flashing a smile as elegant as his pin-striped suit.

"Whattaya gonna do, bust my fuckin' balls?" Moodrow half rose in his seat.

"Now just one minute," Flynn said calmly. "As long as I'm in this room, by Jesus, Mary and all that's holy, we'll have none of that language. We're here to review an investigation and that's just what we're going to do."

Moodrow, recalling, vaguely, that Flynn was president of the Holy

Name Society, dropped his head contritely. "I'm sorry, Inspector. You go ahead, Agent Bradley, and I'll try to answer. Only it seems to me that when I went out to see you in Queens, you weren't very interested."

Leonora Higgins spoke out quickly. "Sergeant Moodrow," she began, "we now feel there's some possibility that the same group responsible for the death of Ronald Chadwick is presently operating as the American Red Army. It's not likely, but it's possible."

"Why?" Moodrow asked and, at that moment, using just those instincts Moodrow had spoken about earlier, Leonora Higgins knew that Stanley Moodrow could, if he chose—and that choice was by no means certain—track down the killer of Ronald Chadwick. "Tell me what's changed enough so you think that now there's a connection where there wasn't one a couple of weeks ago."

Bradley, angry, leaned forward. "We think there may be something you forgot to mention in your last report. Something you missed. Something you want to add."

Moodrow stared contemptuously at the agent, forcing Inspector Flynn to come between them. "Look here, Sergeant. I'm not blaming you, understand, but I haven't got time for this sparring. Do you know any more than you put in your report?"

Moodrow looked down at the floor, as if trying to make up his mind about something, then stared straight into Flynn's eyes. "Inspector, I don't know what kind of BS dragged these agents away from their computers, but it isn't Ronald Chadwick. And if you don't believe me, I'll give you the whole deal and let you decide for yourself.

"First, Ronald Chadwick is killed and an unspecified amount of money taken from him. Then one of his closest aides, a boy who could have supplied the inside information to make the robbery come off, disappears and later turns up dead in a basement on Clinton Street. Autopsy shows that he was killed before Chadwick. Probably. Finally, this aide's best buddy, one of twenty-three people I wanted to question, is missing. Did the aide give out the information that set up Chadwick? Did the missing friend, whose street name is Zorba, kill Chadwick and the aide? Whatta ya think the odds are? Twenty to one? Thirty to one? And, if he did, what's the chance he's still in New York or that he's connected in some way to the American Red Army? Another thirty to one? You want me to find this guy? I'll try my best, but it burns me that when I made my report to Agent Higgins, she practically laughed in my face. Told me there was nothing to it. Now she strolls into my precinct and accuses me of holding back. It's an insult to the whole department.''

Inspector Flynn threw the two agents the darkest look he knew. They had dragged him in here on a hunch when, in fact, they had no solid evidence at all. The sergeant was clearly not derelict in his duty. He had been thorough and professional in his handling of the case. As a longtime cop, Flynn knew that federal agencies universally embraced the delusion that local police departments were at their beck and call, a kind of law enforcement minor league. ''Well, Agent Bradley'' he said, shortly, ''I think the sergeant has done his job properly, don't you? And I'm sure we both commend him on the completeness of his investigation. Now, if there's nothing else, I'd like to be off.''

Bradley, his voice full of contempt, answered, without even looking at Leonora Higgins. ''Perhaps the sergeant could run through the interview he conducted in the course of his investigations.''

''I believe the sergeant,'' Flynn responded before Moodrow could speak, ''has already told you that you have all the information.''

''Then I have no more questions,'' Bradley said, looking over at Leonora. ''Anything further, Agent Higgins?''

Leonora didn't answer, but as she looked toward Moodrow, he caught her eye and winked, tapping his forefinger against his temple and she realized, for the first time, just how big a mistake they'd made in alienating Stanley Moodrow.

10

THE AMERICAN RED ARMY has struck again. On Sunday morning the AMERICAN RED ARMY set off an antipersonnel device at the Robert Wagner Homes, killing two ZIONIST PIGS. Let this be the last warning. Many more may have died, but the AMERICAN RED ARMY chose to spare the lives of its BLACK AND HISPANIC BROTHERS AND SISTERS. The ZIONISTS must leave southern Lebanon. All political prisoners must be FREED. Do not take us LIGHTLY. The AMERICAN RED ARMY will strike swiftly and with greater and greater effect. The AMERICAN RED ARMY demands the restoration of all budget cuts in Medicare and Social Security. We demand that all BLACKS AND HISPANICS be granted their rightful places in AMERICAN SOCIETY. The BLACK PEOPLE must rule in all of Africa. DEATH TO THE FASCIST-IMPERIALIST PIGS. ALL POWER TO THE PEOPLE.

Johnny Katanos drove the van slowly down Vernon Boulevard, in Long Island City, in Queens, listening to Muzzafer read the final draft of their latest media pronouncement. Effie had written it, as she had written the first one, but Muzzafer read it as if it was his own, then waited for Johnny's comment.

"It's perfect," the Greek responded. "It doesn't say a goddamn thing."

"It's not supposed to say anything."

"Yeah, I know. But it doesn't say anything without any style, which isn't so easy to do."

"In that case, it's perfectly fitting, since we didn't really accomplish anything either." Muzzafer was still upset over the failure of their project in Williamsburg. They could have blown the pipe with a radio-activated detonator, but to do so would have put them at the scene when the explosion took place, an added risk in a small Brooklyn neighborhood which Muzzafer had not been willing to accept. Now he was forced to accept the consequences of his decision; he'd hoped to kill half the politicians in New York and succeeded in destroying two unknown patrolmen. Killing cops in Brooklyn and Jews in Staten Island was not likely to bring New York to its knees. But it might result in a bored, unreliable Johnny Katanos.

Johnny, however, even though he'd argued in favor of a remote detonator and had expected to be the one to flip the switch, was neither angry nor bored. He knew the next time, whatever they did, he would be there, watching. Muzzafer could not risk another dud. He could not risk having the American Red Army think of itself as inept. "Listen," Johnny said, his hand resting on Muzzafer's shoulder, "there's no good reason why you should feel bad about what happened in Williamsburg. I know everybody wanted to start off big, but we'll get 'em next time."

"Yes," Muzzafer said, absently. "Next time."

"Look, man, it was a tremendous fucking explosion. Don't minimize the accomplishment. It happened exactly the way Jane said it would; it blew the shit out of that building." Johnny squeezed Muzzafer's shoulder, a sympathetic, brotherly gesture, then allowed his thumb to graze the smaller man's neck as he pulled away. He noted the quick shiver and Muzzafer's hand rising to the place where he was touched. "Anyway, I've got a good idea."

"Say, 'big idea.' " Muzzafer laughed. "It's going to have to be very big. We've done two projects with a grand total of three casualties."

"Shit, man, we were lucky there was even the two cops standing in front when the thing went off. Another ten seconds and all we'd have for our trouble is plaster and glass.''

They stopped at a light by the Roosevelt Island Bridge at Thirty-sixth Avenue and Johnny stretched, flexing the muscles in his arms, waiting for Muzzafer to look over. This whole business, this sexual guessing game which he played and which he suspected, though he wasn't sure, that Muzzafer understood, was becoming almost as interesting as their regular projects, a kind of added bonus for his service in the American Red Army. During their months of training in Libya, he had been too busy and too fascinated, especially with the explosives, to be bored. It wasn't until they'd reached New York and began to set up their operation that he realized how much of a terrorist's life revolved about waiting. Muzzafer insisted that they lead utterly mundane lives—leave the house at the same time every morning, come home in the early evening, watch television. Fighting and drinking in public were absolutely forbidden. They were not even allowed to carry weapons.

Not surprising, then, that Johnny, who understood that, for him, boredom was as potentially destructive as domestic strife, was committed to finding out just how far the Arab could be pushed. Of course, if he actually succeeded in seducing Muzzafer, he would gain control of the operation without losing any of the Arab's contacts. For a moment, he flashed back to his teenage years, to his puberty, spent almost entirely at the Brookshire School for Boys, a model institution for unwanted children who hadn't yet committed a crime serious enough to merit real incarceration. Muzzafer complained constantly of his boyhood in refugee camps, of the hardship, the indignity, but Johnny knew that with his face and body, if Muzzafer had ever been in a place like Brookshire, the other boys would have had him wearing lipstick and a wig before he got through processing.

Just as the light was about to change, Johnny glanced across the car and saw, with satisfaction, Muzzafer's dark eyes flick over to the ropy blue veins lining his forearms. Slowly and deliberately, he tightened his grip on the steering wheel until the muscles bulged. In

Brookshire, one of his nicknames had been 'Coony' because, the others teased, he had even less body fat than the colored kids.

They rode the last few blocks in silence, up to the entrance to a large, fenced yard with a small building set far back. The sign on the building read PELLAGRINO OXYGEN SUPPLY and the yard was filled with orange and green tanks.

"One time," Johnny explained, "after I got out of jail, I took a job as an apprentice welder and I learned to use a cutting torch. Those green tanks are filled with oxygen and the orange ones contain acetylene. If you hook them together, they make a flame hot enough to cut steel. When the tanks are full, there's enough pressure to bust out buildings, but the cylinders almost never blow under ordinary conditions because the walls are an inch thick and neither gas is explosive until it's mixed with the other. But if we were to create some nonordinary conditions, if we were to, for instance, set off a separate explosion that ruptured the walls of the tanks, we'd have a triple threat: concussion, fire, and shrapnel. Three for the price of one."

Muzzafer shook his head. The tanks were five feet tall and very solid. "They look pretty heavy to me. How would we conceal them?"

"Look at the trucks, man." Johnny turned to face his companion. "How do you think they get them from one place to another? Every little gas station has tanks. Every construction job. Every body shop. I checked the yellow pages this morning and found sixteen wholesale supply houses in Queens alone. Look, I guarantee this company has steady customers and regular routes. One day the Bronx, one day Brooklyn, one day Queens. One day Manhattan. It's just a question of putting the right truck in the right place at the right time."

Within the universe of the 7th Precinct, Captain Allen Epstein was a god. He represented the immovable center around which all action revolved. Directives radiated from his office to every corner of the precinct, to each cop from patrolman to lieutenant, to each clerk, to the criminals in their cells, to the janitors and the secretaries. At first, he had viewed himself as a link in a chain of command that began at police headquarters on the Avenue of the Finest near City Hall and spread from there to the various precincts in the five boroughs. But, after several years, the 7th became its own entity to Allen Epstein, like a medieval manor surrounded by similar, rival manors. He had sworn fealty to the barons at headquarters, but he felt his real mission lay in protecting his neighborhood, the Lower East Side, from predation by outsiders as well as insiders.

It finally reached the point where any intrusion was met with suspicion, if not outright hostility. Even printed policy directives were carefully evaluated for fitness and those not found suitable, were not enforced, though they might be displayed on bulletin boards. But directives were nothing compared to visits from higher authorities and, though he faced it with fortitude, inwardly at least, Captain Epstein had reacted to the visit of Inspector Flynn and the two FBI agents as a father might react to the presence of rabid dogs in his children's playground. For the next two days, he stewed, torn between his sense of outrage that anyone could doubt his ability to control his precinct and a nagging suspicion as to Moodrow and what he might be holding back. After all, he, Epstein, was a cop and cops traditionally do not care for the sort of anarchy espoused by the American Red Army. Finally—his gut unappeased by a carton of Mylanta—it was the cop who won out and he again summoned Stanley Moodrow to his office.

"Sergeant," he began.

"Sergeant?" Moodrow inquired, raising an eyebrow. "Take the stick out of your ass. Or at least use some vaseline."

Epstein smiled, suddenly ashamed. "Listen, Stanley, I'm sorry about the other day. I didn't have any goddamn choice there."

"Forget about it. Anyway, they ended up looking like a couple of assholes. Fishing in a dry lake." He leaned back in his chair, comfortable again. "Did I tell you I moved in with Rita? On Monday. It's working out all right. So far. But what the hell, you gotta . . . ."

"Stanley," Epstein said, quiet but determined. "I'm glad to hear that your private life is going well, but that's not what I asked you in to talk about."

"I figured that," Moodrow replied calmly. "And I also figure you ain't gonna ask for no favor, else you would have offered me a fucking beer at least.''

"All right, take a beer, for shit sake.''

"How 'bout you?''

"My gut's on fire. I can't.''

"That's too bad,'' Moodrow said, opening the can and flipping the tab into the wastebasket. "So what's up?''

"I keep thinkin' about the American Red Army. I mean we both know those cocksuckers meant to blow the shit out of the rabbi. I don't care what they said in the papers. I spoke to Captain Marino in Williamsburg and he says the truck was parked there long before the opening was cancelled. Stanley, they coulda took out a couple hundred people. Including the goddamn mayor. That's not fooling around.''

Moodrow broke in, irritated. "So what are you trying to say? You think I know where this fucking Army is?''

"No, I don't think that. I know you're a cop. It's just that I remember you said you could run this guy down, that Greek you think hit Chadwick.''

"Right,'' Moodrow said. "And I'll tell you something else. When I found Hentados' body, I took two ticket stubs from the Ridgewood Theatre on Fresh Pond Road out of his pocket.''

"Is that in your report?'' Epstein asked, his face rapidly changing color.

"No, what difference does it make?''

"Ridgewood's a white neighborhood. What the hell would Enrique Hentados be doing there?''

Moodrow smiled confidently, pulling on an already empty can of beer. "Glad to see you're still a cop. Because that means you know what it feels like to get pulled off a case when you're sure you could bust the dirtball. I went out to Queens and they told me I was an asshole. I came back and you sent me after a fourteen-year-old kid. Case closed, remember?''

"You shoulda put the goddamn tickets in your report,'' Epstein shouted, already clutching his stomach.

"Well, I didn't put the fucking tickets in the report. What good would it do? Listen, you say the word, I'll take an I-DEN-TI-KIT over to Paco's cell and get a picture of the Greek and the two pigs he was working with and go hunting. But if the Greek took Enrique to the movies in Ridgewood because he lives near there, that still takes in a lot of territory. Maspeth, Glendale, Middle Village, Forest Hills—could even be Long Island City or Woodhaven. We're talkin' about three quarters of a million people. Wanna give me a couple of months? Or maybe you got a ten-year-old for me to scare."

Epstein sat back down, overcome by the obvious. "The bitch about it is that we really don't know this guy is connected to these terrorists. I mean you could spend the next two months and not even find the guy or he'll turn out to be innocent of everything, just a poor, scared slob who happened to disappear at the time when Chadwick got killed. It's all a goddamn guess." He paused, got up, walked to the refrigerator and, without thinking, took out two beers and opened them. "You want to hear something?" he continued. "You're the most valuable guy in the precinct. You know everybody. You can do things no other cop can do. Look how easy you straightened that kid out. Any other detective would have wanted me to assign round-the-clock observation teams at the homes. They would have arrested every Puerto Rican kid within twenty blocks. But you just made it all go away. Shit, you're my whole pipeline. I mean two tickets don't make a goddamn case. Maybe he just went to the movies."

"He didn't have no car," Moodrow said, deliberately turning their positions around.

"So?"

"So how did he get to Ridgewood? Times Square is the hangout for kids like him, not Ridgewood, where most likely he'd get his face stepped on if he walked out alone. Somebody had to take him there. Maybe he went to Johnny's home for a day or two. Maybe they tried to persuade him gently. Maybe they succeeded and then killed him. Look, Ridgewood's just too fucking remote to be an accident. People don't go from the Lower East Side to Ridgewood unless they live there or they know somebody who lives there. The story is that they were lovers. Maybe the Greek takes the kid home so he can find a safe place for a blowjob. I don't know, but the answer has to be somewhere in that neighborhood.''

''Too many goddamn 'maybes,' '' Epstein said, shaking his head. ''I can't lose you for that long on that many 'maybes.' '' You shouldn't have held back those tickets, but it's done and if it ever comes up, I'll swear this conversation never happened. I want you to go up to Brattleboro, Vermont, for a couple of days.''

''Brattleboro?'' Moodrow's face dropped. ''Fuck that, Captain. I just moved in with Rita. I can't go.''

''You're going, Stanley. The locals up there got Frankie Baumann on a minor drug charge. Traces of cocaine or some bullshit like that. A crap case, but they picked up our want on him off the computer. We got ten witnesses saw him kill his old lady in that bar and that's murder, and I want him back here.''

''So, why me, Captain? Send someone else.''

Epstein grinned. This was a punishment, for sure, and he was willing to let Moodrow know, even if Moodrow was the man he would have chosen in any event. ''Baumann is our key into the Golden Nomads.''

The Nomads were an all-white motorcycle gang with headquarters in a steel-shuttered storefront on 7th Street and they were heavily engaged in the wholesale dealing of heroin and methamphetamine. Firmly entrenched after five years of operation, it had been initially hoped that they would be eliminated by the Young Warriors, the other white gang on the Lower East Side and a national organization, but after a single clash, the clubs had begun to cooperate. The Nomads bought from the mob and sold to the Warriors, among others, who then distributed on the streets. The Warriors were a street gang, anxious to uphold a reputation for mindless violence, while the Nomads were tightly organized and very paranoid about admitting new members or meeting new dealers. Busting the Nomads was a cherished goal shared by both Epstein and Moodrow and, characteristically, Moodrow found himself slipping into the cop's world of possibilities, though he did not forget about Rita. Whether or not he actually went to Brattleboro, this was a matter that clearly needed discussion. The

Golden Nomads had been the creation of three men: Pete Crosetti, Gilly Baker, and Frankie Baumann.

"So what's the deal?" Moodrow asked, feeling the hook just graze his lip.

"Right now, Baumann's facing thirty-five minimum. He's forty years old with two priors. Bad priors with much violence, Stanley. The kind judges give out the max for."

Moodrow shrugged. "If ever a man deserved the whole fucking thing, it's Frankie Baumann. He was the enforcer. Everyone knew it."

"Which only proves," Epstein said calmly, a smile inching across his face in spite of his best efforts to appear neutral, "that he could be our key into the Nomads. How long have we been waiting? Four years?" He leaned across the desk and whispered into Moodrow's ear. "I already talked to the goddamn DA. If we get the Nomads, Baumann pleads to second-degree manslaughter and walks away with ten. Thank about that shit, Stanley. The guy's forty years old. If he gets the limit, he ain't gonna see daylight until he's seventy-five and that's very old for a con."

"So why me?" Moodrow asked.

The captain let his voice drop another notch, forcing Moodrow to lean into the desk. "All he knows is he's being held on a minor drug charge. Whatta you think's gonna happen when you walk into that interrogation room? This guy's not a faggot, Stanley, but I want that the first time he figures out what's facing him, his heart should drop down into his shoes and his balls should rise up into his throat. Then he'll be ready."

Moodrow sat still for a moment, sipping at his beer. "So how does this get us into the Nomads? You want inside the Nomads, you gotta put Baumann on the street and if you do that, he'll run."

Epstein, energized again, sat all the way back in his chair. "We got a guy working the streets right now. Black kid. Williamson. You know him?"

"Sure," Moodrow smiled. "I busted him by mistake once. It made his reputation. I beat the hell out of him."

"OK," Epstein waved Moodrow off. 'We're gonna let Baumann

introduce Williamson to the Nomads. As a buyer. Williamson's been undercover for a year, so he shouldn't arouse any suspicion. Let Baumann make bail and let Williamson help him out. Or let Baumann sneak into town and then let Williamson hide him out.''

"That sucks and you know it. You wanna run Baumann, you gotta find some legit way to put him on the street and if you do that, he's gonna fly. Like you said, he ain't no faggot. Listen, I got a guy in the slammer at Riker's named Peter Chang, a Chinatown dealer I used to run before Frankie Rosen busted him last month with a couple ounces of speed. He can't make bail and he's waiting for me to help him out. Let's make a deal with Baumann, but don't reduce the charges right away. Let him and Chang become jailhouse buddies or even lovers. Then, from inside, Baumann introduces Chang to the other Nomads; Chang gets out on bail; Chang borrows money from the Chinatown shylocks to go back into business so he can split; Chang buys from his buddy's old gang; we move in." Moodrow paused, his jaw set. "Because I won't help you if you put Baumann back on the street.''

Epstein also hesitated, but for quite a different reason. He allowed the scheme to sink deep into Moodrow's gut, then yanked the hook until it caught. "What do the details matter? Sure, your idea's better, but by the time you're finished, it'll be better yet. The main thing is go up to Vermont and turn Frankie Baumann, make him work for us. And that's what you're gonna do. What'll it take? Two days? Three days? Give my regards to Rita.''

11

Everyone fears something. Even the most battle-hardened military commanders, men who've sent other men to die again and again, who've seen the dismembered bodies of human beings in bomb craters, in instant ponds, bits of legs and arms lying thirty feet from limbless torsos, who've seen all these things and then sat down to a meal in the midst of the carnage, have that one special point of fear, usually kept hidden from the scrutiny of peers, that forces them to acknowledge the fact of their own mortality.

Stanley Moodrow was no exception. He, too, had his point of vulnerability, but, oddly enough, it had nothing to do with the inherent dangers of being a New York City cop. It was not the crazed killer lunging suddenly through the doorway, ten-inch butcher knife descending rapidly, that set him off. Nor was it the black ghetto revolutionary with mini-machine gun pouring round after round into his unmoving body. Even tenement fires, sudden and violent, requiring policemen to evacuate residents, usually nightmare situations for cops unable to judge how fast a fire is likely to spread, didn't give Moodrow a second thought. He'd been in dozens, been burnt a few times, though never badly, and would not hesitate to go in again.

No, fortunately for his peace of mind, Moodrow's fears did not revolve about his duties as a police officer. Like most of us, Moodrow was able to keep his fears at a safe distance. However, also like most of us, he occasionally had to confront them. Occasionally, as for instance, when ordered by his captain to chase after an out-of-town fugitive. Moodrow, it seems, hated to fly. It wasn't while he was in the air that his problem surfaced, nor on the landing. Though he disliked landing, he was always prepared. His problem came along at the beginning of his flight, during the final moments before takeoff. As the plane swung into its approach and the engines revved to a deafening pitch, Stanley Moodrow, all six foot five inches of him, was transformed from a human being into a living fountain, pouring out sweat until the black stains showed plainly on his dark brown suit. Then, as the plane suddenly lurched forward, the sergeant would try his level best to leave all ten fingerprints in the armrest, for he knew that, without fail, seconds after the tires lifted off the ground, the aircraft would bank steeply toward whatever side he happened to be sitting on, while at the same time rattling like dice in the palm of a degenerate gambler. This undoubtedly explained why Moodrow spent the hour before his flight to Vermont in the airport lounge as a prelude to even more serious drinking on the plane. It also explained his headache and his utter lack of enthusiasm at being confronted in Brattleboro police headquarters by Captain Joshua MacDougall, patriarch of Brattleboro Police Headquarters, a fiftyish man, thin as a rail with translucent skin stretched taut across the fragile bones of his face. He sat, Captain MacDougall, legs crossed at the knees, the picture of New England elegance. Marshalling all the resources of his distaste for New York and New Yorkers, he allowed a slight smile to stretch the corners of his thin, white mouth.

"Yes, Cap . . . Excuse me, Lieutenant Moodrow. What can I do for you?"

"Sergeant Moodrow." Moodrow sat quietly, too drunk to react.

Captain MacDougall shuffled the papers on his desk briefly, then looked into Moodrow's bloodshot eyes. "Quite correct. Sergeant Moodrow. What can I do for you?"

"Didn't Captain Epstein call ahead? He said he was going to make all the arrangements. About Frankie Baumann."

"Oh, yes, I recall the conversation. He wanted me to allow Mr. Baumann to be extradited to New York."

"Yeah. We're gonna bury him."

"Bury?"

"Sure, we've got the fucker dead. He'll max out to thirty-five plus." Moodrow, unsure of how much Epstein had confided to MacDougall, deliberately kept any talk of deal out of the conversation.

MacDougall leaned forward, greedily, like a derelict about to suck on his bottle. "It appears we have a problem, Sergeant. We also want to punish Mr. Baumann."

"For what? For a couple grams of coke? What's the point?" Moodrow was sobering rapidly.

"A couple of grams of cocaine," the captain chuckled. "Well, I'm sure that's not very much in New York City, but we take it very seriously in Brattleboro."

Moodrow shifted in his chair, eyes riveted on MacDougall, who sat motionless. The sergeant was trying to figure out what the Vermont detective wanted, if anything. "So what'll he get in Vermont?"

"Get?" MacDougall spat it out.

"How much time?" Moodrow's voice rose, in spite of his efforts at self-control. "How much time in Vermont for a couple of grams of coke?"

"Oh, I see. I would guess about two years served."

"Two years. I could put that prick away forever."

"You'll certainly have an opportunity. As soon as he's released from a Vermont penitentiary."

"Bullshit," Moodrow exploded, half-rising. "Come two years from now there won't be any witnesses left, no evidence. You might as well let the scumbag off right now." For several seconds he couldn't talk at all, then it poured out. "You know what he did? Do you? He thought his old lady was gonna sell him out to the Feds, which she wasn't. So he goes into the Circle X bar on 6th Street and starts slicin'. Doesn't say anything. Not one fucking word. Like fifty times. Small cuts, with the tip, but you know how those things add up when you stick to them. Did the deed in front of fifteen witnesses, too. Now you can imagine that these witnesses are just a little reluctant to point him out in an open courtroom, what with his friends and all, but I got enough persuasions, I could get a few on the stand. But not three years from now. Then it's dead, and you want to hear something else? I was in that bar a few days ago. It's an old bar and the floorboards don't have any varnish left on 'em so the blood soaked right in. All his pals hang out there, and they don't let anybody stand on the stain. They want to preserve it for future generations."

MacDougall sat calmly through Moodrow's tirade, still stiffly erect. "Very moving, Sergeant. Would that you had managed to apprehend him before he came to our city. In any event, we intend to try Mr. Baumann in Vermont."

"What kind of cop are you?"

"I don't have to sit for your impertinence, predictable as it is. This interview is concluded."

"Can I at least see him?"

MacDougall grinned. "You're sure you won't abduct him?"

"Cut the crap."

"We'll have him ready before you get to the jail."

Moodrow left without another word. MacDougall was right. Arguing was fruitless. Later he would phone Epstein and let the lawyers straighten it out. In the meantime, he would try to soften Baumann up, just in case the state of Vermont decided to release him. Still, even though resigned to the situation, Moodrow was not in the best of moods as he walked across the two hundred yards of the macadam parking lot between MacDougall's office and the Brattleboro city jail, nor was his mood improved by the sight of Frankie Baumann's partner, Angelo Parisi, bent over the trunk of a '62 Pontiac Grand Prix, struggling to extract the spare tire. What followed, however, proved to be just the mood elevator the policeman needed to make the afternoon bearable for, as Moodrow passed, Angelo Parisi, stoned out of his mind on Quaaludes, looked up from his flat tire and recognized the sergeant.

"Well, well," he said, from the very depths of his euphoria, "lookee what we got here, the chiefest piggy on the Lower East Side."

Moodrow stopped for a second to absorb two pieces of information. First, Baumann could no longer be turned because having seen Moodrow on his way to question Baumann (and he could be in Brattleboro for no other reason), Angelo would spread the word and Baumann would no longer be trusted by the Golden Nomads. Second, Moodrow realized that as far as Brattleboro was concerned, he was not a cop, but a private citizen and subject to the same laws as anyone else. Nevertheless, grinning with malice, he swung face to face with the very stoned Angelo Parisi.

"Hey," Angelo cried, realizing his mistake. "Youse can't do nothin' ta me. This ain't New Yawk."

Casually, with utter contempt, Moodrow slapped both palms into Angelo's chest, sending the young hoodlum reeling backwards into the side of the Pontiac.

Angelo, not so stupid as to try to fight back, put his hands in front of himself defensively. "Whatta ya gonna do? Whatta ya gonna do?" was the best he could come up with.

"Get in the trunk, Angelo."

"What?"

"Get in the trunk." Moodrow's voice was calm and even, as if he'd made the most reasonable request imaginable.

"I ain't gettin in no fuckin' trunk."

Once again, Moodrow slapped both palms against Angelo's chest and once again Angelo slammed into the side of the car. "Get in the trunk."

Very slowly, as if he was being pushed against his will by a powerful wind, Angelo Parisi began to move toward the back of the car, Moodrow echoing every step. Just as they reached the open trunk, Angelo looked inside, seeing the tire iron and contemplating the feel of it in his hands as it crashed into Moodrow's skull. Then he heard the low rumble of the detective's laughter and, like Paco Baquili, he began to cry even as he stepped inside.

"You got no right, you motherfucker. You got no right." He kept up the chant, each syllable widening the smile on Moodrow's face, until he heard the snap of the trunk lock closing. Then, as Moodrow, the keys to the Pontiac in his pocket, walked toward the jailhouse, Angelo began to kick and shout for freedom.

Once inside, Moodrow paused to consider his situation. There was no hope of turning Baumann, so his original objective was dead, though he was sure the New York district attorney's office would press for extradition. There was a moment when he considered not speaking to Baumann at all, of simply returning to the airport after a quick call to Captain Epstein, but then, on a whim, he decided to see Baumann, to chat for a few moments about Ronald Jefferson Chadwick and a Greek named Johnny Katanos.

Under most conditions, cops and robbers are deadly enemies, even when the robber is a snitch. They simply hate each other. But on occasion, when neither has anything to gain or lose, they relate to one another like corporate adversaries, salesmen for competing firms meeting unexpectedly in a hotel bar and pausing to talk shop. This was Moodrow's position, though not Frankie Baumann's, as they first encountered each other in the small, green room that served Brattleboro as an interrogation cell.

"I am not about to turn rat, Sergeant," Frankie Baumann, taller than Moodrow, but thin, almost spectral, said in his slow, southern drawl. "It is simply not in my nature."

"So who asked you?" Moodrow replied, taking a seat across from Baumann. "I just thought I'd drop in for a little talk. You know, you shouldn't have cut up your wife like that. She wasn't ratting on you. Now she's dead and you're going bye-bye forever. Man, it'll be box time before you hit the streets again."

"Well, I guess that is just the fate God had in store for me. See this here?" He pointed to a jailhouse tattoo on his forearm which read Born to Lose. "I guess I have known the truth of this for a long time. I have no regrets."

"I could see that. I could see you're a tough guy. I wouldn't even bother trying. By the way, you got a little piece of luck going here. Vermont doesn't want to give you up."

Baumann's face, previously grave, crept up into a smile.

"But," Moodrow continued, "we're not quitting yet."

"No surprise there, Sergeant."

"I gotta say, though, the neighborhood's been very quiet since you been gone. I think the last real blast we had was when Chadwick bought it."

"Oh, yes, I do recall the incident. Always wondered about that one. Hurt me, too. Mr. Chadwick was an old rival of ours. Fact is, we were planning a little action. Only problem being, we didn't know exactly when the man was going to be heavy. No sense killing folks if there is no reward forthcoming."

Moodrow leaned forward. "But some asshole must have known the inside, because they took Chadwick for a heavy piece. Least that's the way I heard it."

Baumann, caught up in the gossip, joined eagerly. "Word on the street is only one gentleman responsible. Greek fella name of Zorba."

"You mean Johnny Katanos?"

"Heard that was his real name. But we all called him Zorba."

"Yeah? You think it's possible? I mean one fucking guy."

"Well, now, I can't say for sure, but I must admit that fella Zorba was about as bad as a man can be. Why, one day I saw him tear apart the biggest damn nigger in the whole city. And he did not pick that fight. Fact is, the boy tried to step aside, but when he was faced down, he 'bout killed the coon. Never thought I would feel sympathy for a nigger, but this one took just the worst beating, and right out where the whole street could see. The most amazing thing about it is just how cool that Greek boy made himself. When I get down to a real fight I pretty near go crazy, but not that Zorba. It was like a stroll down St. Mark's Place for all he showed. Shoot, I am just glad I never had to tangle with him myself."

"Sounds like a man after my own heart," Moodrow responded. "I tried like hell to run that prick down, but I couldn't find him. Like he just rolled off the edge of the Earth."

Baumann smiled, knowing Moodrow was probing, but willing to go along. "Now I do believe that boy hailed from out in the boroughs. Queens comes first to mind. We were hoping to recruit him to our cause at one point, but he turned us down. Did a little investigating, though we never did pick up the exact on his home. Just Queens, somewhere."

* * *

A chilly afternoon for late March, crisp and clear; Johnny Katanos with Muzzafer alongside him, parked the van across from 426 West 10th Street, in Manhattan, the home of A&B Oxygen Supply.

"What time is it?" Johnny asked.

"One o'clock."

"We're early." Johnny settled himself in the driver's seat, stretched his legs underneath the steering wheel. "We got a good half hour before he comes out. He's having lunch now."

"How do you know what he's doing?" Muzzafer rolled the side window down a couple of inches, trying to keep it from fogging.

"I've seen him. When it's warmer, the men eat out in the yard." He started the car and flicked on the rear window defogger. "Say, Muzzafer, you know what I always wanted to ask you? What's it like inside an Arab jail? You were in jail what? Six months?"

"Seven."

"But who's counting, right?" Johnny smiled, taking his time. "So what's it like in an Arab jail? They tough or what?

Muzzafer unzipped his jacket. The defroster blew all the heat up to the top of van. His hair was sweaty, his feet cold. "There are two kinds of jails in most countries. In most civilized countries. Even in Russia there are two kinds. We were political prisoners. Criminals were kept away from us."

"You mean, so they wouldn't hurt you?"

"I expected you to say that, but you're completely wrong. If anyone in that prison hurt one of us, he hurt all of us. We have a reputation for getting even. I don't know if you've heard about it." He looked straight at Katanos, a thin smile pulling at the corners of his mouth. "The thing about criminals, their limitation, is that they aren't prepared to die. As revolutionaries, we expected an early death. We embraced the idea. All of our heroes were dead. Many of our contemporaries, as well. We sang in the mornings. Right after we prayed on our knees to Allah, we sang of our willingness to sacrifice our lives. We held seminars, taught ballistics, organization, forgery, smuggling. Most of our jailers supported us. They gave us food, cigarettes, newspapers. I met revolutionaries from every continent but Antarctica. I met Germans, Irish, Afghans, Colombians, South Africans. We'd all been living in Amman, in Jordan, thinking we were protected. Then one day Hussein's secret police rounded us up like cattle, held us while he drove all the Palestinians out of his country, then let us go. The funny part is that while we were in jail, we made associations that still hold up today. You can see it in our own project. A Libyan operation armed by Cubans with American ordnance smuggled by Colombians. Learning how to set that up was what jail was like for me. The criminals, I think, had it a lot tougher.''

Though he read the implied threat, Johnny listened without changing expression. He wore a quilted down vest and a loose, wool shirt tucked into black, corduroy pants. Reaching into his shirt pocket for a roll of Life Savers, he smiled innocently before he began to speak. ''Man, that sounds more like paradise than prison. If American jails were like that, you'd have to lock the poor people out. How old were you when you went inside?''

''Seventeen.''

''Yeah, that's what I was getting at. Kid joints are worse than regular jails. Every day I had to fight and I wasn't even in there for a crime. I was just there because I was between foster families. Like for almost four years. And all those kids ever did was play sports and fight and fuck each other.'' Johnny passed the Life Savers over to Muzzafer. ''Know why I think they used to fight so much? It's because they were so horny. When I was fifteen years old I had a hard-on almost all the time. I woke up hard, walked around hard, and went to sleep hard. And I wasn't the only one. The niggers were desperate horny. Them guys would jerk off under the bench in shop class. Race to see who would come first. God help the kid who couldn't fight.''

''Wait a minute.'' Muzzafer waved his arm in Johnny's face. ''That him?'' He gestured to a truck pulling out of the yard.

''What's the number on the hood?''

''Eight.''

''And what number are we looking for?''

Johnny struggled to keep his voice relatively neutral. The way Muzzafer had answered his question about jail, cool and unafraid, made him wary. The bastard wasn't scared of him and that, in itself, was intriguing. In Johnny's world, prior to meeting Theresa, little guys like Muzzafer, if they weren't actually holding a weapon, were always afraid.

"What time is it?" Johnny asked again. Suddenly he realized that Muzzafer might try to kill him. Not here and not in the near future, but it was possible the Arab would kill him for breaking up the project. That's why Muzzafer wasn't afraid. Because he knew that he *could* do it.

"One twenty-three." Muzzafer kept his eyes on the entrance to the yard. The Greek's patronizing tone was becoming more and more irritating. Under ordinary circumstances, he would slap the man who dared to challenge him, but these circumstances were far from ordinary. Through his superiors, any project leader could arrange for the ultimate lesson to be administered to rebellious soldiers and these same soldiers all knew it, but in New York, under the conditions which he himself had created, there was no higher authority. What could he do? Hit Johnny Katanos? Shoot him? There wouldn't be any Army without him and the oddest thing was that Johnny never challenged Muzzafer when the whole group was together. Never embarrassed him in front of the women. For a moment, Muzzafer tried to imagine himself explaining why he'd had to kill Johnny Katanos. Theresa would tear him to pieces.

They sat in silence, watching the traffic on 10th Street, until Johnny, deadpan, asked for the time.

"It's one twenty-eight," Muzzafer replied.

"Crystal ball time, man. I say in exactly two minutes, right when the lunch whistle blows, truck number 4 is gonna come rumbling out of the yard. The guy driving it'll go east to Sixth Avenue, then north, into midtown traffic. Guess where he's actually headed."

"The Bronx." Muzzafer meant it as a joke.

"How the fuck you know that?" For a moment Johnny was taken aback, the first time Muzzafer had ever seen him even slightly out of control.

"I was kidding." Muzzafer explained.

"Yeah?" He looked at Muzzafer closely for a moment, then flashed his biggest smile. "Well, you win the grand prize, little buddy, 'cause that's exactly where he's going. Most days he takes the New Jersey run, but two afternoons a week he services whatever accounts number 3 can't handle."

"So why does he use Sixth Avenue? How come he doesn't take the West Side Highway or Tenth Avenue and go around the traffic?"

"OK, this is really beautiful. He takes Sixth Avenue because of a little pizza shop at 32nd and Sixth, Gino's Genuine, where they sprinkle their pizza with dope instead of cheese. No shit. Everytime he stops there, the counterman passes him a small bag, a slice of pizza and no change for his twenty. I figure it's probably coke, but who gives a fuck? As long as he goes there."

At 1:30 the sound of an air horn interrupted their conversation and a GMC with an open stake body and the number 4 painted on the hood, pulled out of the yard and headed east on 10th Street, with Johnny and Muzzafer in pursuit. They followed it through heavy traffic to Sixth Avenue between 31st and 32nd, where, as predicted, the driver double-parked next to a stretch limo and ran into Gino's Genuine.

"Son of a bitch," Muzzafer said. "You were right."

"This is some fucking town, partner. I mean these guys are more wide open than a transvestite's cheeks."

Muzzafer ignored the comment. The scenario was perfect for their needs. Manufacturers are forbidden to carry compressed gas in closed trucks in New York and the slats on number 4's stake body offered easy access to the chained cylinders of oxygen and acetylene. Muzzafer could feel the blood rising. This was midtown Manhattan, not Williamsburg, Brooklyn. Every street was crowded and the further north truck number 4 drove, the more crowded it would get.

"Take a count," Johnny said. "Count the cylinders."

"Forget it," Muzzafer responded. "That's the first thing I did. There's twenty oxygen and eighteen acetylene. Let's get out of here."

As they drove toward the Midtown Tunnel, and Muzzafer began to consider the situation, to formulate a plan for the execution of the project, Johnny watched him closely, trying to sense the moment when Muzzafer would be least prepared to hear what he was going to say. For Johnny, it was a kind of stalking, of waiting for the prey to relax before he began moving forward. He would never allow himself to become as lost in his thoughts as Muzzafer. No situation was safe enough for that.

"Hey, Muzzafer, you're not gonna believe this. Guess what happened yesterday afternoon? Guess?"

Muzzafer looked up, startled. "What?"

"I got Janey. I popped her good, man."

"What?" He couldn't believe he'd heard it right.

"I humped little Janey. Humped the shit out of her."

"Are you serious?" Muzzafer felt the news drop over him like a wet snowfall. If Effie found out . . . "Does Effie know?" he asked frantically. "Why did you do that? I ought to kill you for that."

"Relax, Effie doesn't know anything." Johnny laid his hand on Muzzafer's leg, tapping the smaller man's knee. "And Theresa doesn't know, either. And don't look at me like it was my fault. We were down in the laundry room and she got all over me. I mean it's obvious the bitch hasn't seen a cock in a long time and she's tired of plastic." He stopped for a moment, to give Muzzafer a chance to respond, but Muzzafer was too angry to open his mouth and Johnny, quick to seize advantage, leaned close, whispering in his best "buddy to buddy" voice. "But lemme tell you exactly what happened. And don't let me forget about the freckles." He pushed his elbow into Muzzafer's ribs and for the first time, Muzzafer recognized that this whole project, the choice of targets, the location, the method, was entirely in Johnny Katanos' hands. "She's got freckles on her fucking tits, man. They're exactly the same color as her nipples. And real blonde pussy hair that's blonder than the hair on her head, and that's the first time I ever saw that. Would you believe she said if I go down on her, she's gonna kick me in the balls? She said she's had enough tongue to last her into the next century."

Try to imagine your worst nightmare come to life. Imagine you've been having the same dream for fifteen years, at least twice per week, that each time you awaken in a panic and that your dream is so intensely private it cannot be shared with priest or psychiatrist. And then, one sunny afternoon, it jumps out of hiding in the form of two FBI agents and grabs you, Julio Ramirez, immigrant, barber, spy, and whisks you away to a small office in Queens.

If you have a strong imagination, you are shaking the way Julio Ramirez shook, his right knee jerking uncontrollably as he sat in a straight-backed chair across from a smiling George Bradley and scowling Leonora Higgins. For the third time, Bradley repeated his position quietly.

"Mr. Ramirez, we know you delivered a vanload of ordnance to the American Red Army. We know you picked up the van at a garage in Bay Ridge and drove it to 31st Street in Astoria. We know you passed it on to an active member of the Red Army. Why are you wasting our time?"

Julio coughed up the last remaining bits of his courage. "If you know so good, you tell me who tell you?"

"Can't do that, Julio."

"Let's stop the bullshit," Leonora broke in, her voice hard and firm. "Let's just bury the asshole."

"Don't be so hasty, Leonora. Let's give him a chance to come around."

"If you got me," Julio said, "how come you don't arrest me? What you gonna do in court if you can't say who tell you this about me."

"Court?" Leonora broke into laughter, then snapped it off abruptly. "Asshole, the one thing you don't have to worry about is jail. You'll wish you were in jail. Do you happen to know the Havana Moon Bar on Kennedy Boulevard in Union City? Do you know Esteban Perez, the owner?"

Julio shook so badly the coins in his pockets began to jingle. Esteban Perez was known in the Cuban community as the public head of the anti-Castro Cubans in the United States. There were others, of course, whose jobs were to carry out the directives of public figures like Perez, but these names were not well known, and although the FBI had a few in their files, Leonora, in mentioning the name of Perez, was able to scare the hell out of Julio Ramirez without giving anything away. At that point, she was not yet aware of how innocuous and expendable Ramirez was.

"Suppose," Leonora continued, "we mention, in the course of general conversation, that a certain barber, Julio Ramirez, is really a spy who reports to the Cuban Mission every month? Do you think he'll ask for proof? No? What do you think will happen to you when he finds out? What do you think will happen to your family? Do you have children, Julio?"

A long silence followed. The two FIB agents could sense that Ramirez was about to break, but they were totally unprepared for the mixed torrent of tears and words that poured from the hapless spy. No, he did not want to be a spy. He was not a Communist. It had all been a mistake, but how could he get out of it? Now he wanted only to serve his country. He wanted to be an American, like his neighbors. Would the FBI please help him and his family?

They worked him over for the next three hours. He readily named his contact at the Cuban Mission, a man they already knew. He recalled every detail of his delivery of the weapons, except for the description of the man who met him in Astoria. He had been afraid of this man, afraid to look too closely. And it had been dark underneath the el. He wanted to help them, he sincerely wanted to, but this was all he knew.

Finally, it sunk in. Almost at the same time, Leonora Higgins and George Bradley concluded that they were not going to get any closer to Muzzafer and his army by using Julio Ramirez, that they had wasted their time, that they were back at the same dead end. Bradley spoke first.

"OK, Ramirez, out of here."

Ramirez stood up quickly, but remained by his chair. "What do you want me to do? Do you want to use me? What do you want?"

"I want you to get out of here."

"Am I under arrest?"

"Jesus Christ, man, will you just go?" Bradley's frustration finally pushed the Cuban into action and he was out the door without another word.

"I never saw a man open up so easily," Leonora remarked.

"Right," Bradley agreed, his voice tinged with irony. "Why is it only the ones with nothing to tell are willing to tell? Leonora, the bureau's crawling up my back on this one and I just don't have a clue about what to do next.''

Leonora shrugged her shoulders. ''It's not like we've left anything undone. Do they think we're spending our time on the beach?''

''They don't care. They want results.''

''How about Julio?''

''He's not results.''

''Still, what are you planning to do about him? Do you want to use him?''

''Oh, I'm going to use him all right.'' For the first time, Bradley smiled. ''I owe Esteban Perez a favor and I think that favor is going to be Julio Ramirez.''

Leonora sat bolt upright. ''You can't do that.''

Bradley looked across at her, surprised by the conviction in her voice. ''Why not?''

''They'll kill him.''

''So? He's a spy.''

''He gave us all he had. You can't just execute him. It's not right.''

Bradley began to laugh. ''Not right? He's perfect. We have no use for him whatsoever, but he'll make those crazy Cubans very happy. Perez'll take credit and build his own reputation. Then, instead of me owing him a favor, he'll owe me. I like my ledger unbalanced on the credit side.''

''But . . .''

''Enough, Leonora, that's the way it's done. Ramirez was never a player. He was a pawn from the first day. Not even a pawn. A fiftieth of a pawn. No one will miss him.''

''How about his wife and kids?''

12

New York City traffic. If you've been here you know. You know, for instance that, at least once a week, the mayor goes on record as advising (actually, begging) motorists to take mass transit, to leave their cars at home, to use buses and subways. The citizens refuse, of course, even though parking violation fines, as well as parking garage fees, seem to rise monthly, while hundreds of small, brown tow trucks cruise midtown Manhattan, looking for illegally parked cars. The price of the tow, seventy-five dollars (cash only), plus a trip to a pier on 39th and the Hudson River, plus a thirty-five-dollar parking ticket, does not, apparently, deter motorists, because the pier is always full. Every street, it seems, between 57th and 23rd, from river to river, is lined with double-parked cars and trucks and the ten million parking tickets issued each year are accepted as a cost of doing business.

And nowhere in Manhattan, not in the Battery with its narrow, dark streets or at the East River bridges and tunnels, is traffic worse than on the West Side of Manhattan between 23rd and 42nd streets. Sixth, Seventh, Eighth, Ninth, Broadway . . . it doesn't seem to matter what time of the day, 8 AM to 8 PM, the professional driver expects long delays while the occasional visitor squirms behind the wheel, peering around other vehicles, wondering when it will break up. Drivers scream, curse, and cut each other off as double- or triple-parked trucks compete with Con Edison or New York Telephone excavations to create the world's largest moving obstacle course. Here, as many pedestrians walk in the street as on the sidewalk, and the local garment manufacturers transfer materials from loft to loft by means of pushcarts, it is not uncommon for two workers to shove a cart loaded down with a dozen bolts of cloth right up against the bumper of an oncoming car, daring the driver to do anything about it. Then everyone waits. Waits for the altercation to stop, for the cops to show up, for anything that will allow the traffic to start forward.

Northbound Sixth Avenue has its own special set of problems. To people unused to it, the way traffic moves freely between 14th and 23rd streets, only to stop dead at 24th, seems almost miraculous. Yet this pattern repeats itself every day, because at 34th and Sixth, Herald Square, where Broadway crosses Sixth Avenue, the traffic light is split three ways and the endless mass of pedestrians lowers the green time still further. This is also the wholesale plant and flower district and the curbs from 26th to 30th are lined with a jungle of potted tropical plants and with the trucks that ferry them about. The florists occupy most of the storefronts along that part of Sixth, but, scattered here and there amid the foliage, are discount electronic stores, each specializing in the 'guaranteed lowest prices' for cameras, tape recorders, VCRs, ghetto blasters—anything electronic. At the northern end of the log jam is Herald Square, a small patch of concrete featuring an enormous bronze angel poised above a bell, with its two most famous residents, Macy's and the now defunct Gimbels, occupying the block between Sixth Avenue and Penn Station to the west. Herald Center, a newly constructed, seven-story, black glass mall, reputed to be owned by Ferdinand Marcos, fits like a sandwich between the two giants.

Even on normal days, this area in the heart of New York's garment center resembles a beehive, with humans seeming to crawl over one another as they push their way along the sidewalk or thread their way between cars. On Good Friday, however, two days before Easter, with the temperature near seventy and a warm sun flooding Manhattan, the traffic, both pedestrian and vehicular, is virtually at a standstill.

Nevertheless, in spite of these difficulties and every other argument Stanley Moodrow could muster, Good Friday was the day Rita Melengic chose to fulfill her promise to buy Moodrow a new suit with part of her casino winnings. If, while she was at it, she filled out her own spring wardrobe, it, as she patiently explained, couldn't hurt. Moodrow, however, dug in his heels on this particular point.

"I'm not gonna follow you around Macy's all day. Forget it. I hate shopping and you know it," he said, and neither her arms around his neck, nor her breasts pressing against his back, could budge him.

"Well, you're gonna get a new suit anyway. That's a rag you've got on."

"C'mon, Rita, not tomorrow. For Christ's sake, the stores'll be packed. Let's put it off."

"No, A&S is openin' a new store where Gimbels used to be and they're havin' unbelievable sales. We'll never get another chance like this."

"But I gotta work tomorrow."

"Oh, Stanley, don't ruin it."

In the end he could not endure the look of disappointment on her face and had to give in. "OK, OK. I gotta go over to Pulaski's around noon. Meet me on the Sixth Avenue side of A&S around two."

"Sounds good."

"But I could be late. Don't hold me to the minute."

Later on, Rita showed her gratitude by waiting until Moodrow was asleep, handcuffing him to the bedrail, then forcing him to redeem the keys by performing five different acts, three of which are illegal in the states of Georgia, Mississippi, Alabama, and Alaska.

Pulaski's Funeral Home, on 11th Street between First and Avenue A, had been a fixture on the Lower East Side for thirty-five years. Two stories high, it encompassed the width of three storefronts and was, thus, a perfect target for a new breed of entrepreneurs looking to open trendy boutiques, art galleries, and nouvelle cuisine restaurants. It seemed that the East Village, long a stable section for the working and nonworking poor had become, in the insane world of 80s Manhattan real estate, a prime area for upward development. The process was called gentrification by the local press. The reasoning was that if apartments in 'good' neighborhoods go for $1200 per room, there must be suckers willing to pay $800 to live in a tenement. The same principle applied to commercial properties and small businesses like Pulaski's Funeral Home, which upon coming to the end of ten- and fifteen-year leases found monthly rents of eight or nine hundred dollars jumped to eight or nine thousand. There was no way for these "mom and pop" establishments to come up with that kind of cash. Greedy landlords, operating virtually without regulation when it came to commercial properties, often demanded deposits of three months' rent as security, while an utterly indifferent mayor roamed the country, promoting his memoirs.

But Stanley Moodrow was the fixer, the cop with the reputation for straightening out problems and Mrs. Pulaski had called him at the precinct, demanding, "You come. You come," and refusing to take any excuse. So, at twelve o'clock on Good Friday, Moodrow found himself in an empty side room of the Home, a coffee cup on a table by his side, listening to an excited old lady pour out her troubles.

"I come here nineteen and forty-five. I come away from war in Europe. I am Jewish woman and I am afraid of Nazi even if husband is Polish. So Juroslaw bring me here. Right away we use money to buy funeral home. Thirty-seven year on 11th Street we bury thousands of countrymen. Every time we pay rent on first of month. We become citizen. We vote. Our son is lawyer. Son-in-law work business. All good. Now lease running out and building owner is Arab. He say $8,000 every month and twenty thousand for deposit. What we do? Thirty-seven year, Stanley. What we do?"

Moodrow sat quietly, somewhat bored, trying to nod his head at the right times. He'd been hearing the story more and more lately, and he was sorely tempted to beg off, but Sarah Pulaski was a legend in the neighborhood. Her strength and endurance had long symbolized, for him, the tenacity of the residents of this polyglot ghetto. Jews, Poles, Urkrainians, blacks, Puerto Ricans, Italians—for generations the Lower East Side had held on to its identity and now, under the onslaught of the real estate moguls, it was starting to come apart.

"Who's the landlord? Achmed?"

"Yes. The bastard." She made a rude gesture, learned from an Italian neighbor thirty years ago, by placing her thumb under her upper teeth and snapping the nail forward.

"I know him. Tell me, Mother, how much can you pay?"

"Not one cent extra. Eight hundred dollars."

"In that case," Moodrow replied evenly, "you might as well pack right now."

They negotiated for an hour with Sarah jumping up every five minutes or so to consult an enormous ledger, before Moodrow left with a figure he thought the Arab might accept. Being a capitalist himself, Moodrow was not surprised that Achmed was out to extract the greatest possible profit from his investments. However, there was a good chance the Arab, an intensely proud man, would come down somewhat if Moodrow was careful to show him the same respect as on previous encounters. Clearly, if the Pulaskis moved out, the two floors would have to be completely renovated. This would leave the store vacant for months in addition to requiring a heavy capital investment. The Pulaski clan was willing to go to $4,500 with an $8,000 security deposit. They were extremely reliable tenants and not likely to miss payments or walk away from a losing proposition six months into the lease. Moodrow knew he had a chance and the expectation of doing a good deed left him, as always, in a decent mood.

It was 1:00 when Moodrow left Pulaski's Funeral Home. He would have liked to head out immediately for his meeting with Rita, but he had another stop to make first. This one, he hoped, would not take as long. It would definitely be unpalatable. He had to see Mickey Vogel, a longtime junkie-informant who had gone so far into his addiction that he no longer had any names more important than common street dealers to sell. He'd called Moodrow at the precinct the night before and begged for a meeting. Moodrow had no doubt that he needed money to buy heroin and that he would offer some local pusher as his end of the bargain. This Moodrow did not need and, as he drove south toward Pitt Street, the cop knew he would be saying goodbye to Mickey Vogel.

The reality was even worse than Moodrow expected. A single

roach-infested room in a welfare hotel, a desperately sick junkie, snot rolling over his mouth and down his chin, an all-pervasive smell of vomit and sweat hanging over the room—it permeated the bed and the single soiled sheet. Even the walls were filled with it.

"I got a good one for ya today, Sarge." Vogel began, mustering up one last hustle. In his own way and for completely different reasons, he mirrored the emotional condition of Julio Ramirez in the hands of the FBI.

"Forget it Mickey. Not this time."

"Whatta ya mean? I got a big one. I got the Indian. I got the fuckin' Indian cold. All I need's enough bread ta score and he's yours." When Moodrow didn't answer, the junkie tried to go on, but quickly broke into a dry, hacking cough.

"Look, Mickey," Moodrow finally said. "I could have the Indian whenever I want. It's over. You gotta clean up."

Vogel began to cry, almost as Julio had cried. "I'm dyin' here. Don't ya understand? I'm thirty-three years old and I'm dyin' here."

"Methadone. The clinic," Moodrow said softly.

"That's thirty days' lockup. Suppose some of the guys in there know about me?"

Moodrow stood up to leave. "Listen, I'm in a hurry. I just want to say I've seen a thousand junkies in your spot. Look at your fuckin' arms. It's over. You gotta come down now. You say go ahead I could get you in a clinic at Jamaica Hospital tomorrow morning. They'll bring you down slow. Feed you. Give you clothes. In thirty days you'll walk out with a tube of methadone and a feeling like you're a human again. But that's all I could do. Rockefeller ain't got the money to feed your habit. Think it over and call me tonight."

"Ya gotta help me . . . ." Mickey reached out as if to hold Moodrow back, but the sergeant just brushed by him and went out the door. Getting the maximum out of an informant and then dropping him is a common scenario for cops. In this situation, in offering to use his influence to place Vogel in a clinic, Moodrow was doing more than most. In any event, he certainly appreciated the beautiful spring day after breathing the foul atmosphere of the junkie's room. It was two o'clock when he stepped out onto Pitt Street, two blocks from the precinct. For a moment, he considered taking his unmarked car over to A&S, but he knew there would be no place to park, that even the garages would be full, the traffic unbearable, so he drove to the stationhouse and turned the keys over to the desk sergeant. Then he grabbed hold of the first blue and white cruiser he saw, and begged a ride to midtown.

"Surge, Sarge," Patrolman Shawn O'Connell said. "Any time. Hop in the back." O'Connell was a twenty-five-year man, looking for thirty, and an old friend. He was one of those cops who had long ago set aside personal ambition. A heavy, florid man, he was content to patrol his beat and keep out of trouble. He liked the check and he liked having some place to go in the morning. His wife had left him so long ago, he no longer knew where she and his son were living. Or with whom. "Hey," he joked, as soon as Moodrow was inside, "I hear you're gettin' married. And at your age, too. How ya gonna get it up, old man? You gonna watch dirty movies?"

"Fuck off, Shawn. We're only living together. Not married. And we don't need dirty pictures."

"Yeah? So whatta ya got, then, a trained dog?" O'Connell worked hard to maintain the crudity of his sexual imagination.

"No dog," Moodrow answered. "We don't need a dog. Your sister's letting us use her duck."

"You shouldn't say that."

"Why not?"

"Because," O'Connell explained soberly, "what if my sister was dead or somethin'?"

"You don't even have a sister."

"But if I did, she could still be dead. Ya never know. By the way, I got a kid you could use. From the projects. Name of Richard Hatchley. The Rads are fuckin' him around and he wants to even up. I'm too old to bother with that shit, but if ya want him, Stanley, I'll turn him on to you."

"Does he have anything?"

"Maybe now only a little. Like he's still a kid. Sixteen or something. But in a few years, who knows? Think about it."

They drove up First Avenue to 23rd Street, then cut over toward Sixth. Under ordinary circumstances, Moodrow would have requested that O'Connell throw the lights on top of the cruiser so they could make time, but there had been a rash of complaints in the prior two months about the inappropriate use of sirens, so they contented themselves with crawling along with the traffic, until they got to Sixth Avenue, where the radio called all available units to a report of gunshots on 18th and Eleventh.

"End of the line, Sarge," O'Connell announced, finally throwing on the lights and siren.

"Catch ya later, Shawn," Moodrow returned, hopping quickly out of the cruiser. He watched, for a moment, as the car began to cut in and out of the line of vehicles edging toward Manhattan's West Side, then, resigning himself to the inevitable, he began to walk the eleven blocks up Sixth Avenue toward an already impatient Rita Melengic.

He made slow progress, constantly shifting from one side of the sidewalk to the other, trying to avoid the knots of window shoppers and the truckers loading and unloading an incredible variety of wholesale and consumer goods. At every intersection, his path was blocked by Con Edison or New York Telephone or Empire City Subway or the Department of Water Supply or . . . and even when there were no workmen, cars and trucks, desperate to get out of the traffic-choked avenue, cut in front of him, ignoring the lights. Pausing, the sweat standing out on his forehead, Moodrow reflected on the myriad ways New York had of taking the pleasure out of even a beautiful, spring day. Then he heard the sounds of two enormously angry females from across the street, and like everyone else, he was grateful for the interruption.

"You dirty fucking whore. You better stay away from my old man." The girl was slim, but wiry and totally unafraid, though she was dwarfed by her taller, heavier opponent.

"And what're you gonna do about it, hole?" Effie Bloom's laughter rolled over the motorists and pedestrians, drawing everyone's attention in a way no male argument could. Here, with two women involved, nobody felt threatened or had a serious urge to stop it.

Suddenly, Theresa Aviles slapped Effie across the face, much harder than they'd planned at rehearsals. "How about I do that? How do you like that?" She grinned for the crowd and Effie, without thinking, shot a right hand, fist clenched, into Theresa's mouth, sending Theresa to the sidewalk.

In an instant, they were all over each other. It was the plan and it wasn't the plan, though it was certainly convincing and no one, not even Moodrow, suspected that they were putting on an act. Moodrow actually considered crossing Sixth Avenue to break it up, so serious was the fighting, with both women getting marked. But, of course, Rita was waiting in front of A&S and he was already late. He could feel himself pulled in two directions, with one foot in the street, when the situation resolved itself.

"Now, I'm gonna kill you," Theresa screamed, remembering herself and her waiting partners. She reached out, hooked two fingers on Effie's halter and ripped it off the larger girl's body.

That was the final straw. When Effie's huge breasts with their enormous dark nipples tumbled forth, even the most hardened New Yorkers popped their eyeballs, staring at the hapless woman. Hardly surprising, then, that Johnny Katanos, who'd been working his way across the street, dodging cars, was able to slide a package of plastique, complete with detonator, between the steel bulkhead protecting the driver's compartment and the heavy cylinders of oxygen and acetylene chained to the sides and front of A&B Oxygen Supply truck number 4.

"Well, that's that," a young black trucker said to Moodrow as Effie disappeared into 31st Street and Theresa walked triumphantly down Sixth Avenue. Within minutes, both would be safely on subways, their argument forgotten by potential witnesses.

"Sure wouldn't mind gettin' some of that," the driver continued.

"Which one?" Moodrow asked, deadpan.

"Shit, I take both of 'em. They be the bread. I be the bologna."

"And who supplies the mayonnaise?"

Moodrow began walking uptown even as Benjamin Wild, driver of A&B Oxygen Supply Truck number 4, still imagining the sensation of his unshaven face between Effie's soft breasts, pulled out. For the next few minutes, he made only slightly better progress than Moodrow and they arrived at 32nd Street almost at the same time, but then, as the traffic finally cleared an enormous double-parked, tractor-trailer, Ben Wild shot ahead, hooked left and took the cutoff for 33rd Street. Muzzafer and Jane Mathews, noting the move from the other side of Sixth Avenue, smiled at each other. This would bring the truck even closer to the pedestrians, even closer to Rita Melengic, who, by this time, could see Moodrow and was anxiously waving, trying to catch his attention, until the truck carrying Ben Wild passed directly in front of her and Muzzafer, hand inside a large shoulder bag, flicked the toggle switch on his transmitter.

There was no huge blast, as Muzzafer had hoped. The cylinders carrying the oxygen and acetylene were made of cast steel, an inch and a half thick, the industry having long ago recognized the danger inherent in the transportation of compressed gases. Instead, the muffled explosion had two unexpected effects. It blew the valves off the tops of six of the cylinders while at the same time igniting the rapidly escaping gases and creating a small fireball which quickly melted the remaining canisters. The result was a second, much larger, fireball, almost white in its intensity, which instantly spread across the west side of Herald Square engulfing A&S, Herald Center, two dozen cars and trucks and more than fifty pedestrians, including Rita Melengic.

After the explosion, Moodrow found himself frozen, body and mind. The words in his brain kept going around and around, like an endless tape loop, pushing right up to the point of the explosion, then stopping, returning back to the sight of Rita waving from beneath one of the round, green canopies protecting the store's showroom windows. There was Rita. He was walking, stepping out into the street. A truck passed by. There was Rita.

His ears were full of the screams of the injured. He was a cop. A cop was supposed to help at times like these. There was something he'd just missed. He was stepping into the street. There was Rita. He was walking. Rita was waving. What? What? He was stepping into the street. There was Rita.

And then Detective Sergeant Stanley Moodrow, hardened veteran, did what no cop can ever do. He turned on his heel and ran from the scene of a crime.

13

The AMERICAN RED ARMY announces its greatest victory in the war against OPPRESSION. The AMERICAN RED ARMY demands the removal of the ZIONIST DOG from PALESTINE. We demand FULL CITIZENSHIP for the oppressed BLACK PEOPLE of the United States. SOUTH AFRICA must be made FREE. The AMERICAN RED ARMY demands the government of the United States end its WAR OF GENOCIDE against the people of NICARAGUA. The AMERICAN RED ARMY will never end its HOLY WAR until its DEMANDS are fully met. We urge the OPPRESSED PEOPLE of the United States to RISE UP and CRUSH the oppressor. The AMERICAN RED ARMY demands the IMMEDIATE RELEASE of the HEROES imprisoned around the WORLD. ALL POWER TO THE PEOPLE.

For the first time in one hundred years, the Fifth Avenue Easter Parade was canceled. Instead of the usual celebration, the balmy skies of Easter Sunday found a city in mourning. All over New York, families gathered beside the remains of charred, unrecognizable victims. And the mood was not of anger, though that would inevitably come, but of shock, of numbness, as if a deed so awful could not be confronted. The citizens of New York, famous for their impatient rushing about, moved slowly, as if disoriented. They moved with the air of people who'd forgotten something very important, something right on the verge of consciousness.

The Honorable Dave Jacoby, mayor of New York City for eight years, sensed this mood precisely. He understood his obligation to pull his people out of their lethargy, yet he could not bring himself to conduct the press conference called for Sunday evening. He chose to sit it out, turning it over to the police commissioner after a brief introduction. A lifelong Democrat, Jacoby knew it would be political suicide to speak the thoughts crowding his brain, but he was so angry, he was afraid he wouldn't be able to control himself long enough to make a speech.

In my city! In my city! The phrase refused to leave his mind, commanding his attention despite the obvious necessity of organizing his political machine to deal with the fears of the people. If he had his way, he would cordon off the whole town and search the buildings, one by one, until he ran down the animals responsible. Then . . .

He'd made the obligatory visits to Herald Square and to the hospitals where the injured had been taken as soon as the cops declared the areas safe. At every stop, as soon as they recognized his limousine, the reporters, like vultures, tore after him, screaming for a quote. Apparently, no act, no matter how awful, could destroy their armor. Yet it was in avoiding them that his own defenses were thoroughly penetrated. He arrived at Bellevue Hospital to find his way blocked by an army of microphones. His initial reaction was to order the half-dozen uniformed police officers stationed at the main entrance to clear the area, but his town was too jittery to accept any high-handed behavior from its leader, and he finally got through by promising an impromptu press conference when he came out. Only then, like the waters of the Red Sea, did they pull back, still screaming questions and waving microphones in case he should utter some passing words of wisdom. Inside the building, with the cops and the doctors flying about, he took a deep breath and then turned, unprepared, to confront the thing in the stretcher by the radiology-room door. At first, he thought it was a heap of melted candlewax, but candlewax never cries out in pain and it was the sight of a nurse running over, syringe in hand, that made him realize he was dealing with a human being, that the white cubes near the top were teeth and the black spot, an eye.

It didn't get any better. On the morning before today's press conference, as he flew by helicopter to LaGuardia Airport for a quick meeting with officials from Washington, he realized, for the first time, just how big his city was. An enormous expanse of glass and stone that spread beyond the political borders of New York City, to embrace ten million people. The American Red Army could be anywhere, planning anything. Who would protect the city if Dave Jacoby backed off?

In the end, he and his aides gave approval to the speech Police Commissioner George Morgan was about to give. Initially, after a series of hurried conferences with Morgan, they'd created something very similar for the mayor, but then backed off and passed the outline to the commissioner's speechwriters. These ideas, it was decided, couldn't come from the mayor (not until he saw how the voters handled it), but he had made his wishes clear to the top brass in the department. They were not to worry about warrants. They might place bugs wherever they wished. They might tap any telephone. Above all, they were to recreate the old 'Red Squad' of the 50s and thoroughly penetrate the radical community at New York's various colleges, especially City University, which claimed to house a dozen black and Puerto Rican 'liberation' societies.

Thus a short speech of introduction and George Morgan stepped in front of the camera, flashbulbs popping from all angles. His face was stern, mouth locked into a determined grimace. A black man, heavy-set and serious on the most festive occasions, he'd come up the hard way, starting in a violent, crime-ridden precinct in Brooklyn and progressing through the civil service system to the rank of captain before being appointed, first to inspector, then to commissioner. He'd been told by the mayor to keep it brief, businesslike, and thorough. The people of New York, His Honor had declared, must be made to feel the government (his government) was doing something and not merely reacting to situations.

"Ladies and gentlemen," the commissioner began. "I'm going to start with a brief statement, then answer all questions. As of now, we have an investigative force of fifty men working full time on the apprehension of these perpetrators. We expect that number to increase dramatically as we expand the scope of our investigation. Rewards from various sources totaling 500,000 dollars have been offered for information leading to their apprehension. A hotline has been set up and the number will be given out after the conference. All files relating to illicit political activity are being combed. We are going back ten years. Anyone, no matter how remotely tied to radical politics, will be brought in and thoroughly questioned. Anyone arousing serious suspicion will be held as a material witness. Every inch of the area around Herald Square is being searched. We are in the process of questioning people who were in the immediate vicinity before or directly after the explosion. We beg them to come forward and tell us what they saw. Let us decide whether or not it was important. Questions.''

Reporters began screaming, as was their habit, and the commissioner, as was his habit, picked the questions he wanted to answer, repeating them first so all could hear.

''You want to know if any arrests have been made or are close. At this point we are just beginning to evaluate physical evidence. Leads through informants seem more promising, but we are not close to making an arrest.

''Yes, the bomb was set off inside an oxygen supply truck. The driver was killed instantly. We are questioning everyone at A&B Oxygen Supply as well as anyone who came near their warehouse on the day of the explosion.

''You ask about the efforts of the federal government. As you know, First Agent George Bradley is in charge of those efforts and the question is better put to him. However, let me assure you that we are cooperating completely with federal authorities and will continue to do so.''

''The CIA? As far as we know, the CIA is not involved in domestic politics. On the other hand, it's our understanding that the federal effort involves several agencies so, once again, I suggest you put the question to Agent Bradley.

''What are the constitutional grounds for detaining suspects as material witnesses? We are in a crisis situation and emergency measures must be taken. It is my fervent hope that radical lawyers do not begin springing out of their holes to tie up our courts and release these suspects.''

The American Red Army, at the height of their victory celebration, broke into spontaneous applause at the conclusion of Commissioner Morgan's impassioned speech. In recognition of their success, Muzzafer had suspended the rule about drinking and Effie's living room was littered with cartons of half-eaten Chinese food, boxes of pizza, crushed beer cans and two magnums of French champagne, one empty and one three-quarters full.

"It's exactly as I predicted," Muzzafer declared triumphantly. "Democracy is only a bone for their poor, oppressed doggies. I . . . Yowwwww.'' He jumped straight in the air, then dashed across the room, trying to avoid Theresa and the ice-cold beer she was pouring down the front of his shirt.

"It's exactly as I predicted," Theresa mimicked, sending Effie into gales of laughter. "Exactly. Exactly.''

Already high, as were all the soldiers of the American Red Army except for Johnny Katanos, Effie, ordinarily fastidious, ignored the beer puddling on the carpet. She sat on the couch with Jane next to her, in her free hand a huge coffee mug filled with champagne, from which both were drinking, and gestured toward the television set. "It's almost like the stupid bastard was working for us. What'll they do when they find the deed wasn't brought off by some leftover hippy?''

"Then they will arrest people randomly," Muzzafer said, twisting the beer can from Theresa's hand. "And when that . . .''

"No more speeches," Jane declared loudly. "Put on a tape.'' Everyone turned to stare at her. A few hours ago she'd been demanding to be allowed to cook. "Well, I'm a little drunk," she explained, turning to Effie. "Sorry.''

"A tape. Yes, by all means." Muzzafer removed a TDK videocassette from its cardboard holder. It was marked, "Day 1. 6:00 PM/

9:30 PM, ABC," and as he placed it into the recorder, he could feel their attention turn to the screen.

After the explosion, all three networks had suspended local programming for the remainder of the evening. They did this, they said, in order to show their respect for the dead, though no reduction was made in the number of "messages." The ratings, shared more or less evenly, added up to an astonishing 97 percent of all the sets in the greater New York area, due in large part to some especially graphic footage which the networks reran at every opportunity. It seems that two video teams, one from ABC and the other from NBC, were already on hand covering the opening day festivities at A&S and, for the half hour it took the police to seal off the scene, they roamed through the carnage, literally shooting even as the cops dragged them away.

And the footage they got was, indeed, spectacular. With virtually every eye in New York glued to a television screen, network censors had looked the other way as closeup after closeup revealed the damage done by temperatures hot enough to melt steel. Even Muzzafer had been initially rooted to the scene after the explosion. He'd watched the cops arrive, followed by fire trucks and ambulances, until the square, filled with the glare of revolving lights, seemed like a parody of the original blast. Finally, Johnny had pulled him away, leading him to the subway and escape. They'd made one stop on the way to Queens, in an electronics store where Muzzafer bought a dozen blank videocassettes. Then, at home, he had tuned the three television sets, one in each apartment, to the three networks and began to record their triumph. Eventually he hoped to mail these tapes, along with his own description of the project and its methods, to friends in Lebanon who would edit them and pass them on to terrorists everywhere. Even if the American Red Army never completed another operation, Muzzafer knew they could lay claim to the most successful act of terrorism ever executed in the United States. But, of course, he was only just beginning. Just getting up a head of steam.

On the screen, New York's medical examiner, Dr. David Chang, a small, balding man, removed his glasses and began to explain the difficulties involved in identifying the bodies. "Ordinarily," he declared, his voice surprisingly strong, "in cases of murder, each body would have to be autopsied separately, but because of the scope of this tragedy, we are going to release the bodies as soon as they are properly identified. The identifications will be made by relatives, where possible, or through written identification found on the person. Where bodies have been . . ." He stopped for a moment, as if realizing for the first time exactly what he was saying. When he resumed, his voice was much softer. "There are people in there who have been burned beyond recognition. No ID or if there was ID, it's been burned up too. We'll use jewelry, dental records, tattoos— whatever we can find, but it will take some time."

"We seen this tape before," Johnny Katanos broke in loudly. "Let's try another one. What do you say?" He held a tape aloft. "I took this one off this morning's news. Just a quick piece buried in the Macy's coverage."

Theresa shook her head, then staggered slightly. "You know what you are, Johnny? You're a party pooper."

Johnny, calm, glanced at her, then walked across to the television. "Shut up, Theresa."

Though he could not interfere in their domestic affairs, at least not until they threatened his project, Muzzafer nevertheless found himself wishing that he'd stopped pouring champagne several glasses ago. He was not being attacked personally, but the party had been his idea, a brief interlude during which they might savor their triumph, and he felt the need to maintain control.

"Muzzafer, check this out. Tell me if this isn't perfect for us." Johnny walked across the room, put his arm around Muzzafer's shoulders and pulled him down on the couch next to Jane. He could feel the Arab's resistance, that Muzzafer did not want to be handled in this way, but once they were seated, squeezed in next to the two women, the alcohol took over and he relaxed.

Johnny, flicking the remote to start the VCR, said, "If this isn't the best thing you've ever heard, you could cut off my balls." He let his arm slide along the backrest until Muzzafer's neck lay against the inside of his elbow, then smiled his sweetest, most innocent smile. "I swear to God, Muzzafer, when I saw this, I was so happy, I nearly shit."

The report, six minutes long, was by no means unique. It concerned an abandoned warehouse, Parillo Bros. Carting, on North 5th Street, in Greenpoint, Brooklyn, just south of Kent Avenue. Two blocks from the East River, it sat less than half a mile from densely populated Stuyvesant Town in Manhattan. The owners, Guido and Giovanni Parillo, formerly in the private sanitation business, had disappeared, leaving city and state authorities with the job of cleaning up thousands of fifty-gallon drums of toxic waste. There was the usual alphabet soup of PCBs, PVCs, dioxin, hydrochloric acid, cyanide and all the rest, but what made this dump special was an additional five thousand drums of waste oil mixed with as yet unidentified chemicals. If the oil should ever catch fire (though waste oil is very difficult to ignite, the reporter prudently counseled) the resulting cloud of smoke might cause a disaster on the scale of that in Bhopal, India. To make matters worse, the cleanup could not begin until the owners were tracked down or the property and the building condemned, a process that would, in either event, take many months. "In the meantime," the reporter intoned while the camera swept over a damp, gray warehouse, "New Yorkers will just have to live with the prospect of catastrophe hanging over their heads. This is John Brolin, Greenpoint, Brooklyn."

Later, alone with Johnny Katanos in the kitchen, Muzzafer complained about the way in which Johnny had broken up the party. "Your idea was fine," he said, "but it could have waited another day. Before I began this project, before we left Algeria, I met with a friend. To ask for his assistance. He told me that any plan involving criminals would fail. He said you would let your personal feelings get in the way and sooner or later . . ."

Without warning, Johnny turned to Muzzafer, stepping forward until their faces were almost touching. Far from his usual calm self, his dark eyes burned with conviction and for the first time, his smile was unforced and anything but innocent. "Did I let my personal feelings get in the way on Sixth Avenue? Have I ever let you down even one time?''

"Your games with Jane and your tongue with Theresa will break us apart. I've seen it happen before.''

"So what? We don't need the women, man. All they do is go to the fucking library and cook dinner.'' He paused to let his message sink in. "One last job, Muzzafer. We'll do the warehouse, dump the cunts and then take the show on the road. Think about a major project every six weeks for a year. Each one in a different city. You have all the contacts. You can get us the supplies we need.'' He put his hands on Muzzafer's shoulders, his fingers kneading the back of the Arab's neck. "Just think about it, man. Let all the bullshit lessons go. If you got the balls, we can get very high together.''

14

Even as Johnny Katanos and Aftab Muzzafer toasted the successes of the American Red Army, on the Lower East Side, at Pulaski's Funeral Home, the remains of Rita Melengic, shreds of charred flesh peeling off a blackened skeleton, rested in a closed, mahogany coffin, an altar before which rows of gray, folding chairs were arranged, like pews, to accommodate the worshippers. There were no flowers, the nature of her death precluding even the smallest touch of color.

Downstairs, in the smoking room, Stanley Moodrow, expressionless, sat in an enormous, brown, overstuffed chair and listened to the condolences of those who'd come to pay their respects, both to him and to Rita. Off to one side, Sarah Pulaski, crying in spite of herself, for she'd known Rita for decades, still managed to watch the proceedings with that professional eye which never rests. She was amazed by the number of people coming into the building. It was Easter Sunday, a traditional family day and nobody was really obligated to make an appearance before evening. Yet they began to arrive early in the morning. They came from all over the city, mostly cops, in their best uniforms, uniforms ordinarily reserved for official functions, but worn here for an old acquaintance, Stanley Moodrow. For the word had gone out early. Stanley Moodrow had not only lost the woman he loved in the most terrible way imaginable, but had been there, had seen it happen, had seen the fireball mushroom outward to engulf her.

He could see it still. Still hear the same words revolving through his mind, revolving with whirlpool speed, commanding so much of his attention that he appeared to be unaware of the uniformed men who bent over him, whispering, "Sorry, anything I can do. Just let me know. Let me know. Let me know." They were not sure if he even heard them, though he, using whatever concentration he could pull away from his continued involvement with the moment of the explosion, noted every face, added a name and precinct number and filed it away. Because the vacuum which had been filled with Rita two days before had begun to fill again, and he was growing more and more aware of an anger so great as to carry with it all the purpose necessary to avoid grief.

At 1 PM they were still pouring in. The cops came from Manhattan and Queens and Brooklyn, from Staten Island and the Bronx, from New Jersey and Westchester and Long Island. They mingled, united for once, with the people of the Lower East Side, with every nationality, every race. Rita Melengic and Stanley Moodrow were the prince and the princess for people accustomed to hard lives, to struggle and poverty, to roaches and Budweiser, to plastic flowers and junkies in the streets, burglaries and babies. They had no use for the trappings of royalty. Rita Melengic, grown into middle age, alone, finds a big, taciturn cop, a patented one-step-from-the-edge flatfoot named Stanley Moodrow and she moves from her tenement to his. This is love, the blue-collar fairy tale. But she is not supposed to die before the wedding, not like this. Not even the Brothers Grimm would invent such a useless fable.

They came in such numbers that the cops finally closed 11th Street between First and Avenue A. In their own way, they reflected the mood of a battered city. The anonymous phone call proclaiming the victory of the American Red Army had been received by three newspapers and the city's anguish was about to be replaced with rage. Even the reporters recognized the parallel, and though they had spread out to cover nearly a dozen separate wakes, most of them for rich or famous people, several veteran police-beat reporters were on hand at Pulaski's, measuring the crowd reaction, looking for usable quotes, yet, hardened as they were by years of experience, unwilling to intrude on the grief of this small piece of New York. Still, the one thing they sensed, echoing in the accents of a dozen nationalities, in Polish, Spanish, Ukrainian, Italian, Greek, Yiddish, Hebrew, Rumanian, Hungarian, was the wrongness of what had happened. And when they finally pushed their way to the center of that quiet storm, to Stanley Moodrow, a man they knew from a dozen big arrests, a man they would love to quote, his look froze the questions in their throats and they could only mutter, as had all the others, "Sorry, sorry, sorry. Anything I can do. Just let me know. Sorry, sorry."

It went on that way for two days. A parade of humans shuffling between two fixed points, Rita Melengic in her coffin and Stanley Moodrow, silent and still on a chair two floors below. He ate no more than she did, spoke no more than she, almost never left his station until the hour of the funeral when Rita was carried across the street to Our Lady of Perpetual Sorrow, where Father Jarolawski delivered the eulogy along with a Mass. He spoke at length, though all Moodrow heard, sitting by Captain Epstein in the front pew, was "Sorry. Sorry. Sorry."

Then they rode out to Calvary Cemetery in Queens and a dark hole in a new field, a hundred people standing about, watching Moodrow, expecting surely, at the last moment, some sign. When, as the coffin descended, he broke into a smile, they fell away, thinking this cop will not last another month. This cop has already swallowed his gun.

Although Stanley Moodrow was not surprised to get the call, he had not expected it on the afternoon of Rita's funeral. Yet there it was, from a reluctant Captain Epstein.

"Stanley, you know I don't want to do this, but you have to come by my office tomorrow morning."

"Let me guess," Moodrow replied in a neutral voice. "Inspector Flynn and the FBI want to see me."

"What are you," Epstein asked, exasperated, "a fucking prophet?

They been busting my chops for two days and I can't hold 'em off anymore.''

"Don't worry about it, Captain. They have to cover all bases so they can explain how they're working real hard even if they got no results.''

"Listen, Stanley," Epstein said, more softly, "are you okay. You know, if you don't feel up to it, I'll put it off. I don't care what they say.''

"You don't have to play 'daddy' with me. What time tomorrow?''

"Nine-thirty. By the way, if it's any consolation, Bradley isn't coming. Just Higgins.''

"Yeah? I don't know whether to be insulted or stand up and cheer. I'll see you in the morning. And don't worry so much. Worrying fucks up your gut, remember?''

But Epstein did not stop worrying. It was his precinct and one of his men was hurt, injured as if in the line of duty and still under attack. Moodrow's calm tone only made matters worse. Unless, of course, Moodrow was substituting something for his grief, some fantasy of revenge. Unless, like the ticket stubs to the Ridgewood Theater, there were other items being suppressed. This notion kept Epstein awake most of the night, and even as he tried to explain Moodrow's expected condition to Flynn and Higgins, he found himself mistrusting his own words.

"Look," he said, as soon as they'd both arrived (he'd deliberately asked them to show up fifteen minutes before Moodrow), "I don't know if you heard about it, but Sergeant Moodrow's woman was killed in that blast. She was standing in front of the truck. Right in the middle of it.''

Flynn nodded. "Allowances will be made. We're not here to crucify the sergeant." He looked straight across at Higgins, not bothering to disguise his disdain. "I looked through the Ronald Chadwick file on the way over and I'm more convinced than ever that Moodrow's investigation was professional in every detail.''

Leonora Higgins smoothed the skirt of her blue business suit and smiled benignly. Flynn's attitude was no surprise, but as she expected to spend the morning fighting with Moodrow, there was no sense in wasting energy before he arrived.

As if on cue, Moodrow opened the door, walked inside and looked around the room. Knowing his anger and his purpose, he had already decided not to give anything away.

"Good morning, lady and gentlemen," he announced confidently. "What could I do for you?"

"Stanley," Epstein came in first, "why don't you sit down. Do you feel all right?"

"I feel fine." Moodrow sat on a metal folding chair, broken out of storage for the conference.

"Sergeant," Higgins began.

"Excuse me," Flynn interrupted immediately. "I'd like to ask Sergeant Moodrow a few questions first. If you don't mind."

For a moment, Leonora Higgins almost let her annoyance show. She was confident that if it came down to it, she could get to Flynn's superiors with her complaints. But, aside from all the power games, something else struck her as wrong. The cop was too calm. She'd expected a half-broken alcoholic and found an imperturbable, purposeful cop.

"Thank you," Flynn continued, after Higgins sat back in her chair. "Sergeant Moodrow, I'm sure you remember the bombing incident a few months ago—the one where Ronald Chadwick was killed?"

"Sure, I remember it. That bombing's become a legend in the neighborhood."

"Good, good," Flynn smiled his best "we're all on the same team" smile. "Tell me, have you gotten any closer to making an arrest?"

Moodrow twisted about to give Inspector Flynn his best "gee, what's going on here" look. "But you took me off that case yourself. At least, I think you did."

Epstein broke in curtly. "Inspector Flynn doesn't give out assignments, Stanley. I do."

"Sorry, Captain."

"A moment." Flynn, his face reddening, waved a hand between Moodrow and Epstein. "Let's get back to business. Can I assume, Sergeant, that you have moved no closer to the resolution of the case?"

Moodrow looked directly into Flynn's eyes. "To tell you the truth,

Inspector, I haven't even thought about it since the last time I spoke to you. The rumors on the street haven't changed. Some Greek kid they called Zorba supposedly planned out the whole thing himself and he hasn't been seen since the rip-off took place.''

"Well," Flynn continued, trying to anticipate all of Higgins' questions, "how do you suppose the Greek got his hands on a Russian hand grenade?''

"Well, jeez, I don't know. I mean it wasn't like my bust, but I got a friend up in the Bronx and he told me how he went on a raid with some Feds and they caught a dealer with ten AK-47s he was planning to sell off to local street gangs. AK-47s are Russian, right? That's Kalishnikovs.''

Higgins, unable to contain herself any longer, broke in. "That was a dealer with a long record of arms smuggling. Not some Greek nobody ever heard of."

"For Christ's sake," Moodrow complained. "I'm just giving a for instance, not exactly how it happened. I mean I've seen your face twice and both times you told me I didn't have anything. I feel like a yo-yo.''

"Stop playing games, goddamn it." Leonora finally lost her temper. She hadn't wanted this assignment, but Bradley had insisted she handle it alone. More and more she felt Bradley pushing her away. She had expected to become his equal, his partner, but now that he headed up the federal task force, she was kept far from the reporters with the microphones and cameras.

"I won't have that," Flynn said.

Higgins looked him full in the face. "I don't know if you believe this 'oh, golly' face he puts on whenever he talks to his superiors, but I don't buy it for a second. Just for once, I'd like to see him play it straight.''

Epstein jumped to his feet. "You have no right to accuse him of any dereliction of duty on the basis of some kind of female intuition. It's fucking intolerable.''

"Captain," Flynn hissed between clenched teeth. "I cannot have that language here. Let's calm down. Right now.''

Moodrow, his demeanor unruffled, caught Leonora Higgins staring at him and threw her a broad wink. At that moment Leonora's sus-

picions turned to certainty and she found herself convinced that
Moodrow did have the solution. Then she remembered that she'd had
the same realization weeks earlier, but had failed to act on it, failed
to act because her partner, her boss, instead of dealing with her instincts, had patronized her with ill-concealed impatience.

"Sergeant," she finally said. "I assume you have nothing to add
to what you've already told us?"

"That's right," Moodrow returned.

"But there does remain the possibility that you could track this
Greek down?"

Moodrow shrugged. "Maybe."

"And there is also just a possibility that this Greek is connected
to the Red Army."

"Sure, why not? But it's a longshot, no matter what."

"Longshot or not," Leonora declared. "Suppose there's only one
chance in ten thousand that the murderer of Ronald Chadwick is involved with the American Red Army. Does that mean we should
forget about it?" When no one responded, she continued. "I'd like
to have Sergeant Moodrow temporarily assigned to me. Let him work
exclusively on the Chadwick affair. Nothing else. And let him report
directly to my office. We've got a dozen avenues of investigation open.
This'll be the thirteenth. When you're dealing with a threat of this
magnitude, you take any chance, no matter how improbable."

Epstein, protective as ever, interrupted. "But I need him here,"
he complained. "This guy's the heart of a half dozen cases. He knows
everybody."

"Let's not be hasty, Captain," Flynn responded. He turned to Higgins. "I assume you mean that the Sergeant will conduct his own,
independent investigation. All he need do is file weekly reports."

"Twice a week," Leonora said. "In writing."

"Sergeant," Flynn addressed Moodrow, "if there's one truth to be
drawn from this confusion, it's that you are best qualified to run down
the killers of Ronald Chadwick and it seems to me that incarcerating
them, whether or not they have anything to do with these terrorists,
would absolutely benefit the citizens of New York."

There was a moment's silence while all considered Flynn's analysis, then Moodrow broke in, his voice patient and calm. "But I can't take the case, Inspector. See, I'm on vacation."

Flynn nearly jumped out of his chair, turning on Epstein. "Why didn't you tell us this before, Captain?"

"He didn't know," Moodrow announced. "I just went on this morning."

"For how long?" Higgins asked. The move was so perfectly Moodrow, as she understood him, that she almost laughed.

"I haven't taken a vacation in a long time. I'm not exactly positive."

Epstein pressed the intercom on his desk, connecting him to a civilian computer operator.

"Yeah?" The voice crackled in the speaker.

"When did Sergeant Moodrow last take vacation time?"

"Gimme his social security number."

Moodrow gave it and all waited silently until the operator came back on.

"Jesus, this guy ain't took vacation since 1972. Ya believe that?"

Epstein snapped off the intercom by way of an answer.

"Can't you just call him back?" Higgins asked.

"It's not that easy," Flynn explained. "The union'll get involved. Let's face it, we're almost certainly looking at a wild goose chase. If he refuses, the union's going to back him."

"And that's the last word?"

Flynn tried to salvage some shred of his authority. "I suppose I could always assign another detective to the case. There must be leads someone else could follow—" Moodrow surprised everyone by interrupting before Flynn could finish.

"Uh, look, I changed my mind. I mean if you guys think it's that important, I could always postpone my vacation for a few weeks. We are talking about killers here, right? It's my case. I'll handle it for you."

Flynn looked taken aback, then smiled with approval. "Then it's settled. If you need help, just holler and we'll set you up with anything you need." Already tasting lunch, he turned to Allen Epstein and nodded. "Whatever he wants, Captain, let's see that he gets it."

* * *

The thing Moodrow remembered best about the era of the police artist was that his girlfriend at the time, Maria Esposito, got fired when the department bought the I-DEN-TI-KIT concept. All the police artists were fired and then rehired several months later though the I-DEN-TI-KITS were kept when it was found that plastic overlays, no matter how accurate, could not make a suspect appear lifelike, and arrests through the reconstruction of the criminal's features by eyewitnesses were suffering. Unfortunately for Moodrow, Maria Esposito had found new employment in an ad agency on Park Avenue South and in keeping with her upscale job, had also found an upscale lover from within the company, a genuine 3-piece suitor.

But the I-DEN-TI-KIT was still the first line. Artists were more expensive than plastic and demanded better working conditions, refusing, for instance, to accompany cops to the homes of eyewitnesses, who themselves refused to be seen entering a police station. So the procedure changed. The investigating officer now takes his kit and gets the preliminary likeness, which the artist turns into something resembling a human.

The I-DEN-TI-KIT was invented by an artist who worked for a major encyclopedia, creating plastic overlays of frogs whose flesh peeled back in sheets of plastic to reveal deeper and deeper layers of amphibian flesh—the muscles, the digestive system, reproductive system, heart, lungs and blood vessels, skeleton. Why not use the same technique, the artist asked himself, staring at the picture of a fugitive in the *Daily News,* to recreate the appearance of a criminal?

Thus the I-DEN-TI-KIT, which consisted of more than three hundred plastic rectangles upon which had been imprinted head shape, hair lines, mustaches, mouths, noses, etc. The adept officer would begin with the shape of the head—oval? square? round? fat? thin? Add the hairline, then the eyes, eyebrows, nose, mouth, finally finishing with a stack of eight or ten stencils, which could then be photocopied to produce a single image which, in turn, could be taken to an artist who would make the composite somewhat human.

The existence of this I-DEN-TI-KIT made Moodrow's task of creating a recognizable likeness of the Chadwick massacre villains much easier than it would otherwise have been. Under the best of circumstances, it is extremely difficult to smuggle an artist out of a precinct house, but I-DEN-TI-KITS are commonplace and can be taken from the property room at will, never to be missed until the annual winter inventory. After leaving the conference in Epstein's office, Moodrow simply stopped in the property room, put the KIT under his arm and walked out. Moodrow could have checked out the I-DEN-TI-KIT officially, but as he had no intention of cooperating with any agency, local or federal, and no desire to leave a trail that might let Higgins know he was working with anything more concrete than an educated guess, he thought it best to keep his line of investigation to himself.

He went directly to Riker's Island, New York City's enormous holding jail, a place for criminals awaiting trial and unable to make bail, a true house of pain and sorrow and the temporary home of Paco Baquili, whose prior record had earned him a bail far in excess of his potential lifetime earnings. By this time, Paco's sight had been restored, returning on its own as the doctors had predicted. He was also accustomed to the idea of jail, was into prison pleasure and five hundred pushups per day in spite of the pain in his right arm. He had his buddies, old pals from the East Village streets, and was, except for official intra-prison warfare, safe from day-to-day attack. No surprise, then, that the sight of Stanley Moodrow in a small, spare interrogation cell, aroused a defiance as great as his despair at their prior encounter.

"Good afternoon, Paco." Moodrow opened.

"Fuck you, too," Paco replied, unconsciously squaring his shoulders and flexing the muscles of his chest and arms.

"What's the matter? Get up on the wrong side of the bed? Moodrow understood that he was at a disadvantage. Paco had already entered a plea and was awaiting his sentence.

"Just tell me what you want."

"Sure, man. You know Johnny Katanos and his girlfriend? The ones who set you up?"

"No," Paco responded sarcastically. "I can't think who you're talkin' about."

"Well, I'm gonna kill 'em."

"Big fuckin' cop."

Without any warning whatsoever, Moodrow flew from a dead calm into a towering rage and it was the suddenness of the change even more than what he actually did that cowed Paco. In spite of his restored eyesight and all his thousands of pushups, Moodrow was on him before he could move, picking him up and flinging him over the table.

"I'm gonna kill 'em and you're gonna help me. Who the fuck you think got all those charges against you reduced down to felony possession? Who? You think it just flew down from heaven like one of God's angels? I want that Greek, Paco."

"I want him, too." Paco's voice filled with defiance, though in his heart of hearts, he was just as glad that Moodrow was staying behind the table.

"You'll never get him. You're going away. If you could have found him by your methods you'd already have him. But don't worry, man. You help me and I'll do it for you. The prick'll be dead and nobody can do a damn thing to you. Understand what I'm saying? I can't do anything without your help. You're gonna make them dead. All of them. The two cunts and the Greek."

Paco, no longer afraid, came back to the table and sat down. "You ain't sayin' you're gonna bust 'em? You're gonna kill 'em?"

"Kill 'em? I'm gonna line the cocksuckers up with their hands cuffed and I'm gonna go once behind each ear. No jail. No bail."

"Why you gonna do this?"

"Cause I gotta."

"Why?"

Moodrow slammed the I-DEN-TI-KIT down on the table. "Let's just go to work, all right? I'm giving you a chance to get your revenge here. Take advantage."

"I'm gonna trust you, man. I'm gonna give you what you want, Just do me a favor. When you do the fuckin' Greek, say, 'Here's a present from Paco' and let the first one just graze his ear so he thinks maybe he's gonna get away. Then kill him."

"Whatever you want, Paco."

"OK, I help you."

They worked steadily for the next three hours until the sharp features and skull of Johnny Katanos emerged. "He's got a face like a hawk." Moodrow observed, staring intently, as if he could somehow draw the man directly out of the photo.

"You better watch out for this guy. You better show some respect. He's very bad."

"Yeah? Well, I'm looking forward to meeting him."

"How about the two broads he had with him? You want them, too?"

"Sure, but first tell me again about them. When did you first see the women?"

"He brought them bitches around the day before the rip-off. Like I didn't think nothin' about it. There's always New Jersey cunts suckin' up to us, lookin' for some thrill, maybe want us to fuck 'em good before they go back to their boyfriends. You know, man, they come down for a year, two years, dye their hair green, then go back to Paramus and get married. Zorba didn't make no big deal about it. Acted like he didn't give a shit and I figured he was queer for Enrique, so like it all made sense. Next day I see the same two cunts on the street and they're very friendly so I naturally invite 'em inside and the next thing everyone's fuckin' their brains out. I mean like it didn't happen every day in that house, 'cause Chadwick didn't allow no women inside, but they showed up when he wasn't there, so what the fuck. That was what that Greek motherfucker wanted."

They went back to work, despite a correction officer's complaint about needing the room, until they came up with the faces of the two women Paco and the boys had partied with on the night of Ronald Chadwick's death. Moodrow knew when the faces were right even before Paco, and put the finishing touches on the images himself. No surprise considering he had seen both of them less than a week before, seen them engaged in spirited combat on Sixth Avenue, four blocks from Herald Square.

15

After leaving Paco Baquili and returning his unmarked police car to the precinct, Moodrow made three stops. First, he went to see his good friend Pauli Corallo. Pauli had been eking out a living over several decades by buying up junk cars, making them roadworthy, and selling them to fellow East Villagers. He had few rules, but kept religiously to those he did have. He never paid more than a hundred dollars for any car and never sold for over a thousand, even if he spent more on repairs. Most importantly, in a world where ripped off consumers go to the streets instead of the courts for justice, he made sure his cars ran well and honored all guarantees. Pauli was a small, muscular man with a long scar on his right cheek that made him appear to be smiling even when he wasn't. He loved the Lower East Side and had more friends than any used-car dealer is entitled to. His business had grown to a point where he was considering whether or not to buy a vacant lot to store autos ready for sale. He was very sick of moving them from one side of the street to the other when the street sweepers came through.

Pauli was holding court when Moodrow found him, surrounded by a prospective buyer, a Senegalese, and the man's entire family, all of whom were vocally involved in this momentous purchase. It was a loud, but not unfriendly gathering, as the participants struggled to establish a final price on a 1973 Ford LTD, a four-door beauty with only a small scrape on the right quarter panel. The fact that the hood was flat, olive green while the rest of the car was pale yellow was considered only of minor importance, since it was assumed that no one buys a car on Avenue C unless they already understand the realities of keeping a junker together.

"Man, you got to be crazy," Pauli shouted. "Six hundred for a car like this? You can't buy the engine for $600."

"In my country," The Senegalese began, "such a car would not sell for $300." His family rushed in with loud confirmations.

"Don't hand me that shit," Pauli moaned, half-turning away, as if he had some thought of closing the negotiations. "You came here because in your country you didn't have ten dollars to buy a goat cart. Now you want something for nothing. Nobody will give you a better deal."

They fell into a side discussion on the method of payment, quickly agreed that it must be cash, and then began to squabble over the deposit. It was understood that late collections were effected by means of baseball bat or worse.

"Hey, Pauli," Moodrow called, peering over the grandfather's shoulder. "I need a coupla seconds, awright? I'm not busting balls, but I'm in a hurry."

The interruption produced general consternation among the purchasers until Pauli told them, "Hey, this guy's a fuckin' cop and he's my friend, so you're just gonna have to wait." At the sound of the word "cop" the Senegalese had already begun to drift away. In their country, it was understood that relative to them, policemen were gods and they had not yet realized that as legal aliens in America, they might have something so abstract as civil rights.

"Hey, Sarge," Pauli said, instinctively reaching out to touch the back of Moodrow's hand. "I heard about it. I mean what happened and everything. I used to drink in that bar and she was a fine lady. Everybody loved her."

"Yeah, I know Pauli. That's what people keep telling me. But you know how it is, man. I can't let it go. I got to take the cocksuckers out.''

Pauli smiled, revenge being a preoccupation of people commonly ripped off by society. ''I'm hip to it. Just tell Pauli what he can do.''

''I need a car. For a few weeks, probably. Maybe longer.''

''Well, you come to the right man. Pauli Corallo got the most cars on the Lower East Side. I got cars up the ass.''

''Like on a loan, Pauli.''

''No problem. Just bring it back when you're finished.''

''Gimme something with a little room and some kick. I might have to chase.''

Suddenly the Senegalese family, rediscovering their courage, rushed over, totally ignoring Moodrow. ''Six hundred and fifty,'' they shouted in unison. ''The deal is $650.'' Even the grandmother, bent and shrunken, joined in the cacophony. Having reached a decision, they were unable to postpone its deliverance in spite of their fear of the police. Pauli looked at Moodrow helplessly.

''Whatta ya think?'' Moodrow asked. ''Should I bust 'em?''

''Take the whole bunch,'' Pauli said, grinning.

''No, no.'' The youngest of the men reached into his pocket, a quick movement guaranteed to upset a policeman, and Moodrow's gun was in his hand before anyone realized what happened.

''Just leave your hand where it is,'' Moodrow shouted, aware of how bad his joke would look if someone got shot.

''No gun. No gun,'' the old woman admonished. ''Achmed show you his card from the immigration. All legal. You no arrest.''

On cue, Achmed slowly withdrew a small, green card from his pocket, a card which Moodrow had absolutely no interest in seeing.

''All right, Pauli,'' he sighed. ''finish up with these people.'' He walked fifty feet away and leaned against the hood of a parked car while Pauli completed the negotiations. It had been a warm day, but it was cooling down quickly, a reminder of New York's unpredictable spring weather. Finally, a full fifteen minutes later, after Moodrow, trapped, was forced to accept the condolences of a dozen passers-by, Pauli concluded his business and walked over.

"For the price I had to sell," he said by way of explanation, "it would have been better if you shot 'em. Now tell me when you need this car?"

"Tomorrow morning."

"Ah, well, I got just the thing for you."

They walked up Avenue C to 11th Street, then west to Avenue A. There, parked on the corner, was a 1974 Buick LeSabre. The windshield had a long, horizontal crack at eye level and the vinyl top was blistered and torn, but inside, the upholstery was fairly good, all rips having been taped, except for the driver's seat, which had sunken nearly to the floorboards and was stuffed with newspapers.

"I give you this one for two reasons. First, engine and transmission are good, so it's still very fast. Like from the factory. Second, the registration don't expire for six weeks, so you could drive around without piling up tickets every time you gotta park. What you think?"

"It's OK, Pauli. Look, I really appreciate this. I . . . ."

"Forget that shit," Pauli interrupted. "You done me plenty favors and don't forget, she was some of my peoples, 'cause I drink in her bar. You kill those *maricons*. Cut their balls off."

"I intend to."

"That's good. That's very good. You come to my house tomorrow morning. I'll have the key and the registration."

"Thanks, Pauli."

Moodrow walked down Avenue A to St. Marks Place, then cut over almost to Third Avenue, to a very small shop called Fantasy Routes which dealt in every variety of map, from two-hundred-year-old, hand-drawn Italian maps of Antarctica to the most mundane world atlas. Inside, he purchased a five-borough Hagstrom wall map which showed every street in New York City.

From there, he walked east again, to a small liquor store on 7th Street, between B and C. The store inside looked like a bank. Except for a small standing area, it was completely closed off behind 2-inch-thick lucite sheets, guaranteed to stop anything smaller than a howitzer. The man behind the register, Al Berkowitz, perennial cigar protruding from the right side of his mouth, nevertheless managed a rare smile.

"Well, well, if it ain't the Captain," Berkowitz began his usual taunt.

"Cut the crap, Al."

"If you woulda listened ta me twenty years ago, you woulda been inspector by now. With a limousine."

"So where's your limousine?"

"You know what I got? You're a mindreader, now? I live in New Jersey, not in this sewer and what I got, I ain't bringin' here." He hesitated a moment, then continued in a softer voice, a voice ordinarily quite foreign to his personality. "I'm sorry about ya trouble, Stanley."

"Thanks, Al. Just give me a quart of Old Crow."

"Rotgut." The old man seized the opportunity to resurrect his usual irascibility. "Keep drinkin' that shit and watch what happens. You coulda been a big wheel, the people you had lookin' after ya. Nobody in the whole department had arrests like you. You were a legend."

"I'm still a fucking legend."

"See what I mean?" Berkowitz said, shoving the bottle into a paper bag. "Always the wise guy. Stanley knows it all. Heaven forbid anyone should learn the great Stanley Moodrow anything. Big time cop." Still talking, he put the bottle into a sliding drawer and pushed the drawer across to Moodrow's side of the partition, never once stopping. "So how come you're still a sergeant? I knew your mother when she was a little girl. We grew up together, but I live in New Jersey while you never got outta the East Side."

"Close it up, Al," Moodrow sighed. "I'm getting tired of the same song every time I come in here. Maybe I'll find another liquor store and put you outta business." He walked toward the door, opened it, but the old man, chewing his cigar furiously, could not resist a parting shot.

"Fifty years I'm here. A wife and a child I buried and they didn't run me out of here." He began to go off like a windup toy. "I was burglarized fifteen times and I stayed. I got stitches all over my head, but I stayed and now I got something for myself. But you . . ."

"Good bye, Al. Sleep well."

Now thoroughly prepared, Moodrow walked the ten blocks to his apartment, his mind free to consider strategy. Once inside, he pulled down the photographs on the largest wall in his living room, unfolded the map and pinned it up, carefully tugging at the corners to straighten the creases. Then he poured himself half a glass of bourbon, carried it to a small desk along with a notepad and began to work.

First, he listed everything he knew about the American Red Army, from the murder of Ronald Chadwick to the bombing of Herald Square to a catalogue of their weaponry. He knew that at least three of the gang were white. He could trace one of them to Queens County through three sources—Paco Baquili, the tickets found on Enrique Hentados, and Frankie Baumann. He knew that all of their actions had been confined to New York City. He also had good likenesses of three of the gang—Johnny Katanos and two unarmed females which he would take to Andrea McCorkle, an artist and longtime resident of the neighborhood, to have made into something more natural and then to the photocopiers before distribution.

And that was it, the sum of Moodrow's factual knowledge, but from this he was able to draw a number of inferences, as well as to plan a course of action. He reasoned that the terrorists were living in New York City, somewhere in the five boroughs. While this was the weakest link in his chain of logic, he did have several facts pointing to that conclusion as well as the knowledge that if they were not living in the city itself—if they were living in New Jersey or out on Long Island—he had no hope of tracking them down, so he might as well proceed as if he was sure of New York residence. Considering this, he took a black Magic Marker and drew the boundaries of every police precinct directly onto the map, adding their numbers on their exact locations. Then he wrote the name of every cop he knew to be working in a particular precinct on a piece of paper, adding a star to any who'd attended Rita's funeral and taped it within the boundaries of the precinct.

Warming to his task, he began to shade out large areas, New York's totally black or totally Spanish neighborhoods—Harlem, Bedford Stuyvesant, Flatbush, East New York, Bushwick and Brownsville in

Brooklyn; South Jamaica, Hollis, Corona and St. Albans in Queens; almost all of the southeast Bronx including Highbridge, Bedford Park, Kingsbridge, Fordham, Morrisania, Melrose, Mott Haven, Tremont and East Tremont. Proceeding from the opposite end of the economic spectrum, he eliminated the wealthier neighborhoods, including half of Manhattan, as well as smaller sections of the outer boroughs like Bayside and Jamaica Estates. When he finished, the map was quite a bit smaller, with enormous sections of every borough but Staten Island blacked out completely. There was no way three whites and an Arab could live in any of these neighborhoods without attracting attention, and anonymity—the ability to pass their days as unseen faces in the enormous crowd that makes up public New York—would have to be of primary importance in their overall struggle. Without knowing it, Moodrow was following the same line of reasoning as Muzzafer had when he originally sought his "safe" house.

Switching from a black to a red Magic Marker, Moodrow began to draw thin stripes through areas of special interest. First, Middle Village, Ridgewood, Maspeth and Glendale in Queens, the neighborhoods closest to the Ridgewood Theatre, then any very mixed neighborhood. In the 70s and 80s, as in previous generations, New York had experienced a wave of new immigrants, all lusting after the bright lights and big bucks. This time they came from every continent, from Ghana to Bangladesh to Brazil to Lithuania, concentrating in such numbers as to change the character of neighborhoods overnight. Flushing, in Queens, got special attention. It had gone from a white neighborhood going black to an Oriental bazaar in the space of ten years. By now, the signs on the shops were as likely to be written in Japanese or Korean or Sanskrit or Arabic as in English. A small group, a gang, could come into one of the low, six-story apartment buildings and vanish. Forest Hills and Jackson Heights were experiencing similar turmoil, as well as areas of Canarsie and Sheepshead Bay in Brooklyn. It seemed that every vacant lot was being bought up, with two-to-four family homes erected overnight, and the buyers were as likely to be immigrants as native Americans.

Staten Island presented a totally different problem. It was enormous, with few black or Spanish neighborhoods and there were no subways to act as starting points for a search. But Staten Island had two strikes against it as a possible home for the Red Army. There were relatively few apartment buildings. The two-family homes, of which there were a great number, usually had the owner occupying one of the apartments, a situation guaranteed to create a clear and present danger to anyone trying to hide anything. But, more importantly, Staten Island, as most New Yorkers know, is the borough of civil servants, especially cops, firemen and sanitation workers, and the most clannish of New York's boroughs. Moodrow would give it low priority.

Manhattan, too, would receive little attention from Moodrow, but for an entirely different reason. Manhattan was just too expensive. Apartments were almost impossible to find, even in rundown neighborhoods. Parking garages charged two to four hundred dollars a month to park a car. Life in Manhattan was a constant struggle to beat a system designed to crush the newcomer, for while vast areas of Manhattan fell under rent control laws and thus had relatively cheap apartments, none of those apartments ever came on the market. They were passed on from one generation to the next, or else warehoused by landlords who no longer wished to provide services in a losing proposition.

Finally, Moodrow concluded his night's work, by making a list of New York City's neighborhoods, beginning with Ridgewood and proceeding from the most to the least likely to hide the American Red Army. Next to each, he wrote the number of the precinct charged with its protection. Tomorrow he would begin to plod, putting one foot in front of the other in true flatfoot fashion, from precinct to precinct, renewing old acquaintances, calling in debts. His friends would take him to meet the people who see New York's faces—token clerks, newsstand proprietors, hot dog salesmen, check-out girls, waitresses and waiters, bus drivers. He would pass on the likenesses of Katanos and the two women. He would work twelve, fourteen hours a day, pursuing any rumor, any lead. It was what New York cops do best. They just keep going.

* * *

Leonora Higgins had not had to make a real decision since the day she joined the FBI and, sitting in the kitchen of her Park Slope apartment, she realized she was way out of practice. From her earliest training to her assignment under George Bradley, her life had been one long series of directives. It had been so easy. Memorize the training manual. What are the requirements for a legal wiretap? How to make a good arrest. How to avoid entrapment. What do you do if you're offered a bribe? Bradley had not acted any differently. Handle this paperwork. Memorize this list of informants. Interview the complainant. Search the file.

So easy and now this idiot of a New York cop, this ultimate cartoon flatfoot, was forcing her into independence. She did not know how to resist, because, at heart, she had a cop's desire for truth, and all her instincts were leading her to the conclusion that Stanley Moodrow possessed or could find out what she wanted to discover for herself. The fact that George Bradley ridiculed this belief and refused to allocate any manpower to following up on Moodrow's investigation only added to her dilemma.

She knew Moodrow would not tell her anything. He was supposed to be assigned to her, but she had listened to him at Epstein's office and seen his face. Not only did Moodrow know how to find the Greek, but nothing would make him tell her. Nothing she could say or do or threaten would make any difference. She could complain to Bradley—and, if she hadn't heard anything in a week, would—but Bradley wouldn't listen, and even if he did and acted on it, it might just drive Moodrow deeper into his protective shell. Epstein and Flynn would stand up for Moodrow, no matter what. It was all up to her.

What to do? She sat in her kitchen, in a silk slip, her hair still wet from the shower. An untouched Budget Gourmet frozen entree (Chicken à la King) rested on the table in front of her while she cursed Moodrow for complicating her life. At her age, unmarried, she was supposed to be worried about boyfriends, dinners at Lutèce, late nights at the Palladium. Not how to shadow a New York cop.

But that was the best she could come up with—follow Moodrow

and wait for him to catch the crooks. How ridiculous, she thought. The modern FBI agent thinks in terms of wiretaps, sting operations, bugging devices, racketeers turned stoolie. Nobody shadowed criminals, gumshoe style. She imagined herself hiding in doorways, pretending to windowshop, disappearing in the shadows, and laughed out loud. There must be a better method, because she knew she had to do something. In her own way, she was as stubborn as Moodrow.

Wearily, she reached for the phone. She would call her current boyfriend, Alexander, thinking that if he came over, at least she would get to sleep. Tomorrow was time enough to confront her problem. She would retrieve Moodrow's file, copy it, and smuggle it home. Then she would study it for, of all things, clues.

16

The first day of the search and the worst conditions possible—a heavy, unrelenting spring rain. The droplets danced across the pavement, across sidewalks, exploding on rapidly moving umbrellas to create perfect, tiny fountains, silver mushrooms, on every hard surface. But Moodrow was unmoved by the weather, absolutely indifferent to it. He noted the conditions, of course, heard the rain before he left his bed, and shrugged into an ancient, black raincoat and a narrow-brimmed, waterproof hat. Then he walked the two blocks to Pauli Corallo's loaned Buick, got in and turned the key, thinking the weather would be a perfect test of the car's reliability. He was pleased, though not surprised, when the big sedan started instantly. He would not have expected it of a department car, nor the clean windshield and new wipers. Smiling to himself, he flipped on the radio, tuned in the local news, and swung out into the traffic, on his way to Queens County and Victor Drabek, sergeant of the 203rd Precinct.

He headed over the Williamsburg Bridge, into the expected bumper-to-bumper Brooklyn-Queens Expressway traffic; he sat unruffled in the midst of it, not even thinking of the American Red Army or his strategy in trying to find it. This was the nature of his business and he understood that his progress, should there be any, would be slow, his frustrations enormous—a grinding process calculated to produce results in direct proportion to the consumption of shoe leather and tire treads. There would be no shortcuts, no sudden burst of inspiration, only a thoroughness that consumed the clock even as it honed the desire for success.

He drove directly to the 203rd on Juniper Valley Road in Middle Village. He didn't bother to stop for breakfast; he would eat five times before his day's canvassing was over. The precinct ruled over northwestern Queens, including Ridgewood, Glendale, Maspeth and Middle Village, all neighborhoods of prime concern. He drove out to the Long Island Expressway, exiting at Maurice Avenue and turning right onto 69th Street, a route that passed within six blocks of an unsuspecting American Red Army.

Aftab Qwazi Muzzafer and Johnny Katanos, in a 1984 Toyota Celica registered to Jane Mathews, drove through the same rain washing over Stanley Moodrow's Buick. Muzzafer drove down Metropolitan Avenue, to Kent Avenue in Brooklyn, one block from the East River.

"This rain," Muzzafer said wearily. "Always the rain and the cold. I think this is why Europeans are so obsessed with conquest. They will do anything to get to a sunny land."

They were driving through the southern edge of Greenpoint, only a mile or so from the scene of what they called the "Rabbi Action," trying to get a feel for the neighborhood surrounding the target chemical dump. At that time, Greenpoint had the distinction of being the murder capital of New York City, with more homicides per thousand population than famous neighborhoods like Harlem, Bedford Stuyvesant or the South Bronx. On the eastern side of McGuinness Boulevard, remnants of a once dominant Polish-Italian population clung to the old ways. Blue collar from the first, they lived in well-kept three- and four-family homes. On the other side of McGuinness Boulevard, the Puerto Ricans ruled. Violence was characteristic of both sides, but as the Puerto Ricans had yet to crack the barriers that prevented them from finding high-paying union jobs, their violence was filled with extreme poverty, with welfare families and broken-down buildings. It tended to happen in the streets.

But Greenpoint, first and foremost, was industrial, though not filled with the sort of giant factories which dominate the mill towns of New England. Greenpoint was a neighborhood where the young entrepreneur came to battle his way upward. The three- and four-story brick buildings housed businesses of every description—lumber yards, sweater factories, plumbing supplies, paper companies, engine rebuilders and dozens of trucking companies eager to deliver the enormous quantity of goods coming into New York City every day. The owners of these businesses spoke with accents reminiscent of every neighborhood in the city. Typically, they'd grown up in Canarsie or Queens Village, had inherited Dad's business and not found college to their liking. But they were just as determined to move up as the hordes of newly graduated midwesterners who attack corporate Manhattan each spring, and their influence was especially strong in the area of western Greenpoint where Muzzafer and Johnny Katanos were engaged in their reconnaissance. There were few residential buildings left here. There were none, for instance, on North 5th Street between Berry and the East River, though, in spite of the rain, the block was bustling with activity as Muzzafer drove through it. By 7 PM, however, it would be deserted, as all those struggling capitalists made their way back to the tree-lined streets of suburbia.

"Are you fucking crazy?" In a rain that had slowed to a drizzle, Moodrow stood in front of an outdoor newsstand at the entrance to the subway stop at Fresh Pond Road and screamed at an obviously upset Sergeant Victor Drabek.

"Ah, c'mon, Sarge; take it easy." Victor Drabek, short and squat, a fire hydrant next to a refrigerator, folded his arms across his chest.

"You took me to a blind man, for shit sake. I swear to Christ you're just as stupid as the first fucking day you walked into the academy. How in hell can a blind man identify someone from a picture?"

"I don't know. You said where everybody goes, right? Well everybody goes here who lives in the neighborhood. Maybe he could put up the pictures by the magazines."

"Yeah? Well what happens if the assholes see their faces up there? Gone, schmuck. Los Angeles, Chicago, Detroit—where there's nobody like me to keep lookin'. I wanna tell you something. These same boys got Ronald Chadwick? These guys in the pictures? They also got one of Rita's nephews. He wasn't a bad kid, just hung out in the wrong place in a neighborhood that's full of wrong places. I made a promise to Rita I'd get the pricks and I'm gonna get them. Now stop shitting it up and help me out.''

Drabek, awkward as a child berated by a parent, hemmed and hawed, then spotted his redeemer in a 1978 black Plymouth sedan. "What don't we go try Murphy? Let's try Murphy.''

"Murphy what? Moodrow pleaded.

"The guy over there in the cab. He's been around here a hundred years.''

Moodrow looking closer, acknowledged the accuracy of Drabek's judgment. An old, wrinkled man, chewing a cigar behind the wheel of an illegal, though tolerated, gypsy cab, he'd probably driven nearly everyone in the neighborhood at one time or another.

"Now lemme handle this guy,'' Drabek said. "He's a testy little fucker. Lost his medallion fifteen years ago for punching out a city councilman. That's why he's driving gypsy.''

Murphy sat unmoving as they approached his car, as if he was unaware of the two cops, but as soon as Drabek, who was in uniform, bent over the open window, the cabbie started to moan.

"Why don't you bastards just shoot me? Just pull me out of the car and shoot me like a sick dog. Harassment and harassment. That's all you bastards do. Ain't there any young guys you could fuck around out there? What happened ta solving crimes? Remember that? Two weeks ago a spic puts a gun to my head, takes the whole day. Do ya bring him around for me to identify? Do ya bring anyone at all around even if it ain't the right guy? No. 'Forget about it, Murphy,' ya say. 'Too many crimes and not enough cops, Murphy,' ya say. Cause all you bastards are out harassin' old men like me. Maybe if I painted myself with black shoe polish you'd gimme a break.''

"Take it easy,'' Drabek said, his voice harsh. "You wanna get smacked? We're looking for some people and you're gonna help us out. Like real criminals, Murphy. Murderers.''

"Yeah? Who'd they kill?"

"They killed a friend of a friend," Moodrow jumped in, shoving the likenesses of Johnny Katanos and his cohorts at the cabbie.

Murphy scrutinized the pictures for a few moments. "I think I seen this one, but I ain't sure." He held up Theresa's portrait. "Ya don't get such a good look in a rearview mirror."

Moodrow, impartial, with absolutely no expectation of immediate results, nodded his head. "Can ya say when?"

"Jeez, I don't know. Maybe is what I'm talkin' about."

"Well, hold on to the pictures. My phone number's on the back. If you see any of them, give me a call. Might be I could scrape up a few hundred bucks for the guy who helps me out."

"Few hundred?" Murphy studied the pictures more closely, as Moodrow hoped he would. "Sure thing. I'll be watchin' out for 'em."

"Say, Murphy," Drabek interrupted, elbowing Moodrow in the ribs, "tell us how the pigeons are treatin' ya. Any progress?"

Murphy brightened immediately. "Cockroaches with feathers. That's all the bastards are. Pigeons carry more diseases than rats and roaches combined. You know that?" The last was directed at Moodrow.

"Yeah. I read that in the *Post*," Moodrow replied evenly. "Dirty birds."

"Well, I got it down to a science, now. I mean killin' 'em. My kill rate is up to thirty-three percent. If ya don't believe me, take a look at the grille."

"We believe you," Moodrow said. "Tell us how you do it."

"OK, ya know how the pigeons in the street wait till ya come right up on 'em with ya car before they fly away? Even if ya accelerate at the last second, they take off before ya get 'em. First I tried slowing down, then jammin' the pedal to the floor, but they kept escapin'. Seemed like the bastards knew when I took my foot off the brake and flew up before I could get to the gas. Maybe they got pigeon radar or some shit. I mean, it was makin' me crazy until I figured out how ta fool 'em. Now I come up on 'em with my left foot on the brake and my right foot on the gas, so it looks like I'm slowin' down. Then, at the last second, I slide my left foot off the brake pedal, floor the motherfucker and splatter the little pricks all over the radiator. I got about four wings hangin' off the grille right now. Go take a look.''

As Muzzafer wheeled around the block between Berry and Wythe Avenues for the third time and still encountered no guards in front of their target, no apparent security, he could contain himself no longer. He was in the habit of keeping observations to himself until he had all data at hand, but his amazement at Americans and what they took for granted, compelled him to speak.

"There's no one here," he observed.

"Isn't that wonderful." Johnny's smile was almost happy in its intensity.

"It's crazy. In Israel, I would suspect a trap. Even in Europe there would be soldiers here. In Europe, they know what we can do and they try to protect themselves. Americans are afraid of nothing. Except Negroes." Nervous, he began to slap the steering wheel with his left hand, his voice rising in pitch. "I swear, Johnny, it's their arrogance I hate so much. They think we're the shit of the Earth. We're laughable, with our funny talk and dark skins. Even our threats are pitiful.''

"What are you worried about, man?" Katanos answered, his expression unchanging. "So they're stupid? Who cares? Maybe they figure the big ocean will protect them forever. Whatever way they're bullshittin' themselves, it's gotta be great for us. Right?''

"Fuck them and their ocean.''

Johnny looked across at his companion for the first time, fixed him with an unsmiling stare that belied his words. "You know, you're cute when you're mad. And you're always mad, so it works out fine.''

Muzzafer considered half a dozen retorts, rejecting each. He recalled the proposal Johnny had made at the party. On one level, everything the Greek said was true. The women were superfluous; he and Katanos could do it by themselves. Without any difficulty, he pictured the two of them moving from city to city, leaving behind a trail of terror. It seemed so logical, almost easy. They might go for years before they were caught.

"I'll tell you what interests me," Katanos continued. "It's these ugly whores on Kent Avenue over here. I always thought whores were from people neighborhoods, but these bitches must be doin' business with the truckers. Front-seat sex. Blow jobs before breakfast. Man, that is some ugly gash. Looks like it's been on the streets for a thousand years. I gotta come back here some day. One thing I like is fucking bitches that don't get off."

If Johnny Katanos preferred women who didn't enjoy sex, he would not have envied Stanley Moodrow's afternoon. Sergeant Drabek, his friend, with malice aforethought, led Moodrow into Eleanor's Oven, a small coffee shop and bakery on Grand Avenue at the intersection of the Long Island Expressway.

"Everybody goes here for coffee and pastries. Eleanor's famous for her oven," Drabek explained. Moodrow, preparing for his fifth cup of coffee at his fifth coffee shop, was oblivious. He was considering the geography of the 203rd Precinct, the main roads and shopping areas, trying to estimate how much time he would have to give in order to cover the territory fully. Three days, maybe four—he was determined to be thorough.

"Eleanor Allesandro," Drabek said, interrupting the flow of Moodrow's thoughts, "this here is one of my oldest friends on the force, Sergeant Stanley Moodrow from the Lower East Side."

"Please to meet you, Sarge," Eleanor stuck out a large, well-callused palm. About thirty-five-years old, with a broad, open face and a friendly smile, she gripped his hand tightly. Curly, black hair and eyebrows perpetually raised in amusement added lightness to features already beginning to coarsen. She was big-breasted with a butt to match.

"Hey, listen," Drabek spoke up. "Stanley's gonna show ya some pitchers. I gotta use the toilet, so I'll see ya a little later."

"C'mon in my office, Sarge. It's too noisy out here," Eleanor said, grinning broadly. A tiny, four-drawer desk in one corner of a small storage area represented the office. Moodrow, leaning over the desk, pulled out a set of drawings from a small briefcase.

"Ever see . . ." he began his usual spiel, a pitch cut off by Eleanor's reaching from behind to squeeze his testicles, none too gently. The result, of course, was not very sexual from Moodrow's point of view. He jumped so high he cracked his knees on the edge of the desk and ended up on the floor.

"What the fuck do you think you're doing?" he yelled, turning to find his face three inches from the junction of her thighs.

"Don't get nervous, Sarge," Eleanor said softly. "I just like big guys. And judging from that handful, you could take it out and scare half the muggers in Harlem."

Moodrow giggled. As a veteran obscene letter-writer, he appreciated sexual inventiveness. For a moment he imagined himself trying to describe the situation to Ann Landers, then came back to reality. This woman, for whatever reason, was offering him simple, guiltless sex. Not airbrushed, *Playboy* beauty, but sagging breasts, spread hips, cellulite thighs. Sex with Eleanor, he fantasized, would be swift, wet, and odorous. For just a moment, the beginning of a smile tugged at the corner of his mouth as he contemplated taking a quick bite out of the roll of flesh around her waist. A goose was something Rita might have done (though not to a stranger), something she had done. He recalled an argument they'd had, with him continuing to complain even as he bent over the open refrigerator. The quick, hard squeeze she'd given him resulted in a violent collision between his head and the top shelf, followed by an avalanche of butter, eggs, milk, and two-day-old tuna casserole.

"Listen, Eleanor," Moodrow said gently, "it ain't that I don't find your oven attractive, but I can't right now. Just can't." He reached out to caress her cheek with the back of his hand and something in his manner convinced her. "Sorry."

"OK, Sarge," she said, shrugging her shoulders, "but you come back, hear? I know talent when I squeeze it and I'm not hurt, but I wonder why Drabek told me you'd be real eager. He said you were definitely in need."

A few minutes later, after discovering that Eleanor could not recall having seen any of the perpetrators, Moodrow walked outside to confront a thoroughly amused Victor Drabek.

"How'd it go?" Drabek asked innocently.

"Payback coming, Victor," Moodrow responded. "I don't know where or when, but definite, serious payback. Count on it."

The rain had stopped completely by the time Johnny and Muzzafer decided to park the car and walk the block surrounding their target. The building fronted North 5th Street and ran through to North 6th, though there was no entrance on North 6th, only windows. It was nearly afternoon and the morning activity had died down at the various businesses on the block. A heavy, gray mist, the remnants of the previous rain, gave the two terrorists a sense of isolation and safety. Muzzafer was sure they would arouse no suspicion. Once again he expressed his amazement at the lack of security.

"This is too easy," he said to his companion. "Maybe if we ask them nicely, they'll light the fire for us."

"What if," Johnny Katanos changed the subject, "we hijacked a gasoline tanker, backed it up to one of these windows, emptied the motherfucker into the factory and tossed in a match? What do you think would happen?"

"I've seen these trucks everywhere," Muzzafer responded. "How many gallons do they carry?"

"I don't know. Like maybe five thousand. Make a big pop. Suppose we hooked in our ten phosphorus grenades on a timer and spread 'em around those barrels of oil in there so we'd have a little time to get away."

"Yes, that's a problem," Muzzafer nodded. "It wouldn't pay to be in the neighborhood when that factory explodes."

"If we move late at night, we could run up onto the Brooklyn-Queens Expressway and head through Staten Island for South Jersey. We'll celebrate in Atlantic City."

"Can you picture Effie Bloom in a casino?" Muzzafer joked.

"Coming on to the cocktail waitresses."

By this time they were on North 6th Street, at the rear of the building. The windows, not more than five feet above the ground were ordinary, without bars, many of them broken. It was clear to both men that one blow of a heavy sledgehammer would give immediate entry.

"How long do you think it will take to execute this plan?" Muzzafer asked.

"Can't tell. Probably have to go in there at least once. See what's what." Suddenly Johnny's face lit up. "Jesus," he said, "this is the biggest thing that's ever been done by real people. Only governments could beat this record. I wonder if we could kill more than Hiroshima?"

A momentary silence followed, a pious contemplation of the destruction to come, a vision so intense they noticed nothing else, not even the tall, thin, black man with his even blacker automatic pistol emerging from the shadows of an alleyway running between the target building and its western neighbor.

"Welcome to mah worl', gennemens." The man smiled, revealing two missing teeth on the left side of his mouth as well as an artificial gold tooth in front. "Ah calls mahsef Jehovah cause I got the power of life and death here in mah han'." His voice and the sight of the gun drew Muzzafer and his companion out of their reverie. Though he was quite familiar with organized mayhem, Muzzafer had never before encountered ordinary street violence and nearly panicked in the first few seconds. He gained control of himself only after noticing that Johnny Katanos was absolutely calm, his face, particularly his mouth and jaw, completed relaxed.

"Now why don' y'all gennemens step back into mah boudoir." He gestured into the alleyway, smiling his confidence. Perhaps, if he'd been psychic, he would have known how much the dark shadows of the alleyway appealed to the young Greek standing across from him, but Jehovah was far too pleased with his own importance to listen to instinct. "Well, well," he continued, appraising Muzzafer, "it do look like we got oursefs a live, half-nigga in our domicile. What you be, boy, some kinda Potty Rican?"

"I am an Arab," Muzzafer declared, intending to launch into a revolutionary speech, but the soft smile on Johnny's face, the half-closed eyes like a cat waking up from a nap, cut the words off.

"A A-Rab," Jehovah chuckled. "Ah hopes y'all be's one a them richy A-Rabs cause ah needs ta make a big deposit befo' mah bank close. So lets us turn that shit ova and ah mean empty pockets, watches, rings, chains. All nine yard."

Muzzafer, the pistol trained on his face, complied instantly. The thief, seeing this and noting Katanos' hesitation, began to slide the pistol from Muzzafer to Johnny. The Greek waited until the gun was halfway between the two of them and pointed at no one before he began to move. Muzzafer, responding to that instinct which wishes always to surrender to superior force, was at first horrified, then terrified, then fascinated. Katanos was on the man instantly. One minute the gun was moving gracefully between them and then it was flying through the air.

"What're you gonna do now, monkey?" Johnny asked. "C'mon, nigger. Tell me what you're gonna do. Money's right here in my pocket. All you gotta do is take it. Whatta ya say, ape?"

Jehovah said nothing. The gun was lost in the shadows, and only the young man with the black eyes stood between him and escape. He—Jehovah suddenly returned to LeRoy Johnson—was six inches taller, so why was he frightened?

Muzzafer was not, of course, unfamiliar with close-up violence. He had seen many individuals tortured for information, been the instrument of several executions, but he was accustomed to pursuing violence as part of an overall design, as part of a plan. The sudden switching of roles thrilled him; his courage was now as strong as the fear he had felt a few second before. He listened to the sound of repeated blows as Johnny pulled their attacker deeper into the alleyway, like a bat striking the trunk of a tree. The man did not scream. After the first few blows, he did not even struggle. Still, the beating went on, coldly, methodically and Muzzafer, though he knew what would happen if the police had been called, if they came to investigate, did nothing to stop it. He barely breathed until Johnny walked back and took him in his arms. "Were you afraid?" the Greek asked, but the sudden jolt of sensation as their bodies came together, made it impossible to answer.

* * *

"Fuck you,' cried George Tounakis, sole proprietor of Tounakis shoe repair. "Last week you tow my car away. Five minutes I run in to grab newspaper and my car is on West Side Pier Thirty-nine. Seventy-five dollars—no check, no credit card. I spit on police. If your heart on fire, I no even piss in you mouth. Now leave my store or I call lawyer. See, as soon as I say lawyer, all police disappear."

"So what's in it fa you? I mean no cop works this hard fa nothin'." Georgie Bellino, half-owner of one of the last Italian fruit and vegetable stores in New York City, stretched his tall, muscular body, glancing quickly into the mirror above the eggplants, and smiled good-naturedly while his wife, Gina, owner of the other half of the store, peered at Moodrow's pictures.

"These people are killers." Moodrow replied evenly.

"C'mon," Bellino twisted his face into a grimace of disbelief. "For a bunch of nigger dope dealers? Who ya kiddin'?"

Moodrow stepped forward, his patience beginning to ebb as the afternoon wore on, and stared directly into Bellino's eyes. "It's personal, pal. I got a grudge and I'm gonna collect. If that's all right with you."

"Sure, Sarge." The grocer backed away, more amused than afraid. "I don't wanna pry into ya business, but it don't make a lotta sense."

"Hey, Georgie," Gina broke in, her loud, coarse voice belying her petite body and pretty, little-girl features, "how come you gotta make trouble with a cop? You stupit or somethin'? Stop bustin' balls.'

"What kinda talk?" George Bellino demanded. "You got a big mouth on you, bitch? Why don't ya try ta remember—this ain't Palermo where your people come from. This is America. A-MER-I-CA. And I could say whatever I want." Once again he stretched his muscles, letting his shirt fall open to reveal a tangle of gold chains.

"Don't pay no attention, officers," Gina explained. "He's stupit, but he works hard. I respect what ya said about personal."

"Wait a minute," the grocer said, pulling his wife around to face him. "Whatta ya sayin' I'm stupit for? I didn't give youse no cause to be mouthin' off at me. Hey,'' he said to Moodrow and Drabek, ''never work with no wife. It's bad enough what ya gotta put up with at home, but all day is too freakin' much. Look at the bitch. She's bad-mouthin' me over a bunch a dead niggers. Is that right?''

''You put up with me?'' Gina demanded, her breasts heaving with anger. ''If it wasn't fa me and my father you wouldn't have nothin'. You could never get shit on your own.''

''See this, cunt?'' Bellino said, holding up a large, purple eggplant. ''When we get home tonight I'm gonna shove it so far up your ass, it's gonna come out the top of ya head.''

Homosexuality is not a hotly debated issue in the Moslem world. It is considered an abomination (though it exists there as it does in the whole of the human world). Growing up among Arabs, Muzzafer was inculcated with the same values as all of his friends and neighbors and even though he had traveled widely, had, in his own estimation, thrown off the teachings of Muhammad and been subjected to a hundred attempted seductions due to his slender body and soft, feminine features, he had never accepted homosexuals. To him, they were extreme symbols of Western decadence. He presumed the new order would be free of male homosexuality, though women might continue to serve in the manner set forth by the Koran.

Now Muzzafer sat on the passenger's side of a small Toyota while another man, driving casually, used his right hand to caress the length of the Arab's thigh, stopping just short of his groin, teasing with the tip of his finger, then stroking again. And Muzzafer, excited from his toes to his nose, had all he could do to keep from returning the caress. His mind was spinning, reeling from rejection to rejection. He would lose control of a situation that required absolute control. Things would be demanded of him, acts both painful and humiliating. His manhood would disappear; his life would be unbearable, though not, somehow, as unbearable as the idea of allowing this fire to go out. He felt his erection strong against his trousers, looked out of the corner of his eye to see Johnny equally erect. The car came to a halt at a red light. The Greek's face came closer, lips brushing Muzzafer's ear.

"You ever been in a real jail? For criminals, not politics," he began. "If you like read about jail in books and magazines, you get the opinion that sex in jail is rape. Like that's the only sex available, but it happens a lot that two guys just go for each other and ain't neither one of them pussies. They got cocks and the cocks get hard and a man can't jerk off forever, so if you find a dude you like and you can stand putting your lips on his, what's the harm? The hottest sex I ever had was five minutes in a broom closet. Twice a week when the routine ran us across each other and then five minutes in that closet. All hands and ass and come."

"I think I seen this one here."

The two cops were on Fresh Pond Road in the heart of Ridgewood, at Maxell's Donut Shoppe. Millicent Rolfe, proprietor, was sifting through the pictures, pausing to hold up that of Effie Bloom. "I know this one. She came on to me. Imagine? I'm in the church, for Christ's sake. And I do mean butch. Looked like she ate bowling balls."

"When was this?" Moodrow asked, excitement beginning to stir.

"Last year some time. I haven't seen her since then. Tell me something, Sergeant, wouldn't it be easier to put the pictures on TV? Let everyone see 'em at once?"

"Not important enough," Moodrow replied, his interest falling away. After telling the lie so many times, he had it down pat. "If it wasn't personal with me, nobody could care less."

"Sure," Drabek said, "that's the way it goes. My uncle was a cop way back before World War II, and he told me they really used to look hard back then. People didn't kill each other so fast the new bodies piled up before the old ones got buried. Nowadays if ya don't catch them with the gun in their hand, ya fill out the papers and forget about it. Same pension either way."

"Yeah, it's a shame," Millie said. "My first husband, God have mercy, was a cop. Right in this precinct. Never drew his gun the whole time he was on the force."

"Never?" Moodrow said, glancing at his watch. The day was nearly gone, but the wheels were moving. His biggest problem would occur if Epstein caught on. Unlike Higgins, he was sure Epstein would do something. For a moment, as Millicent's voice rolled on, he considered the problem. Would his captain inform on him? Epstein was a good cop; he would have no choice. They would show the pictures on every television station and the American Red Army would quietly disappear into a Cuban or Russian or Syrian safe house. Even if they were caught, Moodrow knew he would be denied his revenge. The state would even protect them from attack by other prisoners.

As Johnny Katanos and Muzzafer walked from the car to their home, Muzzafer experienced a sudden feeling of utter loss. If he was to fail in his mission at this late date, to abandon his training, it would negate his entire life—the early years in the refugee camps, the years of training, the dead martyrs. A complete memory of himself lecturing on the necessity of revolutionary discipline flashed crazily through his mind even as he watched the muscles of Johnny's buttocks alternately tense and relax as they walked up the steps leading to the front door. What would become of the American Red Army and all his dreams? How would he maintain order? He felt as if he'd been smoking hashish for days. The door swam in his vision, but somehow he was not surprised when Jane Mathews, grinning, opened it. For a moment, he thought he was saved, but then, as Jane leaned forward to kiss Johnny full on the lips, whispering, "I've been waiting all day," he knew it was not to be.

"I've brought you a gift," Johnny returned, raising Muzzafer's hand to her lips.

Moodrow, driving toward the Williamsburg Bridge and home, noted the clear conditions, the high winds having blown the smoke and pollution, as well as the rain, out into the Atlantic. Tomorrow would be one of those rare days when the skyline of New York, seen from the highest point on the Kosciuszko Bridge joining Brooklyn and Queens, would stand out against a brilliant blue sky, as sharp and crisp as the fear that held him in place after the explosion that killed Rita. He had a premonition of his future if he was unable to apprehend Muzzafer and his cohorts, but he shut it away by returning to the safety of the task he'd set for himself. The sense of being within a routine performed thousands of times, warmed him, cuddled him. He considered the streets left uncovered, especially Queens Boulevard with the subway running beneath its surface. Hundreds of dwellings, ranging from attached single-family homes to twenty-family apartment buildings had been constructed here over the last decade, as city dwellers exchanged the insane rents of Manhattan for the merely outrageous rents of Queens. Anything close to a subway line and not located in a neighborhood given over to violence and drugs, had become a target for redevelopment. Even Jackson Heights and Forest Hills, which in the 60s had begun to swing over to Spanish and black ghettos respectively, were being contested for by hordes of upwardly mobile young executives, male and female, looking for a base from which to begin their ascent. It would take days, but Moodrow did not yet feel pressed for time. The American Red Army consisted of human beings who had to be fed and housed like anyone else. Clothing had to be purchased, taken to dry cleaners. Cars were washed, gassed and serviced. Newspapers were bought and containers of coffee, usually at the same place every day. Was it possible that none of the three he sought had established any regular patterns in their neighborhoods? Not likely. The Buick rolled smoothly over the bridge and, for once, the cop did not even think about alcohol as he made his way home.

17

Leonora Higgins woke up with a nagging backache, harbinger, she knew, of the onset of the active part of her menstrual cycle. She was a modern woman, modern enough not to see her period as a "curse," yet not so modern as to consider it anything but a royal pain in the ass. Barely into her teens when she began to menstruate, what had bothered her most was the realization that she couldn't get out of it. There were no months off. Like all children, she'd made many an end-run around the "rules," at home and in school, but this monthly obligation defied remedy, emerging almost exactly on time, demanding immediate attention.

At least the backache was no problem. A long, hot shower with the showerhead turned to "coarse" would untie the knots. She shrugged out of her nightgown and padded over to the bathroom, turned on the shower, paused to brush her teeth while she waited for the hot water to come up and jumped in. She stood motionless for the first few minutes, luxuriating in the sensation of hot water pounding her back, then began to soap her body, from bottom to top, working up a thick, rich lather as she hummed a tuneless tune.

It was at this moment that the demons destined to rule this particular day first made themselves known to her. The hot water shut off suddenly. The showerhead unleashed a cascade as cold as any mountain stream, though not quite as cold as the scream Leonora gave out on her way from the shower to the tiles of the bathroom floor. She didn't entirely realize her predicament at first. Reaching unconsciously for the towel, she ran one hand through her hair, withdrawing it immediately to stare at the white soap running between her fingers. Then she looked over at the icy water still pouring from the shower.

"I don't believe this shit," she said softly, almost fascinated. "What am I supposed to do?" But there was only one thing to do. She switched the flow from shower to bath, knelt down on the little rug and leaned into it. It took three attempts and, after the second, wasn't bad at all. Still she didn't even consider finishing her shower. What in the world, she wondered, possessed people to jump into the Atlantic Ocean every winter?

Fifteen minutes to put herself in shape before charging out the door. Park Slope, Brooklyn was a long way from her Queens Boulevard office and she had no car, having long ago discovered that the competition for parking presented her with the choice of paying fifty dollars per week for a garage or a hundred dollars for parking tickets. Unwilling to give up trendy Park Slope and nearby Prospect Park, she'd made the choice of most New Yorkers and opted for mass transit. This meant a two-block walk to the F train, followed by a very long ride on an already crowded subway through South Brooklyn, Chinatown and midtown Manhattan, before passing under the East River to Queens Boulevard and the offices of the FBI. All in all, on a good day, an hour and fifteen minutes. But, as everyone who's ever been there knows, not all days are good days for New York City mass transit. Delays are more common than smooth rides, especially during the busy hours and sometimes these delays can be extensive. Sometimes, as on this particular day, the subways stop altogether, just short of the East River, at the Lexington Avenue station, because of a smoky fire in the tunnel leading to Queens.

Having been in this position before, Leonora ran quickly through the various options, including the N Train, the 7 Train down at 42nd Street, bus and cab. All were bad. The 7 would leave her on Roosevelt Avenue, not Queens Boulevard, a long bus ride away from work. A cab would cost about eight dollars and she would have to fight the traffic out of the city. The buses, if they came at all, had the same problem with the traffic as the taxis and they had to make many, many stops. She would go home before she took a bus.

That left the N Train. She would have to walk to 59th Street, six blocks, but it would carry her directly to her regular station, an ideal solution, except, as she strode up Lexington Avenue, there appeared an ocean of human beings all trudging from unmoving trains on 53rd to the promise on 59th. The N would be packed. Hell, the whole platform would be packed and it would make every local stop, another hour and a half of utter misery. It suddenly seemed too much and Leonora turned into a deli for a container of coffee and a chocolate donut.

The donut lightened her disposition immediately and, taking this as an omen of improved fortunes, she decided to try to hail a cab, walking quickly over to Third Avenue. There were always plenty of cabs on Third in the early morning; they were dropping at the offices lining the avenue and heading back uptown. Lenora was not unaware of the cabbies' reputation for refusing blacks; the papers wrote about it every other week. But she herself rarely had had a problem. Crisp and businesslike as she was in a dark-blue, double-breasted suit, the drivers would expect a midtown destination, perhaps one of the office buildings on Sixth Avenue. They would definitely not be afraid of her. The real problem would occur, she believed, when she asked the cabbie to go to Queens. Nobody wanted to go there, because there was no work and it was nearly impossible to get back.

But the driver be damned. She had important business in the office and if she had to, she'd flash her badge and force the bastard. Determined, she stepped into the street with her arm raised and the first cab to come along made a sharp turn in front of a panel truck, forcing her back onto the curb.

"I want to go to Queens Boulevard in Forest Hills," she said, more timidly then she'd hoped.

The driver stared at her through the open window, fighting a grin. "So?" he asked.

"So you have to take me," Leonora declared.

"Inside or outside?"

"What are you talking about?"

"You wanna get in and let me drive you or do you want I should wish you to Forest Hills?"

Leonora started to get in, already annoyed, but the cabbie reached out a hand to block her.

"There's just one thing," he said.

"Go ahead," Leonora answered, anticipating some half-disguised racial slur. Perhaps he would ask for the money in advance.

"You gotta dump the coffee. I don't allow no eatin' in my car. Sorry, lady." His face remained carefully neutral, eyes blinking innocently.

"I won't open it until I get out."

"Sorry," he repeated. "If it spills, I gotta clean. You don't want I should have to stop everything and wipe the backseat, do ya? But I won't complain if you wanna stay home."

Resigned to this small humiliation, a payback, she realized, for having to go to Queens at 8:30 in the morning, she tossed the untouched coffee into a wire trashbasket and got in. Much to her surprise, the backseat was clean, the floor recently vacuumed, the windows immaculate.

The trip went quickly. Even the outbound 59th Street Bridge, usually jammed because of early morning lane reversals, moved smoothly and Queens Boulevard was virtually empty. Leonora arrived at her office a few minutes after nine o'clock, time enough to get another coffee while she considered the coming confrontation with George Bradley. A thorough review of the Chadwick murder file had pushed the name of Paco Baquili into her consciousness. A simple interview would probably indicate whether Chadwick's murderers were crazed criminals or crazed terrorists, but it would take time and she needed Bradley's permission.

Upstairs, Bradley was in a decent mood for the first time in a month. He'd just gotten off the phone with his strongest source to date. He'd worked for two weeks to put this connection together, tearing through a half-dozen agencies to reach a Palestinian ex-terrorist deep in the Libyan U.N. Mission. The man had insisted that no one at the Libyan Embassy and probably no one in all of Libya knew the whereabouts of the American Red Army, and his insistence rang true. It seemed, to Bradley, that he spent whole days on the phone, contacting various spies and informants, pushing hard and getting nowhere. It had reached the point where the inspector was ready to settle for a weak rumor.

But then, just as Bradley was about to hang up, the man, name unknown, took a quick turn and Bradley had his rumor at last. There was, the man whispered, just the possibility that if the leader of the Army was Aftab Muzzafer, as the inspector suspected, he might have had his features surgically altered in Libya and the doctor who performed the surgery may have taken some photos of Muzzafer and his band while they recovered and those photos might be available. For a price.

The price was a definite problem. The man spoke about one million or perhaps two. He wasn't sure. There were a number of people between him and the photos. He would inquire and call back. Two days? Three? He didn't want to make false promises, but he would have to have money to get started. Part payment to grease the wheels.

"We must meet face to face before any money can change hands. You will have to meet with us personally." Bradley's voice was deliberately harsh. His initial aim was to decrease the likelihood of a con job. The man would have to come into a situation where he would be covertly photographed and eventually identified. His identity, along with the story of how he'd betrayed the revolution, might be sold to those who take such matters very seriously. The meeting would be tantamount to defection and the man talking to him knew it.

"Surely we must meet," Hassan Fakhr answered softly. For his part, he knew he had his fish, but he whispered to make identification by voiceprint as difficult as possible. "However, there is no point just now. I must negotiate with my contacts and you must see if you can get the money. Muzzafer is a difficult man, capable of great violence. If it is him, I do not believe he expects to live." Hassan congratulated himself on his forced "American" English. Who would guess that he'd eaten with his hands until he was twelve? "I think we should look at fifty thousand dollars to begin. If dollars are a problem, gold will be acceptable, at the London exchange rate."

By the time Leonora entered the office, Bradley was very excited. He had not come to his position by making a habit of failure, but here, on the most important case in his career, he'd been utterly stymied. Quickly, while Leonora gulped her coffee, he laid out his conversation with the Libyan. "I pray he's telling the truth. By God, Leonora, I don't believe we've another hope of stopping them until they run out of ordnance and even then, since we don't know what they look like, they might easily sneak out of the country."

"But two million . . ." Leonora didn't bother to finish the sentence.

"Oh, he'll go for a lot less. The Arabs love to stretch it out. Ask for the moon then settle for pennies. Never seem to lose that Cairo shopkeeper mentality."

Leonora blinked in disbelief. Was it possible he didn't understand the racist implications of his words? "Well I have something I've been wanting to talk to you about." She jumped right into it, even knowing it was hopeless. "It's about that policeman, Sargeant Moodrow. He was supposed to make written reports twice a week, but I haven't heard from him at all." She stopped, intimidated by Bradley's paternal frown, then grew angry. "Listen, George, if you don't have any confidence in my judgement, why don't you come out and say so? There's good reason to believe that the robbery of Ronald Chadwick was not just criminal warfare. It appears that this Greek boy came into the drug world suddenly and has now disappeared altogether. Two women were employed in his plan, women willing to have sex with strangers. If these women were whores, why haven't they turned up? Why were they unknown in the neighborhood? Where did they go afterwards? I want to interview the survivor of the massacre, Paco Baquili. He's being held at the Riker's Island jail, pending transfer to an upstate penitentiary."

"And what will you offer him if he's already been sentenced? Why would he want to talk to you? As for the cop—why not pass Moodrow's failure to report to his superiors and let them handle it?'' Bradley took out his pipe and fumbled for his tobacco. An idea had begun to form in his mind and he needed a few extra seconds to think it out. If this lead proved fruitful, if he, George Bradley, developed this path to the American Red Army, wouldn't he be better off if his associate, Leonora Higgins, was somewhere out in the field? Following a false trail at her own request? ''Tell me,'' he said, smiling, ''why do you think there's a connection between this Greek and the terrorists? Omitting the single fact of a Soviet hand grenade? I'm afraid you've become obsessed with this policeman and that's the worst thing that can happen to an agent.''

''What about the killers? How they've all disappeared? That they were strangers in the neighborhood. What have I been talking about all this time? Look, remember last year, that mass murder in Brooklyn? The one where they found the kid crawling in the blood?''

''Sure. Go ahead.''

''They knew it was drugs and they knew who did it the next day, even if it took six months to find the killers. The drug world is just like the terrorist world.''

''No.'' Bradley shook his head.

''Yes. It is. It's a small community engaging in illegal activity, thoroughly penetrated by informers and undercover cops, where everybody knows everybody else. If some group made a quick raid on the Dutch Embassy, got away and never claimed credit, wouldn't you be suspicious? If none of our informants, none of our spies, could give the group a past or a present . . . ?'' She stopped suddenly. Why did she have to justify herself to this man? The word ''racist'' passed quickly through her mind again. It was an easy place to hide and she welcomed the wave of hatred that followed behind it. ''And I know,'' she finished through clenched teeth, ''that cop is holding back. I know it.''

Bradley put on his wisest, most fatherly expression as he paused to relight his pipe. In his own mind, he reeked of masculinity. In Leonora's, he reeked of pompous vanity. Nevertheless, he raised his head to meet Leonora's eyes. ''OK,'' he said, ''if you need to get this out of your system, go ahead. We have no real disagreement here. I know the cop was holding back. I know the surly bastard's playing some sort of stupid cop game. If you want to find out what it is, it's fine with me. Sniff around. Satisfy yourself.''

Leonora kept silent. A memory of her father flashed quickly through her mind. She recalled the moment when she'd put it together and understood that all the problems between her mother and father stemmed from her father's use of drugs, specifically heroin. He was nodding over the kitchen table; her mother was screaming something about ''the money'' and he didn't even have the energy to answer her back. Once again the loathing she'd felt as a child flooded her, and she stared at her superior with angry eyes.

Bradley felt none of this. Oblivious, he stepped forward and gave her shoulder a brotherly squeeze. ''Go get him,'' he said.

Quickly, before she could say something she couldn't take back, Leonora turned and walked to her own office, thinking, this can't be happening to me. How can a day keep going bad like this? Jamming files into her attaché case, she fought a sudden urge to cry. The injustice of it overwhelmed her and by the time she reached the elevator, she was so angry she smashed at the row of floor buttons with the heel of her hand, lighting a cluster of six, and made every floor on her way to the garage and a black, four-door Plymouth Fury with matching black-wall tires, standard bureau issue.

Leonora cut quickly through the late morning traffic on the Long Island Expressway, then wheeled onto the Grand Central Parkway and into much lighter traffic. It felt good to go fast, to glide past the other cars. Taking a deep breath, she felt her shoulders relax, the tension beginning to ease out as she put her attention on the task to come. How would she deal with Paco Baquili? What could she offer him? Unfortunately, her train of thought was interrupted by a glowing set of revolving red lights as a marked police cruiser roared up to her bumper. Leonora could see the two cops smirking as they waved her to the curb. They knew they were pulling over a government car. That's what made it fun.

And sure enough, both cops emerged from the car, highway cops in long, black, leather coats and high-topped boots. They came forward, one to the driver's and one to the passenger's side window, standard practice in dangerous situations, but totally inappropriate here.

"Stopped you for speeding, Miss. License and registration, please," the cop closest to her began.

"FBI," Lenora said, holding up her identification. She was so angry, she couldn't bring herself to look at him.

"Oh, look," the same cop cried, "FBI. Well, whoopie for the FBI." He demonstrated his contempt with an impromptu ballet, turning a complete circle on his toes. The second policeman took this opportunity to express his own feelings on the matter. "What're ya chasin'? A known felon? I don't see any perps here. Ya not allowed ta speed unless you're in 'hot pursuit.' I mean I don't make the rules, but we can't have law officers runnin' over pedestrians, can we?" Like Abbott relieving Costello, the first cop, his dance completed, switched back on. "I'm afraid we're gonna have to give you a ticket, Miss. And I hope it's a good lesson for ya."

Leonora flicked open the clasp on her purse, a reflexive action, which cleared the way to her perfectly legal 9mm automatic, then returned her hand to the steering wheel. It was not a planned move, yet it had its effect. The two cops passed each other an apprehensive look, then disappeared with her identification. Once in the safety of their own car, however, they recovered enough of their original bravado to make Leonora wait a full twenty minutes before the first cop sauntered back. "I'm gonna let ya go this time," he said, laying the papers in her oustretched palm. "But in the future, please try ta watch how fast ya drivin'."

Not to be outdone, Riker's Island demonstrated once again that giving federal agents a hard time had become a permanent part of every city worker's mentality. For the most part, the federal government did nothing to hide its contempt for New Yorkers, considering the payback resulting from that contempt a cause of the contempt in the first place. It was a vicious circle and even though Leonora could have predicted her two-hour wait for Paco Baquili, she could in no way accept it and her mood flipped from anger to self-pity every ten minutes.

Paco, when he finally appeared, did nothing to lighten her disposition. His entire conversation consisted of a single, emphatically offered sentence.

"Paco, I'm Agent Leonora Higgins, FBI."

"Fuck you."

"I want to talk to you about a Greek and two women."

"Fuck you."

"They're the ones who put you here."

"Fuck you."

There's something about being sentenced to seven years in a New York State maximum security prison that brings out the least cooperative elements of the human personality. Paco, in his heart of hearts, just didn't give a damn, though he would have thought twice about doing this in front of a male, New York City cop.

"Sergeant Moodrow from the NYPD was here to see you last week. What was that all about?"

"Fuck you."

"Listen, you little bastard, I'm not fooling around with you. If I don't hear something else this time, I'm gonna make you pay the price for your mouth."

Paco's grin increased to near bursting. "Fuck you . . . nigger." Then he exploded with laughter and Leonora was forced to confront the problem first posed by George Bradley. Paco was a prisoner of New York State, a man convicted of state crimes, a man already sentenced. Leonora had neither threat nor reward at her disposal and Paco clearly knew it. His contempt attacked her blackness and her femininity as well as her professional status. She stood and began to circle, hands behind her back, looking perplexed. Paco's cuffed hands were in his lap and he was very confident. He didn't bother to follow her with his eyes, a costly mistake as she evened up in the only way open to her. She drove a side kick into his right ear, producing an astonishing amount of virtually instantaneous swelling and a strangled sound that in no way resembled, "Fuck you, nigger." Then she quickly circled the room, pushing over the chairs, moving the table out of center.

"What're you doin'?" Paco demanded.

Leonora answered by pounding on the door, which brought in two enormous black corrections officers. "This fool tried to hit me," Leonora explained.

"That right?" The two men stared at Paco like he was an insect under glass.

"He says he doesn't believe blacks have a place in law enforcement. He says we're all nigger scum. I haven't time to file a complaint. Probably never get anywhere anyway. Judges just turn 'em loose. I thought I'd let you know so you could keep an eye on him."

The taller of the two guards threw her a quick ghetto wink. "Don't you worry yourself, mama. We prepared to handle this situation. Happens all the time."

Leonora contained her reaction to the word "mama"; she even managed to smile her way out of the jail, but once on the street, she had to lean against the side of her car for a few moments. She felt like a prize fighter, like a slugger wading into punch after punch before having a chance to deliver a blow of her own. Maybe it wasn't worth pursuing a line of action that met with so much resistance. It was certain that her day would not improve. She had to go to Moodrow now. There was no other path to the knowledge she needed. Even if she interviewed every friend of a friend mentioned in the police report and she came up with a likeness of Johnny Katanos, Bradley would never give her enough time to follow through. It was Moodrow or nothing.

Moodrow was preparing for his last day at the 203rd Precinct when the bell rang. He expected to find the widow Torrez behind his door, armed with a plate of food. Since Rita's death, she'd been after him like an owl on a mouse. The utterly unexpected sight of Leonora Higgins standing in his hallway, brought him up short. "Aaaaaaaaa," he muttered.

"May I come in?" she asked.

Moodrow considered his dining room table covered with notes, the maps pinned to the walls. ''No,'' he said simply, as if such a response was perfectly normal.

''What's the matter with you?'' Leonora asked angrily. She was very tired of being pushed around. ''I want to come in and talk to you about Chadwick and the American Red Army.''

''Not right now, Miss. Sorry.''

''Can't you at least be civil?''

''I'm not trying to hurt your feelings,'' Moodrow shifted gears, ''but, see, I got this girl in there and right this very minute now she's kneeling on my kitchen table, buck naked. Like I would invite you in anyway. Really. But she's a little embarrassed because she's kind of fat. Actually she's real, real fat, so better we should talk out here.''

''I'm getting tired of this,'' Leonora said through clenched teeth.

''Look, lady, I don't care what you're tired of. Anything I got is already in that goddamn briefcase you carry around everywhere.''

''Is it?'' she fired back. ''I know it's supposed to be. You were ordered to file reports twice a week, but I don't have a goddamn thing.''

''So I'm a little behind. Big fucking deal. If I had something important, I would have been to see you already.''

Leonora could stand it no more. ''I need some help,'' she yelled.

Moodrow waited until her voice stopped echoing in the hallway. ''That I don't deny,'' he said evenly, closing the door. ''Why don't you take two aspirins and call me in the morning?''

Despite being totally drunk and in his own bed, Stanley Moodrow could not fall asleep. He had just finished his last day in the 203rd, a session devoted to canvassing the various neighborhood bars. The exercise had produced no result, not even a nibble, and, reasoning that he was on vacation and not on-duty, Moodrow had begun to drink early in the evening. By the time his night was finished, he was far too drunk to drive and had to accept a ride home in an ordinary patrol car.

Upstairs, he barely managed to get off his shoes and pants before collapsing on the bed. He expected oblivion, would have welcomed it, but for some reason, instead of unconsciousness, his imagination kept throwing out instant replays of his walk up Sixth Avenue to meet Rita, a montage of people and vehicles, noisy radios and taxi horns. Try as he might, he could not throw it off until he shifted into what he had come to call "the fantasy."

He'd been having the fantasy several times each day, usually while driving. Alone in a room with a helpless American Red Army (the number varied from four to ten), he tormented them by drawing out the moment of their execution. Sometimes they were chained in a circle; sometimes they were beaten so badly they were unable to move. On this particular night, he had them handcuffed to a vertical hot water pipe in a tenement kitchen.

Several begged for mercy. One, outraged, asserted her right to a fair trial, demanding justice. Still another tried to spit on him. He ignored them. Sitting at the kitchen table, he took his gun apart and cleaned it, piece by piece, spinning the cylinder like a wild-West cowboy before inserting six specially prepared bullets. He held each one up for the Army's inspection before sliding it home. The tips had been cut off so that the .38-caliber slugs would not so much penetrate as smash their way into each body.

Then Moodrow, the gun a toy in his huge hand, stood up and began to move toward his victims. He saw the fear in their eyes, that they knew he was going to execute them without benefit of judge or jury. The fear comforted him. It reached out a dark, enveloping warmth that enabled him, at last, to fall asleep.

18

Allen Epstein, captain, New York City Police, stared, bleary-eyed across the kitchen table at his wife of thirty-seven years, Alma. Watching her transform the contents of their refrigerator into French toast (with blueberries), maple syrup, sausage links, orange juice and coffee, he marveled at her early morning efficiency. His stomach was hurting him again: a sort of borderline pain that might go either way. Not, he reflected, that Alma would make any concessions to his sensitive gut. She played her Jewish mother role to the hilt. Believing that any illness that couldn't be cured with food was not worth acknowledging, she countered all established medical opinion with a single sentence: "So what do they know?" Epstein had stopped arguing a long time before and, truth to tell, loved to eat her cooking.

He knew what was bothering him. It was Moodrow. And the irony that the man he used to handle precinct "problems" had become a problem himself did not escape the captain. He'd gotten a call from a lieutenant at the 203rd Precinct in Queens, a natural pain in the ass who minded everyone else's business, and the details of Moodrow's activities had come to light. The sergeant, as Epstein had suspected, was on a hunt. Of course, that didn't necessarily mean that the American Red Army would be at the end of the hunt. Or that Moodrow wasn't making his reports to the FBI on schedule. But after twenty years in the 7th, Epstein would always have bet his pension that Moodrow was out for revenge. In the last analysis, no matter what Moodrow fed Higgins and Bradley in his "reports," he would take down the American Red Army all by himself.

If the sergeant was wrong it didn't matter, but what if he was right? Thirty-three people had died in the fire at Herald Square. How many in the next attack? A hundred? A thousand? Moodrow, deluded or now, was willing to risk lives for personal revenge. He was throwing dice, betting that he could get to the Army before it acted again, and that idea angered the cop in Allen Epstein. Artist's renderings of the Red Army, shown on television, would at least drive them underground, preventing more bloodshed. A cop could never put his own feelings above society's need for protection. The idea was to put criminals away and the effort was a team effort. Of course, there were plenty of hotdogs who didn't like to share their collars, but they stopped short of allowing criminals to run free. Moodrow was on the wrong side of the line.

And something else, something more important. Epstein was a captain, an intermediate-level survivor of the competition between cops. Intra-departmental warfare was as intense as ever. If Moodrow should be successful (or worse, come close and fail) and it became known that he, Epstein, had knowledge of Moodrow's activities without, for instance, making a phone call to the FBI to confirm that *complete* reports were, in fact, being filed, he would not last a month before being informed that retirement was infinitely preferable to a departmental hearing. Epstein, much as he loved his Alma, was not yet ready to be with her every minute of the day.

"How about a bagel with a shmeer?" Alma asked, breaking his concentration.

"Huh?" Epstein, his glasses still lying on his desk, could barely see her.

"A bagel, Allen. I'm asking if you're still hungry."

"No," he groused. "My guts are on fire."

"It's all that Moodrow's fault, isn't it? I don't know why you protect him; he's like a stone around your neck. Dragging you down. You woulda been inspector by . . .''

"Enough already," Epstein moaned. "You think that makes it better?" He paused a moment, sighed. "Maybe I oughta report it to Flynn."

"An Irish?" Alma cried indignantly. "Not to an Irish. An Irish'll have the poor sergeant's you-know-what's for breakfast."

"For Christ's sake, Alma. You just said I should bury my friend and now . . ."

"But not an Irish. Find someone the boy can talk to."

"Boy? Moodrow's a boy now?"

"For crying out loud, Allen. Why can't you understand about Stanley?" She shook her head decisively. "He's a babe in the woods. The department'll tear him to pieces. I can't believe you could give him up to an Irish without talking to him."

"I get it, now. Lemme ask you this, Alma. If you wanted I should talk to Stanley personal, why didn't you just say so? Why all the shouting?"

"That was for your stomach, dear." She smiled seductively. "I got onion rolls in the fridge."

Stanley Moodrow's apartment was as clean as a whistle when Epstein knocked on the door. Having learned his lesson from Leonora Higgins' unexpected visit, there wasn't a trace of his investigation visible. Moodrow, welcoming the captain, was very proud of his industry until it became clear that Epstein knew almost everything about his activities in the 203rd.

"Well, that didn't take very long, did it?" Moodrow complained.

"For Christ's sake, Stanley, what did you expect? You got friends? I got friends, too. Not to mention guys that're out to protect their own precinct. You can't do this shit in a vacuum."

"I'm running an official investigation. What's wrong with that?"

Epstein looked up at Moodrow and frowned. This was going to take some time, either way. "Could I have a beer, Stanley?" His stomach twisted violently. "Please."

Moodrow made two open bottles of Budweiser and two glasses appear so fast he seemed to have pulled them out of a hat.

"You saying you're making reports on time?" Epstein sipped his beer. "You telling me those pictures of the Greek and his two girl-friends are in those reports?"

Moodrow leaned back in his seat, folding his arms across his chest. "I'm looking for the assholes that killed Ronald Chadwick. If I'm a little behind on my reports, what's the big deal? I don't have anything important enough to report anyway. Don't forget, Captain, right now the Greek is only linked to the Chadwick case. You sound like Higgins, trying to make a big deal out of it."

"Don't bullshit me, Stanley." Epstein was suddenly so mad he was ready to cry. He jumped up and shouted into Moodrow's face. "You're after the scumbags who offed your old lady. You don't give two shits about some junkies on Attorney Street. You believe they're the same people and you want them for yourself. I know you got reasons you ain't telling me. Whatta you think, I'm a complete mo-ron? If I didn't owe you, I'd bury your ass with the department. I want the goddamn truth, Stanley."

"Truth?" Moodrow stared into Epstein's eyes. For a moment he considered telling the captain about the two women engaged in a shouting match on Sixth Avenue. Then he contemplated a future with-out revenge and drew back inside himself. He looked down at his feet, feigning a depression that would be only too real if he failed. "Look, Captain, I'm taking my shot. What's the harm if it's a long shot? I was there. I saw her die. I have to do something, Captain."

Epstein sat down. It was very difficult to pressure a man under these circumstances. Suppose the whole thing was no more than a means to get Moodrow through Rita's death? Who would be harmed? Why not let the man work out his grief? But Epstein could not throw off the opposite line which knew for sure that Moodrow was too good a cop to lie to himself. If he thought the American Red Army was tied to the death of Ronald Chadwick, he had more information than he was sharing. "Stanley, you know what happens to me if you're lying? If I don't take this upstairs?"

"I'm not lying, Captain."

"You lied about those two tickets to the Ridgewood Theatre. You didn't put them in your report."

"But not to you. I didn't bullshit you one second. I told you voluntarily about them tickets or you still wouldn't know. Now you come and say I'm fucking you around? That ain't right."

For all its revolutionary aims, the American Red Army was American in at least one respect—each of its members embraced the work ethic in pursuit of the group's goals. Even as Moodrow persisted in his search and Epstein and Higgins pondered their next move, the Army, minus Muzzafer, who was unexpectedly late, sat around the kitchen table in Effie and Jane's apartment, listening attentively to a taped phone conversation. They had decided, on their own, to follow up on a newspaper article dealing with a Sunday afternoon demonstration in front of an illegal chemical-waste warehouse in Brooklyn. The article had named the Society for a Safe City, a coalition of nearly a dozen ecology-oriented organizations, as the sponsor of the protest and listed the group's telephone number.

Theresa Aviles, scanning the papers each day for any reference of toxic material as part of her general research on hazardous waste, had found the article and thus received the honor of making the inquiring phone call. Not that the others were idle. Johnny Katanos had been inside the building twice. Effie had charted the schedules and routes of three major oil companies with depots on Newtown Creek, a permanently polluted East River inlet, and another on Bushwick Creek, not ten blocks from the target. Jane worked on the problem of igniting waste oil. It was very important that the fire continue long enough to cause a real panic. Hearing about a bombing, a good citizen might congratulate himself on being alive and out of danger, but if there were a cloud of gas coming and continuing to come, anything might happen.

The woman who answered the phone at the Society for a Safe City, Eleanor Satowski, had been more than eager to discuss the situation at the North 5th Street chemical dump after Theresa identified herself as a resident of Greenpoint, a worried parent with three children living within six blocks of the warehouse.

"If I was you," she said, her voice sharply confident, "I'd get my ass out of there. Especially with kids. Kids are more vulnerable to every kind of cancer-causing agent."

"Moving takes money," Theresa responded. "It's not that easy."

"Maybe if I tell you what's in there, it'll change your mind. And I'm not taking this out of the air. We have a number of sources within the Environmental Protection Agency. It's only too bad the media isn't interested in using them. We've put out half a dozen press releases and they continue to print whatever the government feeds them." She hesitated briefly, to let it sink in, then proceeded, rapid-fire. "There are several thousand barrels of oil sludge contaminated with polyvinylchloride, and dioxin. Dioxin, by the way, is the most powerful cancer-causing agent ever tested. This oil sludge is flammable, but only at very high temperatures, and the EPA is taking the position that such temperatures could could not be generated by an accidental fire. They refuse to even consider the possibility of a nonaccidental fire. Just throw a bunch of bullshit about 'budgets' and 'priorities.'

"The long-term effects," she rolled right along, not even pausing to give her caller a moment to respond, "of smoke contaminated with PVC or dioxin aren't that predictable, but there is something that is predictable. Our contact says there are hundreds of drums filled with cyanide and possibly a thousand with hydrochloric acid. If these substances should mix, even without a fire, they would give off a toxic gas that would kill thousands. And all they have to do is touch."

"How could this happen?" Theresa finally asked.

"Good question. And a real simple answer. There was this man named Anastasio Parillo who used to be in the private sanitation business with his brother, Carmine. I guess they weren't making enough money, because one day they sold their garbage trucks to a competitor and bought two big trailers. Then they went up and down the whole East Coast, picking up fifty-gallon drums of whatever anyone wanted to get rid of. They didn't care what it was. As long as it wasn't leaking, they put it in their trucks and brought it back to his warehouse. When the warehouse was full, they simply disappeared. EPA thinks they went back to Palermo.

"Listen, Theresa, do you remember what happened in Cameroon? About two years ago?"

"I don't think so." Theresa played dumb.

"Well, nobody knows exactly how this happened, but somehow a cloud of toxic gas came out of this lake, Lake Nyos, and killed several thousand people. At first, the doctors didn't know what they were dealing with. Just that people came into the hospitals with severe burns on their bodies and in their lungs. It's only after they sent scrapings to the laboratory, that they discovered these were acid burns, the same kind of burns that would—notice, I don't say 'could'—be cause by a fire in that warehouse."

Effie Bloom, grinning from ear to ear, turned off the tape. "Isn't America wonderful? The land of opportunity. That was very professional, Theresa. I don't think you spoke over each other even once. It sounded like she was in the room."

"Thanks."

Muzzafer chose this moment to make his entrance. At first, he refused to listen to the tape, claiming his business was too important, then gave in when he saw the look of disappointment in their faces. He gave it close attention, smiling at the conclusion. "Very good news indeed. You were completely convincing, Theresa. But I'm going to have to postpone this business for a few days. This morning I saw a man I've been waiting a very long time to see. An Arab, Abou Farahad, who sells his friends to Jews. I followed him to his home and I have sentenced him to death. Johnny will come with me."

There was a lull while the Army digested Muzzafer's message, then Theresa reacted. "Is it worth stopping our project just to get revenge? Why can't we do the warehouse first, then take care of him?"

"I have known this man for twenty years, Theresa. We worked together several times, and for a year, when it seemed every country in the world was hunting us, we taught strategy at a training camp in Syria. Do you understand? We were 'drinking buddies' in a country where alcohol is forbidden. He knows how I think and I have to suppose that he's working with our enemies. I cannot risk leaving him alive. Besides, there are certain deeds, among Arabs, that demand revenge. When the Jews first invaded Lebanon, they could not tell who was a freedom fighter and who an ordinary Palestinian. Then, somehow, they captured Abou Farahad and he began to point out our strongholds, one by one. Hundreds were shot immediately by the Christian Phalangists. Thousands were taken prisoner and shipped to Israel, where the best still rot. His death will be very public and very painful, a lesson to all who consider betrayal."

Effie was first to speak, passing Theresa a quick glance before she began. "I want to go with you."

"No," Muzzafer returned. "There's no need for a crowd. The traitor lives in a quiet neighborhood."

"You're deliberately excluding me," Effie cried angrily. "And it's not fair. I've been a good soldier through every action. Didn't I, for Christ's sake, let those repulsive freaks use me for a fucking blow-up doll. Now you're pushing me away. Why? Because I'm a woman?" She looked across at Theresa once again.

Muzzafer, smiling, held out his hand, palms up. "Listen, Effie, do you really think any one of us, including me, can match the skills of Johnny Katanos in this kind of a situation? If you want, you and Theresa can place and set the timer when we do the warehouse. And afterwards I think we'll take a few weeks off. Separate for a little rest and recreation. It'll give us a chance to recover our sense of purpose."

Leonora the Sleuth! The Shadow! Flitting in and out of the darkness. Each doorway becomes an avenue to invisibility. Alleyways offer infinite opportunities. Showroom windows are polished mirrors reflecting Stanley Moodrow's every move. What could be easier than following a gigantic, clumsy cop as he stumbled through the teeming streets of New York City? And Stanley Moodrow, big as an elephant, would lead her directly to the American Red Army. No, better yet, she would snatch his line of investigation before he knew where it was going and arrest the Army herself.

Fantasies come easily at 5:30 in the morning. Standing before her mirror, Leonora figured the whole thing would be a breeze. Uncomfortable, perhaps, but more drudgery than complexity. She slipped the tails of a mauve, silk blouse under the waist of a white skirt, paused to admire herself, than added a small, white scarf in place of a tie. It was a chilly April morning and she grabbed a light wool topcoat, suitably dark in color, and headed out the door, two-inch heels clacking on the marble lobby floor.

For once, she was right on time and Moodrow left his house less than ten minutes after she arrived. Without giving his rearview mirror a second thought, he headed out to Queens Village and the 210th Precinct, which lay on the border of Nassau County. A narrow tongue of working middle-class homes and apartments, it projected, like a buffer, between the more affluent neighborhoods of Bayside and Little Neck to the north and Hollis and St. Albans, both black, to the south. Twenty years before, Queens Village, lying along three main thoroughfares, was filled with empty lots where kids played ball or parents picked blackberries in August. Now it was almost completely developed, though zoning laws kept new construction to five floors or less. The section that most interested Moodrow was a rambling neighborhood of attached, two-story garden apartments called Glen Oaks. Containing more than two thousand units, it was involved in a coop-conversion battle, with the owners wanting to sell and the tenants, who enjoyed the protection of the city's rent stabilization laws, wanting to stay. The result was anarchy. Speculators bought occupied apartments at half-price and took on the obligations of landlords in the hope that elderly tenants would die. Vacant apartments were quickly snatched up and a host of nationalities and races began to move into them. Bedsheet signs proclaiming the immovability of the Glen Oaks Tenants' Association hung from dozens of windows, while the youngsters asserted their own determination with cans of spray paint.

What better place to hide out? Glen Oaks lay on the north side of Union Turnpike, just east of Creedmoor State Hospital. As a six-lane street with timed signals, the Turnpike carried a lot of traffic between Manhattan and Long Island and naturally was lined with shops and restaurants. Moodrow did not have a close friend in this precinct, but he had checked in with the 210th's captain, Luis Alvarado, and gotten permission to hunt in his usual fashion. He parked just past the Cross Island Parkway and began to walk east, stopping in every small business to talk with the owner. In most cases, he was out in two or three minutes but occasionally he stayed to chat with old-timers, to get a feel for the area.

Despite all her fantasies, the instant Leonora Higgins stepped out of her car she felt as if she'd just jumped into the glare of powerful floodlights. Everything about her, from her skin to her shoes, seemed to be shouting "Look at me!" The people around here were resolutely working class and the only female in heels, besides herself, was a heavily made-up beautician with four-inch spikes on her way to work. Leonora looked like she should be hailing a cab on Madison Avenue, not a bus in Queens Village. And on top of that she had to stand around and pretend to be occupied while Moodrow gossiped with the local businessmen. Occupied with what? How long can a person stare at the display in a Woolworth window without being mistaken for an escapee from the mental hospital just down the street?

Then it turned hot. The sun pushed through the clouds and by ten it was seventy degrees. Leonora took off her coat and folded it over her arms. The feeling of relief was so strong she didn't even realize until 11 that her feet hurt. By noon, however, the pain was extraordinary. It came through in sharp jabs whenever her toes pressed together from walking. Sweating didn't help; it merely softened the skin and encouraged blisters. By three o'clock, Leonora had passed from very uncomfortable to absolutely desperate. Still, she never gave two thoughts to abandoning her aim. Instead she concentrated on the problem, turning over a number of possibilities before hitting on the solution.

Here she was, she reasoned, a black woman following a white, male cop through white neighborhoods. Even though Moodrow might never bother looking over his shoulder, she had already been noticed. That much was evident from the looks she was getting. They hadn't bothered her yet because she was expensively and conservatively dressed. They made her out for odd, but not threatening. Still, sooner or later she would be forced to explain her business because, except for workers, there simply were no blacks in this area. Perhaps, she thought, she should approach Moodrow directly. If she informed him that she was going to follow him whether he liked it or not, he might take her on as an unavoidable nuisance. But she knew it was his city and if he actively tried to lose her, if for instance he moved in with friends somewhere, she'd never pick up his trail.

Wistfully, she recalled a surveillance she and George Bradley had kept on a wealthy Arab businessman suspected of ties to the Palestinian cause. A small army of federal agents had placed bugs and homing devices in every room and car the man possessed. They could listen to him fart in the mornings, listen to him snore at night, listen to him huffing and blowing over the upstairs maid. They were invisible because they never left headquarters; now she had to find invisibility on the streets. She kept her eyes on the sidewalk, studying the people. There were black workers in many of the shops, but they were frozen in place and she had to be mobile. Then she heard someone yell and found the solution to her problems.

A meter maid in her brown uniform was being chewed out by a motorist to whom she'd just given a ticket. She stood there, very small and very black, while a full-grown white male screamed his rage into her face. Curiously, it was Moodrow who intervened, telling the man to move on. His bulk accepted no argument and the man drove away quickly, ticket in hand, but Higgins had her idea. She realized that the same woman had been working this same section of Union Turnpike all morning, driving back and forth to examine the cars at the parking meters. Leonora had a good friend, a supervisor, in the Traffic Department. If she could get a car and a uniform and most importantly, permission to conduct an investigation, she could follow Moodrow with almost no chance of being observed. Only then, with the situation in hand, did she retrace her steps to her car, stopping just once, at a small printing shop where she flashed her ID at the owner. The man had a bumper sticker in his window which read, "If Guns Are Outlawed, Only Outlaws Will Have Guns." The signs were put out by the National Rifle Association, a very conservative political organization, and Leonora hoped her FBI status would impress Mr. Rassenberger.

"How can I help you?" the man asked, his German origins quite evident. He was afraid that Higgins' visit had something to do with immigration.

"A cop stopped in here early this morning to talk to you." Leonora was overjoyed at this turn to her fortunes. Sweating foreign nationals was an art well known to her.

"Yes, I remember."

"He showed you something, some pictures, artist's renderings most likely."

"Why don't you go ask him?"

Drawing herself up to her full height, she looked Herr Rassenberger right in the eye. "I want to see those pictures. I want copies of them."

"I must repeat myself."

Leonora spoke from her feet, from the burning pain between her toes and under her heels. "Are you a citizen, Mr. Rassenberger?"

"In six months I will take the oath." He spoke uneasily. He definitely didn't like the idea of being bullied by a black female, but he came from a background of respect for authority. The whole thing was confusing him.

"Mr. Rassenberger, I'm not going to tell you why I don't want to ask Sergeant Moodrow directly. If you doubt that I'm FBI, get the number from the operator and call Queens Headquarters. They'll verify my identity. I'm asking for your cooperation, but if I don't get it, I'm going to see one of my friends over in Immigration and we're going to find something very bad in your file, maybe something about your father being a Nazi. Or better yet, a commie. Wouldn't that be ironic? I doubt that it would stick, but your citizenship might be held up for a couple of years. And don't ever think about getting any family across."

Despite her discomfort and her fatigue, Leonora Higgins, drawings tucked under her arm, was filled with confidence. She couldn't remember a time in the last six months when she'd felt this good. The same words kept running back and forth through her mind, a child's sing-song chant—I'm a cop. I'm a cop. I'm a cop.

19

Eleven on a rainy night—Moodrow had been home for more than an hour. A bowl of wonton soup and two yellow squares of egg foo yung lay untouched on the kitchen table. Though he'd been sitting on a straight-backed wooden chair for nearly an hour, eyes fixed on his dinner, his mind was far away. He was tired; his days began before 6, usually at some bus stop in Queens talking to every driver on the route or making the circuit of the token sellers and motormen in the subway stations. By 10, the stores would open and he could begin canvassing them. The routine continued through the day until too few stores were left open to make further effort profitable. Then back to the East Village, looking for the blinking red light that indicated messages on his phone machine. Inevitably, up until then, they had been from friends, other cops, relatives, but this night he caught a break.

"Yeah, hello. It's aaaaa 6 PM . . . on Wednesday. My name's Anthony Calella, 555-3841. I got a pizza place on Bay Parkway in Bensonhurst. On the border of Bay Ridge. Roma Pizza. Anyways, my cousin, Gina, showed me some drawins youse been showin' her at her grocery in Ridgewood. Youse rememba?'' Well I think I seen one of 'em. The Puerto Rican-lookin' broad. Like, I'm pretty sure, ya know? Anyways, if youse would like ta come here, youse could call me up on my home phone which is the one I give ya, 555-3841.''

Moodrow, his heart speeding up despite misgivings, dialed immediately.

"Hello." A male voice, thin and phlegmy, an obvious smoker.

"This is Sergeant Moodrow. Police. I'm callin Tony Calella."

"Yeah. Speakin'."

"You phoned me," Moodrow prompted. "You left a message on my machine."

"Right. Well, like I says, I seen that spic-lookin' broad. A real piece of ass in them tight spic pants they wear. Comes in a coupla times a week for a slice and a Coke. Hey, I wouldn't mind gettin' a slice myself. Know what I mean?"

"So you're pretty sure?"

"Looks just like the bitch."

"What hours you open?"

"Eleven till ten at night. She usually comes in the afternoon. Probly works around here. Youse don't see too many spic livin' in Bay Ridge. Not too many at all. When it gets dark in Bay Ridge, the darkies go home. Know what I mean?"

Moodrow assured him that he did understand. Bay Ridge and Bensonhurst had reputations as all-white neighborhoods determined to remain all-white. In a celebrated incident, a black subway motorman had been beaten to death for daring to enter a bagel shop at one in the morning. Could a dark-skinned Arab or a "Puerto Rican-looking" woman survive there? The chances that one member of the Army happened to work in Bay Ridge seemed unlikely. Still, the man was positive. Moodrow cursed inwardly. If this was an ordinary case, he would simply assign another detective to stake out the pizza parlor while he went about his business. Now he would have to do it himself. "Listen, I'd appreciate it if I could work inside your place. I don't care if you're making book or running numbers."

"Hey, wait a fuckin' minute." Tony protested his innocence. "I don't do nothin' like that."

"You telling me you never been in jail?" Moodrow followed a sudden intuition.

"Five years ago I come outta there. Jeez, gimme a break. Who's doin' a favor fa who?"

"You're doing the favor," Moodrow said quickly. "All I'm asking is to wait inside instead of on the street. The people I'm looking for don't have anything to do with you."

"Did I say youse couldn't come inside? Did I say fa even one second youse had ta stay out inna street?"

So the deal was struck and Moodrow would interrupt his schedule to spend a few days in Brooklyn. He got the address, thanked the man and hung up. For a few seconds he stared at his food, his fingers resting on the white plastic fork that came with the dinner. Then the fantasy clicked into place, without being summoned—like a video tape machine programmed to begin playing at a certain hour.

He had two of the terrorists, a female and a male, handcuffed, in a room. They asserted their rights vigorously, enthusiastically. Moodrow, expressionless, sat on a low couch and waited for them to realize that he wasn't "the cops" or "the Feds" or even "the pigs." It would take about twenty minutes of silence to destroy thoroughly all of their preconceived ideas of "cops" and getting busted. Then he would begin his interrogation.

At 2 AM on a Tuesday morning, Abou Farahad left the home of his new girlfriend, Sarah Markowitz, and stopped for just a moment at the top of her stoop to consider the prior day's activities. He began with his wife, Estella, and a furious argument with her two children huddled in a corner of the kitchen while he screamed her into submission. The Americans and the Israelis could provide him with citizenship and a new identity—Muhammad Massakan—but they could not erase his Arab belief in subservience as woman's proper role. Coming to America, the first thing he had looked for, finances being no problem, was a wife—vacuum cleaners and dirty laundry were also beneath the efforts of men—and he found a Panamanian with a shaky green card and no hope of citizenship. Estella Ruiz was a hard worker, and did all the housework in addition to her teller's duties at Citibank. Muhammad did not mind the children. He was accustomed to large families and cramped living space, but what he could not accept and what Estella could not control was a hot, Latin temperament. Whenever Muhammad had the urge to spend an expensive evening cruising for women at New York's network of singles' bars (as was his right according to his personal definition of marriage), she became enraged and had to be forced, sometimes physically, into submission. Muhammad figured she was getting off lucky. In his country, he would simply have taken another wife.

So off he went, while his wife calculated the economics of being thirty-five and single with two children. He headed for a bar, The Three Kings, on Second Avenue and 80th Street. At first glance, it might seem that 2 PM is an unusual time for girl-hunting, but the hardened veterans of the singles' scene would have to disagree. They, male or female, are not looking for relationships any stronger than those of two dogs stuck together on a street corner in the Bronx. At night, when the bars were crowded, Muhammad might have to go through a dozen approaches before finding a woman so desperately afraid she feared the end of loneliness more than loneliness itself. In the afternoon, however, all drinkers are serious.

Of course, Muhammad wasn't the only one who knew this, but he was sure his exotic good looks would give him an advantage in the eyes of the experienced New York woman. He was tall for an Arab and wiry-slender, with a strong nose and dark eyes. His skin was more yellow than brown, but not the pale ivory of the Chinese. It was closer to gold, almost burnished. His habit was to stand aloof at one end of the bar in his silk shirt and Italian flannel trousers until he perceived some definite encouragement from his target. He played the part of a Syrian businessman, a banker with plenty of dollars to invest in expensive foreplay. They ate it up—probably because they never gave two thoughts to anything beyond the evening's pleasure. But if they should propose something more permanent, Muhammad would reveal his transience. Sorry, but he was leaving the States in two days.

Proficiency of technique or not, when there is no action there is no action, and The Three Kings turned out to be a dud. He spent the better part of an hour gossiping with the bartender before hitting the streets, then hailed a cab and went over to the Metropolitan Museum of Art on 82nd and Fifth, arriving an hour and a half before closing time. His favorite play here was to cruise the Egyptian section, lecturing any young girl who cared to listen on the perfidy of the British colonialists who stole the highest art of the highest civilization ever to exist. Women were easy to approach in the museum, as if the hallowed halls of art erased the possibility of predation, but their very willingness made it impossible to cull out the amateurs, and Muhammad spent another wasted hour setting up Millicent Perkins, who suddenly discovered she had to meet the rest of her family at Henri Bendel's for one last shopping session before returning to Iowa.

By five o'clock, his ardor undiminished, Muhammad had made his way to the Bad Boy on Lexington Avenue. It was still too early for working singles, but there were some people around. The hunt for sex always made him restless, unable to sit quietly unless there was action. Fortunately, along with the stimulation of a White Russian, came Sarah Markowitz, short and tanned, sporting an obviously muscular body beneath a gray T-shirt and matching, tight sweatpants. She took the seat next to him, smiled a short, New York hostile smile and scanned his fingers for a wedding ring, a ring she hoped to find, a ring sure to make him leave in the morning. Though disappointed, she, as he'd hoped, considered him exotic enough to explore his potential for physical danger.

"I am Syrian," he began. "Muhammad Massakan."

"So?" Sarah sipped at her glass of red wine. In her experience, which was considerable, the over-violent tended to expose themselves right away if she came on tough.

"You are Jewish?" Muhammad smiled his own New York tough smile.

"Right. I'm Moshe Dayan's granddaughter. And you're Yasir Arafat with a nose job."

They laughed in spite of themselves, a laugh of recognition. It is New York's most special game and it echoes in the faces of every fashion model. In order to be really attractive, the female composes her face as if attraction was the furthest thought from her mind while simultaneously thrusting her barely covered body at the nearest desirable male. Some women never abandon the pose, though Sarah, having made up her mind about Muhammad Massakan, was about ready to exchange it for another favorite, what she called "being in lust."

After a few moments of banter, she stood up, excused herself, and took off for the bathroom, figuring to give the Arab a good look at the merchandise. Her body was round and her torso short, yet there was plenty of muscle. She could feel his eyes on her buttocks, on the way her sweatpants rode up between the cheeks of her ass. If he was still there when she came back, the pact would be made. She hoped he was big. Though she needed an all-night session, she didn't fear any lack of endurance; she would keep him aroused and in the morning she could go back to living her normal life.

The intensity with which they came together astonished both of them. Of course, there had been the usual touchings and rubbings as they climbed the stairs to Sarah's third-floor apartment. Sarah was cute in an almost English way, with a spray of freckles running across a small nose. Muhammad found her abdomen was as smooth and firm as he'd expected. But it wasn't her physical beauty that turned him on so strongly; it was the way she went after him, using his pleasure to her purposes. He interpreted her ardor as worship of his own body, especially the way she used her tongue, like a bitch licking her pup, to arouse him again and again. Sarah, however, was in lust, a condition which came over her several times each month and, if attended to promptly, vanished after a single night of sex. The men coming into bars like the Bad Boy were expected to perform. They asserted their abilities just by being there, and, much to Sarah's delight, Muhammad's advertising did not turn out to be false. They fucked for nearly six hours before Sarah fell asleep, the Arab's signal to leave.

So who could fault Muhammad Massakan for pausing to bathe in his own pride? He stood atop the three steps leading to the street and sucked in the night air. Now he could return to Estella fulfilled. If she smelled another woman on him, so much the better. His performance had filled him with assurance, but even so he looked both ways as he came down the steps. Caution is an obligatory quality for anyone operating on New York City streets in the early morning hours.

Standing next to the open door of a half-ton Chevy van parked at the curb, Johnny Katanos watched Muhammad's performance curiously. The irony of the fall coming to Mr. Massakan did not escape him. The street was deserted, yet well-lighted by amber streetlamps. The bar on the corner of Amsterdam Avenue was still going and its neon flashed a welcome. Impulsively, Muhammad decided to have one final drink before returning home and he headed right past Johnny Katanos, making a simple mistake, common to many New Yorkers, which contributed strongly to the series of events leading to the taking of his life. The face by the van was white. If it had been black or Spanish, Muhammad might have crossed the street or walked closer to the buildings. As it was, he passed within six feet of a radiant Johnny Katanos who was on him like a lizard on a cockroach. Muhammad heard the assault more than he actually saw it. Just the blur of a figure in dark clothes and a sudden, sickening crunch as the lead ball in the bottom of Johnny's blackjack crashed into his skull.

While he was unconscious, he dreamed of Sarah Markowitz, of the two of them rolling in sweat-soaked sheets on her bed, each trying to get on top. It was so wonderful; he thought it might go on forever, but then felt himself pulled away from her, realizing that the voice speaking to him wasn't hers, wasn't, in fact, even speaking English.

"Welcome to your death, Jew-dog," Muzzafer said in Arabic. "Wake up, betrayer of your people." He shook Muhammad roughly. "Ahhhh, eyes open at last. Have the Jews taken good care of you in the years since we met? You seem well-fed, perhaps just a little soft around the middle."

"No, please," Muhammad cried, suddenly more awake than he'd ever been in his life, despite the insistent pounding in his skull and the sticky feel of dried blood in his hair and on his neck.

"This softness," Muzzafer continued, "see what it has done to you? It has made you sell your friends so you can come to America and fuck Jews. Perhaps I can help you to get rid of it." He held up a long carving knife for his captive to inspect.

The sight of the blade made Muhammad try to sit bolt upright. It was only then that he realized his hands and ankles were cuffed behind his back. He was physically helpless.

Smiling, Muzzafer brought the tip of the blade slicing down the length of his captive's upper arm, causing the Arab to moan at the sight of the blood. Muhammad had a brief fantasy of screaming for help, but his mouth was stuffed with a rag before he could even finish it.

"Do you know . . ." Muzzafer began again.

"Speak English." Johnny's voice was husky with emotion. He was driving west toward the Henry Hudson Parkway and felt too far from the action as it was. If they spoke another language, he would be left out altogether.

Muzzafer switched languages without switching tone. "When the Jews invaded Lebanon, they came straight to the home of your brothers, of the one who fought alongside you, and killed them. Yes. They pulled them out of their homes and shot them. How did they know which house held freedom fighters and which held ordinary workers? Because you told them." Once again he drew the tip of the knifeblade across Muhammad's flesh, this time down his cheek, hard enough so the tip penetrated into his mouth leaving a gaping wound. "Did the Jews hurt you like I'm hurting you? Did they make you tell them everything about your brothers? Or perhaps you sought them out and made a deal. You have very nice clothes, my friend. I cannot afford such clothes." Muzzafer raised the knife high into the air, so filled with righteousness he would end it on the spot, but he felt the firm pressure of Katanos' grip on his shoulder.

"Don't kill him yet," the Greek said. "I want to do it like we planned."

It was not a pleasant ride for Muhammad Massakan, formerly Abou Farahad, although the morning air was quite warm for mid-April. Johnny drove the van due north on the Parkway to the 155th Street Exit, then turned east, across northern Manhattan to the 155th Street Bridge and the South Bronx to Mott Haven and a level of poverty almost incomprehensible to ordinary Americans, despite the television documentaries and tons of newsprint. In the daylight, it was just possible to see the beginning of a turnaround—many of the burnt-out tenements had been knocked down and the rubble removed so the neighborhood presented the eyes with perspectives unusual in cities, odd configurations of near and far. At night, however, at three o'clock in the morning, it presented nothing but fear. The custom was to break the streetlamps on the day they were repaired. Not that the avenues were deserted. Far from it. It was just that nobody walked alone. Men and women, radios blaring the hottest salsa, huddled in knots, in doorways or alleys—away from even the light of passing automobiles.

Johnny Katanos drove quickly through the desolation, looking neither right nor left. It was their neighborhood and he was just visiting. He took 161st Street straight across to Melrose, then turned south toward St. Mary's Park, a small patch of darkness within darkness at 144th Street. The park, however, was not his objective. Across from it, on St. Ann's Avenue, there remained the first six floors of the Mott Haven Houses, one of the showier examples of the area's failures. In 1975, Jimmy Carter stopped in the South Bronx on his way to the presidency. He made promises that neither he nor the local politicians were prepared to keep. Yet they did get something moving. Money was raised and an enormous, state of-the-art housing project was placed under construction. By this time, however, it was 1979 and Jimmy Carter's fortunes were already on the wane. Somehow, the funds for the Mott Haven Houses were buried in the Reagan landslide. The skeleton that remained was completely surrounded by an eight-foot plywood fence; it guaranteed privacy if the neighborhood animals could be kept at bay.

The method for accomplishing that formidable task was actually quite simple. They would be there for no more than ten minutes, a black van without side or rear windows, bearing commercial plates. Johnny Katanos pulled up to one of the many breaks in the fence surrounding the project, walked to the side of the van, and opened the cargo door. All the while, quite openly, he held a small Israeli automatic rifle across his chest. Both he and Muzzafer could feel the eyes around them, sense the predators moving one step closer, considering the possibilities. But the weapon made it clear that there was no profit to be made from these people, no easy score. The two men pulled Muhammad Massakan out of the van by his feet and dragged him quickly through the fence and into the darkness. Their intention was to be finished before the crazies asserted some perverted version of neighborhood pride and attacked as a matter of principle.

Once inside, Johnny Katanos performed the trickiest part of the operation. They needed to uncuff the traitor and they wanted him to be helpless, but alive. Many methods had been discussed. They had drugs to put him to sleep, but nothing to wake him up before the effects of the drugs wore off. Muzzafer had suggested a second tap on the head with the blackjack, but Johnny had opted for a more personal method. As they'd decided, he put his upper arm across the nose and mouth of Muhammad Massakan and drew it tightly into his own chest, holding it there until the Arab's body went slack.

They worked quickly. Muzzafer turned to remove the handcuffs while Johnny Katanos retrieved the four-pound hammer and the heavy, galvanized spikes from Muzzafer's backpack. The hands were easy, the soft tissue parting and the bones snapping at the first stroke of the hammer. The feet, crossed at the ankles, were another problem. They took turns working at it, but the nails were too short and no matter how hard they hit them, would not penetrate both flesh and wood. So they settled for doing the feet individually. Muzzafer had wanted him to be crucified in the same position as the most famous of all Jews, but the papers would get the idea despite the improvisation.

They finished the crucifixion in nine minutes. Muhammad was awake by this time, of course, and in very great pain. Muzzafer wanted to say something more to him, but could think of nothing. He was very excited; he could feel the heat coming from his lover. If only there was time, they would couple like demons before the devil's throne. But they had to finish their business and what's more, could not chance the possibility that help would come before their enemy died. They must kill him. Muzzafer raised the knife, but was again held back by Johnny Katanos.

"No, no," the Greek whispered. Muzzafer noted that his eyes seemed to glow—like those of an animal caught in a car's headlights. "We can afford a few more minutes. Let's do it right."

He stepped up close and drove his fist into Muhammad's ribs, then stepped back, offering his partner a turn. Muzzafer, in spite of everything he knew about revolution and discipline and putting goals ahead of desire, did not hesitate. Smiling a child's smile of delight, he moved forward and began driving his fists into the flesh of Muhammad Massakan.

20

Captain Allen Epstein, in the waiting room of Deputy Inspector Seamus Flynn at One Police Plaza, felt like a cornered rat. Worse than a rat, for he could not even turn to make a final stand. There was no one to turn against.

He'd been taking the attitude that his men came first for so long, he couldn't begin to accept what he was about to do. And worst of all, he didn't know if he was doing it because he sincerely believed Moodrow to be wrong (which he did) or because he was a coward and wanted to cover his own ass. Naturally, Flynn kept him waiting, standard procedure for cops visiting One Police Plaza, but it was torture for Epstein. A small voice reminded him that it was not too late to leave—Flynn would be mad, but would accept some excuse about an emergency at the precinct. If he stayed, they would crucify Moodrow just as surely as that Arab they'd found the day before in the Bronx.

His agitation increased minute by minute until he desperately wanted to stand up and pace the floor. All the while, one question continued to rumble through his mind—would he be here if there was no chance the department could find out that he knew about Moodrow's activities?

"All right, Captain, you can go in now." A sergeant, young and very male, gestured toward the door. If Epstein had been one rank higher, he would have opened it for him.

"How are you, Allen," Flynn said, as Epstein stepped into the room. He nodded toward a chair, waited just a second to show that he wasn't entirely an ogre, then launched into his standard "dealing with subordinates" speech. "I'm unbelievably busy, Allen. Sorry," he ran his fingers over his hair, patted it gently, "but this has got to be quick."

Epstein tossed the pictures onto Flynn's desk. "Moodrow's handing these out. Canvassing. So far, only in Queens, but I don't know his plans."

Flynn stared at the sketches for a moment, before speaking. "The source?" he demanded.

"The only man who survived the Chadwick massacre."

A look of ultimate disgust passed over Flynn's face. Holding up the pictures he growled, "Do you mean to tell me that you don't have any legitimate reason to associate these people with the American Red Army? I can't believe you came to me with this crap. Tell me, Allen, did we ever question the possibility of apprehending the criminals who murdered Mr. Chadwick? But that, as we noted at the time, is a problem for a precinct leader, often called a captain, not a deputy inspector."

Epstein returned Flynn's gaze, advertising his determination. "I don't think he's reporting to Higgins. I think he's completely on his own."

"Did you call the bureau to ask if he was reporting?"

"For Christ's sake, Inspector, you think I'd go outside the department without talking to you first?"

Flynn, his loyalty challenged, had only a single response open to him. "Of course, you've done the right thing, Captain." He nodded enthusiastically. "One little question, though—has anyone at the FBI complained about Moodrow's lack of diligence?"

"Not to me."

"Then why do *you* want to make a big deal out of it?"

"Suppose the gang that murdered Chadwick is part of the American Red Army? If we put more people on it, we might . . ."

"Hold it, Captain. I've already passed a report on the Chadwick case to the mayor's task force. If they're interested, they're keeping it to themselves. From where I sit, it's the same with Agent Higgins and her people. If they really expected anything to come from Moodrow's activities, they'd be screaming their heads off. Why not let sleeping dogs lie?"

Epstein, his anger tempered by the switch he was about to pull on his superior, leaned forward. "I assume that means you do not want me to go to Bradley with this information."

To his credit, Seamus Flynn did not fail to hear the trap when it sprung. Now it would hang on his ass; he was taking responsibility for a crazy cop on a personal hunt. He sat back in his chair, considered the question for half a minute and realized there was only one move on the board.

"Let's call Bradley and let him decide," he said quickly. He wasn't at all embarrassed to be taken for a coward. "Perhaps you can run these out to him and see what he wants to do."

For George Bradley, FBI, Deputy Inspector Seamus Flynn's morning phone call came as a pleasant interlude in what he hoped would be an extremely significant day. Hassan Fakhr had agreed to a meeting.

"You are a very smart man, Agent Bradley," he'd said. "That's why I'm giving you the American Red Army on a platter. Naturally, the price is slightly more than thirty pieces of silver, but we can chalk it up to nineteen hundred years of inflation."

"Very witty. I just hope you're smart enough not to ask for the treasury," Bradley had answered.

"Try to see it from my point of view, George. Here I am shitting on everything I hold sacred, betraying every one of my living friends. And the nature of my treachery is so all-encompassing that it will force me to take up an entirely new identity. In effect I am to be reborn into any life I want." Hassan's voice was still full of good humor. "Now, I hope you have a portable telephone in the office."

"I have one."

"Get in your car and drive down Queens Boulevard. I'll call you at 4 PM and give you an exact meeting place. Keep this in mind, George—it's going to take at least a week to get the material, even if we can come to terms. If someone on your end betrays me, you might not get another chance at the Army for months. No one can tap a portable phone, so if you're not personally bugged, I won't be caught. Get it, George?''

Bradley had been beside himself with excitement, convinced at last that a nameless, wiseguy Arab was going to give him the American Red Army. Which explains why he suddenly found it important to assert control. "That's absolutely right," he said. "Your freedom depends entirely on me.''

So Flynn's call was a welcome diversion, an interlude to cut the tension. Bradley had insisted on seeing Epstein immediately, much to Epstein's chagrin. New York police captains were not accustomed to being summoned by federal agents. But he went, nonetheless, and without Hassan Fakhr's ability to laugh at his predicament. The best he could hope for, now, was that Moodrow's quest would prove fruitless, that his friend would look like a fool.

Bradley, on the other hand, found Epstein's visit the answer to a knotty problem. Leonora Higgins had been away from her office for nearly a week. When the final report was written, what could he say about her contribution? No matter how innocuous the information, Flynn's call and Epstein's interview constituted ample justification for Higgins' assignment to Stanley Moodrow.

Nevertheless, Bradley took Allen Epstein through his story in great detail, listening, as had Flynn, for anything new. Unlike Flynn, however, Bradley was not so quick to fault the captain. He studied the pictures very carefully, as if he could draw the American Red Army off the pages, then turned back to Epstein. "Tell me," he said mildly, "how long have you been a cop?''

"Thirty-three years," Epstein muttered. He found it extremely difficult to be in the same room with the FBI agent.

"Then why do you come to me with this crap?" He waved the pictures in Epstein's face. "If this was all you had, you would not be sitting in that chair. You must have a legitimate reason for your suspicions and I think I should hear it. If you didn't intend to share your information, why go to Flynn in the first place?''

Epstein cleared his throat. He'd been afraid of this question from the beginning. "I must have had two hundred detectives working under me since I became captain and I never had one better at finding the shortest route to an arrest than Moodrow. In all the time I've known him, he never once went on a wild goose chase."

"Maybe he's in so much pain, he's lost his judgment. It wouldn't be the first time."

"And what if he's got something he isn't telling us?"

"If he's holding back information that could lead us to these terrorists," Bradley said, smiling, "I'll bury him so deep he'll think the sky fell on him."

It was a dismissal, a flip, final word which Epstein refused to accept. "I can't seem to convince anyone that I know how Moodrow thinks. Maybe it's better that way. But if it was up to me, I'd put those faces on every television set in New York." He stopped abruptly. Now that he had put it squarely, he felt more at ease. It wasn't up to him anymore.

Bradley, by way of an answer, held up the likeness of Johnny Katanos so both could see it. "The only thing we know about this person is that he was a friend of a boy named Enrique Hentados. Everything else is speculation. *Everything*. If you put his face on television and even hint that he's some kind of terrorist, and he turns out to be an ordinary citizen, his lawyer's going to retire on ten percent of the settlement. The newspapers already call us a gang of witch hunters. What do you think they'd say if we set the whole city hunting some poor truck driver from Queens?"

By the time Allen Epstein made his obligatory visit to Moodrow's apartment (a visit he'd known he would make even before the day began), it was nine o'clock and he was very drunk. On the way he cursed the stairwell, his own legs, the FBI, Seamus Flynn, and the entire 203rd Precinct so loudly that Moodrow was waiting, door open, before he reached the third-floor landing.

"Guess what, asshole," Epstein shouted. "I just sold your butt to Flynn and the Feds." He broke into a malicious laugh. "And I don't give two shits about it."

Moodrow, who was also drinking that night, was well prepared for this turn of events. He'd been drinking to drown the effects of a ten-hour shift in a Bay Ridge pizza joint, ten hours of tossing dough and spreading sauce while a thoroughly amused Anthony Calella cracked jokes at his ineptitude.

"Come in, Captain," he said formally.

"Thass right." Epstein stumbled into the room and collapsed on the couch. "Sold ya mutha-fuckin' ass to anyone willing to buy." He paused a moment, then turned his eyes up to meet Moodrow's. "But guess what again, Stanley? They ain't buyin'. They don't give a shit. Just another dopey cop."

Moodrow digested the information passively. The truth of it was that he didn't care a damn for what any of them did; for Stanley Moodrow there was no "afterwards." His post-Army future was as uncertain as that of a blind man sleepwalking on the edge of a cliff. Whatever came would find him utterly unprepared.

Nevertheless, his captain needing cheering. He said evenly, "I understand what you did. Look at the bright side. They're not going to do anything and you got your ass covered. What could be better?"

"Oh yeah," Epstein demanded, pointing to the likenesses of Effie, Theresa, and John pinned to the wall. "I know these assholes are the Army. I know this, so don't bullshit me. You're playing a game with the whole goddamn city. And it ain't the right thing."

Moodrow shrugged his shoulders. "Nobody wants it, whether it's true or not. So why get ya balls in an uproar? How 'bout a drink?"

Epstein sank back into the chair. "Goddamn right."

Moodrow went for another glass, filling it halfway with Caulfield's Wild Turkey Bourbon before returning to the living room.

"What the fuck is this shit?" Epstein cried. He looked around wildly for a moment, then fell back. "You really drink this stuff?" he asked in a much quieter voice.

"Listen, Captain, you want I should call Alma and tell her you're gonna stay over?"

Instead of answering, Epstein began to cry in that gross, slobbering way common to men who do not ordinarily get drunk. "I sold out my friend,'' he moaned. ''Sold him out to the cocksuckers. The pencil pushers.''

''I'll call Alma.'' Moodrow went to the bedroom phone and made the call to an unsurprised Alma Epstein.

''Take good care of him, Stanley,'' she said before falling back to sleep.

''I will,'' Moodrow said into a dead phone. He was accustomed to housing local cops too drunk to make their way back to surburbia and had no objection to Epstein's presence. In a way, it eased his obsession with Rita's killers. As the days passed, he was becoming more and more depressed. What if he failed? What if someone else captured them? Or if they were never captured? Only the fantasy, now summoned whenever he was alone, kept him from total immobility. As for Flynn and the FBI—his contempt for them was what had prevented him from discovering Leonora Higgins on that first day in Queens Village.

''Fuck them bastards, Stanley,'' Epstein said as soon as the cop returned. ''There's only one way I can see to solve these crimes. And I'm gonna give it to you on a platter. I never told ya this, but my sister married a Greek. Believe that? A fucking Greek.'' He grinned broadly. ''Disgrace of both families. For years, nobody mentioned their names on either side. Then they had babies and you know how Jewish women get. Can you keep a grandmother from her grandchild? So everybody made up.

''That was twenty-five years ago. Now the bastard's partners in a big diner on Metropolitan Avenue by 69th Street. That's the last stop on the M line.''

''Yeah, I know.'' It was to Moodrow's credit that he did not automatically disregard the random piece of information Epstein, drunk and remorseful, handed him. Instead, he did the prudent thing, performing the act of a slow, thorough clerk in an information warehouse. He went to his notes, remembering how carefully he'd traced the route of the M Train through Ridgewood. For him, the geography of most of Queens had been laid out, like a street map, in small, brightly covered notebooks: Queens Boulevard; Grand Avenue; Metropolitan Avenue; the M Train. The list went on and on.

He'd ridden the M back and forth from Seneca Avenue to Metropolitan, interviewing every motorman he could find. He'd walked the streets at each stop, talking to shopowners. Nevertheless, by his own comments, he did not consider the area thoroughly canvassed. Too many uninterested people, too many stores where the owner wasn't around. His entry under the Metropolitan Diner illustrated the problem. "Moron cunt at the cash register," it read, "knows nothing."

"What's your brother-in-law's name?" Moodrow asked.

"George Halulakis. If you can believe that."

"What shift does he cover?"

"Days. Eight to eight."

Dutifully, laboriously, Moodrow copied the information into his notebook.

Outside of Boston, the pizza business in New York has no parallel anywhere in the country. The telephone directory in Queens, for instance, lists 287 pizza parlors. For the most part they are narrow storefronts worked by a single Italian family. During the day they cater to street trade, especially school kids, selling pizza by the slice as well as Italian heroes and a few pasta dishes. At night, they sell whole pizzas, usually offering a delivery service to housewives too tired to cook. The quality is astonishingly good and visitors fortunate enough to become accustomed to this quality never return to Pizza Hut.

The hours, however, are long and monotonous. Thick loaves of dough are laboriously turned on the wrist until thin enough to spread on a large pie pan. Then sauce and cheese are added and the concoction baked in a special oven for about fifteen minutes. The good chefs work close to the front windows, tossing the spinning dough high in the air to attract the attention of passersby. Moodrow, on the other hand, could not seem to manage even the simplest maneuver and each attempt, much to the amusement of Tony Calella, resulted in strings of dough hanging from his hands to the floor.

"Hey, Salvatore," Calella called. "Maybe youse oughta try Chinese." Salvatore Calella, cousin from Baltimore, was the name and identity agreed upon by Moodrow and Calella. Curiously, although Moodrow was obviously neither Italian nor pizza chef, customers in the close-knit neighborhood of Bay Ridge took him for a fugitive, not a cop.

So Moodrow's day went slowly, uncomfortably, though it was far less boring than sitting outside. Leonora Higgins, who was in fact sitting outside—sitting in a brown Plymouth Reliant with TRAFFIC stenciled across the front doors—would have agreed completely, for in addition to the boredom, she had another more pressing problem. As any cop will tell you, no ordinary human being can pass twelve hours without urinating. Male cops carry bottles just for this purpose. Females, however, are at a terrible disadvantage. By noon, Leonora was uncomfortable. By 2, she was in pain and having flashbacks to her first day trailing Moodrow. But she understood that Moodrow would not be on a stakeout without good reason, that someone must have made an identification from those pictures. For all she knew, the deal might come to a head at any moment. A good cop never left the scene of a stakeout, but good cops worked in pairs and she was alone.

Fortunately for Agent Higgins, the situation resolved itself late in the afternoon. Moodrow, assigned to tossing already cooked slices into the oven for reheating, was in a foul mood—his head ached so bad he was afraid to blow his nose. And Tony Calella, evening up for Moodrow's discovery of his criminal past, stayed on his case, ridiculing him, much to the amusement of the patrons, at every opportunity.

By 4 PM, Moodrow had had enough. He tapped Anthony Calella on the shoulder and muttered, "We better go in the kitchen and have a fuckin' talk."

"Whatsa matter, Salvatore, youse ain't happy in my employ?"

Moodrow, mad as he could get, nonetheless whispered his response so that no one could overhear. "Check this out, wop. Not only have I had enough of your big mouth, but I'm right now only one inch away from pullin' your fucking head off your shoulders. Think I'm kidding?"

"No, no. Youse ain't kiddin', OK?" Calella, looking up into Moodrow's eyes, caught a sudden glimpse of the insanity behind the cop's calm exterior. The effect was chilling and might have had a permanent effect on their relationship. However, just at that moment, and most fortunately for Mr. Calella, a plump, dark, Puerto Rican girl who in no way resembled the wiry Theresa Aviles, walked through the door. "There she is, Sarge. I mean Salvatore. There's the bitch."

Moodrow, after one glance, removed his long white apron and handed it to Calella. His anger dropped off with the apron and was replaced by darkest gloom. It was only then he realized how much he'd been hoping, despite his instincts. He turned on his heel without another word and headed home.

Trailing several car lengths behind, a desperately squeezing Leonora Higgins, much to her credit, followed Moodrow's Buick all the way to the Lower East Side before making a beeline to a coffee shop on 10th Street and Second Avenue. It was still early and she realized the stakeout had failed. Tomorrow, however, would be another day, a more active one, hopefully. At least Bradley had stopped bothering her, though she had no idea why.

In contrast, Moodrow was resisting the aftereffects of the failure as best he could. Stubbornly, in spite of a parade of Ritas floating through his consciousness, he pulled his mind back to his fantasy. He had captured two members of the American Red Army and was about to interrogate them. Slowly, deliberately fixing each image, he ran through the possibilities.

The dream got him into his apartment. Closing the door behind him, he was suddenly aware of the maps on the walls, the stacks of carefully labeled notebooks. He understood that he was buying time the way a falling man clutches at empty air on his way to Earth, but the alternative, to crash immediately, was too frightening. He went directly to the map and began to outline a campaign in central Queens, a campaign beginning on Woodhaven Boulevard at the Long Island Expressway and proceeding south through Ozone Park and Howard Beach to Far Rockaway. A campaign to fill tomorrow.

21

The last weekend of April saw the onset of the coming summer's first heat wave, as low pressure spread upward from the Carolinas to transform the isle of Manhattan into an enormous concrete greenhouse. Flags hung limply from their poles, mimicking the droopy bodies of New Yorkers who fumbled hastily with the winter coverings on their air conditioners. Auto repair shops running specials on cooling system tune-ups (specials which meant, in many cases, a fifty-percent price increase) were doing banner business all through the five boroughs. Only the homeless and the derelicts, free of winter's perils for another nine months, felt much like celebrating and the various forms of city entertainment—movies, restaurants, concert halls—were virtually deserted.

It was, however, perfect weather for the aims of the American Red Army, as a ridge of cold air, forcing itself above the warmer air below, pressed down on New York City. The smoke from the Con Edison stacks on the East River, instead of rising in a cloud, lay in straight lines, like the white contrails of a jet plane, below the tops of the skyscrapers. Driving slowly along Kent Avenue by the old Schaefer Brewery, with the East River and Manhattan within sight, both Muzzafer and Johnny Katanos were aware that the time was getting close. It was the same feeling they'd had before the explosion at Herald Square, only now they were much more confident. No law enforcement agency was willing even to hint that it was close to capturing the notorious American Red Army, and agency heads routinely cancelled press conferences and evaded reporters in order to avoid taking the blame for what all considered to be a collective failure.

"Did you see the *Times* this morning?" Muzzafer asked, then went on without waiting for an answer. "The House Committee on Internal Subversion announced that we're Puerto Rican Terrorists in the employ of Fidel Castro. They've linked us with cocaine and Mexican heroin. That's how we get our money. According to Representative Buckingham of Alabama, we fly into New York, first class, do a project, then sneak back to the jungles of Brazil. Can you believe that?"

"He's gotta say something," Johnny returned evenly. "And it wouldn't surprise me if those Alabama rednecks ate it up. They probably live for that shit. Lay around in the fucking woods, drink home brew and talk about Puerto Ricans flying in from Brazil." He slowed for a red light, then turned to face Muzzafer. "That's the worst that can happen to a human being," he said, seriously. "A life in the backwoods, stoned out of your mind. Start out sharp and then lose it, piece by fucking piece. Better not to have a life at all."

The light changed and Johnny threw the Toyota into first, then eased off the clutch. This was their final reconnaissance and both he and Muzzafer felt entirely at ease. "Take a look across the river. See the smoke from the 14th Street Con Ed station? That's how you can tell which way the wind is blowing. What little wind there is."

The smoke, which seemed at first glance to lay motionless, was actually drifting south and east, slowly crossing the river.

"You know where that puts the smoke from our fire?" Johnny asked playfully. "Have you been studying your geography?"

Muzzafer smiled, a street map open on his lap. "Right down Lee Avenue into Williamsburg," he answered. "Right into the neighborhood where we screwed up with Janey's bomb. I admit I'd rather get Manhattan, but this isn't going to be bad at all."

"It's theme terrorism." Johnny laughed silently. "We're always screaming about the Jews and now we'll give 'em a special treat. It's so humid, the smoke won't drift more than a half mile before it just lays on top of the houses. Killing whatever's inside. Oil sludge burns dirty and the smoke it gives off'll be black and stink of petroleum. When the people downwind start dropping, the whole borough's gonna panic."

They drove down North 5th Street, as they had half a dozen times in the past two weeks. The street was deserted and Muzzafer nodded with satisfaction. "I wish it was tonight. If the weather doesn't hold out until Tuesday, we may have to wait for weeks."

At a group meeting the previous night, Effie had announced the results of her search for an easily hijacked gasoline tanker. Muzzafer, accustomed to memorizing oral reports—of necessity, almost nothing he did could be written down—remembered her strong voice clearly: "There's a large trucking operation on Berry Street. Petroleum Transporters. They're independents who haul fuel oil and gasoline for the big oil companies. They load at the depots, then deliver to homes and gas stations. Truck number 412 fills up with gasoline at the Texaco terminal just off Kent Avenue, by the river, about 6 PM and delivers out to Long Island. After he finishes loading, the driver takes his rig to the Navy Diner, also on Kent Avenue and about eight blocks from the warehouse, where he has dinner. The truck is a diesel and he leaves it running at the curb while he eats. This is a common practice, because diesel engines are often hard to start. It would be no trouble to hijack either him or his truck. But there is a problem. The truck only works four nights a week. Tuesday through Friday. Most likely the guy picks up at some other terminal on Mondays or he works ten-hour shifts, but I haven't seen his truck on a Monday yet."

Johnny made a left onto Flushing Avenue and they drove past the old Brooklyn Navy Yard into Fort Greene, a neighborhood of once magnificent brownstone mansions sandwiched between large housing projects. The area was virtually all black and the hot weather, in stark contrast to deserted, industrial Greenpoint, had brought the citizens out on the streets. "I have a confession to make," Johnny said playfully. "You in a mood for a confession?"

Muzzafer looked over, but Johnny continued before he had a chance to respond. "Last night, after the meeting, I couldn't sleep and I went back to the warehouse for one last look."

"You're not supposed to do these things on your own," Muzzafer said, mildly. At this point he trusted Katanos' instincts as much as his own training. "You're supposed to follow orders."

"Just like you're *supposed* to say that I'm *supposed* to follow orders?"

"What if you were caught inside? Like a common burglar? It would be the end of the project. At the least."

Johnny shrugged. "I wanted to find out exactly what was in there. The other times I ran through it quick because you were always waiting to pick me up. Last night I was more careful. Man, it's amazing what those fuckers did to that building. They got it filled with fifty-five gallon drums, all stacked on pallets. Thousands of them. Two to a pallet, five pallets high. Like an army in formation. The warehouse is two hundred by two hundred feet and there's just enough room to move a forklift between walls of these pallets. I mean it's hard to figure exactly, but a fifty-five gallon drum is only four feet high and the fucking building is really two gigantic open rooms. I have to believe they got about ten thousand drums in there and that, my friend, multiplies out to more than half a million gallons of fluid." He paused a moment, cutting around a double-parked van. "Now here's the kicker. There's drums marked 'Radioactive Waste' against the back wall. I think they're filled with something solid. At least, when I hit one with the side of my hand it didn't make that sound that liquid makes. And I'm not sure how many there are because I couldn't get behind them to see if they ran all the way to the wall, but I promise you this, they're gonna remember us in Mecca. This whole goddamn borough's gonna glow in the dark."

Grinning, Johnny slowed for a red light, turning to face his companion. "But for now, whattaya say we cut across the Manhattan Bridge and eat our way through Chinatown? I'm fucking starved."

The light changed to green and Johnny swung over toward Tillary Street and the Manhattan Bridge, waiting until Muzzafer relaxed before he spoke again. "Speaking of revolutionary aims, the other night, when you told Effie that she and Theresa could go inside and set the detonator, I took it to mean that you don't expect them to come back out?"

"We can't leave them here," Muzzafer said. "They won't last two weeks without us."

"I never thought they would."

Muzzafer smiled and when he spoke, his voice was much softer. "What we've done together? It's more then anyone who came before us. I don't know how far we can take it and I don't intend to stop until I find out." He began to fold the map "Which leaves us with only one question: What do we do about Jane Mathews?"

"Who?" Johnny asked, pulling onto the bridge.

As children and young adults, we pass over so many crossroads, so many points of choice, that we tend to believe opportunities for change will continue to present themselves throughout our lives. Possibilities, once rejected, are not gone forever, but will reappear in new guise again and again. Later on, in middle age, we suddenly realize that dreams left behind cannot be reclaimed. Locked in by money (or the lack of it), by culture and family, by the hopefully slow degeneration of the human machine, most of us make a deal with life: We settle back into whatever circumstances come our way and hope for a swift, painless death.

Hassan Fakhr, on the other hand, was a child of turmoil; he'd never been trapped in the kind of rut awaiting those born into more stable cultures. And thus he longed for precisely that prison which so terrifies those in the grip of mid-life crisis. He'd weighed every possibility before contacting George Bradley and he understood that to be discovered before consummating the deal would land him in the same circumstance as Abou Farahad. Still, he would not simply walk into FBI headquarters and demand protection. Without a heavy cash payoff at the end of the road, he and his new identity would end up scrubbing pots in Peoria, a fate worse than crucifixion for the ebullient terrorist.

But the risks were not great. The world of Arab terrorism, while state-sponsored, was loosely organized and lacked both sophisticated spying devices and the technicians to operate them. Meeting Bradley would seal the bargain, in any event. He knew he would be identified and he knew the Americans were desperate enough to pay a large sum for the American Red Army. He would collect that sum, retire to a slow southern community and enjoy tranquility for the first time in his life.

They met in a supermarket parking lot in Woodside, Queens, and began to spar. How much were the Americans willing to pay? What proof did Bradley have that he could deliver what he promised? Would the FBI guarantee admission to the witness protection program?

"Do you think I don't know that I will be identified? That you are, in spite of my warnings, photographing me at this very moment?" Hassan smiled his fattest fat, jolly smile.

"Then you know that I have you," Bradley returned evenly.

"Oh, was it me you were after? I thought it was Muzzafer you wanted."

"You admit that Muzzafer is behind these attacks?"

"Surely. I admit it. How does this help you?"

They finally agreed to the sum of $200,000, plus all posted rewards, with $10,000 up front, a total which relaxed Hassan immensely. So much so that he failed to respond to Bradley's prophecies of what would happen if he failed to keep his end of the deal. He was as smugly self-confident as he'd ever been in his life and felt entirely superior to the obviously harried FBI agent. It was just at the peak, as Hassan bathed in his own invulnerability, that Bradley pulled the proverbial rabbit out of his briefcase. Passing the sketches across the front seat of his Plymouth, he asked, "Ever see these before?"

As soon as Hassan glimpsed the first drawing, that of Effie Bloom, he had a quick vision of himself nailed to a fence in the Bronx. The image paralyzed him, which was just as well, for had he appeared to be startled, Bradley would not have let him off so easily.

"Well," Bradley repeated.

Somehow, dimly, a crucial idea began to form in Hassan's mind. If Bradley was sure of the identities of the faces he presented, why would he be asking Hassan for confirmation? If he wasn't sure, rec-ognition could be denied. But how could the Arab then return, one week later, with the same photos? He decided to stall long enough for his fear to dissolve. "If you know so much about this, why do you come to me? Do Americans like to give away their money?"

Bradley phrased his reply carefully, so as not to affront the man he believed would take him to the American Red Army. He understood that failure in this situation, with a task force of one hundred and forty men at his command (or to have another government agency get to the terrorists first—the worst possible case), would mean the end of his FBI career. Even if he managed to hang on, they would bury him in some administrative hole in Washington.

"Let's say that someone says they might be part of this thing. I don't think so, but I offer it to you, anyway."

Hassan shrugged his shoulders, the first movement he was able to make, then managed a small grin. "Well, I guess you're out of luck. If I could make an identification personally, we would not have to wait a week. This doctor I spoke of is not such a fool as to let me see these photographs. If he did so, he would have nothing to sell. For all I know, they may well be Army members."

Hassan was pleased with his position. For a moment, his vision of verandahs in South Carolina had been replaced by equally vivid im-ages of greasy dishes in South Boston. "Tell me one thing," he con-tinued. "Where did you get these sketches? That you need to ask me about them?"

"I got them from a cop." George Bradley shook his head in dis-belief. "From a fat, stupid New York City cop."

Even as Muzzafer settled down to wait the few days before he could launch his final assault on New York, and George Bradley, after hand-ing $10,000 to Hassan Fakhr, retreated into his office to wait for the set of photos that would lead him to the American Red Army, Major Dave Jacoby informed his aides that, for political reasons, he could not wait any longer and scheduled a 4:30 PM press conference. He and his aides were in a quandary. They had nothing whatever to offer the hordes of voters screaming for terrorist blood. Nor did they have access to FBI files on potential revolutionaries or a core of political informants such as that maintained by the CIA. Instead, they had had to content themselves with a list of former criminal-revolutionaries supplied by the House Committee on Internal Subversion. Thus, as the police commissioner had promised, hundreds of old-time labor organizers, civil rights activists, student revolutionaries and Vietnam-era peaceniks were called into police precincts, interrogated by hastily formed police "terrorist" squads and held for extended periods without being formally charged. Naturally, the media responded to this avenue of investigation by pointing out its dubious constitutionality, but the public, the *voting* public, according to all the polls, fully supported the police in their zeal to capture the American Red Army. All of which provided the mayor with a surefire. avenue of escape.

Dave Jacoby needed a scapegoat. True, arrested terrorists would be better, but he was realistic enough to know that such arrests could not come about through his efforts. The best he could hope for was that some cop would accidentally stumble across the Army in mid-kill, but until that happened, someone or something would have to be attacked. Thus a Gracie Mansion press conference with national coverage and the mayor spending twenty-five minutes haranguing the do-gooders, pinkos and fellow travelers whose misguided efforts brought aid and comfort to the enemy.

Whether this line of defense fooled the voters or not is a matter of debate, but this much is certain; it did not fool Muzzafer who viewed it as evidence of his secure position. Nor did it fool Moodrow who, at 5:30 every morning, shrugged into his old, black raincoat and began to pound the pavement. He had his dream and his routine so carefully arranged that he rarely thought directly of Rita any more. Like a poorly edited film, whenever his thoughts began to move toward memories of Rita, there was a swift, sharp cut and his attention returned to the day's activities. "Have you ever seen these people? Recognize these? They might live around here. If ya run into one of 'em, my number's on the back." In truth, his lack of success had numbed him so that he seemed like a man standing with one foot in the air, waiting for some push to set him in motion.

He spent four days on Woodhaven Boulevard, an eight-lane road linking central Queens with Kennedy Airport and the Rockaways. The traffic lights along Woodhaven Boulevard are computerized and reverse mornings and evenings to favor inbound or outbound traffic. The cab drivers use it as a shortcut to the airport, especially in the afternoon, and while it doesn't have as many shops as, for instance, Queens Boulevard, the smaller avenues feeding Woodhaven Boulevard—Myrtle, Metropolitan, Atlantic, Liberty—all had to be checked and that meant four days in the butcher's, the barber's, the five-and-ten, listening to every proprietor's opinion on every subject imaginable. The method was simple: Park the car and start walking on the west side of the street. Continue south for six hours, then cross the road and work back toward the car. It's not the most enjoyable way to spend one's waking hours and many cops hate the routine. Moodrow, however, had always loved it. He had never personally been on an investigation in which the culprit was apprehended by gathering "clues." The scientific aspect of police work was only useful after an arrest, to make a strong case where informants or witnesses could not be forced to testify, but the arrests themselves were inevitably the result of direct contact between cops and civilians. Finding the criminals had never been the problem. The dope dealers and the muggers were out there on the streets with the cops. Just that year, in New York, Operation Pressure Point had targeted the drug dealers in Moodrow's home precinct. Without overly concerning themselves with legalities, they began to arrest the criminals they'd known about all along. Most of the arrests were thrown out, but for a brief period the most depraved of the Lower East Side's residents stayed out of sight and the good citizens owned the streets.

So the big cop went at it day by day, like a good bird dog quartering a field, nose to the ground. The dog, like a cop, knows the quarry is somewhere in the field. The trick is not to lose heart, to lift the nose before the trail is crossed. Queens was finished, at least theoretically; every neighborhood had been covered and in the normal course of things Moodrow would have moved on to Brooklyn or the Bronx, but he could not rid himself of the nagging sense of having left something out. Late at night, poring over his notes, a full glass untouched in front of him, he tried to get a handle on the situation. He had good reason to believe that the American Red Army—or at least one member of it—had lived in Queens. In the course of a normal investigation, there would be a half-dozen detectives out in the field. Likenesses of the suspects would have been distributed at every precinct roll call. There were just too many empty spaces in his notes: too many closed stores; too many absent proprietors; too many indifferent sales clerks. He measured the faces he'd seen. How many had really looked? How many just nodded, then turned back to their customers?

Moodrow decided to make a U-turn and go back to Queens. He decided to cover the busier stores, to forget the real estate salesmen, the printers, the plumbing supply houses, the clothing stores. He wanted coffee shops where people came to read daily newspapers, late night delicatessens, dry cleaners, supermarkets. This time he would wait until the merchants could speak to him, until the customers were out of the way, making sure they took a long look at the pictures. They would study them and their negative responses would finally convince him and he would to go the next field with the sense that he hadn't left the quarry behind.

It was nearly 4 AM by the time Moodrow put the period on the last thought. He fell asleep quickly for the first time in a week, a deep, dreamless sleep from which he awoke, at 5:30, in a very grouchy mood. He cursed his way into the bathroom, into his clothes, into his car and headed off to Ridgewood, Queens, with an equally aggravated Leonora Higgins following behind. Too many hours in a brown Plymouth can take the heart out of anyone and Leonora was even more depressed by Moodrow's lack of success than Moodrow himself. It was interminable—not to be tolerated—especially by someone unused to such activity, someone whose idea of patience is sitting quietly while a colleague uses the office copier.

Moodrow first visited the elevated M Train, pounding up the stairs to confront the token sellers. When they tried to push the sketches aside, he slapped the Plexiglass surrounding their booths and demanded that they "try harder." Still, he received negative responses at all three Ridgewood stations, finishing on Metropolitan Avenue in front of the Metropolitan Diner, an enormous twenty-four-hour coffee shop, run, as are almost all the diners in New York City, by Greeks. Gazing at his notes, he recalled his last conversation with Epstein, then trudged inside. He walked directly to the cash register, ignoring the waiters and waitresses in their black pants and white shirts, and confronted the hostess.

"I'm looking for George Halulakis," he said, flashing his badge.

The hostess, resplendent in gold necklace and matching bracelet, curled her full lips into a sneer. Her jet-black hair and olive skin revealed her to be a relative of the owners, as are most of the diner hostesses. Her duties were to escort the patrons to their tables, drop thick menus in front of them, then show her butt, wrapped in her tightest skirt, as she wiggled back to the register. She was fifteen years old. "He's not here right now," she declared without taking her eyes off the *Daily News*.

Her offhand manner made it clear both that she was lying and that she didn't care if he knew it. Perhaps if she'd bothered to look up, she might have realized that the big cop was not prepared to indulge the Greek American Princess (who can make the Jewish American Princess seem like Cinderella) syndrome, but she never raised her eyes.

"And your name, Miss?" Moodrow inquired mildly.

"Hemapolis," she sighed.

"Well, see, Miss Hemapolis, I really have to speak with your boss. Why don't you just get him for me."

Slowly, as if at her own kitchen table, Miss Hemapolis flipped the pages of the newspaper. "I just tell you he is no here."

Moodrow paused for a moment, looking about him as if stone floors and leatherette booths were the only things in life that interested him. Except for a small group of take-out customers gathered at one end of the long counter, the restaurant was deserted. "Tell me," he said, turning back to the young girl, "do you like to eat pussy?"

"What you say?" Miss Hemapolis could not believe her ears.

"The reason I ask is that if you don't get your little hole in motion and fetch Halulakis, I'm gonna place you under arrest for hindering a police officer in the performance of his duty. Then I'm gonna drag your fat ass over to Riker's and lock you up with the biggest, blackest bull dykes I can locate and you're gonna suck them syphilitic cunts until someone goes your bail."

The look on the poor girl's face had Moodrow fighting to maintain his expression. She staggered backward, wide-eyed, with her hands covering her breasts. A decade of religious education had done little to prepare her for this apparently insane giant who stared, expressionless, directly into her eyes. "I go," she whispered, turning away.

"Hope you like fish," he called after her.

Miss Hemapolis disappeared into the manager's office, her mouth moving over the Greek syllables even before the door closed. Moodrow strolled over to the counter and began to question the waiters (all of whom were Greek) and the waitresses (none of whom were Greek) with no result until, as Moodrow knew he would, Mr. George Halulakis, short and very heavy, made his appearance.

"You wish Halulakis. I am Halulakis." He folded thick arms across a barrel chest and waited.

Moodrow waited, too. He stared, unblinking, into the Greek's eyes, as if the man should know exactly what he was after.

"I am Halulakis," the man repeated, fingering the gold chain around his neck. He was a important man, a businessman surrounded by the splendor of his creation, and he was not about to be intimidated.

"Hi, I'm Sergeant Moodrow," Moodrow said, as if nothing had passed between the hostess and himself. "Allen Epstein's my captain and he told me to see you about some people I'm looking for."

Halulakis fell back at the mention of Epstein's name. He twisted his mouth into a bow of disdain. "Why you remind me of this? At least here I come for peace and quiet. All my life ruined by Jewish woman. You know how smart she is? One week after her marriage she tell priest she want to be Orthodox. Now she say no divorce.

Church no like divorce. Bishop himself speak to me. I say if she Orthodox why she no go to Confession? He say she worship in own way. This day I curse when first we meet.'' He snorted once, shook his finger in the air. "You know how to make Jewish girl stop screwing? Marry her. No think is funny? You know how to make Jewish girl start screwing? Give her credit card for Bendel's. Why they all buy clothes at Bendel's? Who knows? But you show wife bill, then she screw you for keep it coming. That is only way to get married Jewish girl in bed.''

Moodrow grinned widely. "You're not gonna tell me you don't have something on the side.''

The Greek returned Moodrow's grin. A mistress was a cultural necessity for many successful Greek entrepreneurs. "Hostess is partner's niece.'' He threw Moodrow a broad wink. "She is nice girl from good family, but very poor. I give her job.'' He shrugged. "She is naturally grateful.''

Moodrow, who'd heard much worse stories, slid the sketches out of his raincoat pocket and laid them by the cash register. "Say, George,'' he said, his voice warm and friendly, "why don't you take a look at this here. I'm looking real hard for these people. They're very bad, George. Very bad.''

"This one I know,'' Halulakis said, holding up the sketch of Effie Bloom. "She has come here many times. Usually in morning.''

Moodrow was was startled by the Greek's response as Hassan Fakhr had been when George Bradley passed the sketches across the car. For a moment, he couldn't say anything, then he managed to grunt a response. "When? When did you see her?''

"Three days before. I throw her out. Every morning she come for change for taking bus. Must have exact change for bus and I give, but she doesn't buy. Never. Not even coffee and her damn face so mean you think she have sandpaper in Kotex. Finally I ask nice, "Why you never buy, Miss? Always change. Why you no buy?''

"You know what she say? She say, 'I hope your cock fall off. As you pull it from father's ass.' This you no can forget.''

"How sure are you?'' Moodrow could not keep the growing excitement out of his voice.

"I call waiter. Theos, come here." A tall, slender waiter detached himself from the fruit salad and walked across the restaurant. "You see this woman before?"

"Sure," the man said evenly. "That's the woman who said that thing about you." He began to laugh. "You shoulda seen your face."

"Enough from my face. Look at these." He passed the sketches of Johnny and Theresa to the waiter. "You are more in restaurant with customers. You know from them?"

"I've seen 'em around. Just once in awhile. But never with the crazy one that cursed you out."

"When do they come in?" Moodrow asked.

"Usually breakfast, but not too often. The other one I see almost every morning. She goes to the 7-Eleven for change now. I was in there this morning for razor blades and I was kidding around with the counter girl about it." He held up Effie's picture. "I think this one likes girls more than men." He winked and returned to his work.

Moodrow put his arm on George Halulakis' shoulder. There was no fantasy, no Rita, left in his mind. He was filled with purpose, utterly joyous. "I'll be back tomorrow," he said. "Do me a favor and keep this between us. I been waiting a long time."

22

Leonora Higgins knew that everything had changed before Moodrow had time to walk from the diner entrance to his car at the curb. His stride was too rapid and slightly unsteady, as if he was being pushed to go faster than he wanted, and he drove, (again too fast) directly to the precinct house on Juniper Valley Road. He left his car double-parked and walked quickly through the metal doors, just pausing to flash his badge at a patrolman inquiring about the old Buick. Higgins wanted to call after him, to demand that he share his knowledge with her as she'd shared all his days of looking, but she contented herself with his back as the doors closed behind him, knowing that invisibility was the price of her ticket to this particular show.

Inside, Moodrow found Victor Drabek and explained that he was looking for the chief of the undercover squad. Without asking questions, Drabek led him to a small, sweaty, black cop, John Anderson, in the precinct weight room. Introductions were made and Drabek went back to work.

"Heard about you," Anderson opened up, his eyes probing Moodrow's. He knew he was about to be asked for something that, at best, should come from higher authority and at worst, would be outright illegal. He had no intention of risking his ass for an insane cop.

Moodrow made a broad movement, as if brushing away a thick cobweb. "I need a private apartment up near Metropolitan Avenue. By the diner. I know you guys got places you work outta when you're on the street. Maybe there's some rooms you ain't used in a while. Just for a coupla days."

"You should go to the captain. Get clearance. I don't have any objection to loaning you a place. Long as the captain tells me to." He made a movement back to the weights, but Moodrow held him.

"I lift weights too," he said quietly. "I mean I used to lift weights. I swear I'm too busy to do anything but walk these days. Sleep, eat, walk. Sleep, eat, walk. Sleep eat walk. I'm sure you know how it is when you've been after something so long you lose track of the days. So you find yourself knocking on empty stores on Sunday." He paused for confirmation, but Anderson just waited impassively. "Only now I'm right on top of what I've been chasing and I don't want no fuckin' brass taking it away from me. Understand what I'm saying? Maybe if I get through this, I could go back to lifting weights."

"Sure, I understand." John Anderson stared ferociously at Moodrow. "I understand that you're a perfect stranger who wants me to do something because you happen to be on some kinda personal revenge trip. I mean, everything I've heard about you makes me admire you, but not enough to put my ass on the line." He hesitated, without turning away, waiting for the idea to sink in, then continued. "Now it just so happens that there's a small apartment building down on Admiral Avenue, by the railroad tracks. It's real old, rundown. People come and go and nobody asks questions in that building, not even about 2H, which's been empty for a long time. You get in there any way you can, cause I'm not giving you no keys. In fact I'm not even talking to you except to say there won't be no one over to that apartment for a long time."

"If you don't tell the boys to stay away, how do you know someone won't come by accident?" Moodrow asked.

"We made one bust too many and the scumbags nailed the place. Best keep an eye out while you're there. Maybe some junkie'll come along lookin' to get even." He laughed, then reached out his hand.

"You're taking a big chance going by yourself. What makes you think you won't be the one to get blown away?"

"Don't know," Moodrow shrugged. "I ain't really thought about it."

Moodrow turned to leave, but Anderson again held him back. "Could be if you don't try the door right now, it'll be open tomorrow."

The building was perfect for his use, a six-story brick apartment house just down from the Long Island Railroad station. When Moodrow went upstairs to get a feel for the layout, he found an anonymous door at the end of a long hallway with the number 2H scrawled on the chipped, gray paint. The walls were covered with the scrawl of would-be graffiti artists, the floor sticky. It was the perfect place for a private interrogation. After running down the superintendent, flashing his badge and explaining that he would be using 2H for a few days, Moodrow left through the basement, walking up a long, concrete ramp to the street, and immediately drove home.

He was in his own apartment before 11 AM and he wouldn't be going out again until the following morning, which left him with a lot of time to think. He felt that he should—that he was obligated—to call Epstein, to say, "Look, Captain, I ran down those motherfuckers who've been blowin' this town to pieces. If we put fifty men out there, we'll have most of 'em tomorrow and the rest'll be running for Libya." The fact that the call was never made did not stop Moodrow's conscience from pressing the issue and they paced—the cop and his sense of duty—the length of the living room for most of the afternoon.

Leonora Higgins, just as excited, sat a hundred feet away from the entrance to Moodrow's building and waited until dark. She, too, considered calling her superiors, specifically George Bradley, and telling him both that Moodrow was very close and that he wasn't about to ask for backup which meant the American Red Army stood a decent chance of escaping, despite the size of Moodrow's ego. But she could not bring herself to share the results of her efforts, any more than Moodrow could share the results of his and so she sat, wishing for a bathroom, in the front seat of her Plymouth until dark.

Moodrow did not begin to prepare in earnest until after sundown. He took an old, blue gym bag from his closet, emptied it of yellowed towels and elastic bandages and carried it into the kitchen, tossing it on a chair. Then he began to lay out his equipment on the table: eight pairs of handcuffs and ten feet of chain with a padlock fastened to one end, a tube of Mace, a pair of gleaming brass knuckles, a blackjack and a sawed-off twelve-gauge shotgun, barely eighteen inches long, followed by a half-dozen shells for his .38-caliber service revolver.

Then he paused to consider the possibilities. This would be the real thing, not a fantasy, and there was no way he would get a second chance. He would grab Effie Bloom, if she was alone (and George Halulakis had insisted that she was always alone), and use her to find the others. But what if he was going into some highly fortified stronghold? He recalled the struggle in Philadelphia to oust the MOVE crazies from one building. They'd used helicopters and bombs, hundreds of policemen; an entire neighborhood had been destroyed by the resulting fires. In such circumstances, a single cop would have no chance. Effie, of course, would give him information, but he would have to guard against accepting a lie just because it suited his needs. In the end he decided that if the situation was impossible, he would call for help.

Satisfied for the moment, he went back to work, dropping two hand grenades—two utterly illegal hand grenades—on the table. If he couldn't get them all, he would get as many as possible. They key would be entering the building (or buildings) unobserved. The American Red Army could not be outwardly militaristic or its headquarters would already have been found. Was it possible they had people in every window? Watching twenty-four hours a day? For all these months? Ronald Chadwick thought he was safe, too.

Moodrow threw a set of lockpicks, an enormous ring of keys, a glasscutter and a short, thick, crowbar into the pile. Then a roll of two-inch masking tape, a package of gauze pads, a set of screwdrivers, a ball of nylon fishing line, a man's necktie. As the pile grew, so did the possibilities. He stripped off his shirt as he flew from room to room, gathering his materials; his breath came hard and the tension grew in his body until the heavy muscle stretched the skin of his shoulders and back.

By 2 AM he'd worked himself into a frenzy, pacing from room to room, his hands in his pockets, eyes on the floor. What if they were separated, in different apartments all over the city? If they had regular check-in times; if one missed phone call would send the Army running? What if they lived with the innocent the way the Vietcong or the Palestinian terrorists had, forcing soldiers to kill civilians? As he shifted from scenario to scenario, he never really considered the possibility that all would be in one building, that there would only be five of them, that he could enter their stronghold at his convenience and pick them off one by one. The Red Army's greatest strengths were its size and its anonymity, its ability to take on the appearance of a normal household. Muzzafer had created his own scenario of being discovered and it invariably involved squadrons of police; it had never crossed Muzzafer's mind that one crazy cop, working all alone, would come knocking on his door.

By 5 AM Moodrow could stand it no longer. His equipment had been packed and repacked and the small gym bag was stuffed until he could barely close it. There was nothing to do but get dressed and get into the street. He began with a jockstrap and a white plastic cup, then a leather groin protector, the type boxers wear, to protect the vulnerable area above the pubic bone. He was preparing for Johnny Katanos. Even though he knew about Muzzafer and understood that the Greek was only a soldier, Katanos stood at the center of his fantasies. He wanted to arrest Katanos in a personal manner; he wanted to beat him into submission. He took a bulletproof vest, one of the old, heavy ones, and put it on. It might or might not protect him from whatever the American Red Army had in storage, but it would certainly protect his chest and solar plexus from Katanos' fists.

He stepped into his black trousers, pulled a sweat shirt over his head and was done. He felt like a snowman and his movements were definitely restricted by the vest, but he knew that he was not going to out-speed the Greek. Frankie Baumann, the gang leader Moodrow'd interviewed in Vermont, was tough and shrewd; if Katanos could impress Baumann, then he was strong enough to offer the cop a challenge. Which was just fine with Stanley Moodrow—the idea that he would hurt Katanos, corner him and hurt him, drove away any need for sleep. Moodrow felt like he was in a locker room before a fight, unafraid but very excited, almost joyous. When the combat began, he would suddenly become calm, but the tension in the lockerroom was as necessary as the weeks of training in the gym.

He left his home at 5:30, speeding across the Brooklyn Bridge and onto the Brooklyn-Queens Expressway with an apprehensive Leonora Higgins, convinced she was about to receive the reward for her efforts, trailing a hundred yards behind. The traffic was light enough to allow her to remain well back without any chance he would disappear. She had a sudden image of herself losing him at this final moment and the idea chilled her. Still, she held back—the only question worth considering was exactly when she would reveal herself.

Moodrow drove straight to the apartment house on Admiral Avenue. Though he checked his rearview mirror a dozen times, the small, brown Plymouth, one of literally thousands rolling through New York's streets, remained just as anonymous as Higgins had hoped; he didn't notice it on the highway, nor on the streets—not even when it pulled past him to stop fifty feet from where he'd parked. He could no more imagine being successfully trailed by a black, female FBI agent then Muzzafer could imagine a city cop coming through his bedroom window. He went up to apartment 2H, found it unlocked and walked inside.

He wasn't there five minutes before he was satisfied—a one bedroom apartment, dirty, with aged furniture that was no bargain the day it was bought. There was a squeaky bed (a set of springs with a thin mattress thrown on top), a kitchen table with several mismatched chairs, and the usual assortment of living room chairs and lamps. Moodrow checked the plumbing, the lights and the gas range, then left to drive the half-mile to the Metropolitan Diner. He parked in a busstop, directly in front of the 7-Eleven Store, prepared to flip his shield if a cop asked him to move on, and settled down to wait.

He had no doubt that she'd come along, just as George Halulakis had said. It was as if he'd done this again and again, thousands of times, each time a rehearsal for some final performance. As he looked around, he felt that he recognized the row of businesses lining Metropolitan Avenue. The faded sign over the printer's dirty windows, the crisp neon flashing in the video store window (a window covered, as were all the closed shops, by a steel mesh that rolled up when the shopkeepers arrived in the morning and down when they went home at night)—were as familiar to him as if he was listening to a roll call in the squad room of the 7th Precinct. He suddenly realized that he'd never been higher in his life, and for a moment he felt he might be drawn into something beyond his comprehension, could actually feel it pulling at him. He handled it by leaving his car for the clean, bright safety of the 7-Eleven and a container of hot coffee.

The two Koreans behind the counter, man and woman, were arguing, actually shouting at each other, in rapid-fire Korean. Though he only understood one word—cash register, which the man kept repeating—their obvious rage calmed him. Almost sleepily, he watched the man raise his fist, as if to strike the woman.

"Stop!" They did stop. Instantaneously. And Moodrow felt confidence surge through him. "Would you mind fixing me a buttered roll? I'm a cop and I'm hungry."

Twenty-five minutes later, right on cue, Effie Bloom walked past the old Buick and into the 7-Eleven. It was 6:45. Moodrow, cold and purposeful, waited on the sidewalk, watching, the way a snake watches a rat, until she was ready to come out. Always the gentleman, he held the door open, receiving a snarl instead of a thank-you, a snarl that disappeared when he placed the barrel of his .38 against her head. "Guess what?" he asked, stripping her purse from her shoulder. "Your life is over."

The morning was warm and humid with a promise of summer by mid-afternoon. Effie was dressed in loose, sloppy jeans and a man's khaki workshirt: No bulges meant no gun. Still, Moodrow pushed her face into the brick storefront with one hand while sliding the other quickly over her body, looking for a knife, a razor, Mace—anything concealable. His pistol was back in the holster, tucked into the waistband at the small of his back. He was hoping she would try to run, but Effie, her right arm locked in the huge cop's grip, allowed herself to be pulled into the front seat of the Buick; she made no effort to resist as he handcuffed her left wrist to his right. In truth, she felt neither anger nor despair.

Still, she was somewhat surprised when they drove, not to police headquarters, but to an old apartment house a few blocks from the 7-Eleven. She'd been interrogated many times, always by squads of professionals, by federal "red squads" created especially for the task. This one, big as he was, had the look and smell of city cop all over him.

They went up the stairs in silence, Moodrow taking the steps two at a time, dragging Effie along. She was not afraid yet; her arrogance kept the fear at bay. She was wondering about the others, if they'd been arrested, too. But that was unlikely. If they had the entire Red Army, there would be dozens of reporters to witness the event and praise the authorities. The cop, whoever he was, wanted information from her and she, of course, would never give it.

Even the loud snap of the closing deadbolt as Moodrow locked the door, a sound cold enough to signal danger in the worst B movie, failed to move Effie. Calmly, without saying a word, Moodrow removed the handcuff from his wrist and used it to fasten Effie's hands behind her back.

"Don't I have rights?" Poor Effie. If she'd practiced her rebellion in South America or in Asia or in Africa, she would have been able to recognize the danger presented by Stanley Moodrow, would have been able to anticipate what was to come, but her experience was solely with agencies bound by constitutional guarantees. Thus the sarcasm in her voice as she repeated, "Don't I have rights?"

Moodrow stood opposite her, swaying slightly, eyes fixed on hers: he was seeing Effie as she'd been on Sixth Avenue, hearing her enraged voice as she and Theresa enacted their charade. If he hadn't stopped to listen, he might have gotten to Rita before.

"You're under arrest," he whispered, raising his right hand to the level of her eyes. Slowly, he curled the tips of his fingers to form a shallow cup, then smiled, waiting until he could see the confusion in her eyes. Finally, without changing expression, he brought his palm crashing against her left ear.

"You have the right to remain silent."

Effie was unprepared for the intensity of the pain. She wanted to cry out, but could not seem to catch her breath. Then something crashed into her lower ribs—she heard the crack of yielding bone despite the intense ringing in her ears. Dizziness overwhelmed her and she would have fallen if Moodrow hadn't caught her by the hair.

"If you choose to speak, anything you say can be used against you." Moodrow's fist traveled no more than four inches, but cartilage is much softer than bone, and blood spurted from Effie's nose as she fell backwards onto the floor. "You have the right to have an attorney present during all questioning." He stared down at her, neither of them moving. She was very frightened and he could see it. For a moment, Moodrow felt a wave of sorrow, sorrow that was not quite pity, that confused Rita with all women and with his personal loss. He wanted to reach down to Effie and was surprised to hear the words coming out of his mouth. "If you do not have an attorney, one will be appointed for you."

He drew his foot back, but despite the pain, Effie rolled away from him. "What do you want? Why are you doing this?" she asked.

"We've met before," Moodrow said quietly. "I don't suppose you'd remember."

"Listen, mister, I don't know why you're doing this to me. You haven't even shown me your badge or told me what I'm supposed to have done. Please don't hit me again." For the first time in years, she allowed herself to feel helplessness.

"It was on Sixth Avenue. You were having this fight with the Spanish girl. You remember? The one who pulled your tits out? That was just before they blew up all those people in front of A&S." He unzipped the blue gym bag and removed a small, blue-black crowbar. One end was hooked and sharp, forked like a fishhook. He held it up for her inspection. "Know what the funny part is? I was walking up Sixth on my way to meet my old lady. Yeah, she was standing in front of A&S. I was a little late and she was really burnt up." He hesitated. "Get it? Burnt up?"

Instinctively, Effie tried to get up and run, but the searing pain in her ribs drove out the last residue of her tough-guy stance. "Please don't hurt me."

"I guess that means you wanna live? Could I take it that means you wanna live? Rita wanted to live, too. And I wanted her to live. Didn't help her, though." He stepped toward Effie, the crowbar in his hand. "Fucked up way to die. Lotta pain." He pulled her onto her back and laid the bar across her mouth, forcing it down between her teeth until she could taste the metal against her tongue. "What're you gonna tell me? You gonna tell me everything I need to know? Huh?"

"Yes." It was difficult to speak with the taste of steel in her mouth, but Moodrow understood her. He pulled her up to a sitting position and propped her against the wall.

"If you bullshit me," he said evenly, "you're gonna think burning up's a fuckin' bubble bath."

23

He took her over it again and again. Until he was convinced she was telling the truth. He couldn't make sense of it at first—five people working without direct help. Where were the Cubans? The Libyans? The Ayatollah? He dragged her through the Red Army's history, from her first contact with Muzzafer in Algeria through the months of training and their entry into the United States (they had walked across the border from Canada, had, with the exception of Muzzafer, claimed American citizenship, their right to enter their own country), then over each separate operation, not even sparing himself the details of the Herald Square bombing. When he finally realized that the American Red Army consisted of five individuals (one of whom was already in custody) living together in a three-family home on an isolated street less than two miles from where he stood, he was hard put to stop himself from laughing out loud. He understood the genius of it: Living in isolation, there was little chance of discovery. But he also knew that no one can act outside the law forever, not while running the same act in the same location. Sooner or later, lines of persistence and coincidence would meet.

"I hope you're not lying," he said for the tenth time. Effie said nothing. " 'Cause if you're lying, you're in a lot of fucking trouble.

See, first I'm gonna crosscuff your hands to your ankles, then I'm gonna gag you and lock you in the closet. You can't live more than four days without water, so if I don't come back, you're gonna have a real dry death.''

"I'm not lying." Effie's voice was flat, indifferent. She'd gotten up that morning, dressed and showered, took her breakfast and walked out the door—just an average day. She remembered, sitting against the wall, Moodrow's face no more than ten inches from her own, that her sinuses had been swollen and she'd had a dull headache. Funny, all the pain was gone now, even the burning in her ribs, though her left ear continued to ring.

"Tell me why there's only five. Tell me that again."

"We were afraid of informants. Somebody ratting us out. Muzzafer said if he even let one other person know, they would get us eventually. That person would rat us out."

"Who gave you the guns?"

"The Cubans."

"I thought you said you bought the guns?"

"We bought them from the Cubans."

"Why did you just say the Cubans gave them to you?"

"I meant we bought them with the money we got from Chadwick."

"Don't 'mean' anything. Say what the truth is and don't 'mean.' '' Moodrow allowed himself to shout, looking for some anger in Effie, something to indicate she had the strength to deliberately lie, but her voice remained soft. In every respect she was a woman resigned to her fate. "Who's home right now?"

"Jane Mathews and maybe Theresa." As she pronounced Jane Mathews' name, Effie felt a wave of nausea building. For a moment she thought she would throw up all over the cop, but it passed and she fell back into indifference. "Johnny's expected by early afternoon."

"And the other one? Muzzafer?"

"Later, but no special time. He doesn't have to give a time."

"And what time are you expected?"

"I told you already."

"Tell me again."

"I have a regular job. It's cover. I get back at six."

"All right, let's do the keys." He held up the ring of housekeys taken from her purse. "Which keys fit which doors?"

They went over it for another fifteen minutes before Moodrow made good on his promise to lock Effie in the closet. He was rough with her and she cried out in pain. Though he did not feel the slightest compassion, her need for medical attention was apparent even to Moodrow, who left her alive only on the small chance that she was lying and that he would need further information. If she was telling the truth, if he was successful in his hunt, he decided he would leave her here to die. To that end he rolled up the thin mattress and stuffed it on top of her in the closet. When he finished, she could barely breathe.

He drove directly to the safe house on 59th Road, aware of the irony in that name. It was just as Effie described it, a row of attached, three-family brick buildings, painfully new, with the sod and the shrubbery, the tiny Japanese maple, looking as if they were planted yesterday. Though it was spring and most lawns were at their greenest, the grass in front of Muzzafer's headquarters was a limp, dead yellow; clearly, the sod had not taken and would have to be relaid. Effie had explained the interior layout. Each floor held one apartment; a narrow, winding staircase (a furniture mover's nightmare) led to individual, tiny landings. Theresa and Johnny Katanos lived on the third floor, Effie and Jane on the first with Muzzafer, the buffer, standing between them. There were tens of thousands of similar buildings in New York and Moodrow had been in dozens. There would be a living room with a kitchen big enough to hold a table, a large and a small bedroom, white-tiled bathrooms with small tubs and a laundry room in the basement next to the oil burner. The walls would be constructed entirely of plasterboard and once a month during the summer, a maintenance man would come to trim the shrubs and mow the grass. Complaints went to a management company that was as inefficient as it was indifferent, but in a new building there were few problems. In order to live in this splendor, the Red Army paid $3100 per month.

Moodrow drove around the block three times, getting a feel for the situation. There were few people about, but he would have to be very careful. This was a residential block and strangers would be noticed. On the third pass he recognized Theresa Aviles, dragging a shopping cart filled with laundry. There was no laundry bag, which meant she would be doing the work herself, a two-hour task.

That left Jane Mathews alone in the house. Investigations were strange voyages; the worst mistake was to force them to be predictable, to fit into preconceived notions of how they should go along. He'd trudged after this moment for weeks and nothing had happened. Now everything was going so smoothly it frightened him. It could not be this easy, he thought. There would have to be a problem somewhere. Of course, it never occurred to Moodrow that the problem might be Leonora Higgins one block away in her Plymouth, calmly chewing on a slice of buttered rye bread.

Moodrow drove around the block again, passing Theresa as she made her way toward the laundromat on Fresh Pond Road. He considered taking her on the street, forcing her into the trunk of the car while he (want) after Jane Mathews. It would be very easy, but it wouldn't make the basic problem—entering the house unobserved—any simpler. On the other hand, once safely inside, he could pick them off one at a time. He pictured the blonde Jane Mathews as Effie had described her, vacuuming the floors, making beds. The front windows, by the driveway, were uncovered and filled with plants. If Jane happened to be looking out as he came to the door, she would know something was wrong. Dressed as he was and big as he was, if she didn't make him for a cop, she would take him for a criminal. There were automatic weapons in each apartment and, according to Effie Bloom, Jane knew how and was unafraid to use them.

He finally parked halfway down the block and circled behind the last building in the row, finding a narrow alleyway leading to a series of back doors. Though they were almost never used, these rear entrances were mandated by city fire laws and led into the first floor kitchens. Moodrow passed by Jane's door, than came in low from the back wall of the adjoining building. He listened for a moment outside the bedroom window, heard nothing, went to the door and listened once again. He was very calm, reaching into the gym bag for the shotgun, pressing it into his chest as he used Effie's key to unlock the door. The mechanism, brand new, turned with a barely perceptible click.

Nothing. The kitchen was quiet and dark. He reached for a clue to Jane's position, a vacuum or television. Silence again, then a faint splash of water from down the hall, from the bathroom. Moodrow, the shotgun raised, eased down the hallway, listening to the sounds of Jane Mathews at her bath. The door was partly open, another indication of how safe they all felt, and he went in without hesitating.

"Morning, Jane," he said, pushing the shotgun forward so that the barrels rested against her eyes. "All cleaned up and ready to go." He made it a statement, not a question. She was a very attractive woman, slim and lithe, but her beauty didn't reach Moodrow, not the spray of tan freckles across her small breasts, nor her white knees making little pyramids above the water.

Jane was surprised beyond thought or speech, and very frightened, too. She sat in the tub, for almost a minute, surrounded by white foam, before it occurred to her that the giant with the shotgun wasn't going to kill her on the spot.

"You're a cop," she said, finally, her voice very small, very girl-ish.

Moodrow neither saw nor heard her. He was hearing sirens—cops and ambulances flying up Sixth Avenue, choking the side streets. There was something he had to do. It was imperative. He tried to step down into the gutter and banged his leg on the side of the tub.

For a moment he wondered where he was, then his free hand reached out, almost by itself, clamping down on Jane's shoulder, yanking her out of the tub. Instinctively, Jane used her arms to cover herself; she could not imagine that, to Stanley Moodrow, she was utterly sexless.

He went about his business routinely, as if engaged in a household task; he had to immobilize her, but he couldn't kill her. He had dreamed it time and again. They were always together at the end, though the number varied, and he was explaining their mistakes in detail. He was explaining why a plan that kept federal agents befuddled was not proof against ordinary cop techniques. It was necessary that he explain it, at least to some of them.

And to that end he dragged a passive Jane Mathews, still naked, into the kitchen and tied her to a chair with a combination of masking tape and two-inch elastic bandage. As he worked, his head and hands passed over her breasts, her legs, her lap, creating a scene that would, in the hands of a modern filmmaker, be extremely erotic. Moodrow, however, felt nothing.

"Are you a cop? You're a cop, right," Jane murmured, unresisting. But if he was a cop, why was he taping her ankles to the legs of the chair?

"Yeah, I'm a cop," he said. She was completely bound and about to be gagged. "You believe that shit? A big, dopey cop and I just grabbed ahold of the American Red Army. Un-fucking-real. See, there's this federal agent named George Bradley. A real big-time expert. He's got about a hundred men workin' for him and he's pulling his dick. Imagine? A hundred fucking guys all went to college. Educated guys. See, you shouldn't of killed Chadwick. That's like neighborhood. You can't get in and out of neighborhoods without leaving traces. Even if you wear gloves.

"I hope you don't mind my running off at the mouth like I'm doing. I'm a little nervous. I never actually killed five people. Not all at one time in one day." As he spoke the last sentence, Moodrow felt a sudden rush of memory, an overpowering image of Rita on their first night together. They'd made love, violent love, for three hours, nearly destroying the bed. Afterwards, Rita had come out of the shower and was dressing for work while Moodrow, clothes on, sat by the edge of the bed, watching. Rita was nervous; she kept her back to him and only lifted her buttocks for an instant as she slid into her panties. Her modesty had tickled Moodrow. The bed reeked of their lust; she had been as abandoned as he.

When he woke up, he found himself hidden behind the leaves of an immense spider plant, Jane's pride and joy; he was sitting on a kitchen chair by the front window. The sun had come out for the first time in a week and with all the lights off, though his view along 59th Road was unimpeded, he was invisible from the street. Curiously, he did not examine the process which enabled him to find the perfect vantage point, which selected and carried the chair from the kitchen. Nor did he wonder why such a long-forgotten memory should suddenly come to the surface. There was nothing to worry about. He had thought it out so many times and it had always gone properly. There was no escape for them.

"Say, Jane," Moodrow called into the kitchen, "did I tell you who ratted? This'll make you crazy. Your girlfriend did it. Yeah. Effie Bloom. She's about twenty blocks away from here. In a closet. I told her I was gonna kill you and she ratted anyway. I think she must be mad at you guys. What do you think, Jane? Mad or scared?

"I say she was scared. Sure. That's because I was very rough with her. I didn't mean it, but sometimes it gets that way. Not that I hit her too many times in the face. I didn't want to break her jaw. I mean if I broke her jaw she couldn't tell me anything, right?" He shrugged across to Jane, his eyes flicking briefly from the window to hers and to the window again. "And I needed someone to tell me where you were and everything about you. I mean if she didn't tell me, I'd probably never find your hideout. She was hard to convince, but she told. She told plenty. I guess that proves it takes more than sucking pussy to make little girls tough."

Jane Mathews, fresh from her bath, was going through a transformation almost identical to that of Effie Bloom an hour before. The affair was finished. The litany of her crimes passed over her, and while she had no sense of having done wrong (it was all necessary, all of it), she could count up the bodies and multiply them by years in jail. The failure of her life with Effie, the impending loss of Johnny Katanos and Muzzafer, decades of isolation from prisoners eager to avenge dead relatives—all poured over Jane, like syrup over fruit. She did not even attempt to find a way to warn Theresa Aviles. Instead, she sat there and listened to Moodrow, listened without really hearing the words.

"Hey, hey, hey. Look at this. Here she comes. And is she ever prompt. She must've left the laundry in the washer, 'cause . . ." His voice trailed off. The transition seemed as natural as in a dream. One moment he watched Theresa Aviles approaching her home and the next he was on Sixth Avenue and Rita was walking toward him, her full lips curled into a pout of annoyance. He found nothing strange in this. "Hey, listen," he called out. "I'm sorry. I had to do a few things and I just couldn't get out of them." He shrugged, completely unaware of Jane Mathews across the room. "Tell me what you bought for me?"

Then Theresa turned onto the concrete walk leading to the front door and Moodrow's attention flipped once again. He stepped back into the shadows by the closed door to Effie and Jane's apartment; he waited for Theresa to open the front door, waited for it to close and lock, waited until Theresa was poised on the landing, then ripped Jane's door open and was on her before she was even aware of the danger. He overpowered her, like a wolf on a hare, yanking her into the room, holding her up against the wall, one hand wrapped around her throat, while he searched her for a weapon.

Though she did not go through a transformation from aggressor to victim, as her sisters had done, Theresa was just as helpless as Jane had been. Her hands were cuffed behind her back; a few feet of tape tied them securely to the back of a chair, then her legs were pulled apart and taped, one to each leg of the chair and she was gagged immediately.

Moodrow, resuming his seat behind the hanging green leaves of the plant, began to talk as soon as Theresa was firmly secured. "Good to see you, Theresa. Paco Baquili says to say hello. Remember Paco? He's the one that should have died, but he turned up to give me pictures of you and Effie. It's funny, but I knew you right away. I've seen you before. I saw you on Sixth Avenue with Effie. You was real mad with each other. You made her tits come out. That's probably why she told me where you were."

They went on that way for the following two hours, Moodrow's voice alternately teasing and threatening. It is common for cops and in some ways very necessary, especially after a very long chase, to twist the knife and Moodrow, a thirty-year veteran, was an expert. "Hey, listen up, ladies," he said at one point, trying to extract every last measure of his revenge. "I think I figured out what I'm gonna do with you. I'm gonna burn you at the chair. Like the Indians used to burn the white guys at the stake? Only we don't have any stakes, so we'll use chairs instead. I got a five-gallon can of gas right out in the car. Once you're all together, I'll tie you back to back, make a little circle with the gas and poooof. Off you go." As he said this, he was overpowered by a smell of burning flesh and clothing, an odor of boiling asphalt so strong he gagged on it. He'd been pretending these glimpses of Rita were memories (though he knew they were not like ordinary remembering), but it was getting harder and harder to maintain the fiction. One moment he was watching the road, peering between the leaves of a potted plant and the next he was in a cellar with Rita and a small boy. He was trying to show her something, to demonstrate some great truth that would allow them to overcome all the small habits which kept them apart. If he could just communicate this one idea, he would not be alone. He would never be alone again.

"Hey," he continued. "I just gotta ask you this one question." His eyes flicked over to the two women, then back to the window. They were dark and cold, in stark contrast to the stifled laughter in his voice. Theresa and Jane saw it and understood, as had Effie. They judged him to be insane which was exactly the effect he'd intended. "Didn't you think even a little bit about the people? I've known plenty of killers. Sure. But they always had a reason for killing the person they killed. Like they wanted revenge or they did it for profit. Or they were just plain angry. You guys leave a package and walk away. You don't know what bodies'll be lyin' around and you probably don't care, neither." He looked at them again, trying to read an answer in their eyes. Later, he decided, when they were all together, he would take the gags off and ask the questions again. Perhaps the order of their executions should be determined by their answers. He would not, of course, make good on his threat to set a fire. Fires had a way of spreading, of involving the innocent, and cops protect civilians. Even if they hate them.

"I guess that was a stupid question. I mean if you really thought about it, you could never do it. Never. But what I wanna know is, did you warn your friends and relatives? Did you say, 'Hey, folks, better not go up to Macy's, 'cause we're gonna burn up thirty people? 'You wouldn't want your friends to get burned up, would you? 'Course not. So you must've let them know somehow. Did you hint? Did you call up and say, 'Look, Ma, that sale down at A&S ain't shit. It's a rip, Ma. Don't go down there?' And did your Momma call you back that night and say, 'Jeez, Jane, it's a good thing I didn't go down to Herald Square, 'cause all them poor motherfuckers got burned up down there'?'' He felt the anger rise in him, felt it blaze behind his eyes. If he allowed it to build, it would begin to affect his judgment and he was having enough problems with his "memories" of Rita. Very deliberately, he picked up a small, glass vase and hurled it at Theresa Aviles. The vase struck her on the shoulder and shattered, nicking her throat. The wound was slight, but several drops of blood dropped to the collar of Theresa's blouse, calming Moodrow so that he returned to his task, eyes sweeping the street in front of the house. It was almost two o'clock and Johnny Katanos would be home soon. He'd hidden his blue bag, along with the shotgun, in a cabinet under the sink, keeping only his .38-service revolver, safely tucked into the back of his trousers, in case the Greek should be armed.

24

It was almost noon and the early spring heat continued to press relentlessly down on New York. The white disc of the sun was at its highest point in the spring sky and the thin layer of haze only seemed to extend its radiance. As he drove his van east along the Staten Island Expressway, Johnny Katanos was playing his favorite game—he was pretending that he'd just that minute been reborn. He did not know how long he'd been dead, nor could he predict how long he'd remain alive. He'd played this game many, many times and though he always lost, always died in the end, the intensity of the life to be derived from the game more than compensated for its inevitable outcome. The premise was that he could keep himself alive by watching for his death, by remaining continually alert, like a cowboy walking down Main Street in some 50s Western. Gunslingers inhabited every window, sat atop every horse, peered down from the rooftops. To defeat his attackers, he must anticipate the attack before it came; he could not hope to survive an ambush, but the ability to see it coming was enough to secure his future existence. The curious thing was that the only way he could know he'd lost was by remembering the game, realizing that he was dead and deliberately resurrecting himself.

But on this particular day, returning from a small martial-arts dojo in Perth Amboy, New Jersey, he was having no trouble maintaining his concentration. He practiced as if doing katas in front of his sensei, a legendary master of half a dozen disciplines who now taught a mixture of styles optimistically entitled Warrior's Way. Katanos' eyes flashed from object to object, evaluating danger (resting them was the first sign of impending annihilation) while his mind tried to put labels on the data. He observed a woman in a car alongside his van reach across the front seat to tighten the seat belt around her child's waist. A truck was coming up behind him, a big Kenworth, rapidly closing the distance between them. His eyes flicked at the rearview mirror, saw the amber signal flashing, darted to the windows of a smoked-glass office building alongside the expressway, explored the small trees lining the shoulder. By definition, the game was over as soon as he forgot to play.

As he approached the Verrazano Bridge, Johnny noted that he was as high as he ever got. He did not use drugs (though he always accepted the ritual marijuana joint when it was passed), because he believed that it was possible to alter, even to elevate, his state of consciousness without them. Danger could do that all by itself, though the fear associated with dangerous situations was enough to drive ordinary humans away. Johnny Katanos had long ago learned how to eliminate the fear while retaining the intensity; and the result was an enormously increased sense of power, a super-alert state in which anything was possible. He had explained the sense of it to Muzzafer on more than one occasion.

"I feel like a praying mantis looks. Nothing can get past me. I'm faster and stronger than anything out there."

"And what happens," Muzzafer had responded, "when some hungry bird comes down out of the sky looking for dinner?"

Johnny's response was more carefully constructed than Muzzafer expected. "It's not that it's real. Feeling like Superman doesn't make you immune to bullets. But it's just then you're most alive. I mean if you're gonna be honest about it, you have to admit that compared to that, regular life isn't worth the trouble."

The game was an attempt to bring about that sense of strength without the danger. The results of the game, the results of the efforts made during the game, could then be applied to situations in which actual danger was present. It was possible to walk into a strange barroom late at night and be aware of everyone and everything; to be present at an enormous drug deal and know beforehand that the man in the blue coat would try to rip you off. And knowing it would keep you alive.

But he was not thinking of these things as he rolled off the bridge and onto the Gowanus Expressway. To think in a straight line required too much attention. It would kill and the game would be over. Thoughts had to be marshaled, pushed in the direction of increased alertness. The Gowanus Expressway was elevated. On his right, row upon row of tenement rooftops, dotted with small, brick chimneys, ran off into central Brooklyn. On his left were the manufacturing lofts of the Brooklyn waterfront, each with its row of enormous, dirty windows. Impossible to see into, yet the Greek remained on guard, reminding himself that his eyes were receiving a complete image. If he could stop himself from getting lost in particular parts, he would be able to sense everything.

Ahead of him, shadows in the haze, the twin towers of the World Trade Center began to grow closer as he neared the northern end of Brooklyn. He was conditioned to the drive from Ridgewood into New Jersey; he made it several times each week. As part of the Army's general cover, it was decided that some of them would leave the house every day, as if going off to work. Effie actually had a job, while Johnny was content to maintain the fiction that he used his van to freelance for one of the many courier services in Manhattan. Nevertheless, though as an independent he could make his own schedule, he had to spend long hours pretending to work, hours put to good use honing his skills in an obscure gym far enough away to make chance meetings with the neighbors almost impossible.

The owner of the dojo, an Italian named Mario Possomani, recognized Katanos for the maverick he was. He had to be treated with respect (in combat, he was every bit the sensei's equal), but he was to be kept away from the true life of the school. He would never be allowed to teach or to spar with the students and no one would ask him to coffee after a workout. However, once these precautions were taken, Mario felt free to enjoy the beauty of this predatory beast who'd come through his front door one day asking to "work out." Katanos would spend hours practicing a move, sometimes just a single kick or punch, exploring one variation after another. He seemed tireless (or, better, simply unconcerned with fatigue), utterly committed and always willing to take direction.

He tried to bring this same commitment into his ordinary life, to charge the most mundane activity with life and death possibilities. The game he played was not an attempt to pass the time while he drove along a too-familiar route. Rather, the trip itself was an excuse, an opportunity to practice the game. It was just as he passed the Atlantic Avenue Exit, as he drove along beneath the Promenade in Brooklyn Heights, that he "died" for the first time. A young woman in a sports car, an expensive Porsche, pulled alongside, then slowed, matching his speed almost exactly. Her skirt was hiked to the tops of her thighs and the Greek entered into a fantasy of them pulling off the highway and searching for a room, before he could catch hold. The woman glanced up, noted his interest, composed her face into a contemptuous little frown and slowly drew the hem of her skirt over her knees.

The action woke Katanos up. He jerked his eyes away from the small car and returned to his rounds. The woman had killed him and this resurrection represented a new game. From experience, he knew that as his attention faded, he would begin to go through these quick deaths and rebirths, only able to extend the game by powerful efforts, the way marathon runners keep themselves going in the last stages of a race. Less than a mile away, as he drove beneath the Brooklyn Bridge, traffic came to a stop and Katanos reacted the way all New Yorkers react to the inevitable traffic jams—he felt the frustration quickly rise into anger, into resentment of a system that refuses to get better, despite the tens of millions poured into it, but this time he was able to pull himself up immediately. Traffic jams were familiar temptations. If you let them, they would drain your energies like vampires drain blood.

Still, this one was a beauty, an utter nightmare with endless minutes spent at a dead stop. Drivers got out of their cars, stepped up on the bumpers trying to see an end to it. Even the exits were jammed with trucks and cars looking for alternate routes. He stayed in it, still struggling with his game, for over an hour. The boredom made it much more difficult. He kept thinking of Jane, hoping that Theresa had decided to spend the afternoon at the library, then bringing himself back, involving himself with the present and only with the present, which was all the game required.

He inched past Flushing Avenue, eyes flashing back and forth to the same cars and trucks that had been alongside him for thirty minutes. As always, the goal was to extend his efforts into infinity (though he would have been happy just to reach home "alive"), but it was becoming more and more difficult. Idle daydreams were beginning to force themselves into his consciousness, little fantasies of the future or replays of past events. The man in the truck reminded him of a counselor he'd fought with in one of the many juvenile facilities in which he'd lived. Another woman reminded him of a foster mother who'd taken him into her bed when he was fourteen. Her husband, a long-distance trucker, was away from home for a week at a time and Lori just didn't like to sleep alone. Johnny saw the woman in her black Chevrolet, flashed to Lori, her blonde hair and especially the salty-warm smell of her breasts, then pulled himself back to the moment.

Finally he told himself to try to make it until the jam broke up, to really believe that every one of these distractions was an assassination attempt. Ahead, where the Expressway merged with Manhattan traffic coming over the Williamsburg Bridge, he could see the flashing lights of a dozen police cars and ambulances. All lanes were closed, but there was just enough room on the left shoulder for a single vehicle to inch past. It took twenty minutes to get to the accident and Katanos managed to hold himself together, struggling the way he struggled with his workouts, demanding the last inch from his body. But as he went by, as he congratulated himself on having made it, he gave in to the urge to rubberneck, to take a quick look at the activity surrounding the accident. A huge tanker filled with milk had swerved over into two small foreign cars, driving them into the railing on the outside of the elevated roadway. Several people were trapped in the cars and, just as Johnny Katanos came alongside, one of them, a young girl, was pulled free. She was obviously dead, her arms hanging limply at her sides, her pink blouse soaked with blood.

The Greek couldn't take his eyes off the sight. He didn't even think of his game. The procession of ambulance attendants was almost stately. The girl was carried to a waiting stretcher and laid on it. Her arms were carefully folded across her chest before she was lifted and carried through the open doors of the ambulance. Johnny, his eyes glued to the passengers still trapped in the cars, slid by the wreck. He wondered why they didn't put the girl into a body bag. Perhaps they didn't want the others to know. Or maybe she wasn't dead. Maybe there was something still alive inside that mangled body. Picking up speed, the Greek reflected on paralysis, the danger of having your choice to live or die taken from you. By the time he reached the foot of the Kosciuszko Bridge connecting Queens and Brooklyn, he was fifteen minutes from home and utterly lost.

The subway ride home from the 42nd Street library, where Aftab Muzzafer had spent most of his day, took almost an hour, but Muzzafer didn't mind at all. The weather, thankfully, had held and he was anticipating the most productive night of his life. Two high school girls sat across from him, gossiping in rapid-fire Spanish. One, a brunette with crimson lips and scarlet cheekbones, wore tight-fitting gray sweatpants and a nylon tank top barely covered by a sky-blue jacket. She was sitting with her heels up on the seat, legs far apart— an open display of her claim to the status of woman. The soft material of her sweatpants had worked its way between her buttocks and into the folds of her sex, reinforcing her assertion as well as advertising her distaste for underwear.

Muzzafer stared openly, undressing her with his eyes, even as he thought of Johnny Katanos. Curiously, the contradiction did not occur to him and when he left the train, he fully expected to conjure an image of this girl as he made love to his boyfriend. He was very excited, but he remembered to check the street as he hurried from the subway toward the safety of his home. Unfortunately, he was looking for an army of FBI men, not a single traffic agent in a brown Plymouth, and he walked past Leonora without giving her more than a glance.

On the other hand, Leonora Higgins recognized Muzzafer without having ever seen him. She was so high she could barely sit still. The arrests were going down, without benefit of backup, just as she'd expected. She should, she knew, call it in, get two hundred agents to block off every street, but she couldn't seem to stop waiting. Everyone in the bureau knew an Arab was running the show. Bringing in an army of cops would spook him. So far, Moodrow had been right in everything and the only real question in her mind was exactly when she should go inside.

Watching Muzzafer stride quickly up the block, she felt that she now understood Moodrow completely. There were no clues, no examination of microscopic evidence. Cops were better off being unimaginative; their work had to be done slowly, laboriously. Everything and everyone moved faster than Stanley Moodrow, but he would never give up. If he was after you, even hundreds of miles away, you would hear his breathing.

Muzzafer, however, as he turned onto the walk leading to the front of the building, anticipated no breath heavier than that of his lover. The plastic panels of the storm door protecting the entrance to the house were nearly opaque and with the sun shining outside, it was impossible to see behind them. Muzzafer, unconcerned, fumbled for his keys, cursing softly, then jerked the door open to find Detective Sergeant Stanley Moodrow standing inside.

"Welcome home, Aftab. How was your day?"

Muzzafer froze, his body rigid with panic. Where was the badge? Where was the gun? The man had called him by name, which made it very likely he was from the Israeli Mossad. Certainly, if he was from an American agency, he would have identified himself by now. In either case, why was he alone?

Moodrow, smile widening still further, wrapped his fingers in the Arab's coat and yanked him through the doorway, closing the door behind them. According to Effie, Katanos would be home very soon and Moodrow didn't want to be away from the front window any longer than necessary. With Muzzafer's hands cuffed behind his back, the detective first taped the Arab's arms to his sides, then his legs to the seat of a kitchen chair. His movements were quick and highly organized and came of learning how to make arrests on hot summer nights in low-income housing projects.

"Tell us who you are," Theresa demanded.

"I'm a relative of one of the victims. I mean, almost a relative." Rita sprang out at him. Rita standing by a craps table in Atlantic City, her hands full of chips, eyes ablaze. So real he wanted to weep.

"Where is Effie Bloom?" Theresa persisted.

"She's tied up right now." Moodrow paused, like a comedian expecting a laugh. "But don't worry. She says to tell you that she's hoping you'll all meet up again. In heaven."

This time his vision of Rita bore no relation to anything they'd done while she was alive. He was in the funeral hall, in the room with the closed black coffin. It was 3 AM and even Mrs. Pulaski had gone to bed. He could see Rita through the wooden sides of the coffin. She was lying on her back and she was not burned as the doctors had said. She looked perfectly natural, even happy, a broad smile dominating her face, as it did when she was playing one of her practical jokes. As he rose from his chair, Moodrow experienced a sense of terrible loss. Instinctively, like a child in a nightmare, he sent out a silent prayer for help. Please, Lord, let me hold together until I take this last one. Please. Let me push it back until after I've killed them all.

"You must tell me who you are," Muzzafer said. Though he expected Moodrow to hit him (which is what he would have done in the same situation), he couldn't stop himself from asking the question. He'd imagined himself being arrested literally thousands of times. Had used his imagination to formulate strategy to prevent arrest. He could name the secret police of almost every nation in the world, but he could not put Moodrow anywhere. Just the one fact that he was alone defied analysis.

"What'd you say?" Moodrow asked calmly.

"Are you a policeman? Are you FBI? CIA? You do not look like a Jew so you cannot be Mossad. Tell me what you are."

Moodrow, his eyes flicking from the Arab to the window, replied matter-of-factly. As if he was passing on a weather forecast. "What I am is the immediate cause of your death. That's what it's gonna say on the autopsy. Cause of death: Stanley Moodrow."

"You can't just execute us," Jane protested. "We're freedom fighters, not criminals."

The words sounded hollow, even to her, but Moodrow responded anyway. "Know how you're gonna die?" I'm gonna take this shotgun and put one barrel on your pussy and one on your asshole, then pull both triggers. Take about a half hour before you stop screaming."

There is no better view to be had of midtown Manhattan, from any of the roads circling the island, than the view from the pinnacle of the Kosciuszko Bridge connecting Brooklyn and Queens. As Johnny Katanos, ten minutes from home, began the climb to the top of the bridge he, like everyone else crossing the narrow band of utterly polluted water called Newtown Creek, turned his head to the skyscrapers of Manhattan. A gray haze lay over the mass of stone and steel across the river and the buildings, with the sun dropping behind them, seemed to float in the dusty air, a colossus dreaming of itself.

Johnny registered the impression automatically, his mind drifting from the haze to the heat to the perfect weather for their coming project. In a few hours, the American Red Army's work in New York would be finished and potential traitors, except for Muzzafer, eliminated. Though he, too, was unaware of Stanley Moodrow's hot breath, he had had enough seasoning in ordinary criminal pursuits to know how dangerous it is to remain too long in one place. Sooner or later . . .

Perhaps they should head north, he mused. With summer coming on, Minneapolis would be entirely appropriate. Or Portland or Seattle. Muzzafer, on the other hand, would probably choose a climate closer to that of his homeland, like Houston or, God forbid, the city they call the Big Easy, New Orleans. Well, he could always apply a little heat of his own to that situation.

Laughing as he cut across several lanes of traffic and darting onto the Long Island Expressway, his attention flicked to an evaluation of their remaining ordnance. Rearming would be extremely dangerous. Too dangerous. Before that could happen, Muzzafer would suffer the fate of the three women and he, Katanos, would remove himself to another country. But that was for the future. There was still enough for months of new projects.

For instance, there were a dozen small, infinitely concealable UZIs, should Muzzafer suddenly develop the balls for close-up work, and a decent amount of C-4 plastic, too, especially if they exploited their environment as efficiently as they had at Herald Square. But it was the claymores that most interested the Greek. American manufactured antipersonnel mines designed to spray jagged metal in an expanding crescent, would, for instance, if set beneath the seats at a baseball stadium, keep manufacturers of prosthetic devices humming for the next two years.

Lost in daydreams, he took the first exit, Maurice Avenue, and ran alongside the highway for several blocks before pulling to the curb and entering a small Italian delicatessen. The fat man behind the counter smiled in recognition.

"Lemme guess," he said. "Prosciutto, salami and provolone with lettuce, pickled peppers and mustard. On a seeded hero."

Johnny smiled his most winning smile, but even though he'd picked a store well away from the main shopping centers, he didn't like the idea of being a regular. If they should ever put his face on television, this guy would pin him in a minute. "Take a pound of German potato salad with that. And a Coke."

By the time he left, he was once again halfway to being alert. What he saw across the street brought him fully awake. Two cops had a black man up against the rear door of a police cruiser. He was in "the position," spread-eagled with his hands on the roof of the car, and he was complaining loudly. Katanos knew, of course, that it had nothing to do with him, but when the bigger of the two cops snapped the cuffs shut, Johnny felt the pressure on his own wrists. He'd been in that situation a dozen times, knew the humiliation of it and could not help being affected. Still, despite the rage, he took his time starting the van, pausing to adjust the side mirror before pulling away.

He drove the few blocks to his home as alert as he had been on the expressway coming out of Staten Island. His eyes darted back and forth, searching the faces, the doorways, the windows. Turning onto 59th Road, he looked for people first, noting the empty sidewalks, then scanned the vehicles parked at the curb until he came upon Leonora Higgins in her brown traffic department uniform. Was she writing a ticket? Unheard of on an obscure residential block like 59th Road. There was too much business on Grand Avenue to make searching the backstreets worthwhile. But there were no blacks living in this neighborhood, either.

Johnny's eyes flicked from vehicle to vehicle, looking for anything big enough to hide a camera or serve as a command post. He found nothing, but still drove by Leonora without moving his head, making the turn at the far end of the block, two hundred yards from the brown Plymouth, before parking the van. Though he was acutely aware of the heat of the sun pouring through the windshield, he forced himself to sit still for ten minutes, counting the seconds on his watch, preparing himself. The urge to flee, to get out while he still could, was very strong. Later, perhaps after dinner, he could call the house to make sure everything was all right.

But, of course, that would mean scrubbing the project. It would mean long, virtually impossible explanations to the others. Besides, what government agency would use a black woman in a brown uniform to carry out surveillance in a lily-white neighborhood like Ridgewood? He left the van and walked directly across the intersection of 59th Road and 60th Lane, just catching a glimpse of Leonora Higgins sitting in the same spot. He walked to the next street and cut behind the houses to the narrow alleyway that Moodrow had used to get to Jane Mathews. At the corner of his building, he put his hand into a small birdhouse which Jane had insisted on putting up when they'd first taken their apartments. There was no bird inside, though, and he was not looking for one as he felt his fingers close around the loaded .38-caliber revolver he'd hidden there months ago, despite Muzzafer's orders.

Quickly, he freed the weapon from the oily rag protecting it. He felt more comfortable with the familiar weight in his hand, more at ease though no less alert. The door to the back of the house was open, a breach of security so flagrant it could not be accidental. As he stepped inside, he heard a voice, Muzzafer's, coming from the kitchen, then another, a stranger's answering from the living room.

"Are you telling me you found us by yourself? That's impossible."

"Actually, I got recommended to you by a Spanish kid named Paco. He says to say hello to Theresa. And Johnny, of course. When he gets here."

"And when he gets here, you're going to kill us?" No matter how many times it was said, Theresa could not seem to take it in. Political prisoners in America were not executed. It might happen in South America. Or even in Israel, in extreme cases. But not in America.

"Fair is fair, right?"

"Not this time." Johnny, satisfied that Moodrow was alone, stepped into the room, the revolver held straight out in front of him. "This time fair ain't fair." Under ordinary circumstances, he would have killed an intruder without another word, but he was anxious to find out if there were other pursuers, if the woman in the brown Plymouth was somehow related to the strange giant sitting by the window, so he held up and instantly regretted it. The "strange giant" somehow managed to grab his own .38, which lay next to the telephone by his knees, and bring it up before Johnny could pull the trigger.

The two weapons went off at the same moment, the roar of the explosion crashing through the room. Moodrow fell back against the window and the gun slipped from his hand, falling to the floor. Johnny, unhurt though stunned by the sound, stood erect, looking for the blood on Moodrow's sweatshirt. The bullet had gone in dead center. If it hadn't, the cop would have pivoted in one direction or the other, but not only wasn't there any blood, the man was getting to his feet.

"If you move another fucking inch, I'm gonna blow your eyeballs through the back of your head."

Moodrow finally stopped, though hatred continued to flow from his eyes. As if he expected to make his enemies pay for the mistake of keeping him alive.

"You wearing a vest?" Johnny said calmly, gesturing towards Moodrow's chest. "Let's see." He pulled the trigger and, again, the .38 echoed in the confines of the small room, slamming Moodrow back into the chair. "Son of a bitch, it is a vest." He raised the gun to cover Moodrow's head. "Why don't we take it off." While Moodrow struggled with the sweatshirt and the vest, Johnny turned his attention to Muzzafer. "How the fuck you let this asshole get you into this position? What'd you do, just walk through the goddamn door? You didn't see the other one out there?"

"What other one? He says he's working alone, a New York City cop out for revenge. Now please, cut the tape off."

"Revenge?" Johnny grinned at Moodrow. "What'd we do, take out your mother? No, not your mommy? Your wife or your girl-friend?" Moodrow's arm jerked uncontrollably and Katanos laughed. "We turn your old lady's cunt into charcoal? We fry the bitch? Well, guess what? I don't give a fuck. It's too trivial to talk about." He began to move across the room toward Moodrow. "Sit down in the chair. That's right. That's a good boy. Now I'm gonna take a peek between those blinds. Wanna see if there's this traffic department Plymouth still parked across the street. You wouldn't know anything about that, right?" He smiled as he came toward the window. "Don't move now. 'Cause I'm gonna be right next to you and we'll bump if you move. Of course, it might be the best chance you're gonna get."

He began to move toward the blinds, he eyes locked on Moodrow's, a half-smile on his face. He moved evenly, calmly, in total control of the situation.

"*Nobody move. Drop the gun.*"

Leonora's scream, designed to freeze everyone and everything, was high-pitched and shrill, a temptation more than a threat, and Johnny, smelling her inexperience, turned instinctively to confront it. Then his hand, the one holding the revolver, disappeared in the hand of the "strange giant."

"You should have killed me," Moodrow said, his voice calmer than he expected. "You should have killed me when you had the chance." He pulled the Greek's hand straight down into the floor, forcing a shot into the floorboards, then slammed it back into the window, rubbing it back and forth across the broken pane until the gun fell to the floor.

At that moment, Katanos knew it was over, that if he should overcome this monstrously strong cop (and he could not even free his hand), there was still a woman with a gun standing ten feet away. For a moment, he nearly abandoned himself to the despair of self-recrimination. He'd spotted the bitch sitting in front of the house. He could have driven away. Only his greed for the coming project had brought him inside the house. His own stupidity.

Then his mind stopped short and his body took over. If he was going to die anyway, he might as well go in style. He struck out with his free hand, driving sharp reverse punches into Moodrow's ribs and groin. Punches that had no effect. As soon as his hands dropped, Moodrow struck downward, a short clubbing blow that crunched into the Greek's chest. That would have knocked him to the ground, if the cop wasn't holding his right hand, preventing him from falling.

"I thought you were a tough guy," Moodrow said. "All those people I questioned? Paco and Frankie Baumann and a dozen other street freaks—they all said you were the baddest thing on two feet. How come you hit like a jailhouse punk?"

Johnny raised his left leg to kick and Moodrow yanked him to the right, pulling him off balance. He struck out at Moodrow's face, tearing with his fingernails and the cop raised a massive shoulder, absorbing the blow.

"Careful, you're gonna hurt yourself." Moodrow's fist shot out, slamming into the smaller man's face. "I guess you weren't centered. Isn't that what they do in karate? They get centered?"

"How about your old lady?" Johnny's voice came raggedly. He could hurt the cop. He knew he could hurt him. Despite the groin protector and the enormous bulk, Moodrow would hurt. "She got a center? Besides the center of a coffin? Or did she survive? Maybe laying in a hospital bed waiting for an operation that'll make her face look like something besides peanut brittle."

He felt Moodrow's right hand curl about his throat. Then he was lifted bodily and his head slammed against the wall. Once, twice. With all his strength, expecting death, which is what he would have given had the positions been reversed, he gathered his strength and tried to spit in the cop's face. But there was nothing left, no strength, no resolve.

"That's enough, Sergeant. Stop. Now."

For the first time, Moodrow considered his rescuer. In his desire to get his hands on Johnny Katanos, he hadn't given a thought to the apparition in the brown uniform and it took a second for him to recognize Leonora Higgins as the well-groomed FBI agent.

"How the fuck did you get here?" he asked. Without waiting for an answer, he handcuffed an unresisting Johnny Katanos and tossed him into a chair next to Muzzafer.

"Instincts," Leonora said. "Just like you told me."

"Instincts don't mean psychic. Tell me how you found me."

"I've been following you for two weeks."

The news shocked Moodrow, shook his confidence. He would not have believed it possible and the revelation opened the door to further mistakes. Nevertheless, after a moment's thought, he began to giggle. "For weeks? Who'd of believed it."

"A brown face in a brown uniform in a brown car? Nobody looks twice, Sergeant." Leonora shrugged. "Not unless they're afraid of a ticket."

Moodrow nodded. "You got that right, Agent. . ."

"Higgins."

"Right, Agent Higgins. But isn't it funny that you're pointing your gun at me? I'm the good guy, remember?" He swept his arm across the kitchen table. "And this is the American Red Army. Reading from left to right, we got Theresa and Muzzafer and Jane and what's left of Big John Katanos. There's one more named Effie in a closet on Admiral Avenue."

Looking at him, Leonora's understanding of the situation became as clear and sharp as the edges of New York skyscrapers on freezing, winter nights. If she put the gun aside, even for a second, he would take it from her and kill them. He would not hurt her, because he had no desire to escape whatever punishment society deemed appropriate, but he would surely kill these people. She glanced over at Johnny Katanos, battered and bloody, at Jane, naked and vulnerable, at Muzzafer and Theresa. She found the idea of being their savior utterly repulsive.

"I can't let you kill them," she whispered. "I know what they've done, but I can't let you."

Moodrow started toward her, slowly, his eyes locked on hers. "What do you mean, 'kill'? Did I say anything about killing."

Leonora raised the automatic to cover the center of Moodrow's chest. "Don't be a fool," she said. "Maybe you don't care about the rest of your life, but I plan on living mine wholly outside of a prison cell. If that's OK with you."

"Sure." Moodrow decided not to deny his intentions. "Why didn't you say what was bothering you? Shit, we could fix this real easy. Just turn around, walk out of here, get in your car and drive away. Who's gonna find out?" Moodrow, his eyes riveted to Leonora's, saw her hesitate, reconsider. "You know what they've done? You've seen all the bodies. It ain't the fucking movies. Real kids. Real mommies and daddies. Real blood."

"So what? You've done your job and I've done mine. We're not judges and juries." She felt the cliches even as she spoke them, yet she continued. "All we do is make the arrest."

"No!" Moodrow slammed his fist against the table. "What do you think is going to happen after you 'arrest' them? Do you have any idea? The first thing is they go into protective custody so no other prisoner can get to them. Then they get to spout their bullshit revolution all during their trial while every asshole dictatorship in the fucking U.N. makes speeches about what heroes they are. Then they go off to some federal joint where the authorities take great care for their safety because, sure as shit, three or four years down the line, some other scumbag's gonna grab a bunch of American tourists and these assholes'll be the price of freedom.'' He paused for breath. ''And five years from now, they'll be killing again. Killing real babies and real mommies and real daddies and we can stop it, Higgins. We can stop it. Just go away for five minutes. Then come back and bust me. You'll be the fucking FBI hero of the century. Bigger than the ones that knocked off Dillinger, and Bradley's gonna look like such a fool he'll probably join the CIA.'' He began to move toward her again. ''They're monsters, Higgins. Look at them. There's no remorse there. There's nothing but death.''

They came to the same conclusion at the same time. Moodrow knew she would not give in, that she was stuck with the definition of ''FBI agent'' given to her when she took her training. There were judges and juries and cops and they never came together in the same person. Even Moodrow, who knew, as do all cops, that the pronouncements of the judges in their black robes only served to keep criminals out of jail, and who had never played by the rules himself, could read the conviction in her eyes. There was no sense in waiting. He shot his hand forward just as her finger tightened on the trigger, just as she realized that he had to do it. That neither had any options.

The bullet crashed into the upper left side of his chest (though she had meant to kill him), two inches from his shoulder, spinning him to the ground. He tried to get up, ignoring the gun still pointing directly at him, but he couldn't move. She read the desire in his eyes, the tremendous effort to remain conscious. This was not the proper reward for accomplishing what several hundred men had failed to accomplish. She let her hand fall to her side as he began to cry.

''I'm sorry,'' she said.

25

Though she rolled the issue back and forth in her mind for more than two weeks, it was the intensity of the first blooming azaleas in Prospect Park that pushed Leonora Higgins into one final trip to the Lower East Side. After five months of wet, gray winter, Prospect Park (two blocks from Leonora's apartment and home to the Brooklyn Botanical Gardens) was a refuge, an Eden to which she and thousands of other New Yorkers retreated as soon as the first crocus made its appearance in late March. By early May, with the temperature in the low seventies and every tree wreathed in a halo of luminous green buds, this pilgrimage had become a drug to her, a free narcotic to be ingested at every opportunity. In spite of the traffic sounds (from which there is no retreat), Leonora could feel the tension begin to leave her body whenever she crossed its threshold. By the time she'd walked into the depths of the park, stunned by gaudy beds of sturdy, unyielding tulips, she would be utterly lost in the enormous power of nature's opening volley. It would not, she knew, last long. By late June, everything would slow down and the park would take on an air of patient waiting. Crowds would thin out. Children would come later, leave earlier and the young mothers, toddlers in tow, would desert the playgrounds in favor of the neighborhood pool.

So it was necessary to get that minimum yearly requirement of spring glory before it was too late. Moodrow had worked throughout the day and Leonora had lost April altogether. Now he was ruining her May as well, for she could not get him out of her mind, not even when walking through the forest of azaleas that covered the central section of the park. She had never seen a man break that way and the memory of him (the blood had run down his arm so fast it dripped from his fingers) trying to rise from the floor while he wept like a deserted child could not be thrown off. She would have to see him one more time or he would haunt her springs forever.

The newspapers had made him a hero. The case had been broken in the classic, flatfoot tradition, and if any of the reporters suspected his injury had been a deliberate attempt to prevent the execution of five people, they didn't write about it. Even Effie Bloom, alive though battered, was keeping her mouth shut while an embarrassed Federal Task Force (in league with an equally embarrassed New York City Police Department) had come to the conclusion that Moodrow's public hanging, fitting as it might be, would only further increase the avalanche of ridicule coming from the media. Moodrow's success (along with his street accent) and their failure had become a regular feature on the five o'clock news.

And there was a debt here as well. She felt that at last she knew who she was (she'd passed her resignation across the desk of an amazed George Bradley the day after Moodrow's victory) and the first push along the road had surely come from Stanley Moodrow, with his mocking laughter and his speech about "instincts." He'd demonstrated the flaws inherent in all procedural thought, the futility of trying to apply the same rules to every situation. Once again she concluded that he deserved better than he'd gotten. If she hadn't been there, he would have had his revenge, for better or worse. Leonora felt like a mother who'd punished her child for breaking one of the family rules. The necessity of the act does not diminish the quality of the tears.

So she made her pilgrimage, driving straight to Moodrow's apartment, and found that the Lower East Side had undergone it's own spring transformation. There were radios everywhere, suitcase-sized monsters blaring rock or salsa. They represented the territorial focus of small groups of young, mostly Spanish kids in T-shirts and head-bands. The radios would go far into the night and the newcomers, the immigrant yuppies in search of affordable space, would complain only to each other. Still, despite their determined posture, the Puerto Ricans now shared the streets with groups of newly arrived refugees from the suburbs. Like exotic birds, these white kids wore crests of multicolored hair and black clothes (leather whenever possible) stud-ded with chrome and steel. They were outrageous, but not threat-ening (though they wanted to be) and they liked their drugs in immoderate doses, so the Spanish kids (who *were* threatening) usu-ally left them alone. Altogether, Leonora reflected, the area had its charms, and not least among them was its tolerance of diversity. The Lower East Side had long been the neighborhood most favored by multi-racial couples.

The lock was broken on the entrance to Moodrow's building and Leonora felt a sudden rush of anxiety as she pushed the door open. What in God's name was she doing here? What would she say to him? As she walked up the stairs, she found herself praying that he wouldn't be drunk. Little visions of him sitting on the couch with his revolver in his mouth kept popping into her train of thought, and by the time she got to his landing, she was ready to bolt.

But his door was slightly ajar. She could see him through the open-ing. He was seated at his kitchen table, his back to her. Bandages covered most of his left side, though he didn't appear to be in pain. At first, she thought he was reading, but when she knocked on the door, the right hand he raised in greeting held a ballpoint pen.

"C'mon in," he called without looking up.

Leonora walked inside, stood behind him for a moment, then fi-nally annoyed, asked, "What are you doing?"

Not recognizing her voice, he turned to her for the first time. "Well, well. I gotta say you have a knack for turning up unexpectedly. I thought you were my landlady."

"What are you doing?" Leonora repeated, moving to the opposite side of the table. Now that it was clear that he was not the suicidal drunk she expected to find, she felt like a fool.

"I'm writing a letter," he answered, breaking into his most innocent smile.

"A letter?"

"Yeah. I'm writing to Ann Landers about one of her reader's problems. I write to her a lot. She's very understanding. Wanna hear it?"

"Sure." Leonora, reconsidering her judgment about his sanity, sank into one of the chairs across from Moodrow. "Let's hear it."

"Dear Miss Landers I am writing you this letter concerning your reader signed FRUSTRATED who said how she had such a problem communicating with her husband about when they wanted sex. She said he would never know when she wanted sex and vice versa she couldn't tell either so both of them would want it when the other didn't and they would feel rejected and hurt. But I would like to tell poor FRUSTRATED about the signals which I have worked out with my wife so we will know in advance if each other wants what we want. For instance it may happen that I will come home from work in a horny mood so bad I would do it with a sock but I don't just grab her because she might not be in the mood and who likes to get their bosoms pinched when they are not in the mood? Instead I just throw out a signal like I say, 'Hey, cunt, how 'bout a little hole tonight?' and if she is feeling the same she might give me a sign by saying something like, 'Sure, scumbag, if ya think ya could get it up for a change.' "

In the silence that followed, Leonora stared into Moodrow's small black eyes, trying to get a fix on what might have brought forth such a document.

"Let me see that," she finally demanded, and Moodrow obediently passed it across the table. She took a few seconds to read it thoroughly, as if trying to will the words off the page, then sat back in her chair. She could feel a grin rush up from nowhere to claim her face. "You know something, Sergeant Moodrow?" she said calmly. "I should have killed you when I had the chance."